MURDER IN THE ZONES

William S Allin

JOKApress

FOR:

Mam (Eira) - who shared her love of detective stories with her
children
and
Dad (Stan) - always happy to show us the
delight to be found in solving a puzzle

CONTENTS

Title Page

Copyright

Dedication

Key references 3

1. The Calm Before The Storm 5

2. Springtime 14

3. Judge Dead 22

4. Back On The Beat 43

5. In The House Of The Lord 53

6. The Interviews Begin 77

7. The Beat Goes On 122

8. A Weekend Off 166

9. A New Week 185

10. The Party Zone 201

11. Getting nowhere, fast 223

12. In the presence of a Goddess 246

13. Brotherly Love 278

14. Reunions 290

15. Gates and other openings 313

16. Unsatisfactory Outcomes 327

17. Juniors' Playtime 337

18. Not your typical fun day 341

19. Repercussions 358

20. Visitors 367

21. Visiting 387

Acknowledgement 395

About The Author 397

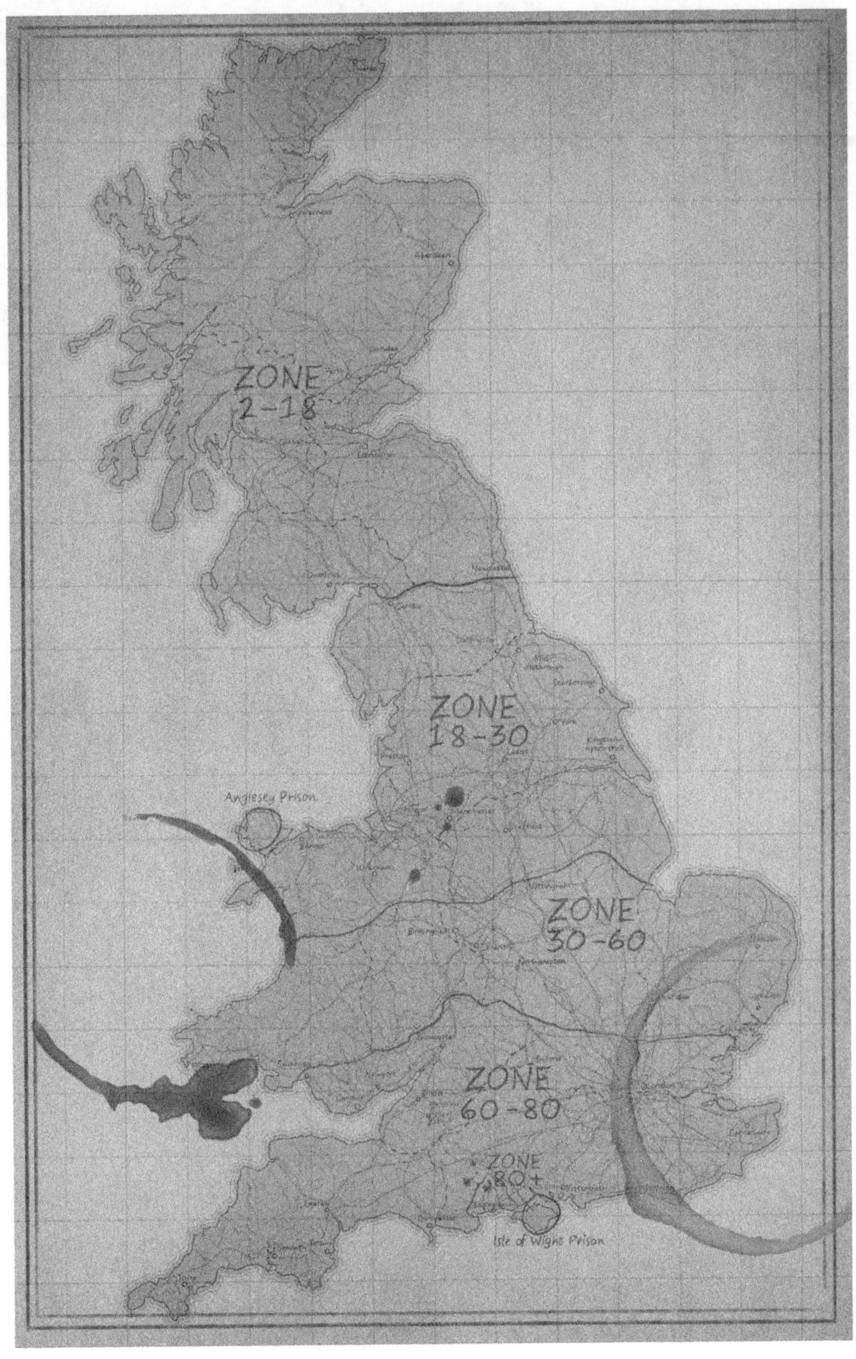
ZONE
2-18
ZONE
18-30
Anglesey Prison
ZONE
30-60
ZONE
60-80
ZONE
80+
Isle of Wight Prison

KEY REFERENCES

Map—The image on the previous page shows the Zones as initially conceived by Lord and Lady Williams, illustrated by Lord Rayer, and stained by them all.

Zone – The zones are from North to South ->

1. Zone 2-18/Z218/Youth Zone.
2. Zone 18-30/Z1830/Party Zone.
3. Zone 30-60/Z3060/Family Zone.
4. Zone 60-80/Z6080/Nearly Dead Zone/Old Gits Zone.
5. Zone 80+/Z80+/Should be Dead Zone/Really Old Fogies Zone (ROFZ).

The ages overlap to allow time for relocation. It is not possible to relocate everyone on their birthday.

Regions – Zone 2-18 has no regions. Zone 80+ has two – inner and outer.

All other zones have four Administrative Regions – West/West Central/East Central/East.

Central Committee – In overall control of the country. Headed by a Secretary General who appoints Committee Secretaries responsible for policy and delivery in areas such as Economy, Security, Employment, Energy, Education, Food, etc.

New Committee members are selected and appointed by existing members. Proposals for elections were developed but never implemented.

All Committee Members are awarded the title of Lord.

ChiZA – Chief Zonal Administrator. The person appointed to lead a zone. ChiZAs sit on the Central Committee but are not Lords.

LeRA – Lead Region Administrator. The person appointed to lead a region.

Administrations – One for each region, providing all essential services for citizens in that region. Responsible for everything from schools to hospitals, policing to road sweeping and housing allocation to food supply.

Administrators/Admins - Committee-appointed workers who deliver for the Administrations

Tranzers – Citizens of a younger zone who are allowed to work in an older person's zone.

The Nobles House - occupied by the remaining Dukes, Marquesses, Earls, Viscounts, Barons, etc. The House has no formal say in government, but members sometimes influence decisions of the Central Committee. The number of members of the House depletes year after year, following the decision only to allow blood relatives to qualify for succession. No new titles are created.

1. THE CALM BEFORE THE STORM

Her finger hit the pause button as the other hand removed the pods from her ears - enough of that nonsense. Amelia Duggan stopped momentarily to reflect on the torturous preceding moments.

Bismillah. Did they say bismillah? Is that even a word? What does it mean? There was little doubt that it was the strangest song she had ever heard. Merely listening to it was challenging. It was so weird. Bizarre. One minute, the singer wallows in self-pity after committing murder. Next, he's performing a mock comic opera with falsetto accompaniment before spouting words she'd never known existed. Bismillah? What the....

Amelia pushed her sunglasses onto her head to read the track listing. That was only the third song, and she dreaded thinking what the others would be like. Next up were Windsor Davies and Don Estelle.

"I've never heard of them either," Amelia mumbled, stuffing the CD player and case into her bag. She would keep that delight for her walk home. With luck, it would be a high-energy dance track that she could jog to. She doubted it could be any worse than that operatic nonsense. Amelia would be happy never to hear that again.

Her stepfather often sent her CDs from his collection, but he was no closer to expanding her musical tastes beyond classical. Some of his selections were tolerable, but Amelia doubted she would ever be a fan of seventies music. She was much happier with a touch of Schubert.

It dawned on her that she'd only brought one disc and her portable radio was still on the sofa, where she used it last. With nothing to block out the outside world, she had no choice but to endure the sounds of everyday life. She glanced around, saw she was not alone in the gardens and prepared herself. Some of the noise she was about to hear would be almost as bad as that Bohemian rubbish.

She was accustomed to being the brunt of the gardeners' jeers, sarcasm, sexual innuendos, and rude gestures. Initially, she suggested they would be better off focusing on doing their job, but that only encouraged them. They slated her accent and dress sense, called her names and told her to return to her own zone. Latterly, she ignored them and often made a display of turning up her CD player and walking away. That usually worked.

The worker's comments were more irritating than hurtful, and Amelia had grown bored of the repetition. The remarks would never lead anywhere. She knew she was safe; nobody would lay a finger on her. Not even the poorly educated grasscutters and rubbish collectors would be that stupid.

Citizens and workers knew the punishment for serious offences, including assault and robbery, in this zone might be death or, even worse, banishment to the Isle of Man. The law was applied fervently, and even minor violations, such as dropping litter and jaywalking, often resulted in relocation. Nobody risked it. No sane person wanted to leave the safest and best-paid region in the country. As far as Amelia was concerned, her new town was a perfectly safe place to live, albeit frequently dull. Nothing exciting ever happened around here.

A worker shouted, "Oi, Lady Muck, I saw you here yesterday. Why didn't your lot put your rubbish in the bins like decent people? Do you think you are too good to do that?" He saw Amelia turn away. "Go on, ignore the truth. Just because your rich parents got you a job in a big house working for a rich old fart doesn't mean you don't have to keep the place tidy. You ain't any better than the rest of us."

Amelia turned to smile at the man, raised her left arm, keeping her fist flat, knuckles facing the floor, and extended her middle finger. She used her spare hand to blow the man a kiss and moved on. The man repeatedly cursed her, and his colleagues soon joined in. Amelia walked on up the hill and out of hearing range.

She looked back at the gardens and accepted that the workers might have had a point. There was a mountain of debris. Her gang did not usually leave so much litter. Her guilt lifted as she remembered what a splendid time it had been. The sun had finally emerged, and they were compelled to make the most of it.

Amelia's fellow revellers were her age and employed on similar contracts. Their working days were Monday through Friday, and they were contracted to remain at work for as long as needed. For Amelia, that was never later than 6 p.m. The weekends were theirs to enjoy, and they did.

The merrymakers spent many hours on the beach as the weather became much warmer, but they used the sheltered gardens when there was still a risk of cold winds.

The previous two days had been sunny, and a large gathering quickly settled on the grass by the bandstand. They drank alcohol, cooked food on improvised barbecues, consumed copious amounts of drugs, sang, and generally larked about. The fun began on Saturday morning, continued into the early hours of Sunday, and started again soon after lunch.

Amelia smiled at the memory of a fun-filled, spontaneous, fabulous weekend, but all good things…

Today was her return to reality. It was time to resume her tedious job working for a partially incontinent nonagenarian who rarely spoke to her. She took little comfort from knowing what to expect. There would be the usual mix of vacuuming, polishing, tidying, and laundry sorting. She anticipated a dull day. There would be no real challenges, nothing to get her blood racing, certainly not enough to cause her stress or anxiety.

She continued walking, debating whether to begin her work upstairs or down. Her decision would depend on her employer's location.

The house was a short distance from the park. Amelia

exchanged pleasantries with the gate guard. He was always polite but tediously dull. She did not loiter after telling him His Lordship's clothes would not clean themselves.

Not that she had any plans to trouble the washing machine. In recent weeks, Amelia discovered a way to make that part of her job easier. A new laundry service had opened in town. She dropped off the dirty items on her way home on Monday and collected them, washed and pressed, the following Friday on her way to work. The only drawback to this arrangement was the impact on her funds. Washing the old man's clothes, however smelly they may be, was part of her job description, and she could hardly ask for reimbursement for outsourcing costs. Fortunately, the old man left cash hanging around and never noticed if Amelia helped herself.

The heavy wooden door opened slowly, and she entered silence. This was normal.

Amelia never received a welcome greeting. Nobody wished her a good morning, enquired if she enjoyed her weekend, or asked how she felt. The only sound was the clip-clop of her footsteps as her shoes hit the stone floor in the lobby.

Amelia did not care that her employer ignored her arrival. She knew he was a private, shy man who took time to accept strangers. His tight circle of friends had shrunk in the fourteen months Amelia worked for him, and he did not appear in any hurry to acquire replacements.

The agency had forewarned her about His Lordship's peculiarities when they offered her the job. They had triple-checked that this would not be an issue. She was confident it wouldn't be. The arrangements suited Amelia. She and His Lordship occasionally shared the briefest of discussions, usually when he had indulged in too much wine, but she never encouraged it. She preferred to be left to herself.

Amelia was self-assured enough to believe she could win him over if she chose to, but that was not on her agenda. There was no need. She saw no benefit in forming a friendship with the old man. What was the point? They would never hang out together. In any case, he probably wouldn't be around much longer.

Amelia had heard plenty of horror stories about rude, abusive, and demanding employers, and she often counted her lucky stars. Some of her cohort, including young men, received unwanted sexual attention, often bordering on the perverse. She wanted no part of that action, thanks very much.

A few of her acquaintances stopped attending the gatherings when they started a relationship with their employers. Some had gotten married. They lived a high life for a while, but sadly, none secured long-term happiness. The new spouse was always much older, typically over eighty, frail and lonely. When they died, the families divided any assets and forcibly repatriated the younger partners to their age-appropriate zone. Her association with His Lordship would remain distant and purely professional.

She entered the main hall. The house was previously a boutique hotel built by a long-dead local business owner. To the left of the entrance, the old reception area was adorned with hand-painted scenes of Bournemouth in its heyday. Amelia had become so familiar with the images that she barely noticed they were there.

Her eyes surveyed her wider workplace. The stairlift was on the ground floor, which probably meant the Judge was at work in his study. That room could wait until later when it would be empty. Her work would commence in the kitchen.

Amelia kicked off her shoes and walked barefoot over the cold floor toward the rear of the building.

Her cleaning materials, including her apron and work shoes, were stored in a concealed cupboard under the back stairwell. She slipped on the overall, wrapped the cords around her waist and tied them into a large knot at the front.

Amelia pushed her feet into the mules. They were not the most expensive shoes she had ever bought, but they were ideal for work. They were comfortable and light.

The kitchen looked untouched since the previous Friday. She

was not surprised. The Judge often ate with his driver, MC, on weekends. MC meticulously washed every dish and saucepan and wiped every work surface before departure. Nothing was left out of place.

Giving the chrome work a cursory wipe with the soft cloth, Amelia Duggan admired the pristine kitchen full of top-end gadgets. She spotted the new coffee maker. She knew where His Lordship kept his supply of beans and, all being well, thought she might enjoy a cheeky espresso before leaving.

An inspection of the fridge confirmed that His Lordship had not touched the leg of lamb he had received the previous week. That would need to be eaten soon. It would probably go to a friend of MC's. There was no point in her taking it, as it would be too much for one. Amelia was not jealous. Lamb was not her favourite meat.

She opened the freezer. The top shelf was stacked full of steaks. A quick peek to the right told her the vegetable cabinet contained potatoes, greens, and mushrooms. In a cupboard, Amelia found a variety of powdered sauces. She clapped her hands. She knew what she was having for her supper.

She danced the vacuum cleaner on a whistle-stop tour of the downstairs rooms, wiped shiny surfaces with her cloth and sprayed copious amounts of air freshener around rooms the Judge used regularly.

Standing outside the study, Amelia sniffed the air but could not pick up an aroma. The smell of urine usually revealed His Lordship's presence. Perhaps she had been wrong, and he wasn't where she expected him to be.

Amelia tapped a knuckle on the study door before entering. The room was empty, with no papers cluttering the desk.

The downstairs bathroom was next door. It smelled fresh and appeared spotless, and she saw no evidence of recent use.

Returning to the entrance, she opened the mailbox to find the broadsheet had yet to be collected. This was unusual. The judge made a point of gathering his paper when he reached the lower level. Amelia could not understand why it was still there.

Perhaps His Lordship had not made it downstairs. He might still be in his bedroom. She shivered. What if he were dead?

Amelia told herself not to be so melodramatic. MC had probably taken His Lordship on another of their little trips. The pair had taken many journeys recently, but Amelia could not recall them leaving before her arrival. Why had they left so early? Her concern left as quickly as it arrived. There was no need for her to dwell on such matters. She was only his cleaner, not his nanny. He could go where he pleased. Amelia preferred having the house to herself.

She wiped what needed wiping, polished where necessary, and barely overworked the vacuum cleaner as she completed the downstairs in close to record time. Amelia usually took a tea break before moving upstairs, but as her employer was out for the day, she thought she might get away early and enjoy a swim before the pool closed.

She carried the vacuum cleaner up the splendid front staircase to the first floor, stopping now and again to run a cloth over the brass handrail. Her thoughts returned to her evening meal. She might as well select a bottle from the Judge's wine cellar. Her preference was for red, but which one should she take? Her choice was delayed by a stubborn fingerprint requiring attention. As she lifted her head away from the rail, Amelia became further distracted.

His Lordship's house stood on the cliff above Bournemouth seafront. When seen from the upstairs landing, the large windows at the front provided stunning panoramas of the beach and coastline to Boscombe and beyond. Amelia loved this scenery. She rested her arms on the railing, taking it all in while considering the choice of wines. Which would go better with steak? She opted for something French. The final selection would depend on the variety with the most bottles. His Lordship kept a wide and varied cellar, although Amelia could never determine the source of his fresh supplies.

Her duties on the upper floor began with cleaning the Judge's bedroom. Her routine involved opening the windows, stripping the bed, spraying the air freshener and leaving it for five minutes before fitting the clean sheets and duvet cover. She remembered that the previous week's laundry had not been unpacked and would be in the back bedroom. It made sense to unpack it while she let the fresh air and the spray do their work.

Amelia stopped and stared, confused at finding the door closed. His Lordship insisted on his bedroom door being open. Amelia thought it ironic that the man who was afraid of no living being and had committed the most vicious criminals to a life behind bars was terrified of the dark.

She was about to turn the knob when her fear of the Judge being dead in bed returned. Amelia was unsure what to do. Should she call Alan, the boring gatekeeper? Should she ring MC?

Her mother's voice echoed in her head. *'Get a grip, Amelia, stop being such a drama queen.'*

The first thing she needed to do was to check if the room was occupied. She would probably find it empty. MC had almost certainly taken the Judge out for the day and had inadvertently closed the door. That made sense. Amelia was relieved she hadn't called for Alan. She would never have lived it down had she called him, and they had found the room empty.

Confident in her assumption but opting to play it safe, Amelia tapped on the wood and, hearing no reply, smiled as she turned the handle and pushed the door.

She immediately regretted that decision.

The morning sun blazed through open curtains, floodlighting the room and providing Amelia with an unobstructed view of the naked Judge suspended above his wheelchair with puny arms tied above his head.

The man's scrawny, freckled body did not make a pretty sight. A plastic bag covered the head, which lay awkwardly on the chest. The pale, wiry legs were cable-tied at the ankles, and a cylindrical block of wood was wedged between the knees. Not that much remained of his knees. Splintered bone and a colossal blood stain covered the carpet under the body.

Amelia stood open-mouthed, transfixed by the scene. Her eyes drifted from the Judge's head to his feet and back as she absorbed the horror. It took the buzzing of flies that Amelia had not initially noticed to bring her out of her stupor and her breakfast out of her mouth. She sprinted from the room, stopping only to vomit again over the landing floor.

Amelia Duggan was desperate to get outside. She darted to the staircase, collided with the vacuum cleaner, and sent it tumbling down the marble stairs. She fell after it and passed it before it made the bend. Her shoes slipped off.

Hitting the bottom step, Amelia was disoriented as she searched for the front door. She screamed and wailed while racing down the drive. Seeing no sign of Alan, she passed the garage and guardroom and sped through the open gate onto the street.

She did not think about the steak, the sauce or the wine. Amelia Duggan had lost her appetite. She no longer cared about 'Bohemian Rhapsody' and 'Whispering Grass', the next track on her CD, would have to wait.

2. SPRINGTIME

The trees were recovering from a harsh winter's ravaging. The birds chirped happily on the roofs and branches, and the temperature had climbed a few degrees. Spring had arrived. He was thrilled. He loved this season. Life could begin again.

Jeff Cleveland admired the long lines of daffodils growing on the border between his lawn and the path which ran the length of his expansive garden. The concrete paving ended at his sizeable, expensive (at the time) greenhouse, which had been carefully positioned to run parallel with the back wall. It remained in the sun most of the day.

Every year at this time, he told himself it felt good to be alive. The last time he believed it was fifteen years ago.

The garden looked splendid. His efforts at putting everything in order before winter had paid off. The lawn was healthy. The trees were sprouting new life, and the daffodils were coming to full bloom. The grass would need a cut, but he was content to let the bees use the weeds and wildflowers for a while longer.

The handmade bird table stood beside him in the centre of his lawn. Jeff held a bag containing seeds and nuts, which he gently emptied onto the wooden table. When the bag was empty, he folded, rolled, and placed it in his cardigan pocket.

So much had happened since he and Felicity purchased the bird table and bench, which they placed on the patio, but he remembered every second of the day they bought the items.

The pair visited friends in Exmouth to celebrate his 48th birthday and stopped at a craft market outside Exeter. Flissy spent ages haggling with the woodworker and walked away ecstatic to receive a substantial discount on her two purchases. The bench would need to be delivered, but she insisted they take the bird table with them.

Jeff beamed as the memories flooded back. He had never been proficient in practical matters and struggled to adjust and lower the rear seats of their estate car. Flissy had embarrassed him by asking a passerby for help. She teased her husband and compounded his discomfort when they arrived home by getting an elderly neighbour to help him return the seats to the correct position. Jeff remembered that he had struggled to conceal his irritation and could still hear Flissy chuckling at his displeasure. The image soon faded as Jeff's thoughts wandered to much darker images.

He visualised the torrential rain that fell on the day the bench was delivered. The appalling weather did not let up for weeks. Felicity boasted about going to the continent for her work as a wine buyer for a supermarket chain. She worked hard trying to persuade Jeff to accompany her. He had plenty of annual leave, and she believed a few days in the sun would benefit them both. Jeff was tempted by the offer of good food, wine and sun, but things were difficult at work. He could not drop everything and fly away. Flissy understood and agreed to his compromise that they take a holiday later in the year.

Hardly a day went by when he wished he had chosen differently.

After waving goodbye at the airport, he never saw his beloved Flissy again. She became one of the billions lost when repeated earthquakes, typhoons, tsunamis, and shifting tectonic plates caused insurmountable global damage.

Strangely, Britain emerged relatively unscathed from the catastrophic events that ravaged everywhere else. Speculation about survivors in some parts of the World circulated frequently without concrete evidence. All communication beyond the UK was severed, leaving the average Brit with little knowledge of the outside world.

There was no formal explanation for why the UK survived largely intact, but the matter remained a popular topic of conversation over a pint or two.

Whatever the reason, the prevailing belief was that the country had been fortunate.

Jeff couldn't consider himself lucky. He often wished his island had succumbed to the same fate as everywhere else. It would have spared him the unbearable pain of loss. He still found it difficult living without Flissy.

As the rest of the country adapted to the new world order and began to recover, Jeff wanted no part of it. He shuffled around his home, his heart heavy. He rarely washed, seldom ate, and spent long periods indoors behind closed curtains.

Their children became his lifeline. When the Universities shut, and the pair returned home, they became his pillars of strength, helping him come to terms with his new life.

Jeff was never sure if things moved quickly or if he was incapacitated for longer than he had realised. When he returned to reality, he found that the Government had abandoned elections, revoked all human rights, and introduced rationing for food and clothing. The Internet had been shut down, personal computers were confiscated for other purposes, and some mobile telephone networks had been abandoned. All media came under State control.

If that was not bad enough, what came next threatened to send Jeff back into the darkness.

To reduce the risk of anarchy and an escalation in crime, people between the ages of eighteen and thirty were moved into a fenced-off zone where they could study, work, and live without impacting others.

Jeff did not want to live alone. He threatened to end his life if the children left him. They told him that desperate times called for extreme measures. It was not as if they would be far away. They had been fortunate to survive. Billions of people worldwide had been lost, and any survivors in other countries were unlikely to have it so good.

Their constant reminder, *'Mum would hate to see you like this'*, motivated Jeff to keep going. The pair promised to ring him regularly, and once they had completed their studies and secured employment, they could return. In the meantime, everyone had to accept the situation, and they would never forgive him if he did *'something silly'*.

Things did not turn out the way they suggested.

Once the first zone was established and proven to work, the wider population was relocated to areas where they could be kept safe. The oldest people were moved nearer the coast, and those displaced by their arrival were offered new accommodation further inland. Slowly, everyone lived in a zone with people within the same age band. Formal borders and barriers to travel were established to ensure compliance with the new arrangements.

The area around the family home became part of Zone 6080 for those between the ages of sixty and eighty. Technically, when it opened, Jeff was too young to stay there. He should have volunteered for relocation, but could not face the upheaval. For once, Jeff benefited from looking much older than his years. His already prematurely grey hair had turned white almost overnight after he lost his wife. Everyone assumed he was over sixty.

Jeff kept his head down and slowly began to integrate. He found the incoming population friendly enough, and, as a local, he was called upon for advice and guidance. Nobody questioned his eligibility for Z6080. He played boules, cricket, and walking football and made many new friends.

By the time the Administration caught up with him, Jeff had settled into the new ways and was popular with neighbours and teammates. He was allowed to stay after an unexpected intervention from an old friend who had secured a senior Admin post. The downside was that he could not participate in sports until he turned sixty. The authorities believed it would be unfair if they allowed Jeff to compete as he was at least five years younger than the competitors. Now sixty-three, Jeff was once again actively participating in sports and pastimes.

He and his children remained close. That weekend, Jeff had a pass to the Family Zone, Z3060. He would visit his daughter, Jill, and her husband and hoped to see his son, George, and his daughter-in-law.

A robin landed on the bird table, causing two slightly larger birds to fly off. Flissy always reckoned that Jill was like a robin. She was small but not to be messed with. Her brother would testify to that. Jeff smiled as the creature enjoyed breakfast without competition. Having taken its fill, the Robin flew off to be replaced by several other feathered friends.

Jeff's birdwatching lasted until it was time for his mid-morning cuppa, which he enjoyed with a biscuit while listening to the radio.

As it was a Wednesday, in keeping with his established routine, after tea, Jeff collected the cardboard and paper to take to the recycling depot at the other end of the village.

He left the back door unsecured. Everybody in the area knew everyone else, and leaving doors open was a safe, commonplace practice.

On the return journey, Jeff fulfilled one of his monthly rituals. He checked that his pension had arrived. There was never usually a problem, but he saw no harm in checking. It gave him something to do. He used the cash dispenser at the Post Office. A small queue had formed at the ATM, and Jeff stood behind Mr and Mrs Chopra, who lived nearby. The pair acknowledged his arrival with broad smiles before ignoring him and continuing to bicker. Villagers wondered how the pair's marriage had survived so long. Jeff could not recall the last occasion he was in their company when they weren't squabbling.

He took his mind off their disagreement by looking up and down the street. The shops were busy, and he imagined the market, which used to be a school, would be heaving. Not having the internet meant there was no home delivery. If residents wanted something, they had to shop locally for it. As a result, the butchers, bakers, and greengrocers always did a roaring trade. Jeff pondered what meat he fancied.

A stranger approached carrying a brown leather satchel. Jeff read the logo on the bag and assumed the visitor worked for the telephone company. The man had a thick grey beard, sunglasses, and a flat cap pulled down onto his forehead. He saw he had caught Jeff's eye.

"Sal…" The man stopped and coughed into his hand. "Good morning."

Jeff thought the stranger was about to add something else, but changed his mind. The outsider nodded at him, touched the peak of his cap and strolled away.

"Good morning." There was something vaguely familiar about the individual, but Jeff did not have time to dwell on it. The queue had shortened, and the lady behind him, whom he did not recognise, was ushering him, reminding him she was in a hurry.

"Sorry," Jeff shuffled along the path.

The Chopras discussed how much money they needed to withdraw. Mr Chopra was overruled as his wife was saving for their holiday in Brighton. Mr Chopra turned to Jeff and pulled a face.

Jeff checked his balance and withdrew enough to cover his shopping. The lady behind eased him aside, her card in hand.

With his provisions acquired and having caught up on what constituted local news, Jeff returned home intending to spend the afternoon in his garden.

The daffodils reminded him of one of the most famous poems ever written. He knew it off by heart and recited it softly.

"I wandered lonely as a cloud.

That floats on high o'er vales and hills."

The next lines of Wordsworth's finest never got out of his mouth. His doorbell rang.

Two men waited on his doorstep. Both were about his age and wore white shirts and a red tie bearing the crest of the local Administration. The epaulettes on their shoulders were identical, bearing the initials 'HQA', which Jeff recognised as the insignia of the regional administration headquarters.

Jeff had little time for Admins. He sided with those who believed them lazy, corrupt and untrustworthy. He had no idea why they were bothering him, but had already decided they would have to work to get what they came for.

"Yes, can I help you?" Before either man had time to say anything, Jeff added, "I have no money to buy anything. I am not interested in politics. If you are collecting for charity, you've wasted a journey."

Both men held out their right arms, showing open leather wallets containing a badge and an identity card.

Only one of the men spoke. Jeff detected a trace of a Geordie accent.

"Good morning, Mister Cleveland. We're from the Regional Administration, and we would be grateful if you could accompany us to our Zonal Headquarters. Your assistance is required on important business."

Cleveland was intrigued, but not enough to resist having fun at the Admins' expense. He peered over his glasses as he carefully examined the passes, checking that the badges related to the correct zones. He made a show of comparing the photographs to the faces.

"Thank you, gentlemen. I think you both need to update your security passes. Those photographs are more than a few years old." Neither man commented. "What do you want with me? I've done nothing wrong."

Geordie spoke again. "We didn't say you had done anything wrong. We want you to come to HQ to see if you can help us."

Jeff spotted his good friend and neighbour on the street and waved, then shouted, "Pat, come over here a second." He pointed at the Admins. "These men want me to go with them, but won't tell me why."

The talkative Administrator turned to Pat as he walked up the drive. "There's nothing for you to worry about, sir. Mister Cleveland is perfectly safe. We need his assistance for a brief time. He has not done anything wrong."

Pat studied the bulkier Administrators, who towered over him. The men could not see Cleveland's cheeky wink at his friend.

Jeff spoke again to Pat. "If I'm not back by three, make sure my lawyers, family and the media know where I went and who took me."

"Will do."

Jeff prodded one of the men in the back, "Tell Pat who you are and where you're taking me. Where are you forcing me to go?"

The other Administrator responded, "Calm down, Mister Cleveland. We are not forcing you to go anywhere. We are asking you to accompany us to help with a matter that we cannot discuss here. If you refuse, that is not a problem. We will return to HQ without you."

Pat saw Jeff nod and wink at him, turned, and retraced his steps to the street.

"This sounds serious." Jeff leaned out to look at the road. A third Administrator stood by a large black car with tinted rear windows. It resembled a limousine. "I see that you've brought a car too. Can we stop at the supermarket on the way? I need a few groceries." Cleveland trotted inside to swap his cardigan for a sports coat. It was not a cold day, but he never felt dressed without his jacket. The pockets already contained everything he was likely to need.

He dropped a trilby hat on his head. "Right, gentlemen, I am all yours. Shall I drive?" The Administrators remained silent as they walked behind him to the car. Reaching the pavement, Cleveland shouted, "Hey, Pat. Come back here. We'll give you a lift to the surgery."

Pat walked toward them with a wide grin on his face.

"You don't mind, do you, gentlemen?" Jeff whispered to the chattier Administrator, "Pat is having terrible trouble with his piles. These seats will be far more comfortable for him."

3. JUDGE DEAD

The Administration Headquarters for Z6080, known colloquially as the '*Nearly Dead Zone*' or '*NDZ*', was in Cardiff.

Back in the day, Jeff visited Cardiff many times and usually completed the journey in under ninety minutes, depending on motorway traffic. He anticipated a much shorter trip this time as there would not be enough vehicles to cause a delay.

Jeff reclined in the rear seat and watched the world go by. He had not been in a car for over a year, the last time being the weekend he visited his grandchildren in the Youth Zone. His son had been given access to a work vehicle.

Cleveland's movements usually involved the State-run bus service. The buses were frequent, punctual - at least in his zone - and cheap. However, bus seats were nowhere near as plush as those in the black Mercedes-Benz State car. Jeff became sleepy. He yawned and forced himself upright, shaking the weariness out of his head.

The driver was obviously under orders to drive efficiently. The vehicle rarely exceeded sixty miles an hour. The journey was comfortable, and the views were pleasant, but Jeff considered his companions poor company. They seldom spoke and obviously resented Jeff's attempts at conversation. Perversely, their attitude made Jeff more determined to talk.

"Have you been with the Administration long?" He asked the one sitting next to the driver.

"Five years."

"And what were you doing before that?"

"I worked in local government."

"What did you do in local government?"

"None of your business."

Fair enough, Jeff thought, planning a new approach. He turned his attention to the man behind the wheel. "You look like you're quite fit for your age. Do you go to the gym a lot?"

"No."

The third Admin, who sat beside Jeff, admitted to working in a factory but ignored all other questions. Jeff returned his attention to life outside the car.

They joined the M5 and headed north. When Jeff asked why they were taking a detour, he was told they had to deliver documents to the Family Zone. The Admin in the front held up an envelope as proof.

A traffic jam had formed at the border crossing, and vehicles queued along the motorway.

"Why is this taking so long?" Jeff looked on as border guards studied passengers' papers, checked the boot of cars, crawled underneath lorries, and searched larger vehicles. "What's going on?"

The driver answered. "They are hunting down illegals."

"Illegals?" Jeff took a moment to comprehend. "Do residents try to sneak out of my zone? Who would do that?"

The driver nodded. "You'd be surprised. We catch loads trying to change zones without the necessary permissions."

"Not that many get a permit to live permanently in a younger zone," the driver added. "The Committee is determined that people stay in their age zones."

"Unless there is a good reason to relocate. To do that, you must prove you are economically or socially active." The Admin in the passenger seat sneered. "It also helps if you know someone in authority."

"Very true." The Admin sitting next to Jeff stirred from his slumber. "Does paying backhanders to the local Admins qualify as economically or socially active?

The driver found that funny. "I am sure the local Admins would say it does."

Jeff's children had briefly explored the possibility of him joining them in the Family Zone, but the request was declined as Jeff had retired. He was not sorry. He had no wish to be a burden. "Why would anyone risk it?"

The front passenger looked his way. "Some people get lonely

without family and try to cross over,".

"They must know they'll get sent back," Jeff suggested.

"You'd have thought so," the rear Admin said. "It's probably worth the risk if the family or friends on the other side have a large property with plenty of room. The local Admins might not notice they were there."

"Especially if the family or friends have plenty of money and can pay our regional colleagues to turn a blind eye." The front passenger looked at the driver.

"That's true enough."

All three Admins laughed. Jeff rubbed his chin.

With documents delivered, they rejoined the M4 toward Cardiff.

The vehicle eventually turned onto a road behind the Millennium Centre in Cardiff Bay and stopped before a barrier. Two guards, each carrying automatic weapons, stepped forward, and one shouted, "Out."

The Admins left the car, but Cleveland stayed where he was. One of the armed guards, waving his gun, repeated the order for Jeff to leave the vehicle. All visitors had to be searched.

When Jeff refused, the guard said they would not let him in unless he complied. The Admins he travelled with assured him this was standard practice, that it would only take a minute, and urged him to comply.

Jeff did not move. He had not asked to visit in the first place, so they could take him home if they did not want to let him in.

It took several minutes and a few telephone calls before the barrier was raised and the car was allowed inside without the visitor getting frisked.

They parked outside a red brick office block behind the two-storey glass-fronted building that once housed the Welsh Parliament.

Like its counterpart regional governments in Scotland and Northern Ireland, the Welsh Parliament was dissolved as part of the Emergency Measures in response to the Shift. Those measures were never repealed, and Cleveland doubted they would be. People had accepted the changes, and there was no appetite for a return to the old days from the Welsh, Irish or Scottish. The populations of those countries had been dispersed across the country, meaning there were no longer any homelands. Most people classed themselves as British.

Cleveland took a lift to the fifth floor and was told to wait outside a door labelled "OFFICE OF THE CHIEF ZONE ADMINISTRATOR Z6080."

Jeff doubted that the ChiZA role provided much in the way of job security. There was no nameplate, which Jeff recognised as a sign that the job had recently changed hands. He mentally counted the postholders since the role was introduced. Five names came quickly. He thought there was a sixth, but the identity eluded him.

It irritated him that he could not recall the current occupant. He wondered if the name would come to him if he thought of something else. That often worked. He needed a distraction.

Magazines lay scattered across the small table next to his seat. He ignored them, knowing what they would contain. They would be full of state propaganda and advertisements showing what the State wanted people to see and purchase.

Deciding he did not care what the ChiZA's name was, Jeff stretched out his legs, tucked his glasses into his pocket, slid his trilby down over his eyes, folded his arms and closed his eyes. If he had to wait, he might as well get comfortable.

A loud cough stirred Jeff, and for a moment, he was unsure where he was. He flicked his hat back onto his head, sat upright, stretched out his arms, raised his legs off the floor and wiggled his feet in the air.

"Mr Cleveland, the ChiZA is ready for you." Jeff noted that the man pronounced the title as 'Caesar'. Jeff typically referred to the post as 'Cheeser.'

The short older man wearing the official Administrator's uniform straightened as the visitor stood.

Cleveland replaced his glasses and checked his watch. "About time, too. I've been waiting for ages," he said huffily.

"I have been trying to wake you for five minutes." The man opened the office door. "Mr Cleveland for you, sir."

A rotund man, also wearing the Admin uniform, rested his significantly sized backside on the edge of a wide desk. He spoke slowly with a deep, gruff voice. "Thank you, Stephen. Would you fetch us tea and perhaps a few Welsh cakes? I hear they made a fresh batch this morning." The large man studied the stone-faced Cleveland, whose eyes surveyed the room.

"Yes, sir." The other Admin departed from view.

The large man stepped closer to Jeff. "Good afternoon, Mister Cleveland. My name is Frank Purcell, and I am honoured to be ChiZA for this zone. I am pleased to meet you." He held out a hand, which Cleveland ignored.

"You haven't been in the post very long. Did your predecessor resign?"

Purcell had expected a friendly greeting but kept his composure as he said, "Yes," and withdrew his hand.

"What is it with this job that the postholder changes so often? No sooner have I learned the ChiZA's name than someone else gets the job."

"I think it has something to do with the residents of Z6080 being such a grumpy bunch of bastards." Purcell grinned to let Jeff know he was joking.

Cleveland thought he might warm to the man, not that he was ready to go easy on him. "I'm sorry. I had no idea it was our fault that you are so terrible at your jobs."

"Touche." Purcell took a seat behind his desk. "Our performance is, as you probably know, judged by several targets, one of which is to keep complaints to a minimum. Unfortunately, my predecessor hit the number required for a review."

"And he was found to be lacking."

"He was."

"Who undertakes this review?"

"The four Lead Regional Administrators."

"Nice. The four natural successors to the throne review the head's performance and fitness for office. They are not going to have a vested interest, are they? Little wonder ChiZAs don't stay around very long." Jeff waited for a reaction, but Purcell merely offered a polite grin. "Which region did you lead?"

"I was in the West, but I did not seek promotion. I supported my predecessor, but sadly, my three colleagues outvoted me. I did not stand in the election."

"But here you are. Why didn't you want the job?"

"I was keeping my head down, hoping to move to Z80+, but my three peers could not agree on which one should get the promotion, and I felt uneasy about having to vote for any of them. It remained a stalemate until the Central Committee demanded someone step up. I was selected."

"You were the compromise candidate. That's unlucky." Jeff sat on a wooden chair. "How long do you think you'll last?"

"I have no idea. The last ChiZA was unfortunate because last year's intake contained many ex-military personnel. That type doesn't like to grow old gracefully. They always need a battle to fight. They complained about everything from the quality of the free bin liners to the colour of the bus seats. Numbers went through the roof."

"Have things calmed down now?"

"Yes, thankfully. We introduced a wide range of services to keep the folks busy."

"Ah, you are responsible for constructing the bowling green in our village. I am sure it will be nice when it's finished."

"I regret that it has taken longer than expected, but the wider policy has succeeded. The groups we established for volunteers, gardeners and ramblers are very popular."

"Okay, there's no need to go on and on about the ramblers." Purcell cringed. Cleveland added. "How will you cope with the next lot of incomers?"

"There won't be such a major influx for a year or two. I have time to research names and interests."

Jeff had not expected such honesty. It might be worth his

listening to what Purcell had to say. "Why am I here?"

"Well, Jeff, do you mind if I call you Jeff?"

"I'd rather you didn't call me anything at all."

Purcell looked perplexed. "But I must call you something. Not to do so would be impolite."

"I don't see how using my name has anything to do with manners. It annoys me when people insist on calling you by your name, even if you've never met them. They do it because it creates an illusion of familiarity. One that marketing and customer service gurus have accentuated over many years. I find it a crass, unnecessary practice. I dislike people repeating my name during a conversation."

"I only wanted to put you at ease."

"Do I look worried or stressed?"

"Not at all."

"Then don't fix what's not broken." Jeff looked around the office. "There are only two people here." His finger pointed at Purcell, and his thumb flicked back at himself. "When you speak, I will assume your words are aimed at me and vice versa. Does that sound sensible?"

"Yes. Yes, I suppose it does."

"Good. In that case, you don't need to call me anything."

"Fair enough." Purcell was still unsure about what had just happened. "I will not mention your name."

"Thanks." Jeff had yet to finish. "Before we talk business, I wish to get something off my chest. Please do not record it as a complaint. At least, not at this stage." Purcell nodded, encouraging him to continue. "I want you to know that I do not appreciate being collected from home at short notice and driven halfway across the country only to be kept waiting while you finish your lunch."

An embarrassed Purcell asked why Jeff would think such a thing. Cleveland pointed at the crumbs on his desk, the empty wrappers in his bin and the remains of the sandwich partially hidden by the file on his desk. "Elementary, my dear ChiZA."

"I am sorry about that, Je… my previous meeting overran, and there was a queue in the canteen, but I still thought I had enough time to eat before you arrived. I was not expecting you to get here that quickly. I do apologise."

"Accepted." Cleveland dropped his hat on the floor beside him, "Talking of food. Can you get Stephen to fetch me a cheese and pickle sandwich, brown bread, with not too much butter? I haven't had any lunch, and a Welsh cake isn't going to do it for me."

"Of course." Purcell picked up his telephone, dialled a number and placed the order.

The ChiZA rested his hands on his desk as he pondered how to regain control of the discussion. "Your sandwich will be here very soon. Is there anything else?"

"No thanks."

"In that case, let me explain why I asked you to come in today."

"Please do. I'm all ears."

"Thank you." Purcell leaned on his desk. "I am sure you will have heard of Lord McGregor?"

Cleveland nodded. "Of course. Lord Kendal McGregor, the eminent Judge. I gave evidence before him many times. He presided over who knows how many trials and put an end to the police force in this country."

"That is a bit harsh. It was not His Lordship's fault. It is up to individual Administrations to decide whether to have a police presence. The fact that none of them does is not down to Lord McGregor."

"But he recommended giving Administrations the power to defund the police and do the work themselves."

"His Lordship did not take the final decision. He undertook the review and submitted recommendations."

"I accept that, but his report highlighted police shortcomings without acknowledging how thinly resources were stretched."

"I fear we will have to agree to disagree on that. From my memory, the actions of corrupt officers brought about the police force's demise."

Cleveland considered reciting his counterargument but saw no point in raking over the coals.

He was the lead officer in one of the cases subsequently used to support the case for scrapping the police. One of his young constables, PC McCallum, was accused of planting incriminating evidence. At the time, there was nothing to substantiate the claims against the officer, and Jeff was confident McCallum would be cleared. Then the Shift hit, everything stopped, and Jeff had retired by the time the country got moving again. Sometime later, the investigation reopened, and multiple witnesses came forward to implicate McCallum in a multitude of cases that were subsequently dismissed because the police were found to have acted illegally. Subsequent, exhaustive inquiries into police corruption identified failings that no government could ignore. An independent review panel, chaired by McGregor, was established. The recommendations included allowing the new Zonal Administrations to defund the police.

"Anyway, enough of the history lesson," Jeff scratched his chin. "What's Kendal done now?"

"Lord McGregor has been murdered."

Cleveland lurched forward in his seat. "When?"

"His body was found the day before yesterday at his home in Bournemouth."

Cleveland rested his elbows on his knees, clasping his hands. "Murdered?" He found it difficult to believe what he'd been told. "He's been murdered in the ROFZ?"

"ROFZ?"

"The Really Old Fu…Folks Zone."

Purcell's face showed the slightest glimmer of a smile. "Ah, I see. I had not heard that phrase. I know some call it the SBDZone - The Should be Dead Zone – but I've never heard of the ROFZ. However, perhaps we can use the correct terminology from now on. As you know, Bournemouth forms a part of the Inner Region of Z80+."

"I'll try. Why are we discussing this? What does it have to do with me? Surely you cannot suspect me of murdering the

Judge?"

"No. I do not think that at all. I have invited you here today because I would like you to investigate the murder to see if you can find something my Administrators missed."

"You want me to investigate?" Cleveland's fingers pulled at his chin. "Why would I want to do that?"

Purcell's answer came quickly. "We would pay you, and we could arrange extra time with your children. You have grandchildren, I understand."

Cleveland nodded. "I do."

"Well, I'm sure extra visiting permits would be convenient."

"It's a long journey to make on my own."

Purcell smirked. "The permits would also cover your children and their partners. You could make a family holiday out of it. We'll even fund your accommodation."

Cleveland's smile briefly expanded. "I'm sure we could find time for that. If that is, I was interested. You must remember that His Lordship brought about the downfall of an institution that…well, let's say, I held very close to my heart. Why would I care who killed him?"

Again, Purcell had anticipated the question. "Because you relish the challenge, you enjoy the thrill of the chase. But most of all, I am prepared to bet that you would love to show the Administration a thing or two."

Cleveland nodded, appreciating that Purcell was close to the mark, but was not convinced this was a job he fancied. "I've been out of action for a long time. I am not sure I am the best choice for this role."

"Don't be so modest. You come very highly recommended, and we are not expecting you to solve the case. We merely want you to investigate to see if your trained eyes can see something others have not."

"That's all."

Purcell nodded.

"Tell me more. How was he killed?"

"He was tied up, with a block of wood rammed between his

knees, which someone smashed with a sledgehammer."

"Nasty." Cleveland let out a faint whistle. "I remember reading something about that. Weren't there similar cases in Leeds many moons ago? The Admins blamed it on gangs torturing so-called informants."

"You have a good memory."

Jeff ignored the compliment. "Was the Judge tortured?"

"We don't know, not for sure, but we think it is likely."

"But why torture an old man.... how old was he? Early nineties?"

"Ninety-three. What difference does his age make?"

Cleveland slumped back on his chair, crossed his legs and folded his arms. The fingers on his right hand moved over his lips. "None, I suppose. Murder is murder. It just seems a particularly callous, inhumane way to kill an old man. He was frail the last time I saw him, and that was years ago. I cannot believe he fattened up since then." He pulled his cheeks as he considered his next question. "Do you have any idea who did this?"

"None."

"Was he unpopular? Had he trod on the wrong toes?"

"Apart from everyone who used to serve in the police force?"

Jeff gave a wry smile. "Obviously. But it is unlikely that ex-police officers were involved. We upheld the laws. We didn't break them."

"That is a contentious point."

"Moving on. Has the Judge upset anybody in the last few years?"

"I don't imagine he has. By all accounts, he lived a peaceful life."

"Any indication of what his assailant might have been looking for? Did he have valuables in his house? Was the Judge working on anything that might have had value to someone?" Purcell shook his head. "Were there hidden rooms or safes where he stored his valuables?"

"As far as we can tell, nothing was stolen. We can find no

evidence that anything is missing. His Lordship did not have much by way of valuables. It appears he lived off his pension. He had already donated most of his personal and family wealth to his children. I am told that he no longer needed it. I very much doubt that his death is linked to a robbery. From what I have been told, the contents of the house look untouched."

"Then why kill him?"

Purcell guessed, "Maybe it was revenge? You mentioned that he heard many high-profile cases."

"Hmm...but why the torture? What is there to gain from torturing an old man? He probably wouldn't have survived long enough to make it a real sport." He pursed his lips and then put his upper teeth into the bottom lip as he pondered again. "You say he was tied up?"

"His hands were suspended above him, tied to a light fitting."

"That sort of thing takes time to arrange. Why would they take the risk? He died at his home in the ROF...sorry, Z80+?"

"He did."

"Whoever did this would either have to live there or have access to the zone." His brain worked quickly to put his thoughts into words. "His neighbours are unlikely to have the strength to pull that off, which suggests it was an outsider. Who could have gotten in? It's not easy to access the Inner Region of Z80+."

Purcell's words cut him off. "There is nothing unique about that area. Zone rules dictate that inhabitants of a younger zone cannot infringe on an older zone without the correct documentation. That rule is applied equally across the country."

Cleveland waved a hand, dismissing the interruption. "That's rubbish, and you know it as well as I do. The Inner Region of the ROFZ is the most securely protected of all the zones. It's where the Committee's rich and famous friends go to die. Pegging it there is a thank you for your efforts or wealth."

"You are more cynical than I expected."

"I'm only just warming up." Cleveland focused his thoughts on the case. "Do you have a list of recent visitors to the Zone?"

"We do and have already checked it. There is nothing unusual about it. Everyone on the list has permission to be in the area."

"All the same, someone ought to check visitors' movements. You know the sort of thing. Check if anyone hung around longer than expected. Whether any of them took a detour."

"I will get someone to look into that."

"Was there any evidence of forced entry at the house?"

"Not as far as we can tell."

"I will need to see the house."

"Of course."

"Where's the body?"

"The body?"

"Yes, the body. Did forensics find anything? Has the post-mortem been carried out?"

"The body has been incinerated, and the remains are probably on their way to Norfolk to be used as landfill. I am sure I do not need to remind you that corpses are removed within eight hours, as we no longer have space for burials."

Jeff knew the score but could not believe the body had been taken. "But this is a murder. A murder of a prominent man."

"Rules are rules, no matter who you are."

"What about forensics?"

"We have none. Those services were defunded at the same time as the police, and the computer hardware and software were reallocated to where they were needed most. Even if we found evidence, we couldn't do much with it."

This was not welcome news. "Let me get my head around this. There is no body, evidence, suspects, or police to investigate this matter."

Purcell pursed his lips and nodded. "That's about the size of it. There may be evidence at the Judge's house. We have Administrators at the property to keep an eye on things, but they are not equipped to undertake an investigation."

"Who found the body?"

"Amelia Duggan. She is a Trans-zoner employed to provide

domestic assistance to His Lordship. She reported the body to the Administrators who have remained at the house."

"Amelia is a Transzer. Where would I find her?"

"She has a flat close to His Lordship's house."

"A flat? How did she manage that? I thought you ferried Transzers in and out."

"We do if they live in an adjacent zone, but Amelia didn't. She is in her early twenties."

"Early twenties," Jeff's eyebrows could not reach any higher. "Who fixed that? Amelia would have crossed…what…three age zones? How was that allowed?"

"Certain individuals are granted permission to cross multiple zones where they can provide services not readily available in their new area."

Jeff still did not understand. "But plenty of people in my zone would welcome the chance to earn extra money doing domestic services for the wealthy old folks. How did this twenty-something-year-old get the job?"

"I don't know. I was not involved in the decision. I think it helps if you have friends in the right places."

"I see." Jeff nodded. "Who helped Amelia?"

"I believe her mother is very well connected."

Jeff nodded again. "I might have guessed."

"You will have an opportunity to meet Amelia. From what I hear, she is very personable."

"If I accept the role."

"Is there a doubt?"

"There are a few issues. The biggest being I am not sure how much help I will be. There is little, if anything, to go on."

"I did not expect you to quit just yet."

"I didn't say I was giving up. I am just being honest. I'll visit Bournemouth to see what's what, but I'm not promising anything."

"I understand. Thank you."

"How will I get there? Bus? Train?"

"We will provide you with a driver for your investigation."

Jeff liked the sound of that. He thought about his diary for the rest of the week. Other than Saturday, he had nothing planned. "In that case. I want to go tomorrow. Can you ensure Amelia is available to chat? I also need to speak to the first Admins on the scene."

"I can arrange that." Purcell scribbled notes on a nearby pad. "There are a few other things we need to sort out."

"Like what?"

"We need to establish a few ground rules, such as the scope of your involvement, what role you will play, your fee, to whom you will report, etcetera."

"I haven't accepted the job yet."

"I am well aware of that, but it is probably best if we both know what arrangement we are entering into."

"That seems sensible." Jeff leaned forward in his seat. "I need to ask a question first."

"Another one. Please go on."

"Why me?"

"I don't understand."

"Why do you want me involved in the investigation? I am one of the bad guys, remember? It was partly due to one of my cases, indeed one of my team, that the purge of the police forces started. Now, you want to bring me back into the fold. Why? You have plenty of Administrators, including ex-coppers, available to do the job. Why bring me out of mothballs? I'm old, retired, and haven't been a policeman since the Shift..."

"You mean the Great Pearl?"

Cleveland's eyebrows raised and fell. "You can't still be using that?"

"I can, and you should too. The Central Committee wants us all to refer to the events of eight years ago as the Great Planet Earth Lurch."

"You won't hear me saying it. It's a crap acronym. That was another one of Lord Williams' bright ideas, wasn't it?"

Lord Williams was the current Committee Secretary for

Communication. He developed and introduced the Zones with help from his wife and Lord Rayer.

"The Secretary-General wants people to use it. The Great Pearl was the moment the balance of the World changed, allowing Britain to blossom."

"Bloody hell! I cannot believe anyone spouts that nonsense." Cleveland placed his face into his hands. "I will never understand how Lord Williams earned a living before the Shift…"

"He was in marketing…"

"I know, but I doubt he was any good at it."

"Why would you think that?"

"Ignoring the grief and hardship caused by the Zones, his catchy phrases and soundbites leave much to be desired. He thinks people are stupid."

"In what way?"

"Take the Admins' motto, 'Civility, Attentiveness and Politeness'. That was lifted from the NYPD's 'Respect, Professionalism and Courtesy'. He claims the words came out of his head. They probably shot out of the other end. I am not sure that spouting such rubbish justifies his significant salary."

"Lord Williams, like all members of the Central Committee, works to serve the people of this country. He is not out for personal gain."

Cleveland leaned back in his chair and stretched, overstating his imaginary struggle to restrain a yawn. "Okay, okay, save me the sermon. I hear those words every time a member of the Central Committee appears on the screen, trying to justify their existence." Jeff's elbows rested on his knees. "You still haven't answered my question. Why do you want me to investigate this murder?"

"You have the necessary experience and gravitas, and you come highly recommended."

"Even with the blot on my CV?"

"I am aware of issues with a member of your old team, but the full extent of those problems did not come to light until after you retired."

"I let my colleague down. He got hung out to dry. I would not have accepted retirement had I been fit for work, but ..."

Purcell interjected. "There is no need to dwell on that. The fact remains that you retired with an exemplary record. We have many ex-police officers working for the Administration, but very few have your experience in cases of this nature. We need someone whom the residents of inner Z80+ will accept and trust. The area is primarily left to its own devices. The residents don't engage much with the outside world."

"In that case, isn't it better to let the local Admins work on it?"

"Z80+ does not currently have its own Administration. There is talk about establishing one, but my people get drafted to look after residents in the meantime. They are not universally popular. Our role is limited to organising transport, arranging domestic support, keeping the streets and public gardens tidy, and providing support where necessary. We maintain border security but try to remain invisible as far as the residents are concerned."

"You could easily investigate this without causing consternation. The Judge's neighbours are bound to know what's happened. They will be reassured to see a presence. Any presence."

"The Inner Region is full of highly influential people. Many of them hanker after the old days of the boys in blue."

"Put your people in police uniforms and send them in."

"People would soon find out. The residents would feel uncomfortable with Administrators investigating the murder of such a prominent person. Whereas, I believe, bringing Chief Inspector Cleveland in to investigate will help reassure them."

Jeff was not convinced his presence was necessary. "Is the real reason you want me involved because you know there is no chance of me finding anything? My failure will allow you to perpetuate the myth that all police are useless."

"Not at all. We have complete faith in your ability and want to demonstrate to the great and good that we are taking this crime very seriously."

He waited for Jeff's response.

Cleveland scratched his ear. "I very much doubt the residents of the ROFZ know who I am or what I used to be." He leaned forward again. "Why me?"

"I just explained…"

"Who chose me? You had probably never heard of me until today."

Purcell pondered how to respond. "It was Lord Wilson, the Committee Secretary for National Security."

Cleveland's face lit up. "My old Chief Constable. I always knew he would make a better politician than he was a policeman. He's a nice enough bloke but not always the best judge of character."

"I don't know about that. He was adamant that it had to be you. Before you ask, he did not explain his reasons."

There was a knock on the office door.

"Enter," Purcell shouted.

Stephen entered, pushing a trolley.

"Good timing," Purcell pointed at the table. "Put Mr Cleveland's sandwich and the other items on there." He rose from his seat and held out an arm, inviting Jeff to join him. "Would you like to eat as we discuss the terms of your employment?"

"That's an excellent idea," Cleveland agreed, slowly standing.

"Don't forget your sandwich."

As they sat at the other table, Jeff asked, "Are you sure you can afford my rates?"

"I am, but money won't be the deciding factor here."

"What will?"

"The chance to solve a high-profile murder. If what I heard about you is true, then you are influenced more by the challenge than by monetary gain. You will be very hard-pressed to find a bigger challenge than this one."

Cleveland already knew that. "We'll soon find out." Cleveland thought about his ex-boss and allowed himself another wry smile as he munched his cheese and pickle sandwich.

Lunch over, terms agreed, and chain of command established. Purcell used the telephone.

A moment later, there was a knock on his door.

"Enter."

A grey-haired man of average build, wearing the uniform of a Lead Administrator, entered. "You wanted to see me, sir."

"I did. Come on in, Norman. Close the door behind you."

Jeff studied the Administrator. Norman worked for the Western region of Z6080. He looked the part, apart from his open-toed leather sandals and grey socks. Jeff turned away to stop himself from laughing. He had often told Flissy and his children to shoot him if they caught him wearing sandals and socks.

"This is Senior Administrator Norman Draper. He is one of the region's best. Norman, this is Jeff Cleveland. I should say ex-Chief Inspector Jeff Cleveland. He is going to investigate the death of His Lordship."

"Very good, sir." Norman held out a hand. "Pleased to meet you. Do I call you Chief Inspector? Mr Cleveland? Jeffrey or Jeff?"

"We'll get to that, but certainly not Jeffrey, as it is not my name." He shook Norman's hand. "How do you do?"

"Very well, thank you. However, my feet are rather painful today. I wouldn't normally wear sandals. I also have a slight twinge in my knee."

Jeff wished people could understand when questions were rhetorical. "Sorry to hear that. I hope it doesn't stop you from doing your job."

"Not at all."

Purcell told Norman to drive Jeff home. It would provide an opportunity for them to get acquainted. He asked Norman to return to his office after dropping Cleveland off. Purcell would arrange for the delivery of relevant papers and for Jeff to get an ID card and a mobile phone.

"Just one last thing," Jeff said, "I assume my investigation will not be restricted by the Administrators either here or in the other zones?"

"Zones as in plural?" Purcell's eyes narrowed. "How many zones do you think you will need to access? The death occurred in a neighbouring zone. I see no reason for you to travel elsewhere."

"But if my investigations lead me in a different direction, then I have permission to follow my nose, and I will not face problems with your counterparts?"

"Not at all. Secretary Wilson has already issued a decree for you to get full support from all Administrations. He probably intended that to cover this zone and Z80+, but the order was not specific. It could, therefore, be interpreted as applying equally to all zones. It's probably best to speak with me before crossing into other areas."

Jeff was happy to comply. "And I have carte blanche to investigate this as I see fit?"

"You can do whatever you believe is necessary to find who killed His Lordship. If you encounter any resistance, let me know."

"I will."

"There is one proviso. An Administrator must always accompany you. We need to know where you are."

Norman and Jeff headed to the car.

The M4 was quiet. Cars were few and far between, and Norman did not care about saving petrol. They made rapid progress.

The Admin spoke as they approached the road to Jeff's village. "What time in the morning, and where do you want to go first?"

Jeff had opted to sit in the back seat and could only see Norman's eyes via the rearview mirror. "Eight, and I think we should start at the crime scene."

"That's fine. I will ensure the tank is full."

"Thanks."

"Can I ask you a question?"

"Of course."

"What is your Christian name? Everyone refers to you as Jeff Cleveland, which I thought was short for Jeffrey, but you said that is not your name. Were you registered as Jeff?"

"No. When my father discovered a dead American President who shared our family surname, he became obsessed with everything to do with the man and his country. I was named Jefferson Grover, and my brother is Lincoln Roosevelt. Everyone calls him Lin. I think I had the better deal." He waited for a chuckle, but nothing came. "Take the next right."

4. BACK ON THE BEAT

What the hell have I done? Why did I agree to get involved? Ex-Detective Chief Inspector Cleveland felt his stomach turn as he attempted to focus on his breakfast. He tried another mouthful of the cereal but quickly spat it back into the bowl. He was too nervous to eat.

Jeff emptied the cereal into the food waste and rinsed his bowl under the tap. His cup of tea was still warm. He carried it with him to the stairs, where he raided the cupboard for items that might be useful for his new role.

The old, battered leather briefcase contained what remained of his time as a policeman. It had been an age since he opened it, and he had long forgotten what was inside.

He gathered unused notebooks, pens, pencils, and his old extendable baton and laid them on the dining table.

The biros were useless. The ink had completely dried up. The pencils had life in them. He sharpened the blunter ones with a knife as more memories came flooding back.

Dad, Malcolm Cleveland, was an electrician who used a sharp knife to cut cables and trim wires. He was always keen to pass on tips to his sons. Malcolm patiently instructed Jeff on handling a knife by getting him to sharpen a pencil. Jeff recalled the bloodied fingers and mumbled swear words that had made his father laugh loudly.

Malcolm hoped his sons would take over his electrical business, but Jeff made it clear he had neither an interest in nor any aptitude for electrics and wanted to join the police force. His brother, Lincoln, heeded the lessons, inherited their father's talents, and acquired the firm. There was never any animosity. The brothers remained close whilst not living in each other's pockets.

Jeff rang Lin the previous evening to tell him about his new role. His brother could not believe the Admins were desperate enough to recruit a *failed old fart* to do their policing before he congratulated his brother and wished him well. Jeff suggested it might be the shortest appointment ever. The odds were stacked against him, but Lin told him to be optimistic. He reminded Jeff that he was a good copper and could solve this case standing on his head.

Lin promised to visit soon to see how things were progressing. He admitted to having an ulterior motive. He and his wife had a special anniversary on the horizon and wanted to see what Jeff was buying them. Jeff suggested Lin was as subtle as a brick.

Cleveland had also spoken with his children to update them on developments. Both were pleased for him but warned their father to be careful. The country had changed significantly since he last worked, and not everywhere was safe. Jeff thought it ironic that they were worried about him. He dismissed their concerns and assured them he would be fine.

Having had the night to think about it, he wondered whether he had made a colossal mistake accepting the job. This was an impossible task. Not everyone would be supportive.

Jeff tried to rid his mind of doubts as he stuffed a couple of notebooks and pencils into his jacket pockets.

He rested his hands on the rim of his kitchen sink and breathed deeply. He felt like he would be sick. He told himself not to be such a stupid old man. This was just another day in the office, another stroll down a once familiar path, but deep down, he knew this was different. This was something new. He had not expected to do this job again and feared being out of his depth. Jeff tightened his grip on the sink, tilted his head back, closed his eyes, and calmed his breathing. He held the position, emptying his mind of thought and doubt. His arms loosened, and he dropped his chin to his chest. He opened his eyes in time to catch a chaffinch helping itself to the scraps on his bird table.

Cleveland wriggled his head and shoulders before running a hand over his hair.

"Come on, you sad old man, you've got a job to do," he muttered, moving into the hall to await his lift.

Norman tooted the horn and, by the time Jeff reached the car, had opened the rear door.
"A nice trip to Bournemouth. I know where that is. I won't go too fast. Purcell reminded me that I need to save fuel."
"Have you got the address of the Judge's house?"
"I have." Norman started the car and fought to get the seatbelt across his chest. "These things are ancient and don't want to move." He finally secured the clip. "Purcell asked me to give you papers." Norman looked at him through the mirror. "Details of visitors to Z80+ on the day the Judge died. Nothing exciting, nobody you wouldn't expect to find there. I don't think you'll find it of much use."
Jeff would make his own decisions. "Can I see them, please?"
"Of course." Norman grabbed the canvas bag and lifted it into the back.
"Thank you. I will read this as we go along."
"I can't read in a car. I have never been able to. It makes me throw up." He pondered his words for a second, "Not just cars either. Travelling by bus or in a lorry has the same effect. I am okay on a train, though."
"Right, I will try not to make a mess." Cleveland opened the canvas bag and removed several bundles of paper. He put his glasses in his breast pocket. He read better without them.
Norman made steady, if unspectacular, progress on the road toward Warminster. Cleveland kept conversation to a minimum, concentrating on the documents from Purcell.
The first was a yellow ring binder containing a list of everyone who signed in and out of Z80+ in the forty-eight hours before the body was discovered. He was pleased that someone had cross-referenced the lists of those arriving against those who had left the zone. This provided an estimate of visitors' time spent in the zone. A large "R" had been placed against the names of residents re-entering the zone.

The list identified seven individuals who had entered the zone but were not shown to have left. Five were Administrators, and the other two were categorised as 'Resident Support Workers'. The address of each resident who required support was listed in the margin. Cleveland made a mental note to make further enquiries about the movements of these seven.

The second document was a blue binder containing the names, addresses, and previous professions of every registered resident of the Bournemouth area. Where an individual had no noteworthy previous occupation, the form explained why they had been allowed to live there. As he read a few descriptions, Cleveland despaired, *'Grandfather to Committee Secretary for Defence'* and *'Family money invested in State enterprises.'*

The Judge's immediate neighbours were in their mid to late nineties, and most suffered from disability. Cleveland decided that these were unlikely to have committed the crime without assistance. There was another reason to dismiss the neighbours as suspects; why would they kill the Judge on their doorstep? Jeff was sure the killer was an outsider.

The third bundle of papers, tied with red string, was the most voluminous and gave details of everyone with a permit to access Z80+. Cleveland was astonished by the number of pages in this list, but was relieved when he saw that the bulk of it gave names, but not addresses, of all the Administrators allowed in the zone. He quickly flicked through the pages until he reached the end.

The last dozen pages provided personal details of the Resident Support Workers, including their name, address, age, previous history, and, for those allowed to live in the zone, the details of the person who had sponsored them.

A red ink circle had been drawn around the name of Amelia Duggan, who was listed as a support worker to Lord Kendal McGregor. Aged 23, she had been a language student at Leeds University, where she passed with honours. She spoke Spanish, French and German. Cleveland read a manuscript note, scribbled in black ink across her list of qualifications, *'Not much use now then'*. He wondered if Purcell had seen that.

Reading on, Cleveland saw that Amelia was the granddaughter of Lord Fulmer. Her sponsor, Lord Wilson, Cleveland's old boss, assisted in her quest for a job in Z80+.

He ran a finger down the column, noting the ages of the other support workers, and was surprised at how many came from Z1830. He could not begin to comprehend how much influence had been exerted to get them there.

In Amelia's case, the influence extended beyond employment. She was allocated an apartment close to Bournemouth's main square. There was no evidence of a boyfriend or flatmates. She did not pay rent and appeared to have a higher salary than her counterparts. Cleveland wondered again how such privilege was justified.

His eyes drifted out the window as he deliberated why a young girl would want to live in the SBD zone. She would probably have very little to do besides work. That seemed a strange life choice. There had to be a reason for her relocation.

Jeff had heard that female Transzers encountered significant problems in their new zone. Rumours abounded about them being forced into prostitution, marriage, childbearing and other undesirable activities. Several widowers in his neighbourhood had expressed a desire for a young wife, but could not afford one.

He revisited the bundle of papers and read Amelia's Agency application form. Her hobbies were swimming, cooking, cleaning and reading. Cleveland had no idea whether these were actual interests or simply what she had been told to list.

It dawned on Jeff that Amelia had been watched. There were comprehensive details about her activities. He could not decide whether that was for her protection, because she was seen as a threat or because the Administrators were lustful. Reading on, he decided the latter was closer to the truth. Somebody had scribbled in the margin next to her hobbies, '*AD likes to flaunt her young, firm body in front of the old men on Bournemouth beach'*. Jeff expected better. Comments about how

Amelia '*Looks great in her red bikini but gorgeous in the black one*' made him uneasy. A few of the other scribbles were even more sexist and offensive.

Jeff tried to work out who had been watching her. If Purcell had told him the truth about the Administrators' lack of presence in the zone, then who had made the notes about Amelia, and why were they allowed to record such irrelevant comments in official records?

He wondered who made the scribbles. It looked like they came from the same hand, but what were the chances of someone repeatedly arriving just as Amelia visited the beach? If it were a local Admin, how could they monitor her without getting noticed?

The answer came quickly. Amelia had been watched on CCTV. Jeff surmised that, although the Bournemouth area had few Administrators on the beat, it still had operational cameras. He took out a pencil and wrote, '*Check CCTV. Check the other Transzers. Who owns AD's flat?*

Norman proposed a shortcut. He claimed to know this road like the back of his hand. The lane had many bends, but did not stop Norman from speeding. Cleveland felt queasy getting bounced about in the back. He stopped reading, took deep breaths, and bundled the papers into the bag. "Take it easy on the bends. I want to get there in one piece," he said, replacing his glasses.

"Yes, of course." Norman eased off the accelerator. "We should be there soon."

Entry into Z80+ proved more difficult than Cleveland expected. As the car approached the West Gate, close to Blandford Forum, the guards refused entry and told Norman to check in at Central Gate, Salisbury.

Jeff studied the high metal fence alongside the road. Barriers across the road restricted access. Administrators were everywhere. All were armed, and most were accompanied by a sniffer dog. Norman guessed the Judge's death had raised the security level.

Their trip to Salisbury was interrupted by more stops as Administrators checked all vehicles. Pedestrians and cyclists were also searched. Jeff guessed the Judge's death was the cause of the increased security.

Cleveland and Norman got stopped, searched, and sent on their way again eight times. Jeff joked that the day before, he had not got in a car for over a year, and now he had been in and out of one ten times in two days. Norman did not even smile. He lectured his passenger on the need for vigilance. Cleveland was silent for the remainder of the journey.

The vehicle pulled off a main road and onto the grounds of a large, detached property. The driveway allowed vehicles to enter through the gate and make a loop before exiting.

The gardens were perfect. The gravel border adjoining the drive contained well-tended bushes, flowers and elegant shrubs. The lawns could have hosted a game of championship bowls. Cleveland was envious. By comparison, the green at the recently established Marshfield Bowls Club looked like a wasteland.

The car stopped behind a white van just outside the front door. Cleveland checked that they had the correct address. Nothing suggested this was a crime scene. The front entrance was unguarded, and a workman was cleaning windows. He wore a flat cap and white overalls.

"What do you think you are doing?" Cleveland asked as he climbed out of the car.

The workman stopped and looked around. Not seeing anyone else, he sensed the man in the jacket, wearing a Trilby, had spoken to him. "I'm riding my bike. What do you think you're doing?"

Cleveland was happy that sarcasm had not been wholly eradicated from everyday life. "Never mind me. What are you doing here? You are interfering with a crime scene."

The man dropped his chamois leather onto a rung on his ladder, removed his cap and scratched his head with his free hand. "I'm cleaning the windows. That's what I do: I clean windows. I get paid to clean the windows twice a month. I would normally have done it yesterday, but the Administrators wouldn't let me through."

"But they let you through today?"

"No, they stopped me at the gate, and I'm still waiting there." He smirked. "Of course, they let me through. I wouldn't be here otherwise."

Cleveland scanned around the exterior of the property. There was no sign of anyone in uniform. "Where are the Administrators?"

"I have no idea. The guy at the gate checked my papers and asked me what I wanted. He asks the same question every time, and I always give the same answer. We had a bit of a chat, and then he sent me through." He looked around. "His mates are probably around, but he's the only Admin I've seen, apart from you and your driver."

"I am not an Administrator," Cleveland surveyed the surroundings. There were none of the usual signs of a crime scene. No control centre had been established, police crime scene tape had not been used to mark the perimeter, and, most surprisingly, there was no sign of an Admin. He pushed his hat back and scratched his forehead. "How long have you been here?"

The window cleaner checked his watch. "About an hour."

"What were your movements before that?" The question came automatically.

"I left home at seven and got through the zone gates just after quarter past. I had a few other houses to do on the way, so by the time I got here, it was after nine. Security is tighter than ever this morning. If they searched my van once, they must have searched it half a dozen times."

"But once you got here, nothing? Nobody stopped you from entering the building?"

"No."

"And you haven't been told where you can and cannot walk?"

"Nothing at all." The window cleaner pointed at the entry gate. "As I said, he wanted to check why I was here, but I showed him my papers, and he let me in."

Cleveland folded his left arm across his body and rested his right elbow on his left wrist, pulling at his face as he thought aloud again. "It would be much easier with a Scene of Crime Team."

"Sorry? Who? Scene of Crime Team? Are they like the CSI?"

"Yes, that's them." Cleveland was not paying much attention. His thoughts were elsewhere. "We called them SOCO - Scene of Crime Officers."

"I used to love the CSI series." The man nodded. "They don't make shows like that anymore. Television is just not the same nowadays. All we get is those boring documentaries and news broadcasts. I miss decent entertainment. They should make more drama programmes."

Jeff often complained to his friends about the amount of state-controlled propaganda the Government broadcasts. "Yes, you're right there." Jeff needed to get on. "I assume they have your details at the gate?"

"Yes, every gate between here and Weymouth, I imagine."

Cleveland spoke to Norman, "Do me a favour. Go and have a word with the man at the gate. Get him to come up to the house to see me. Make sure he brings his paperwork."

Norman checked the distance between him and the gate. "That'll be a waste of time. He'll never leave his post," he replied. "Anyway, you'll need my help inside."

Jeff wanted time alone to assess the scene. "Well, think of an excuse. Tell him that you'll take his place for ten minutes. I won't keep him long."

"But I'm a Senior Admin. I am not a guard."

"I thought you were here to make things easier for me?"

"I am your driver, not your slave."

Cleveland fixed his stare on Norman and did not blink. "Are you going to see him, or shall I?"

Norman eventually said, "Okay, if that's what you want." He

set off down the drive. "It might take me a while, though. My feet are killing me."

"Take your time," Jeff replied. "I'll be inside."

5. IN THE HOUSE OF THE LORD

Cleveland stood in the open front entrance and shouted, "Hello". His voice echoed around the house.

There was no obvious evidence of forced entry. He examined the wooden door. The locks appeared undamaged, and the wooden frame was intact and smooth. Whoever entered the property to kill the Judge had not broken in this way, assuming there was a break-in.

Two Administrators appeared. One hurried down the stairs, and the other came out of a room off the hall. He carried a sandwich.

The man using the stairs spoke first. "Yes? Can we help you?" He looked at Cleveland and then motioned for his colleague to lose the sandwich. The man hid it behind his back.

Cleveland recognised the food carrier but made no greeting. The man's eyes widened, and he subtly shook his head, urging the visitor not to say anything. Jeff stepped inside. "I am here at the request of ChiZA Purcell."

"Really?" the chewing Admin spoke between swallows. "And why has the ChiZA asked you to come here?"

"To investigate the murder of the Judge," Cleveland studied the sandwich eater. The man stood just over six feet tall, had short, cropped light hair, and wore the administrator's regular uniform.

"And did ChiZA Purcell give you any documentation to this effect?" The man from upstairs stepped nearer.

Cleveland showed the identity card and an envelope he had removed from the canvas bag. "Indeed, he did. Here it is."

He handed both to the man from upstairs, who put on his glasses before opening the envelope and reading the letter aloud. His colleague stood beside him, biting into the remains of his sandwich.

Both men read and re-read the letter before putting it back in the envelope. They studied Cleveland's identity card, nodded at each other, and returned both items to their rightful owner.

The man from upstairs spoke. "Thank you, Mr Cleveland. We have been expecting you. I am Administrator Steve Lauren, and this is my colleague, Administrator Mark Harding. We will give you whatever assistance we can, as instructed by Lord Wilson."

"Thank you. I should be grateful that I am dealing with Lauren and Harding rather than Laurel and Hardy." He found his comment funny and giggled.

No trace of a smile from either Admin.

"How can we help?" Harding asked. "What do you want to know?"

The pronunciation of 'know' as 'nore' reminded Cleveland that Harding was from the North.

"Have you two been here all day today?"

Harding replied. "We've been here since Monday. We were the first Administrators on the scene. We came here after the girl was found screaming down by the pier."

"Our seniors ordered us to stay put until told otherwise," Lauren added. "We still haven't been told." His head moved as his eyes circled the interior. "I've been stuck in worse places."

"I bet," Cleveland said. "Can one of you show me where you found the body?"

Lauren and Harding looked at each other again. Lauren mouthed something at his colleague, but Jeff could not tell what it was.

Harding said, "I'll take you up."

Jeff thanked him. "Is there a murder weapon?"

Lauren nodded. "The hammer and the wood block have been taken to Regional HQ for safekeeping."

"Z6080 HQ?"

"Yeah. They collected that at the same time as they came for the body, and that's when we were told to stay put."

This was progress. "Good," Cleveland said. "Has anyone checked for evidence? You know, fibres, footprints, hairs, etc."

He knew the answer before Harding confirmed nobody had.

"Ok. It would be useful to know how many people have wandered through this house since you've been here."

Lauren counted with his fingers. "We were here first, and then the four came to collect the body. That's six."

Harding joined in. "That workman from down the road helped us cut the ropes. He makes seven."

Lauren looked at Harding. "Those three blokes from HQ who come to collect the Judge's papers." He saw Cleveland look surprised. "They heard the Judge was working on a top-secret project."

"But we have no idea what that was," Harding said.

Jeff understood. "Was much taken?"

"A couple of boxes," Harding said. "They brought a pile of those easy-to-assemble cardboard things, but only used two. I think they expected to find more. They walked out with faces like slapped arses."

"So that's ten," Lauren continued counting. "Plus, the two who collected the hammer, wood and rope."

"Twelve," Harding said.

"Do you have any of their names?" Cleveland asked.

Harding's response came quickly. "No."

Lauren raised a hand in the air. He had remembered another detail. "I almost forgot the four old farts from the zonal residents' committee who visited last night. That makes sixteen.

"Zonal committee?" Cleveland asked. "What's that? What does it do? What did they want?"

"Nothing much, really," Lauren said, "they told us they are a liaison group forging closer links between the residents and the Administration." He breathed, relieved at finishing his explanation.

Harding took over. "They only deal with the bigger fish. They looked down their noses at us. Fortunately, they didn't stick around for very long. They helped themselves to get what they wanted from the fridge, the freezer, and the drinks cabinet.

There was not much left after their visit. They were like locusts."

"Yes, I quite fancied that leg of Welsh lamb myself," Lauren confessed.

Cleveland raised his eyebrows at the mention of the Welsh lamb. Only the privileged few had access to such rarities, reinforcing his prejudices about how influential and well-connected the late Judge and his counterparts were. "And you just let them take what they wanted?"

"Yes," Lauren was unapologetic. "It's standard practice these days for neighbours to rid the house of perishables after you die." He looked around the hall again. "The furniture and stuff go back to the State, but the food, well, it's every man or woman for themselves. Our Seniors told us not to take any of it away, but we can use what we find to keep us fed."

Cleveland scanned the area again. This was a crime scene. However, with over two dozen feet wandering around the property, he doubted any untarnished evidence remained, even if he had the means to identify it. "I don't suppose you have the names of these zonal committee members?"

"No," Lauren said. "We are under orders to keep a low profile and not to upset the natives."

Cleveland changed tack. "Did anyone take photographs of the scene? Possibly of the body and where it got found?"

Lauren looked at Harding, then back at Cleveland. "Not as far as I know."

"Okay, thanks." This investigation was going exactly the way Jeff feared.

Harding wiped his mouth before leading Cleveland towards the stairway. Lauren shuffled away to the kitchen.

When his colleague was out of sight and earshot, Harding shook Cleveland's hand. "Good to see you again, sir. Sorry about that charade back there. They don't know I used to be in the force. Admins take a dim view of ex-coppers."

"I've heard that. How are you doing? You're looking well. Is the family okay?"

"Fine, thanks, sir. The kids are settled, and me and the wife are doing well. Touch wood." He tapped his head. "How are you?" Harding's face turned solemn. "I meant to visit after …you know, but it never seemed the right time."

"Don't worry about it. I am not sure I would have been much company. I was a bit of a mess back then." He patted Harding on the back as they reached the upper floor. "By the way, stop calling me sir."

"Old habits." He leaned closer to Cleveland and whispered. "You know you asked about photographs." He waited for Cleveland to nod before continuing. "Well, I took a few." Harding took out his mobile phone. "When we arrived, and the house was empty, I took a few snaps. I don't know why. It's probably due to my training. The funny thing is that I haven't seen a dead body for many years. The shock never leaves you." He handed over his phone.

Cleveland looked at the small screen and nodded in appreciation. "Well done, that was a good move." He quickly checked through seven photographs and was pleased that Harding had captured the murder scene from several angles. The images showed the location of the hammer and how the Judge was tied. The last two were slightly blurred but might still prove helpful. "Thank you. Can you send them to me? Purcell has promised me a mobile."

"Yes, of course." He pulled out a business card and handed it over. "Text me when you have your new number."

"Thanks."

"Just keep them to yourself. My life wouldn't be worth living if they found out what I used to do. Since the purge, ex-coppers are treated like second-class citizens. If anyone found out I was still acting like a copper, word would soon get around. I'd have to find another job."

"Would you get kicked out for being an ex-copper?"

"No, just re-assigned. They don't like being reminded of what we were. The Administration is nothing like the Police. A lot of Admins have served time. A few senior ones in this zone have such dodgy backgrounds that they don't want anything to do with ex-police. They wouldn't hurt me, not physically, and couldn't sack me because they need workers. But it wouldn't do me any good to get excluded if you know what I mean. If they think I am one of them, I get the better jobs, which bring other rewards. If I were outside, I would probably end up on litter patrol, and there's no fun or money in that."

"Fair enough." Cleveland had long suspected that not all was well in the Administration. He spotted the stair lift. "Has anyone used that?"

"No, not while I've been here. I wondered how his Lordship got up when the chair is down here?"

"Exactly," Cleveland wished he could take fingerprints. He studied the lift and gently lowered the seat, ensuring he only touched the corner. "Do you know if there is any powder around here? Talc or similar?"

Harding knew what he intended. "It wouldn't do any good if we did. They destroyed the fingerprint database, so we'd have nothing to compare it to even if we found anything."

"When did they do that?"

"About two years ago. They wanted to compile lists of residents in each zone, but because of a shortage of computer space, they had to delete other stuff. From what I hear, the fingerprint and criminal records databases got scrapped."

Cleveland removed his hat and scratched his scalp. "There is no way we can compare fingerprints or check whether similar crimes have been committed before?"

"Not as far as I know."

"This is a nightmare." He walked up the stairs. "What possessed them to do that?"

"It was to do with the shortage of computer equipment, but I think it had more to do with civil liberties."

"I thought we were done with all that?"

"We are, but telling everyone the fingerprint and records data got wiped gives the impression that the State is not gathering records on everyone. It is, but they don't mention it."

"Do they collect much data?"

"A bit. They've started to build new computers. I saw one last week. They are basic, but they can store quite a bit. The chips aren't yet available to make them do everything as quickly as we'd like, but once they get going, I am sure they will build better and faster machines." Harding had overtaken Jeff and was nearing the top landing. "Technology moves very quickly. Remember what computers looked like when we finished work compared to when we started? There was no comparison."

Cleveland appreciated optimism but seriously doubted whether the UK's fledgling IT companies would quickly recover lost ground. Having reduced the manufacturing base before the Shift, the state was not finding it easy to rebuild. There was a shortage of expertise and raw materials.

Harding showed him around the upstairs rooms. The two back bedrooms looked like they had not been used in a while. Three oversized laundry bags sat on the bed in the larger room, still full.

The upstairs bathroom was clean and tidy, and the landing was spotless apart from a stain by the entrance to the Judge's bedroom. Cleveland took a closer look at the mark. Harding told him this was where the cleaner had thrown up after finding the body. The vomit had started to smell, so he and Lauren removed it.

Cleveland opened the door to the Judge's bedroom. There was a faint aroma of urine. Light filled the room through the open curtains and expansive windows. The bed did not appear to have been slept in. All drawers and cupboards were shut. An upturned chair lay beside the bed, with small pieces of reddish-white matter scattered around it.

"Was this how you found it?"

The Administrator looked around the room. "Yes, pretty much." He pointed across the room. "The chair was right under the light fitting, and the Judge was tied to it. His ankles were fastened to the chair legs. He had a block of wood between his knees." Harding swept his arm in a clockwise, quarter arc. "The hammer was left there, just beside the occasional table. It was upright, resting on its head."

"Could it have been placed there?"

Harding considered the question. "I guess that if it had been thrown away, it would probably have landed on its side, but it was upright, so I imagine it could have been placed there. Why is that relevant?"

Cleveland poked his tongue into the gap between his bottom teeth and lip. "I'm not sure. The scene makes me think that whoever did this was calm and collected. Everything is as I'd expect it to be. There is no sign of panic. Whoever did this knew they had plenty of time to torture the Judge to get what they wanted. They were confident they would not be disturbed."

"I see."

"Was the Judge clothed?"

"No, he was completely naked."

Cleveland's tongue explored his left cheek, pushing out the flesh as he did so. "I wonder what they…if it is they…wanted?" He looked at the furniture. "All the cupboards and drawers were shut when you arrived?"

"Yes, every one of them."

"Thieves don't usually bother to tidy up afterwards." Jeff looked around. "If they weren't searching for something, did they want the Judge to either give them what they wanted or to tell them where to find it?"

"If they did, they went about it the hard way. They made it hard for the Judge to tell them anything."

Cleveland looked at Harding, "Why?"

"Because of the bag."

"What bag?"

"The bag they put over the Judge's head." Harding saw that this was news to Jeff. "When we found him, he had a thick plastic bag over his head, covering his mouth. It had been tightened at the back. He wouldn't have been able to breathe much, let alone talk with that on. They would have to put it on and then take it off. That's a lot of effort for a frail old man. My guess is that he probably suffocated before he bled out."

Nobody had mentioned asphyxiation. "Let me see the pictures." Jeff studied the images on the mobile and saw the plastic bag in place. "I never spotted that." He was unhappy and disappointed at his failure and shook his head as he pulled at his lower lip. "Why bag him when you need information? They could not have been sure the Judge would survive very long." Jeff stepped away to view the scene from another angle. "Would they need to kneecap him and choke him? That seems over the top. Did they come to kill him and not search for anything?"

"Sorry?"

Cleveland rubbed his temples. "I thought they were looking for valuables or information. But that theory falls because there is no evidence of a search. Everything is neat and tidy. In any case, the Judge couldn't say much with a bag on his head." Jeff was confused. This made no sense. "Why bag him when you are already breaking his knees?"

"Perhaps they bagged him first." Harding guessed what his ex-boss was thinking. "In which case, why kneecap him?"

"Exactly." Jeff folded his arms. "Perhaps they wanted to hurt him and, in doing so, demonstrate they could do what they wanted. This might not be about gathering information, as I assumed. It could have more to do with proving a point - reminding the Judge that he held no power. It's still torture but for different reasons."

Harding considered the scenario again. "They might have bagged him to make sure nobody heard anything?"

"Possibly, but how much noise could a ninety-three-year-old make? And anyway, who would hear him? This house is vast, and the next-door neighbour is probably the same age but a long way away."

"Perhaps it was a ritual killing? They did it out of habit?"

Cleveland nodded slowly, "You may be onto something there. I heard that the Party Zone gangs used similar techniques, but I don't know if such things happen often in this area."

"Nor me, but it won't take me long to check. There are very few records."

"Don't crimes get logged these days?"

"There is so little crime around here." Jeff's face showed that he didn't believe it. "It's true. Anyone found committing a crime in this Zone faces serious punishment and, as a result, not much happens."

"Can we check for similar crimes in the other zones?"

"I can try, but in the current climate with apathetic administrations, I am not sure we'll find much."

"Why? Don't the Admins record murders?"

"It's a different world nowadays. If someone gets hurt or murdered, the tendency is that their friends and family take revenge. Natural justice. If nobody reacts, then nobody cared in the first place. Why should the Admins do anything? The same goes for lesser offences such as robbery or assault. Those who feel strongly act, but why should Admins intervene if people can't be bothered to remedy problems themselves?"

Cleveland had never been a fan of the 'eye for an eye' system of justice. He accepted that trial by jury was a thing of the past but assumed that the authorities would investigate. "Then why are the island jails full?"

"Admins have a wide range of powers and send all sorts of people away without proving guilt and with no legal representation. Criminals and enemies of the state get hauled off to the islands and remain there until somebody decides they have served long enough, or they buy themselves out. For the most part, they get forgotten about. I've heard about citizens confessing to crimes they had no chance of committing because they're happy amongst friends on the islands. Nobody says or does anything. It makes life much simpler for those in control."

"But that's abhorrent. I thought Admins were supposed to serve and help the public."

"We do, but we do it in different ways. If a Judge or another bigwig in this zone gets bumped off or is a victim of crime, we can't let that go unnoticed. If a crime occurs elsewhere, we leave people to sort it out themselves. Of course, we get told which dissidents and anarchists to lock up. Our leaders spare no effort in removing opposition, but most criminal activities never get reported, so they don't exist."

"How did things end up like this?" Jeff studied the bedroom floor, taking care not to walk on possible evidence, including the still-damp blood stain. There was abundant hair, fibres, dirt, bone fragments and blood, but he could not differentiate between what the killer left and those of the other visitors.

He looked to the ceiling. A small length of rope hung from the ceiling light. "Can we get that down?"

"Yes, no problem," Harding examined the knot tightly wrapped around the metal arm of the light fitting. "I might be unable to untie it, though; I might have to cut it. There are knives in the kitchen."

"Good. And don't forget..."

"I know. I'll try not to touch anything with my bare hands and place evidence in a clean, sealable bag." Harding thought for a moment. There are food bags in the kitchen. I'll use them."

"Thanks," Cleveland said. "Can you collect a few bone fragments while you're at it? And try to get a few carpet fibres from this blood stain."

"You know that you'll struggle to find anyone to do anything with all this evidence."

"I'll worry about that later." Jeff knelt by the large bed, examining a substance resting on the expensive carpet. He prodded the substance with his pencil. "This looks like jelly."

The Admin stepped nearer. "I think it is. The cleaning girl thought the Judge had been off his food recently, so we guessed he had eaten a bowl of jelly."

Harding moved to pick up the blob, but Cleveland moved his arm away. "No, bag it. It is evidence, remember." He sniffed at the substance. "It smells a bit off."

Harding's expression showed that he was unsure what use the jelly would be, but he accepted the instructions. "Fine. It's your call. I'll go and get the bags."

"Thank you." Cleveland continued his search.

Harding returned a few moments later with two rolls of food bags, one of which he tossed to Cleveland.

"Do you want all this jelly and bits of bone?" Harding detached a bag from the roll, opened it, and then turned it inside out. He placed his hand inside the bag.

"Not all, just a few samples."

"Your driver popped in to say the guard refuses to leave his post. You'll have to go down to see him."

"Great." Cleveland wondered why Norman had taken so long to discover nothing. His driver had not impressed so far. "Where is he now?"

"Lauren is making him a sandwich in the kitchen."

Cleveland pointed at a couple of larger fragments he wanted Harding to collect. "He made himself at home very quickly."

"Yes, he knows Lauren from the old days. They seem like long-lost friends." Harding tied another bag. "But then Lauren knows loads of people. You know he is surprisingly well-connected, considering he was only a bookie."

"That profession would bring him into contact with people from all walks of life." Jeff put the chair upright and tested it for stability to check that it would take his weight. "Did you get a knife?"

"It's on the edge of the bed."

Cleveland grabbed the short, sharp knife and placed it between his teeth as he climbed onto the chair. He touched the rope with his bagged hand, but, as feared, it was too tight to undo, so he cut off a piece, secured it in the bag and dropped it onto the bed before dismounting the chair.

"Right, I think that's enough from here. Let's look downstairs." Harding collected all the evidence bags and joined Cleveland on the landing. He leaned on the railing, admiring the view. "This is a cracking house."

Jeff concurred but was more interested in Harding's recent history. "When did you leave the force?"

"I was there until the wind-up."

"What was that like? I often wondered how it felt to see the force coming to an end."

"It was sad. I was still a Sergeant and had only done twelve, but, as you know, others had put their whole lives into it. They broke their hearts and were given shit jobs because they got tarred with the same brush as those accused of being bent. I had already been moved to a desk job in records."

"And what became of those records?"

"I have no idea. We expected the files to be transferred to a central depot or warehouse, but nobody seemed interested. They might still be at the station."

"Did you join the Admin straight away?"

"No. I was in Z3060, to begin with, and got a job repairing the roads. I had a small contracting company. Then, when I moved to Z6080, my cousin helped me join the Administration."

Jeff was again reminded that connections counted. "Things are so much different from the old days."

"They are. The Shift brought about major changes."

"It did. It allowed those in power to make changes, and they took full advantage."

Harding was not sure if Jeff was serious. "You reckon?"

"Absolutely."

Harding looked around to check that the coast was clear, then whispered, "Would you care to elaborate?"

"They used the Shift to implement policies they had wanted to introduce for years."

Harding smiled as he turned away. "Don't tell me you are one of those conspiracy theorists. You'll be telling me next that the Shift never actually happened?" He immediately thought of Mrs Cleveland. "Sorry, that was..."

"Don't worry about it," Jeff said, shaking his head. "I believe that the tragedy was used to their advantage. I didn't notice it then, but looking back, it's amazing how quickly they removed human rights, scrapped elections, introduced the zones, did away with Parliament and replaced it with a Central Committee that we, as citizens, do not select."

"Desperate times and all that."

"That's what my kids used to tell me." Jeff smiled. "I think it was a concerted attempt to gain control."

Harding did not look convinced. "Steps had to be taken to keep the population safe."

"Then why confiscate all personal computers and the like?"

"Because they needed to build up a supply of parts to keep the important systems going. Don't forget we couldn't import products, and all our IT stuff used to be made overseas."

"I can't imagine an antiquated tablet or laptop would be much use to the state."

"Those machines had parts that could be recycled. Anyway, why else would they want them?"

"To restrict access to the internet."

Harding chuckled, dismissing the notion. "The internet fell apart. The satellites and cables were lost in the fallout."

"Hmm. I can just about believe that international connections were lost, but not domestic ones. We still have landlines and can use the ATM, so the connections are good. Where is the internet? I think it is still there, but they don't want us to use it."

"Nah, I can't see that happening." Harding shook his head. "Do you have any other evidence of a power grab?"

"The police force."

"But...

Jeff held up an index finger. "Just before Mother Earth's waters broke, do you remember the case against young McCallum? He was accused of planting evidence."

"That was the case that kicked everything off. I knew Connor. He was a good kid. I can't believe he would do anything as stupid as they claimed."

"I agree. Those accusations were complete rubbish. All investigations ceased when the Shift occurred. I was not much use to anyone then. When I was told to retire, I asked what was happening in the case and was assured another officer would take it up in due course. I was promised McCallum would be looked after."

"If I remember correctly, the case was reopened by a DCI from the Met." Harding tried to recall details. "Her name was Phillips, I think…but she moved on quickly."

Cleveland nodded. "I heard things ground to a halt and assumed it had all gone away. I was so wrapped up in my problems that I barely noticed what was happening in the outside world. The next thing I knew, we had Admins rather than police officers. I read McGregor's Review and could not believe that zones were allowed to do what they liked. McCallum and a few other young bobbies were mentioned a lot in the report because they faced multiple allegations of corruption, which the force failed to act on. The so-called fresh evidence, which I had never seen or heard of before, bore no relation to what was considered originally. All manner of ridiculous claims came out of the woodwork. Do you know they stated, not claimed, that McCallum was at a party in Brogan's house the night the girl was attacked? Where did that come from? McCallum was on duty. I know because he was with me at the time. McCallum's name was mentioned in the press, and hundreds came forward to complain about him. He was hung out to dry."

"It wasn't just McCallum. He was one of many." Harding said. "I can't remember where, but I spoke to our old boss…"

"Wilson?"

"Yes, and he made it abundantly clear that the number of allegations of police corruption made it impossible for him to help McCallum or any others. He pinned his hopes on the Review clearing them. I remember thinking that the allegations against the Police had become more and more incredible. Things got blown completely out of proportion. Almost every case in which the so-called suspects were involved, even if they only made the tea, became tarnished.

Most of the claims were fantastic and laughable, but nobody argued against them."

Jeff knew that. "Lies and more lies were fed to the press, and fresh enquiries opened almost weekly. It was too well orchestrated to be spontaneous. Someone set out to shut down the force and succeeded. All they needed was an opening." Jeff rubbed a hand over his mouth. "Nobody cared if the allegations were valid. The police force, as we knew it, was disgraced and disbanded. The public was promised something better, but I am afraid to say that it still hasn't had it. Present company excepted, of course."

Harding's face looked sad. "You really believe it was a set-up? That someone worked to get rid of the police?"

"I think that someone achieved their goal."

"But how could they have known the situation would develop like it did?" Harding asked. "Talk about good luck."

"As the Roman philosopher Seneca once said, *Luck is what happens when preparation meets opportunity*."

"You seriously believe someone engineered events to bring about the end of the police?"

"I do, but the police were only part of it. In addition to the other things I mentioned, the justice system was torn apart. Look what happened to the automatic right to a trial. That ended four years ago and was replaced by Trial by Peers, where other citizens resolve disputes within the zone. There are no judges or lawyers, and the Administrators arrange everything. They are gamekeepers and poachers. No disrespect, but the outcome will be what the Admins want."

Harding frowned. He was not persuaded. "But we still have judges. One lived here." He spread his arms. "Although I accept that we are one short at the moment."

Cleveland appreciated the dark humour. "The services of certain judges were retained to hear the more controversial cases and to advise on legal matters, including new legislation. For the most part, the legal system as we knew it has been destroyed."

"And you think all this came about because somebody seized the opportunity presented by the Shift? Nah, I can't see that myself."

"Someone spotted an opportunity and seized it."

"I don't know. It seems a bit farfetched." He faced Cleveland, holding his attention. "Who would have the time to prepare all this? How come nobody mentioned anything? Somebody would have blabbed."

"It depends on who was involved, and in any case, a long time passed between the Shift hitting and the adjustments being made. People changed jobs and locations. A lot was going on. The Shift took its toll, and the rest of the world was in crisis."

"I accept that, but I can't believe someone set it all up."

Jeff straightened and stretched his back. "It's up to you what you believe, but I believe the purge was carefully planned during that hiatus. When the floods came, it suited the government to use the police to maintain law and order domestically while the armed forces searched for survivors elsewhere. They needed new arrangements when they were ready to introduce the zones. They wanted something cheaper, less burdensome and easier to control."

Harding admitted he had not considered that possibility. "That would take some organising."

Cleveland agreed. "I know, and that's probably why they started so slowly. They knew they were only lighting a fuse when they began implementing the changes. Others would add extra explosives."

"But how come nobody said anything?"

"It was probably in their best interests to stay silent." He realised the mood had become very dark. "Just so you know, if you breathe a word of this discussion to anyone, I will deny it."

"I thought you might."

"But if this case develops as I think it might, I will need help. Would you be interested?"

Harding took a moment before responding. "I would, providing the terms and conditions were acceptable."

"I am sure we can sort something out." The pair shook hands. "How do you get on with Norman? He's been allocated as my driver."

"Everybody needs to get on with Norman, whether they want to or not. Nobody wants to be his enemy."

Jeff noted but offered no comment.

They reached the ground floor.

Cleveland pointed to an empty table in the hall. "Let's leave our evidence bags there and look around," he said.

They found little of interest in three of the four downstairs rooms. The bathroom had been adapted for a disabled man, but offered no clues. Cleveland paid particular attention to the windows, but, once again, there was no sign of forced entry. Norman and Lauren were still busy catching up in the kitchen and ignored their two visitors.

The Judge's study was full of law books and journals. The desktop was clear, but the drawers were crammed with papers. Cleveland found nothing of interest. "You say the other Admins extracted a couple of boxes of papers?"

"That's right."

"From where?" Jeff opened one of three filing cabinets and removed a couple of files. "These are linked to old cases." He opened the next drawer. "This is mostly boring administrative stuff. So, what did your colleagues take, and where did they find it?"

"I have no idea," Harding confirmed, adding that nothing had been removed from the three filing cabinets. "They are as full as I found them."

"How did they find two boxes of papers? Were there other papers on the floor or scattered around?"

"No. As I said, this is exactly as we found it."

"Did you see where the other Admins searched?"

"We were told to remain in the hall. We had no idea where they went."

The third room was a large, long, rectangular dining room.

An enormous oval, dark wood dining table filled most of the space, with twelve matching chairs. The centrepiece was a silver three-pronged candle holder. Various elegant serving dishes decorated the table.

Cleveland stopped to admire a painting close to the door. It was an oil painting of a courtroom scene with a young barrister addressing the jury. Behind the barrister, an attractive young lady sat in the public gallery, transfixed by the young man.

Cleveland's eyes moved to the next painting. It was an almost identical scene, only this time, the man who had been the barrister in the previous portrait now sat in the Judge's chair. The attractive young lady sat in the gallery with her arm around a young child. Cleveland believed it to be her son.

He stepped back from the picture and looked around the room. Three large paintings were on each of the long walls. Another sizeable, framed painting hung on a wall next to the door they had used to enter the dining room. Five smaller, framed portraits were on the short wall at the other end of the room, by the door leading back into the hall.

All the large paintings were of a similar courtroom scene and included the same characters, but in different roles. He moved to get a closer look at the solitary painting on the wall by the kitchen door. He saw the young barrister in Court. He thought this represented the lad's first appearance as a barrister. Jeff studied the next first painting, on the outward-facing long wall to the left of the table. This showed two young barristers in Court. The young man's opposing counsel was the lady sitting in the gallery in the first painting he had studied, which hung on the opposite wall.

He pointed back to the previous painting. "So that is the Judge's first day in Court." Jeff turned to the very first painting he had viewed in the room. "There, he's a little more accomplished, and the young lady is watching him." He turned to the image of the boy and girl, both working as barristers. "Here they are rivals."

His eyes moved on to the next frame on the opposite wall. "In this one, he has become a Judge, and his, I assume, wife is now in the gallery with their son." Do we know if the Judge has any family?"

Harding was not sure of the relevance of these paintings and was happy to think about something other than conspiracy theories and murder. "His wife died years ago. He has a son and a daughter still alive."

Cleveland narrowed his eyes and nodded slowly as he walked down the room. He pointed at another frame. "In this one, he is in Court, and his wife watches with their two children." His eyes darted across the room. "In that one, it looks like his son is now an adult watching the proceedings from the gallery. Could that be his sister? She looks like him." He moved to the smaller portraits. "These are pictures of the Judge and his wife. A beautiful woman by her looks, their son and then her daughter holding a man's hand. There is no sign of the son's partner."

"He only recently married and became a father."

Cleveland studied the remaining pictures and guessed they were portraits of grandchildren. "A family story told in Art. I have never seen that before. His Lordship must have been a committed family man."

"Hmmm." Harding thought differently. "More money than sense if you ask me. Those frames cost a fortune, and artists don't come cheap."

Cleveland was studying the edges of the paintings. He struggled to make out some letters. "K.M. MC, it looks like. If that stands for Kendal M McGregor, he painted them." He blew air through pursed lips. "The Judge was a very artistic, skilful and talented man."

"The M stands for Murray. It's a family name."

Cleveland asked Harding how he knew this.

"There's a family bible on the desk, and it is open to the page showing the recent arrival. I guess the Judge's whole family is listed in that book."

"I thought that practice died out years ago," Cleveland walked to the desk.

"His wife was Elizabeth. She was a Bairstow before marriage."
The name meant nothing to Cleveland, and Harding picked up on his ignorance.

"The Bairstow family are well known up North. They used to run a prominent legal practice in Leeds. Elizabeth Bairstow qualified as a barrister working in Manchester but then moved to London to become a QC."

"I see." Cleveland turned a page. "They had a daughter named Fiona, now married to Simon Cadwallader. They had two daughters, Abigail and Elizabeth. The second daughter was born the same year Elizabeth died. The Judge's son…"

"Lawrence Murray."

"Thank you. Lawrence has just had a new son?"

"That's right."

"This must have happened recently. The page has not been updated."

"It was in the last few weeks. There is a pile of press cuttings in the drawer there."

Cleveland read the birth dates. "Lawrence must be sixty now?"

Harding nodded. "Almost. He is fifty-nine." He sensed something was puzzling Cleveland. "What?"

"He left it late to settle down. I wonder why that was."

Harding turned to another page containing details of weddings. "He divorced his first wife and married someone almost forty years younger than him."

"A marriage of cross-zone convenience?"

"Probably. A lot of it goes on with the rich and powerful. It's all right for some to be able to select a younger kid to become their breeding machine in return for a life of luxury in an older zone."

"I suppose it was ever thus, but I hope he sticks around for her sake. It can't be much fun returning to another zone if he dies on her."

"She would certainly struggle fitting back into Z1830. Going back to the Party Zone must be a shock when you've had it so good elsewhere for years. Have you been to that zone recently?"

"No," Cleveland said,

"It's absolute mayhem, complete madness. Not that the new Mrs McGregor needs to worry about that yet. Will she become Lady McGregor?"

Cleveland admitted he had no idea.

Harding provided more background. "They live in Oxford, where he works as a legal representative for the food industry, and she sits on several charities. Word has it that she can't wait to be pregnant again."

"And you got all that from your stay here?"

"Yes, well, the Bible and the newspaper articles about the family. His Lordship also kept a scrapbook. It's on a bottom shelf in the library."

"You had a good look around."

"It helped fill the time."

Jeff examined the frames of the paintings on the wall, moving them to see what was behind them. He found that the painting of the family attending court had been hinged. One side of the frame moved away from the wall, exposing a giant safe.

"That's where they got the papers from." Jeff tried the handle, but it was locked. "They must have come armed with the combination."

"Is that important?"

"It tells us that your HQ friends knew what they were looking for and where to find it. The Judge must have revealed the combination to someone. Maybe he told them in case he died."

Cleveland took one last look around the room, confirming that the windows were undamaged, then tipped his hat back into the correct position. "That's enough. I don't think we are going to find anything here. I'd better see what the guard on the gate can tell me about what he saw. Could you put the evidence in a bigger bag and give it to Norman to put in the car?"

"Of course. There are ice cubes in the freezer. I'll see if there is a cool bag in one of the cupboards. The bits of blood and bone will start to stink before long."

"Thanks. I'll have to see where I can get them analysed."

"Good luck with that. They shut all the labs when they did away with the police. The Administration does not need such luxuries. No crime, no evidence, no crime labs. There's a certain logic there, don't you think?"

Cleveland thought he would enjoy working with Harding again. "I'll be in touch."

It took Cleveland over an hour to learn that Alan, the gatekeeper, had seen nothing unusual in the days leading up to the murder. The Judge had received no visitors, but the log showed that he had been taken out in his official car several times in the week leading up to his death. Some days, he was gone for over twelve hours, and Alan thought the Judge went straight to bed on his return. On other days, the Judge was away for less than half a day and returned to supervise the gardening. Alan doubled as a gardener as a favour to the Judge, who paid well. He hoped this could remain a secret as the Administration frowned upon moonlighting. Cleveland promised not to say anything and learned that the Judge's regular driver was an ex-army Colonel called Max, "MC", who could be found at the Administration's Wimborne Minster depot.

Cleveland thanked Alan for his time and asked where he could find him should he need to ask any more questions. The guard was unsure of his future, but he handed over a business card.

Jeff re-entered the main house to find an improvised cool bag – a large plastic sack containing the bags of evidence and ice blocks, waiting for him on the table in the hall. Next to the bag, in a comfortable leather chair, sat Norman, enjoying a gentle snooze.

"Come on, sleeping beauty..." Cleveland kicked the soles of his driver's sandals. Norman woke with a start but rose slowly. "I need to speak to the girl who found the Judge."

"Right." Norman eventually stood up straight and shivered.

"Ready when you are." They walked on until Norman stopped suddenly. He took a piece of paper from his trouser pocket and held it out for his companion. "Here's the address."

"Thank you," Cleveland said, taking the paper and stuffing it into his jacket pocket. Seeing Amelia's file earlier that day, he already knew where she lived, but did not admit it. Harding had suggested there was merit in keeping Norman on his side. "How would I manage without you?"

6. THE INTERVIEWS BEGIN

After several false arrivals, Norman confirmed they were parked outside Miss Amelia Duggan's flat. Cleveland could have walked it quicker. As the crow flew, the apartment was less than a mile from the Judge's house. Jeff kept his thoughts to himself, not wishing to suppress Norman's evident pride in his navigational skills.

"What do you want me to say? What do we want to know?" the driver asked.

"You can stay in the car," Cleveland instructed.

"No chance. I am under orders to accompany you."

"But I want you to wait here."

"You heard ChiZA Purcell. I am to stay with you."

"I will only be in there, and Amelia might prefer meeting just me. Do you have an official mobile?"

"Of course."

"Good. Contact your HQ and get me the whereabouts of Doctor Martin Rowe.

R. O. W. E."

"I know how to spell, but I am not doing it. In case you'd forgotten, I am not your dog's body. I am a Senior Administrator. I do not work for you."

"No, you simply drive me around. Nobody mentioned you getting involved in the investigation."

"Nobody told me that I should not. I was told to accompany you, and I'll do that. I will not sit here twiddling my thumbs while you play at being a copper again. I have no idea why we needed you anyway. The Administration has a good record in solving cases, so we don't need your help."

"Not everyone agrees with you," Cleveland got out of the car. He was tempted to say more. He found it hard to hold his tongue.

The detached building housed two flats, one above the other, with a common entrance. Amelia lived in the downstairs flat. Cleveland pressed the button on the intercom under her name. A lady answered almost immediately. "Hello. How may I help you?"

It had been a long time since Cleveland had heard such refined tones. "Good afternoon. Am I speaking to Amelia Duggan?"

"You are."

"My name is Cleveland. I am looking into Lord McGregor's death for the Administration. I wonder if I might ask you a few questions."

"Does it have to be now? I am rather busy."

"I am afraid it does. I am only in the area today, and it would be beneficial if we could chat. It won't take long." He left space for a response, but Norman did not.

The Admin leaned across Jeff, shouting into the microphone. "Of course, you could always meet us at the Administration headquarters tomorrow morning."

"Would there be a car?"

"No chance," Norman said, adding quickly. "But I hear there is an excellent bus service between here and Cardiff. We would expect you to be there by ten, so you'd have an early start."

"Cardiff? You would expect me to travel to Cardiff?"

"We would," Norman smirked as he winked at Jeff. "That's where the office is."

"I have no intention of going to Cardiff."

Norman stood in front of Jeff, monopolising the intercom. "I am sorry to hear that. Lord Wilson tasked us with investigating His Lordship's death and expects a full report as soon as possible. We need your help with that. I would hate to have to report that you are being unhelpful, especially since the State has generously found you an easy job and a fabulous place to live. But I imagine you have friends in the party zone and look forward to seeing them again."

The silence lasted seconds. "You'd better come in."

A buzzer sounded, and an inwardly seething Cleveland pushed the door. He knew that the old Jeff would have told Norman to back off. There was no need for threats or bullying. Building a rapport was a much better way to engage with people. The big difference between the old and new Jeff was that he used to have power, authority and respect. Now, he had none of those things and needed to tread carefully.

The hallway was well maintained, if a little bland. A metal rail ran up the concrete steps.

He tapped the glass of the door to his right.

Amelia Duggan opened the door wearing a full-length dressing gown and a towel around her head. "Please come in."

Cleveland reached into his pocket and removed the letter and his identity card.

Amelia waved the paper away. "That's not necessary. I was advised that you might visit me." She held the door to allow Norman to follow Jeff into her lounge.

"Do take a seat," Amelia waved her arm toward one of the two sofas in the small room. "Would you like some tea?" Her nervousness was evident.

Cleveland held his hat as he stood by the sofa. "No, thank you."

Norman slumped onto the sofa. "What sort is it?"

"Indian."

"That will be fine. Just milk for me." Norman picked up the pillow behind him and dropped it on the floor.

"I'm afraid milk is all I have. I do not use sugar." She collected the pillow as she walked to the kitchen, stopping to place it on her dining table.

"I can see you are sweet enough as you are." Norman saw her glance back and gave her a wink.

"That's enough, thank you." Jeff stood over Norman, staring hard at the Admin.

"Only a bit of fun. You know…banter."

"Is it banter, or is it intimidation? This young lady has already witnessed a terrible scene and is probably still shocked. I want to build her trust, and we will not do that by making threats and lecherous comments."

"Okay, keep your hair on. Once a cop, always a cop." Norman

mumbled, "Until the cash runs out."

Cleveland ignored the comment and remained standing to admire the beach views and examine the room.

Amelia's flat had all the creature comforts. The sofas looked new and expensive. Luxurious rugs partially covered the hardwood floors, and the windows were filled with vertical blinds and lined curtains that hung from the ceiling to the floor. Her television was massive, and the long wooden unit on which it rested also held a CD/DVD player. The number of cases on the floor in front of the unit and on the shelves to the right suggested that Amelia made much use of the media player.

The walls were neutral, off-white, and perfectly smooth. A few framed prints hung around the room. He moved closer to inspect the artwork. Two scenes of London included the obligatory red buses. One had Buckingham Palace in the background, and the other was Trafalgar Square. The paintings' detail and perspective were superb.

It had been many years since he had visited London. He recalled his previous visits when he had taken the children to see the sights - Trafalgar Square, the Tower, and the Science Museum, to name but three. Those were great days.

He studied the Palace scene very closely, and it brought back memories of the only time he got inside the gates. He could still feel Flissy's pride at him collecting his Queen's Police Medal.

Amelia re-entered the room as he looked for an artist's name.

"Do you like the paintings, Mr Cleveland?"

"Yes, very much. They are quite excellent."

"I would never have classed you as an art connoisseur, but thank you. I think so, too. I wanted to tell him he should exhibit them, but it was not my place. In any case, he never wanted any fuss. Personally, I think he wasted his talent." She eased her bottom onto one of the sofas and placed the tray on a nearby table. She had lost the towel, and her damp blond hair was left to hang loose. "He gave me those for my twenty-second birthday earlier this year. Of course, he painted them many years before, when London was not like it is now."

"Indeed not." Cleveland sat. He studied her face. Her eyes had red edges, suggesting she had cried a lot recently. Her cheeks seemed drawn, and her lips were pencil thin.

Amelia poured the tea into China cups, resting on matching saucers, added milk and then placed a spoon beside each cup before raising a saucer and holding it for Norman to collect, which he did without thanking her.

Cleveland nodded at the paintings again. "Who is the artist?"

Amelia showed her surprise at the question. "You mean you don't know?"

"No clue."

"Kendal, Lord McGregor. He once told me that the four great loves of his life would be his wife, his kids, art and law, in that order." She looked at the paintings again and appeared to lose herself momentarily.

"You were close to his Lordship?"

Amelia appeared to shiver as she returned to the conversation. "No, not really. We rarely spoke to tell you the truth. I seldom saw him."

Norman stopped slurping his tea long enough to ask, "Did he give you these paintings, or did you steal them?"

Their host was horrified. "He gave them to me. I have a signed letter from him to prove it." Her finger waved at the bedroom. "It's in there somewhere." She rose to get it.

"That won't be necessary," Jeff spoke softly. "We believe you, but we needed to check." He motioned for her to sit again. "Can you tell me how long you worked for him?"

She thought about this before committing. "Just over a year. I left University, moved into .... that place for a bit... and started here in March."

"That place?"

She took a slow sip of tea, gently licked her lips and composed herself. "After I left University in Harrogate, I had to leave the Uni region and endure a move to Manchester. It's an appalling place, dreadful."

Jeff nodded, appreciating that Harrogate, Ripon, and York had established themselves as three of the best Universities in Britain. Because of this, student places and accommodation in the area were much sought after. Once a course was completed, students relocated. Resettlement involved getting a job on the other side of the Pennines. He imagined Amelia had not relished the move to the heart of Party Zone, also known as Z1830.

Jeff knew postgraduate studies were available at Oxbridge universities, but they were the domain of exceptionally bright, super-rich, or well-connected students.

"You did not go to Oxford or Cambridge?"

"Regrettably not. I was never the most diligent student. I liked the social side too much. Mummy refused to throw good money after bad."

Norman chuckled but stopped when he saw Jeff glaring at him.

"How did you come to work for his Lordship?" Jeff wished he had accepted the offer of tea. His throat had dried.

Amelia sipped and swallowed slowly. "Aren't you going to take notes?"

The question caught Jeff off guard. "No, why would I?"

"Isn't that what policemen used to do? Write things down that might be used as evidence?"

Norman could not stop himself. "He is no longer a policeman. He is merely helping the Administration investigate the death of His Lordship. He will not be taking notes." He waited for her to show that she accepted his position, which she did by nodding. "Carry on, Cleveland."

Jeff tightened his lips and breathed out through his nose. "Where was I? Oh yes, could you tell me how you came to work for the Judge?"

"That was down to Mummy. She knew His Lordship and arranged for me to be accepted by a relocation agency. I was jolly lucky to get this gig."

Cleveland wondered whether Amelia tried to hide her accent during her brief spell in the Party Zone. He doubted she would have done a very good job.

"Are you happy here?" Norman asked.

She sighed softly. "It was quite lonely to begin with. Luckily, I have made friends with other Transzers in similar circumstances." Her face looked sad. "I am unsure what I will do without His Lordship."

"You'll miss him?" Jeff suggested.

Amelia nodded.

Norman spoke sharply. "You just told us you rarely spoke to him. Why would you miss him? What you really mean is you will miss the easy life and all the perks that go with it."

Jeff did not appreciate the outburst. "Norman, that's enough, thank you. I'll ask the questions."

The Administrator did not back down. He pointed at Amelia but snapped at Jeff. "Her connections got her this job. She's given a fabulous flat and an easy job. Her kind spend all weekend getting stoned or pissed and leaving a mess for others to pick up. If my wife took a job in this zone, she would have to take the bus every day, but this one can wander around doing what she likes. She didn't give a toss about His Lordship. He was just her meal ticket. Most people her age would not be so fortunate and would have no choice but to live and try to survive in the Party Zone. If I had my way, I'd send them all back."

Jeff took a breath. "Luckily, you won't get your way because your opinions do not matter." He turned his attention to Amelia, who was shocked and upset. "Ignore my Administrator. As you can tell, he carries a rather enormous chip on both shoulders." He saw the faintest trace of a smile. "What did your role involve?"

"Cleaning, cooking, shopping, laundry, and generally providing support as required or requested. But he never asked me to shop or cook for him."

"How many clients could you have at any one time?"

"A maximum of three, but I only had the one, His Lordship, although I don't even have him now." She held her manicured index finger to her nose to stifle a sob. "My friends are confident the Administration will find me another client very soon." Her eyes met Cleveland's.

"Not if Norman here has his way, but I am sure he won't. And what will you do in the meantime?"

Amelia touched the corner of her eye with her middle fingertip. "Nothing much. I can stay here on gardening leave until I am re-allocated."

"Well, I suppose that's not so bad. How will you manage?"

"What do you mean?"

"How will you keep this place going and look after yourself without a salary?"

Amelia stiffened, "I don't think that is any of your business, Mr Cleveland." She put her head in her hands. "I'm sorry, I didn't mean to be rude. It's been a testing couple of days."

Norman wanted to speak, but Cleveland held out a hand to stop him. "That's okay. I understand. I didn't mean to ask personal questions. I guess my old habits die hard. I am sorry about that."

"Offer him some cash. He'll be putty in your hands." Norman placed his empty cup and saucer on the tray. "These old coppers are all corrupt."

Jeff had no wish to embarrass himself or Amelia by arguing with Norman. He wanted the Admin out of the room as soon as possible. "I can see that you are upset, so it might be better if we return at some other time."

Amelia nodded.

Norman stood and headed to the door.

Jeff waited. "Thanks for the tea. I am sure it was very nice."

Amelia faked a smile, and her shoulders loosened.

"You say you didn't see the Judge very often? Why was that?"

"He was an extremely busy man. He was always on the move."

"When was the last time you saw him?"

"At the house, briefly, last Friday morning. I arrived late, and His Lordship and MC left as I got there."

"Did he mention where he was heading?"

"No. As I said, we rarely spoke. He was a very private man."

"You have no idea where he was going?"

"No, sorry."

"How often would you see him? Every few days? Weekly?"

"It varied. I visited the house daily, apart from weekends. Recently, he had often left by mid-morning and returned after I had finished for the day."

"Recently, as in how long? Days, weeks, months?"

"Several weeks."

"You have no idea where he went?"

"No."

"Were you at the house on Saturday or Sunday?"

"No, I don't work weekends."

"Nor me." Jeff forced a chuckle, and Amelia smiled. "Did you do anything nice? The weather was good."

"It was. Some friends and I had an impromptu party in the park."

"That sounds lovely. I remember parties like that. Music, food, alcohol."

Amelia nodded. "Yes, all of the above with lots of Oasis, Blur and Pulp."

Jeff had not expected the Britpop bands to be still popular. He liked his music but did not have time to engage in a conversation about it. "Would you happen to know what the Judge had planned for last weekend?"

"I have no idea, I'm sorry. I saw him on Sunday at the Royal Exeter Hotel on his way to lunch." She looked at her feet and then at Jeff. "At least I saw his car. I can't imagine MC driving it without His Lordship." She fell silent. "It's been restored, you know. The Royal Exeter."

"I didn't know. Was that a regular eating place for the Judge?"

"It may have been, but he visited so many places. He ate out quite a bit - not that he ate much - I think he had a stomach problem."

"Why would you think that?"

"MC used to prepare lots of soup because His Lordship had little appetite. I put two and two together."

Norman reappeared, tapping his finger against his watch. "You said we were making a move."

"Just a second. Amelia and I are discussing something." He looked at her, "Why would MC mention preparing soup?"

"It was mentioned in passing. MC complained that the blender was a beggar to clean after combining the ingredients. I would have done it, but MC insists on leaving things spotless."

"I see, but you had no evidence of a stomach problem?"

"No."

"Do you know what his Lordship was working on at the time of his death?"

"Why would I?"

"I just thought that you might have seen papers hanging around. If we knew what he had been doing, it might explain why he died."

She thought for a moment. "I did see some papers. He had three pieces of work in progress. One is…was concerned with the law on the abolition of elections. Another involved work with the Prison Reformers. He kept the third one private. It was strictly on a need-to-know basis, and I didn't need to know." She forced a smile. "MC would leave me a note to tell me that the study was locked as the Judge was working on his special project and did not want the papers disturbed. I delayed my chores until those papers were locked away."

"Did you read any of his other papers?"

"Yes, sometimes." She feared she had said the wrong thing. "I had to tidy his study. Kendal used three secure filing cabinets, one of which was always kept locked. It was one for each task. If I arrived and found papers on his desk, I would file them. To do that, I had to read them. He knew I was trustworthy and would never say anything. The papers were rather interesting, very enlightening and beautifully crafted. As well as being a talented artist, his Lordship had a wonderful way with language. His arguments were compelling, and he was very clearly very selective in his choice of words."

"It sounds like he was an extraordinary man."

"I don't know whether he was any more special than anyone else, Mr Cleveland, but he was a very generous and caring man, and they are not abundant these days."

Cleveland's thoughts returned to the paintings. "He must have liked you to give you these paintings. I would have thought they were very personal to him?"

She tightened a little. "As I've said, he was a very generous employer. What else do you want me to say? I did not ask for them or take them without permission. The fact is that these paintings were stored in the small back bedroom of his house. One day, after I had been working for him for about a month, he caught me looking at them and asked me what I thought. It surprised me when he spoke, but he had been out for lunch and probably had too much to drink. I told him they were superb and made me think of happier times."

Cleveland understood this sentiment.

Amelia continued, "MC turned up here on my birthday carrying these paintings. He also brought a small food hamper and a bottle of wine. MC said His Lordship wanted me to take the day off. Millie would cover for me."

"Millie?"

"Millie Small. She does for...sorry. It is easy to slip into colloquialisms. She provides support for several residents in the zone."

"Did Millie often...do for the Judge?" Cleveland pulled a face, recognising his clumsy comment.

Amelia giggled. "Yes, she did. Not that anyone ever knew officially." She slid one hand across the other. "The truth is, Mr Cleveland, I am not very good at domestic work. Everyone knew. Millie regularly came in after me to ensure everything was spic and span."

"Couldn't you have done something else instead of cleaning?"

"There was nothing available. I hope to secure something different after...this." She rubbed her hands together again. "I speak several languages and am a rather talented musician. I am being considered for several orchestras. In the meantime, in the current climate, one must tick the boxes on the citizenship charter. This means that either I return to Z1830 and get a job." She shivered again at the prospect. "Or I undertake menial duties in other zones." She parted her hands and held them out. "Norman is quite correct. There are worse places to be."

The Admin used the mention of his name to say he never understood people learning languages they would never get to use. There was also an overabundance of skilled musicians waiting to be discovered.

"Ignore him," Jeff said. "I think being able to play music and speak other languages is a gift. I am sure those skills will help you soon."

They were close to the entrance. Norman had left, closing the door behind him. Jeff asked a few questions about finding the body, but learned little that he did not already know or had guessed.

Amelia repeated that she had set about her routine tasks on the fateful day and saw that the bedroom door was closed. This was unusual. She opened it, saw the body and ran. She had not intended to head to the pier, but that's where she was stopped by two other support workers, who then called passing Administrators. She was taken to Wimborne Minster, the regional HQ, and asked questions by the staff there. She was driven home but told to expect further visits.

Amelia spoke about the body's position and how it had been tied, which corresponded with Lauren and Harding's descriptions.

"Do you know if the Judge had many callers?"

"No, he didn't welcome visitors. His house was his sanctuary. As far as I could tell, he went out to entertain and came home to work. You could not get to see him unless he authorised it. The gates were there for a reason."

A thought struck him, which he vocalised without realising. "Where was the guard on the gate?"

Amelia opened the door and held it. "Sorry?"

"The guard on the gate. I was just wondering where he was when you found the body?"

Amelia was slow to connect, so Cleveland helped her. "You ran from the house and made it to the pier before you were stopped. Why hadn't the guard tried to stop you?"

She raised and lowered her head as she understood his meaning. "We had an informal arrangement. He would sometimes leave for breakfast once he knew I was at work. I would keep an eye on the place. In return, he brought me little luxuries I could not get in the shops. The Administrators know where to find the best quality products." She looked at Norman, who stood outside with his back to her.

Jeff hoped the Admin felt uncomfortable, but doubted it. The man seemed to have no shame. "I can imagine. Would the gatekeeper normally shut the gate after you had arrived but before he went for food?"

"Yes, why?"

Cleveland ignored her question. "Was the gate open or closed as you ran from the house?"

Amelia pictured the moment she fled the scene. "I think it was open now that you mentioned it. I don't remember entering his hut to press the button, so it must have been open. I imagine he had forgotten to close it."

"And how long were you cleaning downstairs before you went upstairs?"

Her face showed impatience. "We have already been over this - no more than fifteen to twenty minutes. I cleaned the kitchen, put the vacuum on the floors, polished where necessary, and checked the downstairs toilet. Once I saw everything was fine, I headed up the stairs, carrying the vacuum cleaner, polish and duster."

"I see."

Amelia sensed an edge in Cleveland's voice. "What does that mean? What do you see?"

"I was just thinking of something."

"What something?"

"It's probably nothing. It just occurred to me that the killer or killers might have been in the house when you found the body."

Amelia's face lost colour, and she recoiled against the wall. "You think I might have been alone… in that house… with the killer?" She saw Norman smirk and focused on Jeff, awaiting a response.

One of Jeff's gripes about ageing was the frequent loss of the filter. If a thought entered his head, it usually came out of his mouth. He never intended to upset her, but now that the damage was done, he could not think of an easy way to end the conversation. She was bound to ask more questions if she did not get a complete response.

He chose his words. "I don't know, but it is possible. The body was taken before we could get it examined. I had assumed his Lordship had been dead for some time before you found him, but I cannot be sure if it had been hours or minutes."

Norman eagerly added his contribution. "For all we know, the killer could have arrived after you. You might have unlocked the door for him…or her. It's possible that the killer was upstairs doing the deed while you were cleaning downstairs. Whoever it was might not have left the scene until after you ran away. You may have had a fortunate escape."

Amelia started to cry. "Why would you say that? How do you know?"

Norman's obvious delight in Amelia's misery made Jeff's discomfort worse. "I don't know, and we might never know. It just dawned on me that my earlier assumptions that the Judge was killed while he was alone in the house might be way off the mark."

Amelia folded her arms around her body and then covered her mouth as she sobbed.

Jeff felt terrible. "I'm sorry if I've upset you. I was thinking out loud. It is more likely that the Judge was killed while on his own. If anyone else had been there, you would have heard something. The sound echoes around a big house like that. The most important thing is that you're safe."

Norman was in his element. "You are a lucky girl. Who knows what might have happened to you?" He patted her shoulder, which made Amelia jump. "Thank you for your time, and good luck finding a new post. In the meantime, don't forget to lock your doors." The leer was evident.

Jeff gave a half-hearted smile. Amelia let the door swing shut behind them. Jeff heard her crying as he returned to the car.

"I hate those pampered pooches who get all the best jobs simply because of who they know."

"I can tell. You didn't hide your feelings." Jeff secured the seatbelt.

"Why would I? We were promised a fairer, more equal society, but the rich still get the best pickings."

Jeff accepted that the man had a point but did not vocalise his agreement. "Can you ask the office to check on Martin Rowe and then take me to a public toilet? I need a wee?"

"You should have used the one in her flat. I bet the toilets are plush."

"I am not sure I wanted to leave you and her alone. I might have had another body to deal with."

Norman found the comment hilarious and roared with laughter. "Snooty little bitch had a lucky escape."

Jeff looked at the outside world. He had not intended it as a joke.

"Do you want me to lean on her?"

Jeff's attention returned to his driver. "What do you mean?"

"You know, lean on her, get her to talk."

"What will she talk to you about? Her choice of soft furnishings? How her parents acquired their money? What she did to get such a comfortable home? I doubt Amelia would tell you very much."

"You'd be surprised how persuasive I can be."

"I'll take your word for it, but I struggle to see any benefits from you and her chatting."

"I could get a confession out of her."

Jeff leaned forward. "You seriously think she might have killed the Judge?"

"She must be a suspect. She was in the house on her own, and you said yourself that we have no idea if the Judge died before or after her arrival. It would make things easier if she admitted doing it."

"Easier? How?"

"We close the case. You could return to your comfortable retirement. I go back to my day job."

"I don't believe I am hearing this."

"Don't tell me you've never fitted someone up to close a case."

"Never."

"Well, you must have been an exception because the police force was discredited and defunded because it was so corrupt."

Jeff struggled to control his anger. "We had a few bad apples in the force, but I'm starting to think that the Administration has rotten orchards."

Norman pulled a face. "We get the job done. In any case, it's not as if Amelia would get much punishment. With her connections, she would be released in no time."

"But her reputation would be tarnished."

"Nobody will care. She'd probably return to the party zone for a while before getting another move, or mummy and daddy find her a rich husband."

"I am also protecting my reputation. I have never knowingly convicted an innocent person, and I don't intend to start now."

"Nobody cares either way. All the bosses want is an early result. They can tick the box and forget about it. They won't give a toss if we send Amelia to the island jail. As I said, she won't be there very long."

"She isn't going there at all unless we find evidence to implicate her."

"Suit yourself. If not her, then who? Alan on the gate is a boring old sod, but I'm not sure he'd have the energy to commit a crime like this. Do you have anyone else in mind?"

"Unbelievable." Jeff soothed his neck. "You might think I'm old-fashioned, but I'd prefer to find the real culprit."

Norman started the engine. "How are you going to do that? You've got no body, no clues, no suspects, apart from Amelia. You've got no chance."

"It's nice to know you have confidence in me," Jeff said, sitting back. "It's only my first day on the job, and you've already written me off. Just to make myself clear, I have no intention of stitching anyone up, and I certainly won't be pressured into making an early arrest. I was taught to look at the evidence..."

"I know means, motive and opportunity, but I don't see the point. You might as well quit now because you have no chance of solving this murder. Give it two weeks, and nobody will care about it."

Jeff wanted to say he would still care, but didn't think there was much point. "Let's see what we find. In the meantime, can you get me to a toilet?"

They found a public convenience by the pier. When Jeff returned, Norman handed him a sheet of note paper with a telephone number and address for Martin Rowe and asked him where they were going next. He pointed at the dashboard clock and reminded his passenger that he was usually home by five.

Jeff ignored him and told him to contact HQ to ask where they could find Millie Small. The answer came quickly.

The journey from Bournemouth to Boscombe was memorable only for the number of vintage cars parked on the promenade. Jeff doubted he had ever seen so many Bentleys, Rolls, Mercedes and Jaguars in such a short time. He did not want to think how much it would cost to run them.

The residents of Z80+ were out in force. Pavements and roads were awash with wheelchairs carrying old people, wrapped up in blankets, shawls, caps and gloves, being pushed by marginally younger people, enjoying the warm spring air.

"Isn't it nice to see the old ones enjoying themselves?"

It had been a tiring day, and Cleveland was fed up with

futile conversations about meaningless things. He was tired of listening to Norman and could not forgive him for his treatment of Amelia. Norman's failure to listen to travel directions did not help.

"For God's sake, we were not supposed to cross that junction. You should have taken a left back there, as I suggested."

"Not a problem. I can take the next turning."

"But the sign says no left turn."

"The signs don't apply to Admins. I can turn wherever I like."

The State car sounded its horn and turned sharply, sending the backseat passenger into the door.

"Ouch," Cleveland mentally added to the extended list of things he disliked about Norman.

"Sorry."

Cleveland rubbed his shoulder.

"Anyway, we're here now." Norman pulled into the driveway of number 12 Owl's Road.

Cleveland reached for the handle. "You wait in the car. I won't be long."

"No chance. My orders are to accompany you. ChiZA Purcell was quite clear about that. He isn't going to be pleased if you interview Millie alone."

"Okay." Jeff gritted his teeth.

No sooner had he put his foot outside the car door than a petite, grey-haired lady appeared before them on the driveway. "Hello, my dear. I'm sorry, but if you've come to see Lord Stephen, you're out of luck. His son is taking him for a walk." Her strong Liverpudlian accent gave her no chance of hiding her origins.

"Mrs Small?"

"Yes." The lady stepped back. "Who are you, and what do you want?"

Jeff explained the reason for his visit and asked if they might chat. Mrs Small eyed Norman and pointed at him. "What does he want?"

"I'm helping..."

Jeff cut off Norman's response. "I am afraid that, as I am not an Administrator, I must be accompanied everywhere by Administrator Norman here."

"That's Senior Administrator..."

Norman got no further.

"Just call him Norman. He's here to look after me and won't bother you."

Millie beamed, although it looked like her brain had forgotten to inform her eyes what it had planned. She had the saddest expression Jeff had ever seen. Her eyes were lifeless. "No problem, dear. I will do anything to help find those who did this to that lovely man."

Mrs Small took them into the living room of the house. It was very sparsely furnished, and Cleveland thought Amelia's place was palatial by comparison.

"Lord Stephen only allows guests in this room. He is cautious about security and is terrified of getting robbed. I always tell him he is perfectly safe around here, but I'm not so sure after what happened to His Lordship." Millie invited the visitors to sit on the scuffed sofa. "Would you like some tea? I can only use the Bristol blend if His Lordship is out."

"There's nothing wrong with the Bristol blend. I use that at home, but we won't, if you don't mind. We have a bit of a journey back to Wiltshire, and there are no service stations these days."

Millie did not require further explanation. She sat in the high-backed chair. "No, I don't suppose there are many places to stop these days, are there? Long journeys can be a pain as you get older. In which part of Wiltshire do you live, dear?"

"Marshfield, just outside..."

"I know Marshfield very well. We used to live in Bristol before ..." she stopped herself, unsure of the correct terminology. "... things changed. We had friends in Marshfield. They ran one of the pubs there. Have you lived there long?"

Cleveland was accustomed to Bristol being pronounced as *'Brizol'*. It was how his neighbours referred to the city. It was weird hearing it pronounced correctly. "Too long, I sometimes think. I have been there the best part of thirty years."

"You're one of the lucky ones then. Most people were moved around after the disaster."

Cleveland had told this story so many times. The words came automatically. "Yes, I was lucky enough to be in the right place at the wrong time of my life. I was technically too young to live in Z6080, but that's where my house was, and I kept my head down. By the time they got around to moving me, I was almost sixty, so they let me stay where I was."

"That's nice, dear," Millie replied with little sincerity. "I've moved three times in the last five years. We were living in Clifton when they brought in these zones, and because my husband and I were only fifty-five at the time..."

Cleveland had assumed she was much older.

"...they moved us up to Shrewsbury. I got a job in a chocolate factory, and my husband went to work on reopening the pits. Then, when he died..."

"I am sorry to hear that."

"Thank you, dear. It was a shock at the time. He was helping to reopen a coal seam when the roof caved in. Five of them were killed, and they moved me over to Melton Mowbray to work in the food plants." Millie fiddled with her apron and sat back. "My job was to rear chickens, but that ended when they abolished the free-range programme. I suppose intensive production has its benefits, but I wouldn't say I liked seeing all those poor little animals stuck in their tiny cages, so I applied to change roles. I argued that I should get a priority move because my husband had given his life for the State. Eventually, someone agreed, and I was moved into domestic work. I was lucky to be allocated Z80+." She looked around the room. "This is one of three I clean, but I am not complaining."

Cleveland again compared Millie's life with Amelia's. He doubted Amelia would have needed to make a case for a move. All she needed was a phone call to one of Mummy's friends. His eye caught sight of a mobile phone in Millie's bag. It dawned on him that he had yet to get the mobile Purcell had promised.

The room had a distinct lack of personal effects. There were no ornaments, knick-knacks, or keepsakes on view; everything appeared functional by nature. There was also a complete absence of photographs. He found this unusual and recalled seeing at least three framed photos at Amelia's place. "Does Lord Stephen have any other family apart from his son?"

It was Norman's turn to interrupt. "That is none of our business. We should keep to the matter in hand."

"Of course." Jeff resisted the temptation to say more. "Do you have any family, Millie?"

Millie clasped her hands together and stiffened. As she spoke, she avoided eye contact by looking at the ceiling. "I have a daughter…she lives up North somewhere… her brother lives in Nottingham, and I have a grandson in Scotland, but I can't get up there much. It's too expensive, and they won't let him visit me. I get letters and cards and the like." Millie's hands tightened around each other.

"That's nice", Cleveland wished he had minded his own business. He changed the subject. "How long had you worked for the Judge?"

A wry smile broke across Millie's face. "Officially, I never worked for His Lordship. I was merely a friend. I couldn't have worked for him as I had three employers, and the Judge was already allocated to someone else."

Cleveland grinned. "How long were you friends?"

"Just over a year, his old support worker was repatriated when they moved her family on. They were religious people who refused to give up their faith."

Cleveland had been deeply troubled at religious people being forcibly moved to Ireland, allowing secular people to travel in the opposite direction. There were no longer any recognised religions in the UK. All places of worship were stripped of their treasures, which were donated to the national coffers. However, it was common knowledge that informal, illegal religious services still took place.

"When Naeema was sent away, His Lordship got Amelia. She's a lovely girl, but not a patch on Naeema. She was a hard worker. I don't think Amelia is cut out for domestic work. She is probably more used to having things done for her. She's not the most committed, if you know what I mean. She doesn't have much oomph."

Cleveland had gathered as much. "How were you and the Judge introduced?"

"His driver, MC, came to see me and asked if I would be interested in a part-time job, cash in hand, no need to declare it. I agreed right away. I mean, who was going to argue with the Judge? I started the next evening. The money comes in handy, and he was a pleasure to work for, such a lovely man." She leaned forward. "You know that he never complained or moaned about anything. He never had a bad word to say about anyone, including Amelia. She was taking him for a ride, and I told him as much, but he didn't care. Most others would have sacked her and got someone else in, but he was happy to keep her on and pay me as well. He used to say he could afford it and couldn't take the money with him. I used to go in three times a week and give the place a good going over."

"Was the Judge there when you visited?"

"Always. He used to like me to call around in the evenings, and we would chat as I cleaned." She thought of bygone days. "He used to tell me about his family and some of the cases he had been involved in. I used to talk about my Jim, my late husband, and our kids."

"When was your last visit to the Judge's house?"

"Sunday afternoon. It was about five. I called in to see him on my way back from here. He said he wouldn't need me until Tuesday."

"How did he seem?"

"He was fine, in good spirits. He was a bit squiffy." Millie chuckled. "We had a nice little chat."

"What did you discuss?"

"Family things. He had visited his son a couple of days before.

His Lordship wanted to see his new grandchild before the little one was taken to Scotland. He enjoyed that and told me all about it."

"Was he alone?"

"Yes, as usual. He had lunch with friends at the Royal Exeter on Sunday. Not that he ever ate much, but he had a good time. He liked a drop of wine and had a couple, or possibly several couples."

"Did he have many friends?"

"Not really. He knew lots of people, but not many real friends. He didn't like visitors. If he wanted to see somebody, he would get MC to drive him to their home. He liked it that way. It allowed him to decide when the visit would end."

"Did you notice anything or anyone unusual around the house?"

Millie fell silent. "No, nothing, dear. It was just like any other day. It was all very tranquil."

"Can you talk me through what you did that day?"

She retraced her movements. "I left here about half four, arrived at the Judge's about six. Alan, the gatekeeper, let me in, and I found his Lordship in the kitchen. He was getting a glass of juice. We discussed the weather, his day, and the lunch. He told me about his visit to Oxford and told me he would be busy the next day. He didn't need me to work until Tuesday. I did my work and left. That was it, really. I caught my bus." She put her finger to her eye to catch the tears. "I didn't know that would be the last time I saw him." Millie reached for the end of her apron and pulled it to her eyes. "I'm sorry, dear. It just upsets me to think of anyone hurting that lovely old man...."

"That's okay," Cleveland said. "Take your time." He tried to take her mind off the killing. "Do you always travel by bus?"

"I do, yes. I live just over the border in a place called Stourpaine. There is a regular bus service, and the guards know me now."

"Does the travelling get you down?"

"Not at all, I read my books. The return journey can drag if I have to catch the last bus. It goes all around the houses to pick up stragglers."

Norman spoke. "The last bus picks up everyone without a reason to be in this zone."

"I see," Jeff said. "Did the Judge often talk about his family?"

"Sometimes he did, yes. His wife died many years ago at roughly the same time as their daughter had her second baby. He missed his wife a lot. Have you seen those paintings in his dining room?"

"I have."

"Brilliant they are. Do you know what? On the second day, I worked for him, I mentioned the paintings and how good I thought they were, and His Lordship talked me through each one. He could remember the exact day he sought to depict the cases they were hearing and the verdict. Now, what do you think of that? The man was in his nineties but could still remember all those details."

"Amazing," agreed Cleveland. "Did his children visit him?"

"No, not really, dear. Passes into Z80+ aren't the easiest things to get hold of, even if your father is a famous Judge. He used to visit them, though. He also liked to see his grandchildren and would go to the youth zone to see his great-grandchildren. Of course, he could afford it."

Cleveland had not considered a fourth generation. "Great-grandchildren? How many of those did he have?"

Millie closed her eyes as she recalled the names. "Abigail had two sons, Kendal and Ewan. Elizabeth had two girls and a boy, Mary, Louise, and Jeffrey. The Judge was annoyed that Jeffrey did not have the middle name Murray. It was a family tradition."

"What calmed him down?"

"What, dear?"

"The Judge was annoyed. Do you know what had calmed him down?"

"Oh well, he could never be angry with Elizabeth for very long. His two eyes she was. Every time he spoke about her, his face lit up, and his old grey eyes twinkled. Then when Mary died...."

"Mary? That was…err…his great-granddaughter?"

"Yes, that's right. She died a few years ago."

"How? Do you have any idea?"

"I only know what the Judge told me. She was at the University in York. She started as an English student and did ever so well. Then, the Judge arranged for her to stay on to study law as a second degree, and by all accounts, she flew through that too. She had a great career ahead of her, but died in a terrible accident."

"Go on."

"Well, there's not much I can tell you. Mary was changing jobs and was celebrating in Scarborough. They say she fell off a cliff. She landed on some rocks and was dead by the time the Administrators reached her. She broke her neck. It was tragic for the family. The Judge was devastated. He had arranged for Mary to work with him, but she had delayed her arrival by a fortnight to complete a task. He never got over it, believing if Mary had arrived as originally planned, she would still be alive."

"That's very sad." Jeff felt the Judge's pain. "What happened to her siblings?"

"I think they're doing well for themselves. The girl is married now and lives in Lincoln with an older man. The boy is a trainee accountant in Grimsby. Abigail's boys are involved in their uncle's food business. They are management trainees or something like that, his Lordship said."

Cleveland listened as Millie summarised more of her conversations with the Judge. He believed most of it irrelevant, but he let her continue anyway. Eventually, she mentioned something about the Judge visiting London, providing a convenient opportunity for him to interrupt.

"London? What was he doing in London?"

"I'm not sure, dear. I think he was meeting the …what do they call them nowadays, Secretary for something or other?" She thought hard. "Security, that was it. He went to visit the Secretary for Security."

This was the third time his ex-boss had been mentioned in conversation in less than 48 hours. "Did he tell you why he went to visit Lord Wilson?"

"No." She noticed a change in Cleveland's expression. "Sorry, dear. All I knew was that it was to discuss something he was looking into."

"Thank you. Did the Judge say anything about what he was looking into?"

"I think it was something to do with elections." She moved her hand quickly across the space above her head. "All that stuff is way above me, dear. I don't worry about things like that these days. My Jim always reckoned that Governments do what they want to do, never mind the rest of us. I used to listen politely to his Lordship, but it never made much sense to me."

"Did you ever see any of his papers?"

"Papers, dear? What papers?"

"Work papers, possibly in his office?"

"No, I never set foot in his office. That was Amelia's area. She used to look after his papers and all that sort of thing. You'd have to ask her. Me and the Judge used to talk about stuff, but I never read his papers."

"I understand that the Judge had been travelling quite a bit recently. Did he mention where he was going and why?"

Millie nodded slowly as she shuffled forward on her cushion, "Yes, he had been out and about a fair bit in the last couple of months. I don't know all the details, but he mentioned that he had visited Wrexham several times. He quite liked it up there. He enjoyed the scenery."

"Wrexham? North Wales?"

"That's right, dear."

"What was he doing up there?"

"Not sure. He mentioned something about interviewing prisoners from the island jail. That would be Anglesey, wouldn't it?"

Cleveland nodded. "Yes, I believe it would."

"I thought so. We went there once when the children were

small. We rented a caravan in Rhyl, and Jim drove over. From what I remember, there were lots of lovely castles."

"I'm sure. Did the Judge mention any names?"

"No, not to me, he didn't. I knew he was meeting prisoners because I asked if it was safe. They would be under lock and key and brought to him. But if you want to know more about who he was meeting, you will need to ask MC."

"His driver."

"That's right. MC is lovely." She heard Norman cough and asked him if he was okay.

Norman confirmed he was fine.

"Do you know anything else about MC?" Jeff asked, focusing his attention on Millie.

Norman interjected. "I don't think MC is relevant to this discussion."

Jeff frowned at his driver. "Don't you? It is easy to see why you were not asked to investigate this case. I think MC could be a key witness." Norman's face reddened. Jeff asked Millie, "How much do you know about MC?"

"Nothing, really. Used to be in the Army, but no idea what part."

"Do you know where MC lives?"

Millie pushed out her lips and furrowed her brow as she considered the question. "Someone mentioned something about a house in Christchurch, but that's all I know. You'd have to check the rest. They'd probably have the details at the Administration. I am not sure if they will give them to you."

"It's worth a try." It was time to leave Millie in peace. He doubted he would learn anything new. He studied his watch. "Goodness. Is that the time? I'd better be going." He rose slowly from his seat and waited for Millie to stand. He held out his hand. "Thank you very much, you've been a great help. I appreciate you taking the time to talk to me."

Millie gently grabbed his fingers. "No problem, dear. I had better think about making tracks, too. I can't be late tonight. I'm going to Bingo at the social."

"Why don't we give you a lift home? It's on our way."

Norman did not welcome that offer. His expression turned sour.

"I don't want to be any trouble. I've still got to finish upstairs."

Norman relaxed a little, and the smug smile reappeared.

"It's no trouble. How long will you be?"

Norman's smile disappeared again, and he waved a hand to catch Jeff's attention. Jeff ignored him.

"About half an hour, I suppose."

"You take your time. Norman and I will have a walk on the front. We'll return in half an hour, but if you're not ready, no problem. We can wait. Can't we, Norman?"

"Looks like it," Norman gave a shake of his head.

Jeff felt a perverse satisfaction at getting one over on his driver. "Just one last question before we go. The Judge didn't eat much. Do you know why that was?"

"Stomach problems. He had tablets that he took regularly, but I don't know what they were for. You'd have to ask MC."

Millie lived in a row of terraced houses, having a garden between the pavement and the front door. Jeff insisted on accompanying her to her property. He waited until Millie had entered her hall before returning to the car.

Norman was in discussion with an older man. The newcomer wore a shirt, trousers, slippers and a flat cap. His driver was not enjoying the man's company and appeared aggravated.

Norman's voice was firm and loud. "I have already told you there is nothing to report."

"But it's been weeks now. A car can't just disappear like that."

Norman saw Jeff approaching and shooed the man away. "I will be in touch when we find something."

"I need that money to survive."

"So you keep telling me. I repeat, we are doing our best. If you excuse me, I must take this gentleman home."

The man shuffled up the street.

Jeff leaned on the roof of the car. "What was that about?"

The engine started. "Nothing, really. Old Loony Gibbons. He's a pain in the arse."

"Hang on. Switch off the engine. We are not going anywhere yet. Why is he a pain? What has he done?"

"I would like to get home. Can I tell you as I drive?"

"No, you cannot. What has he done to annoy you?"

Norman explained that Mr Gibbons, Jeff admonished him for repeating the Loony term, owned a vintage Rover 70. It was one of only four left in the country. When Mrs Gibbons became ill, the couple used all their savings to pay for some pioneering private treatment and care. Sadly, she passed, leaving her husband short of cash. He advertised the car for sale but then reported it stolen. Norman had visited a few weeks previously to speak to the man but had not been convinced by what he had heard. Jeff was intrigued by why Norman was dubious.

"Isn't it obvious? He sold the car and either forgot about it, which is quite likely as the bloke has been all over the place since his missus pegged it, or he pocketed the money and wants to claim off the insurance."

"We'll park the first option for a moment. Have you checked his bank balance?"

"Yes, but that doesn't prove anything. He was probably paid in cash?"

"What about the vehicle registration document? Has it been updated to show the new buyer?"

"No, but not everyone does that anymore. We have no idea how many cars change hands or when."

"Mr Gibbons doesn't appear to be benefiting from any ill-got gains. His trousers looked worn, and his slippers had seen better days."

"That could be an act. He might have a fortune stuffed in his mattress."

"It would be quite an act. You think he's forgotten he has sold it?"

"Yes, and he can't find the money. He told me that several people had called about the car. He gave us names for some of them, but there were a couple he could not remember. I imagine he sold it to one of them, but it's conveniently slipped his memory."

"Or he could be telling the truth. His car has been stolen, which is why he is struggling and anxious about his future."

"No chance..."

"Still, I would like to speak to Mr Gibbons."

"But it's getting late. I have to take you to Marshfield before I can go home."

"I'll drop you off on the way and drive myself. I'll collect you in the morning. We are coming back here to speak to MC."

"I can't do that. Only Admins are allowed to drive these cars." Norman opened the rear door. "Get in. I'll take you home."

Jeff slammed the door. "You go on home. I am going to have a chat with Mr Gibbons."

"This has nothing to do with your case. You have no jurisdiction in this matter."

"It's not in my job description, but as I will be acting in a private capacity, I can do what I want."

Norman inhaled loudly through his nose. "This is your last chance."

Jeff stepped back. "Are you still here? I thought you were in a hurry to get home."

The driver's chest rose and fell as he nibbled his upper lip. "I don't see why you are wasting your time. Gibbons is crazy. He's a nutter."

"What happened to the mantra about treating the public with civility, attentiveness and politeness?"

"I do for most people, but Gibbons is out of his tree. He also claims that someone is stealing his electricity."

"Where does he live?" Jeff looked up the road, but Mr Gibbons had disappeared.

"In the next street."

Jeff walked away from the car.

The houses on Gibbons' street were much larger than those on Millie's. Norman had changed his mind and moved the car. Jeff found it parked outside the last detached dwelling.

It was a warm, bright evening, and most houses had curtains and blinds open. The street was mostly silent. The one exception was Gibbon's next-door neighbour. All curtains were closed, and every room was well-lit. Loud music bellowed from upstairs while a television played at maximum volume downstairs.

"Who lives there?" Jeff asked, seeing Norman get out of the car.

"The Bishops. The wife is senile, and the husband is deaf. His son and wife were allowed to move her to care for his parents. They occupy the upstairs. It can't be easy having the television blaring through the ceiling."

"Hmm," Jeff said.

Mr Gibbons's property had a resin drive leading to a double garage. The side entrance was a glass door. Jeff tapped it with his knuckles. Gibbons welcomed them warmly and asked them inside.

The house was a mess. Newspapers lay scattered across the carpet, and clothes, some clean, others not, were strewn over the furniture. The place had a strange, stale odour.

"It's okay, I won't stay long." Jeff pointed at the Senior Administrator. "Norman here has told me about your car going missing. Can you repeat what happened? I always prefer to hear it from the horse's mouth, so to speak."

Gibbons spoke of his wife's illness and how they had paid for a new treatment which failed. They had used most of their savings, and he was now finding living on just his pension difficult. He had enough to survive but could not afford essential repairs to his property, and the flat roof needed replacing. He had owned the Rover 70 for many years. It was in superb condition. The car was his pride and joy. He stored it in the garage, covered with a tarpaulin.

Even though it did not go far, the car was cleaned inside and out at least twice a month. The engine was pristine, the bodywork was immaculate, and the interior was spotless. The front and rear seats were leather, and the dashboard was walnut with shiny brass fittings.

It broke his heart to part with it, but he had no choice. He advertised the car for sale and had several expressions of interest, including a visitor, Billy Jensen, who seemed keen initially but backed out. On the day the vehicle disappeared, Gibbons had gone to see an old colleague in the hope of securing part-time work and, on his return, found the garage empty.

"I have no wife, car, or money, and I didn't get the job. I am not sure what I am going to do."

Jeff promised to do what he could to recover the car, but Gibbons said he would be happier to get cash. He had already submitted a claim to the insurance company, but they would not process his claim without confirmation from the Admins that they had completed their enquiries and were satisfied the vehicle had been stolen. To date, he was unsure if Norman had even started making enquiries.

Norman snapped at the man. "That's rubbish, and you know it. We've enquired with the people you identified, but it's not our fault you could not give us all the names."

Gibbons tried to respond, but Jeff interjected.

"What about Billy Jensen? Did anyone speak to him?"

Norman nodded. "Of course, but Billy is a very successful businessman and a great friend to the Administration. He also has friends on the Central Committee. Billy is one of the good guys. He said he was interested in the car but changed his mind, and that is good enough for me."

"Well, someone took it," Gibbons insisted.

"We only have your word for that," Norman retorted.

Jeff was determined to move forward. "Let's not dwell on what has been. Norman and I will revisit the case and see if we can find anything new. If not, we will ensure you get your letter to continue your claim."

"You must be joking," Norman said. "I'll never agree to that."

"The decision will not be yours to take." Jeff gave him a piercing stare, suggesting Norman had better not push him before thanking Gibbons for his time and promising to be in touch.

"Thank you. Next time you come, would you mind looking at my electricity meter? I am sure there is something wrong with it. It costs me a fortune, and I am no longer running the medical equipment."

"Of course," Jeff was embarrassed by Norman's tittering. "Let's deal with the car first." He jerked his thumb in Norman's direction. "You know these Admins. They can only deal with one thing at a time. Let's not confuse them."

Gibbons was still laughing as he shut the door.

It was after eight o'clock when Jeff Cleveland climbed out of the car outside his home. He felt exhausted, hungry and thirsty.

The journey back had been soundless. Norman was sulking and did not even wish his new colleague a good night. Not that it bothered Jeff. It was water off a duck's back.

His street was empty, with not a soul or animal to be seen. He could hear people talking and sounds of gentle laughter, but could not see anyone. He guessed someone, somewhere, was enjoying the evening.

He unlocked his front door and stepped inside. There were no letters or pamphlets. Jeff discarded his hat and jacket onto a hook in the hall.

The evening sun beaming through his patio windows lit up his living room. The small red bulb on his answering machine flashed, telling him he had a message. He placed the dripping wet, cool bag on an old newspaper on the windowsill and then pressed the play button on the machine. He waited for the automated voice to tell him he had just one message.

The message, timed at seven fifteen p.m., came from ChiZA Purcell enquiring whether there was anything to report. Purcell asked Cleveland to ring him on his office number before nine that evening.

Cleveland was in no rush. He needed his supper. There was no harm in making Purcell wait.

He collected the makeshift cool bag and carried it into the kitchen. Placing it on the draining board, he reached for some old newspapers, which he then wrapped around the bag, depositing the reinforced packet on the bottom shelf of his freezer. Jeff removed a tray of ice cubes, which he banged against the table until five cubes fell out. He returned the tray and closed the door.

He kept his whisky in the cupboard by the cooker, next to his favourite glass. The small, crystal tumbler had a *'Johnny Walker'* logo on the side, although the gilt had faded over the years, evoking a sense of nostalgia. The whisky in the bottle was not excellent quality, but the good stuff was in short supply and only available at premium prices.

He poured what he believed to be a sensible amount into the glass and added two of the five ice cubes from the table. He placed the other three into an empty cup.

The first sip awoke his taste buds, and he savoured the flavour, swallowing slowly. He took another sip and then placed the glass on the table.

His meal for today was supposed to be chicken leg, potatoes and peas, but Cleveland had lost his enthusiasm for cooking. He was hungry but not picky. He prepared a sandwich and transferred it to a plate, put that onto a tray, added his whisky glass, and walked to his living room.

With plate and cutlery left in the sink, Cleveland topped up his whisky, added the remaining ice cubes, and took his glass to the hallway.

Felicity purchased the telephone chair as a surprise. She was fed up watching her husband trying to juggle the receiver while making notes. The unit had a shelf where Jeff could put the book.

He placed his drink on the floor and called the ChiZA.

Nobody answered. Cleveland checked his watch. It was only 8:50 p.m., and he silently chastised the Administrator for sneaking off. He called Purcell's home number and left a message with his wife. She sounded much younger, and

Cleveland initially asked her to take a message for her father. She cackled so loudly that he had to move the receiver from his ear.

The next person on his list was Martin Rowe.

"Hello, Martin Rowe."

"Good evening. It's been a long time, but no see. It's Cleveland. How are you?"

There was a momentary silence. "Cleveland? The ex-Chief Inspector Jeff Cleveland?"

"The very same."

"Good God, there's a blast from the past. How are you? Where are you? What are you doing?"

Cleveland found it amusing that Rowe never asked one question at a time. "I'm fine, thank you. I am still in Marshfield, still retired, although I have a project on the go that you may be able to help me with."

"Good, I'm glad to hear it. How is the family? Where are they now? What are they doing? What's the project?"

"Glad to see you don't change. Slow down, will you? The family is fine. I am a grandfather now, and the children are both in Aston. The grandkids are…well, you can guess where they are. I will tell you about the project in a moment. You haven't given me a chance to ask about you. How are you?"

Rowe chuckled into the phone. "Yes, sorry. I am fine, thanks. I'm living in Reading, still married to Carol, and the offspring has finally settled in Nottingham, where he works in the health service." He took a breath. "It's good to hear from you, Jeff, but what is so important that you are bothering me at this time of the evening? What is it that you want?"

"That's charming. Can't a man phone an old friend for a chat?" Jeff took short, deep breaths to stop himself from giggling.

"No, you can't, not after all this time." Rowe lowered his voice. "The last time we spoke, you were reviewing the evidence in that Brogan case. Then I heard you'd retired. Brogan walked free with his head held high, and young McCallum was made the scapegoat, destined to be marked down in history as the man who brought about the end of the police as we knew it."

Cleveland no longer felt like laughing. "I had no idea that would happen. You do know that, don't you?"

"I guessed as much. I couldn't imagine you treating McCallum like that, but where were you?"

"I did try to help him, but ..." He struggled for his next sentence. "When I heard that my wife was missing in the Shift, I lost interest in most things. There's nothing else I can say. I didn't care what happened to anyone else. My children were all I cared about."

Rowe offered his sympathy. "That must have been a rough time. How are you? Are you fit and healthy?"

"I'm fine, thanks. I hit rock bottom, but I'm over it now. Ironically, it was my kids who brought me through."

Rowe said that was good news. "Do you have any idea what happened to McCallum? Where is he? What's he doing?"

"I have no idea. Since the introduction of the zones and the lack of internet, it's nigh on impossible to track people down. It was a while after the Shift when I learned what had happened. Those accusations against him were complete rubbish. He hadn't even worked on half those cases. He had no chance. You know the rest."

Rowe tutted into the mouthpiece. "Yes, I do. It wasn't just the police they brought down. It was the whole justice system - the Courts, criminal lawyers, forensic services - everything went down the pan."

Cleveland wanted to forget all that. "What are you working on now?"

The question caught Rowe off guard. "Me? Oh, I have a plum job."

"Glad to hear it, tell me more."

"No, seriously, I have a plum job. I work as a scientist in the fruit industry, trying to increase the annual yield of plums."

"And what are your qualifications for this post?"

"I was a scientist."

"Yes, but a forensic scientist."

"Ah, but since the Shift, one must be prepared to extend, learn new skills, adapt, develop, improve, survive."

Cleveland chuckled at Rowe's recounting of the Committee mantra. "If anyone is listening, can I just say I completely disagree with his views?"

It was Rowe's turn to laugh. "It is weird how things turn out, but I enjoy it. Production was up 30% last year, and we reckon it will be higher still this year."

"Is that just plums? I don't like plums."

"Today plums, tomorrow, I don't know. How do you feel about apples?"

"Love them."

"I will work on them next. How about a bumper crop of Orange Pippin?"

"Great, I look forward to it."

"Now, will you tell me why you rang?"

"Do you still have access to lab equipment?"

"Which part of me being a scientist did you not understand?"

"Fair point. What I meant was, do you have access to forensic equipment?"

"Depends on what it is you want done?"

"I am working for the Administration at the moment, investigating the death of a prominent figure."

"Not Kendal McGregor?"

"Might be."

"You are kidding me? You are investigating the death of the man who destroyed the organisation you treasured?"

"I am, but Kendal didn't do it alone. He was one of three on that panel, and they were merely the public face of the review. I believe bigger sharks were behind them, waiting to destroy the police, and I don't care who knows it." Rowe chuckled. "I would also take great comfort from discovering who did this, just to prove that good old-fashioned policing can still work."

"Good for you."

"Do you have the equipment to test some bone fragments, some blood particles, and a lump of gooey stuff that I am told is jelly? It doesn't smell very jelly-like to me."

"As I said, it depends on what you want done. What are you looking for?"

"Anything you can find."

"Bring it over, and I'll see."

Cleveland took down details of his office address and proposed to visit the following day.

Wishing Dr Rowe a good night, Jeff replaced the receiver and retired to his lounge.

The conference call was supposed to occur earlier, but had to be delayed due to a late arrival. Norman Draper sat across the desk from his Lead Regional Administrator, LeRA Martin Cormack. They sat silently, listening as the voice at the other end of the line asked for an update.

Draper coughed and said, "There was nothing for him to find. Any evidence that might have existed has been cleared away. He has hit a brick wall. There is no way he can make any progress." He listened as the others praised his efforts. "I nearly forgot; I found out today that Wilson's Admins collected boxes of papers, but we have no idea what was in them. They kept our boys in the lobby while they took what they wanted." He stopped to hear a question. "Yes, they seemed to know where to look. Lauren said they marched in, secured the room, filled the boxes and left without saying a word." Another question. "No clue. The boxes were sealed and kept well away from prying eyes."

"Tell him about Cleveland poking his nose into other matters," urged Cormack.

"What's that?" the voice at the other end asked.

"Nothing to worry about. I have it all under control." Draper sipped the whisky provided by Cormack as the third person made it clear that an explanation was required. "Cleveland is trying to poke his nose into Admin business. Looney Gibbons ambushed me on our travels, and PC Plod wants to investigate his missing car." More comment. "No, Billy Jensen has nothing to worry about. I've already shut the matter down. I rang Percy on my way here and put him straight. He's going to speak to Cleveland tonight. He'll tell him to keep his nose out. Give it a week, and Sherlock will be off the case. He has nothing to go on."

Jeff was dozing when he heard the telephone. It was ChiZA Purcell. "Good evening. I did try you at your office, but you must have left early." Cleveland allowed himself a silent smile. "I do have other matters to attend to." Purcell did not sound the least bit fazed. "How are you getting on?"

"Not very well, if you want the truth."

"I am sorry to hear that. Problems?"

"Where do I start? I have no body, which means I only have other people's word that a murder has taken place."

"I can assure you that Lord McGregor was murdered."

"Yes, but assurances aren't always facts, are they? I was taught to deal in facts."

"We all need to adapt, develop, improve, Mr Cleveland."

He smirked. "I suppose so, but the crime scene has had more visitors than the bingo hall on pension day. There is nowhere to process any evidence, even if I could find some. Taking fingerprints is pointless because the National Register has been deleted. I imagine the same is true for the DNA databases?"

"Yes. We were extremely short of computer capacity. We had to make choices."

Cleveland ignored the reply. "My investigation can be little more than a token effort with so little to go on."

"Perhaps you should concentrate on just the one case."

Jeff had not expected Norman to get to Purcell before him. "You've spoken to Norman?"

"Yes, he rang earlier. He is concerned that you are poking your nose into matters that are not relevant."

"I am surprised you wanted me to look at this case. Norman could do the job on his own."

"There's no need to sulk. He doesn't understand why you are so interested in this missing car. I cannot see a connection either."

Jeff yawned loudly, knowing the sound would travel down the

line. "Can I ask you something?"

"Yes."

"How could someone move around the Old Fogies Zone without being noticed?"

"I don't follow."

"Norman and I walked along the seafront today and were immediately clocked as outsiders, strangers. If Norman had not been in uniform, the local Admins would have stopped us and checked our papers."

"What has this got to do with the missing car?"

"I am coming to that. What is the best way to travel across that zone without being noticed?" He fell quiet momentarily and then added, "In a vintage car. Nobody pays any attention to a classic vehicle. There are so many in that zone that they go unnoticed. Residents would probably pay more attention to an old banger. If our murderer had driven through the ROFZ in a battered Vauxhall Astra, I am sure people would have remembered seeing something."

"That makes sense, but from what Norman told me, Gibbons' car went missing weeks ago."

"And there's been no effort to find it," Jeff replied. "If this murder was planned well in advance. Whoever is responsible might have stolen the car when it was first advertised and stored it until it was time to visit the Judge."

"Speculative, to say the least."

"But you cannot prove I'm wrong, just as I can't show I'm right. There is nothing to suggest the two incidents are linked, but we cannot be certain they are not. We need to keep an open mind and explore all options."

"I think I get the point. Don't spend too long barking up the wrong trees. Your priority is finding out what happened to His Lordship."

"You knew he was working on various important projects before he died. Is that why you arranged for someone to remove all the papers?"

"I did not know what His Lordship was involved in. As for the suggestion that I removed evidence, that was not down to me. I only found that out this afternoon. The order to remove them came directly from the Secretary for Security. The papers were taken to London."

Cleveland's ears pricked up. "Why would Wilson want them?"

"I don't know. I assume what they contain must be important to him. It is not my place to question Lord Wilson."

Cleveland wondered whether the projects the Judge was working on might have been enough to get him killed. The only one Jeff considered controversial was the work on elections. He thought he would test whether the Administration felt the same. "Does Wilson think the Judge was murdered because his work might see a return to elections?"

Purcell took a long time to answer. "I do not know what Lord Wilson thinks. There is no evidence to suggest the death is due to His Lordship's work."

Jeff pressed on. "I need a pass to see Lord Wilson in London."

"Mr Cleveland, I do not…" He didn't have a chance to finish his sentence.

"I am trying to establish a motive for the killing. Without one, I am looking for the proverbial needle in a massive haystack. The information in those papers might help me learn why the Judge was murdered."

"I can appreciate that this is not an easy investigation for you, but I cannot simply agree to you going to London. I am not dismissing the possibility, but I must be satisfied that you have exhausted all other avenues first."

"In that case, I will need assistance."

"Accepted, and we agreed you could use Norman."

"Err, yes, but I am not sure Norman is… equipped for this particular task."

"I can assure you that Norman is…" Again, Purcell was interrupted.

"I know you think highly of Norman, but he is not the best man for this job."

"Why not?"

"I need somebody who understands investigative work. Someone who can ask the right questions, seek out witnesses, and take instructions. Norman can't keep his mouth shut, refuses to do as he's told, and he bullied a witness this afternoon."

"He mentioned you were unhappy with his assertiveness when questioning Amelia..."

Norman's honesty surprised Jeff.

"...but that says more about your dislike of being challenged than Norman's abilities. You would do well to remember that you are no longer a police officer. Things are different these days, and you need to approach things differently. I am grateful you agreed to help, and I will allocate what resources I can, but you are not in command as far as the Administrators are concerned. That is my role. You will stick with Norman."

"Then let me use Harding, too."

"Harding? Who's Harding?

"Mark Harding."

"How do you know him?"

"I met him at the Judge's house today with his colleague Lauren. Harding showed me around, and he was a great help. I think he could prove useful." Jeff wanted to avoid revealing Harding's past. "I will need all the help I can get."

"Did Harding offer to help you?"

"No. He knows nothing about this request."

Purcell fell silent. "I will get you Harding, but you keep Norman involved. Try to engage with him more. He has many skills and lots of contacts. You'll find him very useful."

"I will try," Jeff said, not believing the relationship could work.

"Do me a favour. Make it clear that Harding has been appointed against his wishes."

"Why on earth..."

"Otherwise, his colleagues might give him a hard time when this is over. The Admins mistrust the police. It will help Harding if you emphasise that he is doing this against his wishes."

"I can do that."

"Thank you. By the way, I am taking some bone fragments and a lump of jelly to a scientist friend tomorrow." It was an open secret that the Administration listened in on telephone calls, so Jeff guessed Purcell already knew his plans. He wanted to appear open. "I doubt he can do anything with them, but I thought it was worth a try. You don't mind, do you?"

"Not at all. I told you I would be happy to explore all options if it helped determine who committed this heinous crime."

"Thank you."

"Was there anything else?"

"Yes, I need to speak to Colonel MC Sands."

"I wondered when you would want to speak to MC. What are you hoping to discover?"

"Details about the Judge's activities in the last weeks of his life. Who he met, where and why. That sort of thing."

"I will arrange for MC to speak to you tomorrow. Ring me at my office in the morning, and I'll give you a time and a place. You are aware that MC is not the easiest to deal with?"

"I've met many awkward people. I'm used to it."

"I very much doubt you have met many people like this one. MC is ex-military and used to authority and obeying rules, but can be obstinate and prone to be up and down."

"What does that mean?"

"One minute friendly, the next...MC might be about to rip off your head. Don't expect answers to all your questions. MC will probably want to size you up before saying very much."

"I am sure I'll be fine."

"Good luck. Is that it?"

"Can I see the footage of the surveillance cameras you have around the Judge's property?"

"No."

Cleveland was startled to get such a definite negative answer. "Would it make a difference if I told you why I wanted to see it?"

"I presume it is because you want to check who was in the area on the night in question and see if anyone entered the Judge's house?"

"That's about the size of it."

"You're out of luck. The cameras are live feed only, and the images are not recorded anywhere."

"What is the point in that?"

"I told you before that our role is only to observe Z80+ and ensure there is no trouble. My men watch the screens all day. If anyone has a problem, we send help but do not record anything we see."

"Is that because of an agreement with the residents?"

"I would like to say it is, but it is because we have nothing to record on to. We cannot waste valuable computer space, so it is a live feed only. As there are no trials, there is no need for evidence."

The response caught Jeff off guard. "Oh, I see." He quickly scanned his notes again. "Right. Looking at tapes is a no-no. What's next? Oh yes, the lists you gave me showed that five Administrators and two residents entered the zone on the night in question but didn't leave again. Can we find out why that was?"

"Presumably. Remind me of their names, and I will check where they are and what they were doing."

Cleveland wanted to interview the seven, but he already had enough to do. He read out the names slowly so that Purcell could write them down.

"I will ask the questions tomorrow and tell you what they say. Is there anything else?"

"Not from me. Do you have any questions?"

"There is nothing that cannot wait until tomorrow. If you don't mind, I will say good night and return to my dinner."

"Of course, good night."

Cleveland replaced the phone and downed what was left of his whisky. The ice had melted, slightly diluting the impact on his tongue, but it still tasted good. He thought he had earned a nightcap.

7. THE BEAT GOES ON

Having made his telephone calls the previous evening, Jeff took Purcell's lists to his bedroom with another glass of whisky, pulled up a chair, sat beside the bed, and spread his papers over the duvet. Leaning over made him tired and uncomfortable. He undressed and climbed into bed to continue reading.

The next thing he knew, the bin collectors shouting at each other in the street woke him. It was 6:45 a.m. Jeff had attached himself to several sheets of paper, with lists stuck to his face and torso.

He lifted his head, stretched his arms, yawned loudly and began peeling. He had no idea when he last slept so well. He vaguely recalled being woken by what sounded like a 4x4 vehicle in the early hours, but had not been bothered enough to do anything about it and drifted back to sleep immediately. It was probably the milkman making deliveries.

He straightened out the creased pages and considered putting them back into some resemblance of order, but decided it could wait until he had a cup of tea. He switched off his bedside lamp and went downstairs.

The birds were gathering in the branches around the bird table, and Cleveland duly obliged them by taking out a bag of food. There was a chill in the air which he had not expected, and he shivered as he emptied the pack onto the table.

Back in the sanctuary of his kitchen, he studied the birds indulging in a feeding frenzy. He and Felicity enjoyed their breakfasts together, watching their feathered friends coming and going. She had become quite adept at recognising the different species. Jeff could barely tell one bird from another, but that did not stop his enjoyment of them.

He ate breakfast and enjoyed a leisurely shower before calling Purcell, who confirmed he had requested Harding's help but had not yet received an answer. MC had agreed to meet Cleveland at the Wimborne Minster office at midday. Jeff made more tea and sat at his kitchen table, planning his day.

Before heading to Wimborne Minster, he would travel to Reading to deliver the evidence to Rowe's laboratory. He also wanted to make another stop on the way to meet MC. He doubted Norman would be happy, but the visit would not take long.

Jeff considered how best to approach the issue.

Purcell had suggested he build bridges with Norman, but Jeff was not convinced that would be possible. The man was a pain. Jeff would be happier with a new driver, but for the moment, he was stuck with Norman. He would need a solid case to move the man on. In the meantime, he thought they should try to get along. A fresh start was required. Jeff rehearsed lines he might use.

His driver arrived on time. Jeff spotted Norman had changed his socks. He doubted the new pair showing yellow and red ducks was a regulation issue, but kept his thoughts to himself. Instead, they discussed what Norman had done the previous evening, and Jeff apologised if Norman felt he had spoken out of turn. Jeff was used to giving orders and needed time to come to terms with his new role. His teeth gripped his bottom lip when he heard Norman's reply.

"No problem, Jeff. Just so long as you know your place."

Dr Martin Rowe was on a conference call but had forewarned the receptionist to expect a delivery. She placed the damp plastic bag on a tray and instructed one of the messengers to take it to Dr Rowe's office. Cleveland left contact details in case the doctor needed to speak to him.

He used the vending machine in reception to purchase two teas and took them to the car. Norman leaned against the back door, basking in the sunlight.

"I got you a tea. Not sure if you take sugar, so got one with and one without."

"With, please. I prefer this Bristol stuff with sugar. He took the card cup from Cleveland. "Cheers."

They drank their tea in silence, admiring the surroundings. Rowe's laboratory was the smallest of three low-rise buildings nestled amongst trees planted around an enormous, manufactured lake. The London to South Wales railway line lay at the far end of the lake, and their peace was disturbed by the familiar rattle of a passing train.

"I thought they had electrified this line," Norman took another sip.

"Me too, but that was a diesel train. You could tell by the noise."

"And the smell," added Norman. "That diesel stinks. You notice it more now that the air is cleaner." He discarded the rest of his tea onto the grass and dumped the cup into a bin. "Right, we'd better get a move on if you want to be in Wimborne Minster by noon."

Cleveland studied his watch. "It's not that far, is it?"

"No, we'll get there soon enough, but we might have to stop at the checkpoints."

Cleveland had not factored in time for the security checks. "Of course," he dropped his cup into the bin. "Let's go," he said, climbing back into the car. Seeing Norman was comfortable and about to set off, Jeff said, "I want to visit Sherborne, so let's go that way." He waited for the reaction.

"What do you want in Sherborne?"

"I want to see Billy Jensen."

Norman turned, resting his arm on the back of his seat. "What for?"

"Just to help me with my enquiries."

"This has nothing to do with your case. This is because of that nutcase, Loony Gibbons. I've told you that man has lost the plot..."

"You did, and I told you to have some respect. I want to go to Sherborne."

"It is a waste of time." Norman faced the front.

"You may be right, but I want to speak to Mister Jensen. Are you prepared to drive me, or must I catch a bus?"

"This is outside your remit. You have no jurisdiction in Administration matters. What do you think you'll learn? What good will winding up Billy do?"

Jeff took a breath before answering. "As I explained to ChiZA Purcell yesterday evening…"

Norman scowled into the rearview.

"…the car might be important in establishing how the perpetrator travelled through Z80+ without being noticed."

"Billy wouldn't have anything to do with this. Gibbons is a nutcase."

"Yes, you keep saying, but I want to check."

"There is nothing to check. You are no longer a policeman. Your role is to investigate the murder. That's it."

"That's what I am doing. I want a quick word with Mister Jensen to ask him a few questions about his dealings with Mister Gibbons. It might be nothing, but I feel the missing car could be important. Billy Jensen's house is on our way…"

"It is not. It is out of our way, and I am under orders to minimise fuel consumption."

Jeff was losing patience. "You also have a duty to investigate theft, but you don't appear too keen to do so."

Norman turned again, clearly irritated. "That car has nothing to do with this case. It did not get stolen. It got sold, and Gibbons has either forgotten about it or is pulling a fast one."

"Either way, let's see what Mister Jensen has to say, and we can, hopefully, eliminate him from our enquiries."

"This is your enquiry. I want nothing to do with it."

"Noted. Now, are you going to take me to Sherborne?"

"No."

Jeff opened the door and stepped outside. He leaned back to say, "Tell Purcell that I will likely be out all day today making enquiries and will see MC tomorrow. Also, advise him that I will be speaking with Lord Wilson to tell him that his instructions about my getting the full support of the Administration are not being followed." He slammed the door and walked away.

He had taken no more than twenty steps when Norman shouted after him.

"Wait. I'll take you."

"Are you sure?"

"Yes. I don't suppose there's any harm in putting your mind to rest." Norman left the car, holding up his mobile. "I'll just ring HQ to tell them we might be late."

Billy Jensen lived in a sprawling old vicarage which had, until recently, served as a care home. Scaffolding adorned the east wing, and the multitude of workers appeared busy.

The man walked to meet the car as they pulled up outside. He was tall and walked with a straight back. His leather-soled shoes scrunched over the stones on the drive. Jeff thought Jensen did not look old enough to be a resident of Z60-80.

"Hello, Norman. Good to see you again. Is the family all well?"

"Fine, thanks, Billy. How are you settling in?"

"Very well, thank you."

Norman spoke to Jeff. "Billy was allocated a place in Amesbury but needed something bigger. This place became empty when the sad old farts were finally moved to Scotland."

Jeff had heard that all state-run care homes in the south were closing, and the residents moved further north. Private homes continued to operate in the zone. He nodded to show he understood.

Billy pointed at the workers. "As you can see, the house needs a lot of work. We completely gutted the interior, and I hope to get the exterior work completed before winter, providing this lot gets their fingers out."

Billy and Norman laughed. Jeff forced a smile.

Norman had another question for Jensen. "Did you get those permits for the Weymouth apartments?"

"I did and wanted to thank you for being so helpful."

"No problem."

Norman explained to Jeff that Billy managed many properties

providing holiday accommodation around the coast. He had recently helped Billy to acquire an apartment block for holiday accommodation in Weymouth and several camping sites.

Again, Jeff uttered no words and offered a weak smile. He had already marked Jensen's card. The score was not good. Jeff neither liked nor trusted this man.

Billy stepped nearer. "I'm afraid I haven't had the pleasure."

"No reason why you should have." Jeff introduced himself and apologised for arriving unannounced. He explained the reason for his visit. He did not mention the murder of the Judge but spoke about Gibbons' mysterious car disappearance and how Jensen might have been one of the last people, other than the owner, to see it.

"Of course, I am always happy to help however I can. Let me think for a moment…"

Norman helped him. "It was the Rover 70, blue with leather seats." He turned his attention to Jeff. "Billy is a real petrolhead and sees so many cars. He probably can't remember everything he's seen."

"If only he could buy them all," Jeff suggested.

"I would love to. Sadly, I don't have the space. I do see a lot of cars because, as my old fella used to say, you have to kiss a lot of frogs before you find your prince. I am very selective."

An awkward silence followed until Billy filled the void. "As it happens, I do remember that one. I was looking forward to seeing it. I always had a soft spot for Rovers. My dad sold them, and my granddad worked in the factory." He checked that he had Jeff's attention. "The advert claimed it was in pristine condition, but it was a bit of a rust bucket, to be honest with you. The interior was in pretty good nick, but outside…" He forced a shiver. "Big disappointment. I offered him a fair price because I planned to dismantle it for bits to use on my car. The parts are ridiculously expensive nowadays. You have to get them tailor-made. There are not many old Rovers around."

"How did Mister Gibbons react?"

"He threw a wobbly, telling me about his wife's death and

how he needed the cash. I told him I was sorry to hear of his problems, but I wouldn't pay the asking price. I offered him more than my original offer, but he wouldn't listen to reason."

"See, Jeff. This is what we are dealing with. Gibbons is a nutcase." Norman stepped between Jeff and Jensen. "He gets offered a fair price but still wants more. If you ask me, he's sold the car and is trying to get the insurance."

Billy placed a hand on the Admin's shoulder. "Hang on a minute, Norm, I am not suggesting Mister Gibbons is trying to defraud anyone. He probably genuinely believed the car was worth more than it was. I wouldn't mind betting that after I turned it down, Gibbons met someone pretending to be interested in buying it, and that bastard nicked it off him. He pointed at Jeff. "If I were you, I'd be looking at the scrap metal dealers, and I don't mean the pukka ones. This sounds to me like the work of a dodgy dealer."

"You think it might have been stolen for parts." Jeff scratched behind his ear.

"In my opinion, that is all that car was good for. Do you want me to put the word out that I'm looking for bits for my Rover 70 in the hope that someone offers something?"

Norman's response came very quickly. "That would be very helpful, Billy. Thank you."

Jeff disagreed. "There's no need for that, Mister Jensen. I don't want to put you to any trouble. I am relieved that you believe Mister Gibbons' car was stolen. We can file the necessary report, and he can get his money. Is that okay with you, Norm?"

"If it gets him off my back, then I suppose that's fine."

"Just one more thing, Mister Jensen..."

"Call me Billy, please."

Jeff had no intention of doing that. "Did you tell anyone else about the Rover?"

Jensen's eyes narrowed. "Like whom?"

"A fellow vehicle enthusiast, perhaps? Someone who might be interested in vintage cars, maybe for spares, etc."

"No. I was only interested in that vehicle for my own purposes. I was gutted it was in such poor condition."

"Of course." Jeff nodded. The conversation was almost over. He had one more question. "Is there any chance I could see your Rover 70? I vaguely remember seeing one when I was younger but can't recall much about it."

Billy's eyes lit up. "Of course, come this way. I am happy to cooperate even though I know you have no jurisdiction in this matter, and had I declined, you could do nothing about it."

Jensen was very well-informed. Jeff guessed Norman's earlier call had not been to his colleagues at HQ. "Thank you."

"No problem, as Norman here will testify. I have nothing to hide and am always ready to help our Administrators continue doing such a fine job." A sneer appeared on his face. "You used to be a copper, didn't you?"

"I did."

"Well, I wasn't sorry to see the last of your lot. If you don't mind me saying, you were a corrupt bunch of bastards. We are much better off with the Admins taking direct action locally without needing all that palaver involving the Courts. Justice these days is seen to be done and gets delivered quickly."

"I'm sure," Jeff said, thinking this was not the time or place for an argument.

They followed Jensen to a shed at the rear of the property. Jeff was only half listening to the man bragging about his car collection. He waited while his host tapped in a code and stepped back as two massive doors slid open.

The space was crammed with vintage cars. The Rover was only partially visible at the back. It was behind an original Land Rover and a Porsche SUV.

Jeff circled the car, studying its condition. Jensen unlocked the driver's door and told Jeff to sit, but he refused, claiming he did not want to dirty the leather. Instead, Jeff took another long, slow look at the vintage classic. He noted bubbling paint on the wheel arches and the slightly different colouring of the front panels compared to the rear. He kept his thoughts private.

Jeff tried to appear nonchalant while listening to Jensen and Norman discuss Gibbons. They openly mocked the man. Norman was delighted that they had found a way to close the case. He felt obliged to tell the insurance company that the car was not in as good a condition as had been claimed. The pair moved to the door, and Jeff struggled to hear the details of what Jensen said about a week in Cornwall. He realised what had been said when Norman announced how overjoyed he was with the offer and hugged Billy for his generosity.

Jeff had seen and heard more than enough. He thanked Jensen for allowing him to see his collection, shook the man's hand and walked to the State car alone. Norman updated Jensen on ticket sales for the Summer Ball and shrieked when Billy offered to buy two more tables. Jeff looked back to see the pair hugging and heard Billy say how much he appreciated the advance warning about the visit.

Jeff sat quietly in the back, trying to absorb what he had learned. The Administrators were more lazy, crooked and biased than he previously thought. He supposed it was bound to happen with so few checks and balances to their activities. It came as a surprise when Norman spoke to him.

"You are very quiet. Pouting, are we?"

"Why would I?"

"You hoped Billy was responsible for the disappearance of Looney's car, but now you know he wasn't, and you are not happy about it. You could have saved us time by listening to me. I told you Billy had nothing to do with it. He wouldn't get involved in anything like that."

Jeff could not decide whether Norman was gullible and a poor judge of character or a knowing participant in Jensen's broader activities and, therefore, corrupt. He feared the latter. Jeff listened in silence as his driver recounted the numerous good deeds his good friend, Billy, had done, quoting to the pound how much Billy had donated to Administration charities.

The longer Norman extolled Billy Jensen's virtues, the more

Jeff thought about the chair. His father's beloved chair. That unique antique piece that held such substantial historical significance for the family. Dad described it as '*a bespoke combination of top-quality design and craftsmanship specially created for a world-renowned name on the Cleveland family tree*'. Nobody else, not even a museum, owned such a rare artefact. It had been Malcolm Cleveland's pride and joy.

Back in the day, Jeff regularly used the 'Chair' speech to welcome new detectives. This was an opportune time to repeat it, not that he thought Norman would take much notice. The man would never make a detective.

"Would you mind if I told you a little story?"

"Not at all, providing it is not boring. The last thing I need to do is fall asleep at the wheel."

"I will try to keep it interesting." Seeing Norman nod, Jeff commenced. "My father's name was Malcolm, and he hated school. He paid little heed to academia and the benefits of reading. He left school with few qualifications and even less ambition. Despite his lack of formal education, he was a sharp cookie, and it took a very clever person to get one over on him." He took a breath. "Dad had a swift mind and absorbed information without being told twice. He was also very astute and could read people. I might have inherited a little of that trait, hence my job. Anyway, I digress. My grandparents insisted that Dad would not be allowed to join the army as his career officer suggested and persuaded him to apply for an apprenticeship with the local electricity company. It turned out to be the best thing he did. He took to electrics like the proverbial duck..."

"Is this going anywhere? Because if you are going to tell me your life story, I'll ring Purcell and get reassigned."

In that case, I will keep my fingers crossed and continue, Jeff thought. He forced a chuckle. "During his first visit to America, a tour guide mentioned that Dad shared a surname with the 22nd and 24th Presidents of the United States. My father was more impressed that the lady could recite the names and numbers of all the US presidents. He had trouble recalling the names of recent prime ministers, let alone knowing the order in which they had been elected." This usually resulted in titters of laughter, but Norman did not even smile. Jeff was not put off. "He returned home eager to know if there was any family connection between the Derbyshire Clevelands and Stephen Grover Cleveland, US president. Dad used online ancestry sites to trace our heritage. The sites put him in touch with American namesakes who were equally keen to discover English relations. One connection produced documentation proving we were related to Grover and offered to help Dad establish links with the wider family. That man's name was Calvin Cleveland, and he soon sent Dad extracts from family histories showing how we were directly linked to the great man."

The response was as flat as Jeff had expected. "Yippetty do dah."

Jeff carried on. "Utilising the services of a successful American historian recommended by Calvin, Dad paid seven hundred dollars for a personalised family tree, which he eventually received in the post. He framed it. It hung on the living room wall until he died."

"Nice." Norman openly yawned.

"My story rolls on a few months now. Dad was saddened because Calvin ceased all contact. Then, out of the blue, he rang, apologising for his absence and explaining that his wife had surprised him with a demand for a divorce. He believed they were happy, but she left him and their children to move in with a musician. Calvin had been busy raising money for a quick settlement. He was desperate to keep the children. His wife threatened to take them to live with her new man on the other side of the country unless he found the cash. Calvin used up all his savings, cashed in his pensions, and downsized. Dad had seen images of Calvin's homestead and could imagine how different things would be for the family. Calvin was particularly aggrieved at selling his family heirlooms to pay off his wife. He cried down the line, saying he had no choice. His kids were the most important things in his life, and he had to provide for them."

"I hope this has a happy ending. I'm almost in tears here."

Jeff ignored him again. "Luckily, there was a keen interest in items linked to past presidents, so Calvin's things earned good money. The proceeds exceeded his expectations, and he earned enough to pay her and buy a car. He was particularly excited about the auction for the last of his Grover possessions, a chair made for President Cleveland by a furniture maker in Chesterfield. They made it to commemorate his presidential election. The auction house told him to expect it to raise between six and ten thousand dollars, but the pre-sale offers exceeded twenty-five thousand. Calvin couldn't believe his luck. He would get a much better car and take his children on holiday. Dad was thrilled for Calvin but wished he had been aware of the sale, as he would have bought something. Owning an item passed down through the generations would have been very special. Calvin felt terrible about letting down his newly discovered relative and offered to cancel the sale. Dad could have the chair. My father appreciated the offer but would not accept it. Calvin needed the money, and it was his chair to sell. Calvin was adamant that Dad should have it. Eventually, after much discussion and several long phone calls, Dad offered to buy it. They agreed to a price of ten thousand dollars, the higher end of the original estimate. The deal suited both parties, was a reasonable compromise and eased Calvin's conscience."

"I love a happy ending," Norman could not sound less interested.

"I haven't told you the best bit yet. That was a fortune for Dad, but he took out a loan and used the savings he intended to put toward a house. He was confident that this represented a better investment. Calvin refused to accept payment until the chair reached England safely, but agreed with Dad's suggestion to place the money into a holding account to be released on delivery. My father thought that was fair, as Calvin didn't know if Dad was genuine. Dad also agreed to pay the transport costs and enhanced insurance, further depleting his funds. Anyway, the chair arrived safely, and my father fell in love with it. He released the payment immediately. Dad was ecstatic to read the supporting documentation verifying what he had bought. He framed the documents and hung them alongside the family tree on his bedroom wall, immediately above the chair."

"Did he ever use it?"

"No, he never sat in it. He kept it covered with a plastic sheet. When my parents married, the chair and family tree became the focal point in the dining room of the marital home. When my brother and I arrived, it was moved to safety in a spare bedroom."

"I used to have a brother. Is there just the two of you? Your brother's name is Lin, isn't it?"

"Yes." Jeff had no idea why this was relevant. "There are just the two of us."

"Who is the elder?"

The question surprised him. "Hmm. I am, by a couple of years."

"My brother was older than me. He died in the shift. He was in Turkey."

"Sorry to hear that. Was he on holiday?"

"No. He was having a gastric band fitted. He was a big guy." Jeff thought he saw tears in his driver's eyes. Norman added, "Did you ever get to sit in this chair?"

"Never. Nobody used it. We could only look at it when Dad was around. We used to love hearing how he bought the chair and seeing the other smaller items his distant cousin sold him. My father was devastated to learn Calvin had been killed in a car crash. He never forgot his generosity."

"Generosity? He paid ten grand for that chair."

"But Dad thought it was worth every penny, and Calvin could have got much more. I can still visualise the pride on his face and hear the enthusiasm in his voice whenever he recounted the history of the chair. Some visitors had to hear the story many times, but never complained."

"It's my first time. Please promise never to repeat it."

Again, Jeff did not react. "I was astonished when Dad gave me the chair and the framed family history to celebrate my promotion to Chief Inspector. Lin had always been more interested in the family's history, and I expected it to go to him. Dad insisted it went to the older son, and my promotion was an opportune moment to hand it over. He felt we had something to celebrate, and, in any case, they had no room for the chair in their new bungalow."

"Were they moving then?"

"Yes, because Mum needed full-time care."

"Sorry to hear that."

"Thanks. He said it was up to me if I used the chair, but I treated it with the respect it deserved. It remained under plastic in our spare room until we moved house. My wife was worried sick about it getting damaged in transit and called in an antique dealer friend, Mitchell, to give us a value for transportation insurance." Jeff shivered, recalling the valuer's verdict.

"How much was it worth?" Norman was finally interested.

"Well, Mitchell began by explaining that the chair was not as old as had been suggested. He highlighted several features which were not in keeping with the period. He also said the Certificates and Family tree were worthless. The dates listed did not correspond to actual events. I questioned how he could be so sure and was told that the manufacturer had not started business when the chair was supposed to have been made. I was furious, embarrassed and became obsessed with tracing Calvin."

"I bet your father felt stupid?"

"I never told him about the fraud. I contacted American colleagues and discovered Dad was the victim of an elaborate scam orchestrated by Chester Z Hill, one of the many names of a fraudster whom the US authorities estimated had made hundreds of thousands of dollars by selling fake items online. Hill was eventually convicted and jailed, but as so few victims came forward, his punishment was lighter than it should have been. No money was recovered for those who helped with the police investigations."

"The chair was rubbish?"

"I thought so. I remember saying to my wife that *'the piece of shit is too crap to scrap,'* but she insisted the chair had value, although nowhere close to what had been paid. I only told my brother after Dad passed. I keep the chair under cover in a spare bedroom."

"Why did you feel the need to tell me all that? Your father got ripped off. It happens all the time. Some people get taken for mugs. Get over it."

Just for a moment, Jeff thought he had been getting somewhere. He was mistaken, but wanted to finish his tale. "I know it happens all the time, but that chair is a constant reminder that not everything is as it first appears. Sometimes you see things as you want them to be and not as they are, and certain people play on that...desire."

"Shit happens."

"It does, but it is worth remembering that nobody is infallible. Everyone makes mistakes and can be misled. You should never put emotion over logic and reasoning. People play on your emotions and get you to do things you might not want."

"Okay, I get it, but what does that have to do with me?"

"I think you should be careful. Billy might not be the top bloke you believe him to be."

"How would you know? You've only just met him."

"How long have you known him?"

"Six months. Since he moved to the zone."

"About as long as my Dad had known Calvin."

"Yes, but I am not your Dad, and Billy is not Calvin. I can trust Billy. Anyway, he is not trying to sell me a chair."

No, but he might be using you, Jeff thought, deciding to let Norman make his own mistakes.

It was Jeff's turn to do the listening. Norman babbled enough for them both. He bragged at length about how, with Jensen's help, this year's charity events would raise more money than ever.

By the time they reached their destination, Jeff could still not decide if Norman was complicit or naive. He had, however, made up his mind on one thing.

The Z80+ headquarters were once a hotel on the town's main square. Norman claimed to have been instrumental in selecting the building because of its ideal location. He ignored Jeff's suggestion that Poole might have been a better choice, as it already housed many old municipal buildings, was better known, and was far more accessible.

It was just after noon when Jeff entered the HQ. The Administrators knew Norman and waved them through. Jeff was taken to a large room next to the main office on the ground floor. Norman had reserved this room for as long as needed.

MC was waiting for them.

Norman stifled a chuckle at Jeff's expression when he first saw MC. From Norm's description, Jeff had expected an overweight, grumpy Administrator, but MC was anything but that. In his brother's terminology, MC looked like *a mean machine*.

Jeff wavered slightly as MC stood to attention. The Admin was huge - about six feet, in great physical shape, broad shoulders with muscular arms projecting from the short-sleeved official shirt. MC's head was a shiny dome with no hair.

Jeff tried to keep his jaw under control. He held out a hand. "MC. It is good to meet you. My name is Jeff Cleveland."

MC grunted and sat back down, making no effort to shake hands.

Jeff leaned on the back of the chair and carried on regardless. "I think you know why I want to talk to you. I am keen to learn about the Judge's last few days. Before we start, can I get you any tea or coffee?"

"No." The Judge's driver pointed at Norman. MC's voice was deep and rasping with the faintest trace of a West Indian accent. "You can get him out of here. I am not talking to you in front of that prick."

"Tough luck, MC. You are not in the army now. You are not my leader. You don't get to decide. You can't get rid of me." Norman sneered and stood firm.

Jeff moved his head, suggesting Norman leave the room. "I think I can manage. Go and get a coffee. I'll find you when we're done."

MC smirked. Norman was dumbfounded but not finished.

"In case you've forgotten, Jeff, ChiZA Purcell insisted that you always have an Administrator present."

Jeff was mildly impressed at the speed with which Norman regained his composure, but took delight in saying, "I haven't forgotten that. As luck would have it, MC is also an Administrator, and Purcell never suggested I needed two of you."

"But…"

"No buts. Off you go and ask someone to bring me tea, milk, and no sugar. MC?"

"Water. Still not sparkling."

Norman shuffled out of the door. MC found Norman's departure amusing.

"You don't like Norman?"

"He's a prick."

"You are a shrewd judge of character." Cleveland sat and took his notebook and pencil out of his pocket. "Let's start again. Thank you for agreeing to see me today."

"I was ordered to be here." The words were delivered calmly, clearly and deliberately. "I did not have a choice."

Cleveland nodded. "Right, so I take it ChiZA Purcell has explained who I am and what I am doing?"

"He did."

"You also know I am not an Administrator. I am an ex-policeman, but don't hold that against me…"

MC stared impassively.

Jeff moved on quickly. "I want to ask you a few questions about your time with the Judge. Is that okay?"

"Do I have a choice?"

"I suppose you don't."

"In that case, get on with it."

"Thank you, but before I begin, I must advise you that I have no formal jurisdiction. My role is purely advisory. Whatever I find during my investigations will be handed to ChiZA Purcell, who will decide upon the next steps. Is that clear?"

"As day."

"I may make notes during our conversation. Is that acceptable?"

A tilt of the head, then eyes forward again.

"I don't know about you, but as I get older, my memory gets worse. I would forget where I am if I didn't write it down." MC sat stone-faced. Jeff hurriedly added, "Is that enough background?"

"Yes."

"Do you have any questions at this stage?"

"None."

Cleveland stood long enough to remove his jacket and place it on the back of the chair, which he pulled away from the table. He crossed his legs as he sat and intertwined his fingers, placing them around his right knee.

"Okay, so you are Colonel Sands, also known as MC."

"I am."

"Distinguished soldier, veteran of Iraq, Afghanistan and Bosnia."

MC's tongue pushed between the top teeth and lip before the head slowly nodded.

Jeff continued. "Very impressive credentials, I must say. You've been through some traumatic times, I would imagine?"

MC grunted.

Jeff removed his hands from his knee, uncrossed his legs and stretched them under the table. He asked more about MC's service history but learned nothing. MC stared at him, looking bored. This was proving to be a challenge. "That was just intended to break the ice, but I get the impression you would like to get this over with."

"I would."

Jeff folded his arms across his chest. "Let's talk about your time with Lord McGregor."

MC's face relaxed a fraction.

"Tell me about your time with the Judge, what you did for him and where you went."

"No."

Jeff did a double-take. "Why not?"

"Your question is not specific. You hope asking open questions will get me to say more than I need to."

"Are there things you'd rather not tell me?"

"You do not need to know everything that happened while I worked for His Lordship."

Jeff scratched the back of his head. "Okay, take me through the last few days of your employment with the Judge."

"No. You need to be more specific."

"Okay. How long had you worked for him?"

"Two years"

"Did you apply for the post, or were you appointed?"

"Appointed."

"Did you have any choice in the matter?"

"No."

"Why you?"

"I was available."

"Okay. Thanks. What did your role involve?"

"Driving and protection."

"Protection from whom?"

"Anyone. Anything."

"You were the Judge's bodyguard and driver?"

"Yes."

"What sort of relationship did you have with him?"

"Define relationship."

"Did you get on with him? I heard the Judge was a shy man. Was he the same when you were around?"

"He knew me better."

"Would you say the pair of you got on well?"

"We got along."

"But you wouldn't say you got along famously. Things were okay between you?"

"We got along."

"Did you ever have any problems with his Lordship?"

"Define problems."

"Did you ever argue?"

"No."

"You never had words or disagreed with his instructions?"

"I refer you to my last answer."

"Thanks." Jeff could not pretend that he had not been warned. This certainly wasn't easy. He sat up, pulling his chair closer to the table. "When did you last see him?"

"Sunday."

"Sunday? That was four days ago?"

"Correct. The day after Saturday but before Monday."

"What happened on Sunday?"

"I saw His Lordship."

"Please tell me what you and he did that day."

"I collected him from home and took him to the Royal Exeter Hotel for lunch. Later, I collected him from the hotel and returned him to his house."

"And that was it?"

"It was."

"How long were you with him?"

MC did not need time to calculate an answer. "About an hour before lunch and two hours afterwards."

"How was he during this time?"

"Alive."

"Yes, of course. How was he?"

"Same as usual."

"Was he in a good mood?"

"He was in a better mood on the return journey."

"Why do you think that was?"

"Because of the wine."

"I get the picture. Did you often drive the Judge around on a Sunday?"

"I worked most Sundays. Sometimes, it involved driving. Other times, I was on hand to help His Lordship."

Jeff was happy to get a fuller answer. "Help? How?"

"In any way he wanted me to."

"Doing what?"

"Whatever."

"Would you mind expanding on that a little?"

"I helped him shave, bathe and sometimes prepared his food."

"Ah, yes, soups. I heard you made him soup. Why was that?"

"He liked soup."

"Any particular favourite?"

MC looked like Jeff was about to have his head removed. "Tomato. Why is that relevant?"

"No reason. I was just being nosey." Jeff decided that was enough food-related questions. "You dropped him off last Sunday, but you must have done more than that."

"What makes you think that?"

"You spent two hours with him. The journey from the hotel was what? About ten minutes."

"Approximately."

"What did you do for the remaining hour and fifty minutes?

"Why is this important?"

"You might have been the last person to see him alive."

"I wasn't. Millie was. She called in to see him later that evening."

"How do you know that?"

"She told me."

"You've spoken to Millie?"

"How else would she tell me?"

That was a reasonable response, thought Jeff. "Do you often speak to Millie?"

"Define often."

"Do you have frequent conversations?" Jeff guessed what was coming and quickly added, "Do you speak daily, weekly, or monthly?"

"A couple of times a week."

"About what?"

"I relay His Lordship's instructions, check her availability and note what materials she needs."

"Thank you." Jeff had enough information on MC's dealings with Millie. "How did you fill the remaining time with His Lordship?"

"When?"

"On that Sunday, after you dropped him off."

"I helped him change his clothes, sat him in the lounge, put on some of his favourite music, and opened a bottle of wine. He talked for a while, and then I left."

"What did you talk about?"

"I didn't speak. He talked. I listened. He spoke about his family and the old days."

"Any old days in particular?"

"No."

"Did you put him to bed?"

"No. If he needed help, Millie would provide it."

"Where did you go when you left the house?"

"Home."

"Can anyone verify that?"

"No."

"Nobody saw you for the rest of Sunday?"

"That is not what I said. Nobody can verify that I went home. Later, I went to the pub, and people saw me there."

"Had you seen the Judge on Saturday?"

"No."

"Why not?"

"He had visitors."

This was new. "Who were these visitors?"

"I don't know. He informed me on Friday that I was not required on Saturday as he was receiving visitors."

"But he didn't say who they were?"

"I just told you he did not."

"I heard he didn't like having visitors."

MC offered no comment.

"Were you with him all day on Friday?"

"Most of it."

"And was Friday a normal day?"

"Define normal."

"Did anything unusual happen?"

"No."

"Where did you go?"

"When?"

"Friday."

"Oxford."

"Why Oxford?"

"Because His Lordship wanted to go there."

"Do you know why he picked Oxford?"

"He wanted to visit family."

Cleveland recalled the discussion with Harding at the Judge's house. He picked up the pencil and tapped it on the notepad.

"Did he often go there?"

"Depends."

"Depends on what?"

"How you define often."

Jeff felt as though the walls of the windowless room were closing in. He considered asking MC to be more cooperative, but as their eyes met, he knew it would do no good. MC would see that as a sign of weakness, making matters worse. "When was the last time he went to Oxford?"

"Friday."

Jeff groaned. "Before that?"

"Three, possibly four weeks ago."

"Do you know why he wanted to go there on Friday?"

"Yes"

"Please tell me."

"He wanted to see his latest grandchild before he relocated to the youth zone."

"What time did you depart for Oxford?"

"Eleven-thirty."

"And you arrived at that time to collect him?"

"No"

"What time did you arrive?"

"Eight forty-five."

"Why so early?"

"To help him."

"Help him? How?"

"To get him down the stairs.

Cleveland recalled the house. "He has a stair lift. Did you have to lift him onto it?"

"No."

"His Lordship could get from his wheelchair onto the lift?"

"He could."

"How did he manage if his wheelchair was on a different floor?"

"He had another wheelchair. He left one on the lower floor and one upstairs, but he was old, not totally disabled. He regularly walked from his bedroom to the stairs."

Jeff resisted asking MC to specify how regularly. "Why would you need to help him down?"

"His stairlift had been playing up recently."

"Playing up? How?"

"It goes upstairs okay, but sometimes it jumps and sticks coming back down. His Lordship was nervous about making the journey on his own. He liked someone there to watch him."

"And had the lift played up that weekend?"

"Not as far as I know."

"So, it worked fine."

"As far as I know."

"How did he manage on days when you were not there?"

"I was there most days."

"What about on your day off?"

"I don't take days off."

"Unless the Judge tells you to?"

"Affirmative."

Cleveland tried to hide his frustration. He knew he was losing this battle. All his working life, he had prided himself on his interviewing technique. He thought he had mastered getting a conversation flowing, even with the most challenging customers, but not today. MC was proving to be a hard nut to crack.

"Okay, tell me what happened after you helped him down the stairs."

"What do you want to know?"

"Tell me about what happened before you left for Oxford."

"He had a cup of coffee and toast. I waited in the hall."

"Did you make his breakfast?"

"No."

"Why not?"

"He didn't want me to."

"But he was a very old man."

"He could do it himself."

"What happened next?"

"He went to the bathroom and then to his bedroom. I helped him dress. I helped him downstairs. Would you like more detail? Shall I describe what he wore?"

"No, thank you. What happened next?"

"We drove to Oxford. Do you want a description of the journey? Shall I tell you the route we used?"

"No need. Thanks. Did you speak much on the journey?"

"No."

"And once you got to Oxford, what happened?"

"I helped him to the front door, and his daughter-in-law took him into the house."

"Did you go inside?"

"No."

"What did you do?"

"I looked around the city."

They spoke briefly about the merits of the famous City. It was the only time MC showed any form of emotion. The visits to Oxford had evidently been enjoyable.

"What time had you arranged to collect him?"

"Seventeen hundred hours."

Jeff mentally transferred that back to standard time. "Was the Judge waiting for you when you got back?"

"No, I was early. I sat in the car."

"And was he ready at five o'clock?"

"He was late."

"Why?"

"He took his time bidding farewell to his family."

"That would be his son's family?"

"Yes, but his daughter was there too."

At last, MC had volunteered information. Jeff's energy level rose slightly. "Oh, really?"

"Yes"

"Had she been there all day?"

"She arrived as I was leaving to go to the city."

Cleveland rested his elbows on the table and brought his hands together under his chin. "Did she live in Oxford too?"

MC's shoulders rose and fell slowly. "No."

"Where does she live?"

"I never asked."

Cleveland's energy disappeared sharply. He would find her address via other means. "What time did you get him home?"

"Nineteen hundred hours or thereabouts."

"Did you accompany him into his house?"

"Yes"

"And you spotted nothing unusual?"

"No."

"You didn't see anybody or anything suspicious?"

"No."

"What about inside the house?"

"It looked like it always did."

Jeff rubbed the end of his nose. He knew he was allowing MC to give too many one-word answers.

"So, how does it work? This arrangement you had with the Judge. You lift the old man into his wheelchair and take him into the house?"

"Yes."

"Then what?"

"Once he was safely inside the house, he would tell me what we were doing the following day and our departure time. If he wanted something to eat, I would get it for him. Once I had tidied up, I went home."

Jeff used the reference to home to take the conversation in a new direction. He wanted to learn about the driver's personal life. He asked about MC's house, neighbourhood, family, interests and relaxation. He learned little apart from the fact that MC enjoyed attending the local pub.

Jeff returned to MC's time with the military, but MC stonewalled his questions. Jeff half-expected to hear MC's name, rank and serial number. That might have been preferable to the awkward silences that frequently befell the room.

Jeff focused on the more recent past.

"What time did the Judge want to see you on Monday?"

"He didn't."

"Why not?"

"He wanted to catch up on paperwork."

"He planned to stay around the house on Monday?"

"Yes."

"Was that unusual?"

"Define unusual."

"Did it happen often, say, a couple of times each week?"

"No."

"But you were there most days?"

"I was."

"Right. How would he get down the stairs without you there? Presumably, this would be before Amelia arrived?"

"It was. If I weren't there, the gatekeeper helped down." Cleveland raised his eyebrows. It had the desired effect. MC provided extra detail. "There is a telephone link between His Lordship's bedroom and the gatehouse."

"Did the Judge regularly ask the gatekeeper for help?"

"I have no idea."

Jeff scratched his cheek. This was painful. He studied MC's face, but the ex-soldier did not change expression or position. MC sat, staring back at the ex-policeman, brown eyes unflinching, face sombre, indicating no thoughts or feelings.

"Did you enjoy working with the Judge?"

"Define enjoy."

"Did you find it stimulating, rewarding or interesting? Or was it just okay, bearable, acceptable?"

"It was satisfactory."

"That's all?"

"It was a job."

"A good job, I would imagine."

"It was a job."

"Was it a dangerous job?"

"Define dangerous."

"Were you ever called upon to act as his bodyguard?"

"I was his bodyguard."

"What I meant to ask was, were you ever forced to take action to protect the Judge because his life was in danger?"

"No."

Jeff probed MC's experiences as an Administrator and driver in the days before the Judge. Again, he gained little new information. He adjusted his glasses as he prepared his next question. "What can you tell me about what the Judge was working on before he died?"

"Not much."

"Do you know anything about the projects he was undertaking?"

"Yes."

"Good. Can you tell me how many there were?"

"I can."

Jeff winced. "How many?"

"I knew of two."

"What were they, and who asked him to do them?"

"One was to look at how prisoners were treated. He was asked to do this by an old friend in Government. The second project came out of the first."

"What was the second project?"

"He was reviewing the powers of the Administrations."

"And who asked him to do this?"

"Nobody did. As I said, the second came out of the first."

Cleveland leaned on the table. "I'm sorry, I don't understand. Can you explain that to me, please?"

"The deeper His Lordship delved into the lives of prisoners, the more he realised that the same issues were arising repeatedly. Many prisoners protested that they should not be in prison. They complained about the Administrators who put them there and the unbridled powers the Admins have. His Lordship decided to investigate a little further."

"I see." Cleveland softened his tone and angled his head a little. "You must have been very close to the Judge?"

"Why?"

"Well, for him to tell you these things."

"He told me nothing. I heard it when he was interviewing the prisoners."

"You sat in on these interviews?"

"No."

"Why not?"

"My job was to make sure the prisoners were shackled. Then I waited outside."

"Why didn't you stay in the room?"

"Because I am an Administrator, and he was investigating the Administration. He wanted to put the prisoner at ease. I was instructed to leave the room."

"How could you hear what he said?"

"His Lordship had a routine and would introduce himself at the start of the interviews while I was checking the prisoner was securely shackled."

"Why would he do that?"

"He was only allowed an hour with each prisoner. He didn't

waste any time.”

“And he would always start by introducing himself and explaining the projects?”

MC thought about this. “Usually.”

“But not always?”

“If it were something he always did, I would not say usually.”

“Fair point. What changed?”

“He began to focus on just one project. He rarely mentioned the other.”

“Which project took precedence?”

“He stopped talking about the prisons project.”

Jeff sensed he had heard something important. “He was focusing his attention on the operation of the Administrations?”

“Yes.”

“When did that change?”

“Recently.”

Cleveland nodded, encouraging MC to continue. “Define recently?”

MC gave a faint hint of a smile. “In the last six months.”

“Why was that?”

“No idea.”

“Do you suspect that he discovered something untoward about the Administration?”

“Possibly.”

“Could one of the prisoners have told him something?”

“Possibly.”

Jeff followed with several questions, trying to get MC to expand on what the Judge might have learned and why he had focused on the second project. MC’s answers came quickly but were no help.

“How did he select which prisoners to interview?”

“I have no idea.”

“Did he ever interview the same prisoner more than once?”

“Yes.”

“Which ones?”

"I don't know their names."

"But you know he made repeat visits to certain people."

"I do."

"But you don't know any names?"

"I do not."

"Then how do you know they were repeat visits?"

"I saw the same man at least four times. And there were others I recognised from previous visits."

"You noticed them while you were checking the shackles?"

"I did."

"But the Judge never explained why he had called them back?"

"Not in front of me."

"Do you know how many interviews were conducted?"

"I did not keep count."

"Were the interviews always held at the same venue?"

"Yes."

Not for the first time, the words blood and stone sprang to Jeff's mind. "Where was that?"

"Wrexham."

"Wrexham, North Wales?"

"I am not aware of another."

"But why there?"

"It's where the PHC for that zone is located."

"PHC?"

"Prisoner Holding Centre."

"What is a prisoner holding centre?"

"It's where prisoners are taken before they go to the island."

Cleveland did not understand. "Why don't they just take them straight to the island?"

"They take them to the PHC to search, wash, and shave them. If the Admin guards at the PHC know and like a prisoner, or the prisoner has plenty of cash or good contacts, they might release them."

Jeff wanted to know more about how often this occurred, but decided it could wait. "Is there a PHC in every zone?"

"Yes."

Cleveland thought about the Isle of Wight, the island jail closest to zones Z6080 and 80+. "Where is ours?"

"Portsmouth. The PHC is in the dockyard."

"Why would the Judge meet them at the PHC? Surely, he would have wanted to visit the island jail?" Cleveland rubbed the bridge of his nose, causing his glasses to rise to his forehead.

MC offered no response.

Jeff rephrased. "What I mean is, if the Judge was keen to see how prisoners were treated, then wouldn't he have wanted to visit the prison?"

"He tried."

"And?"

"He was refused."

Jeff's eyes narrowed as he repeated the word. "Refused?"

"Yes. They informed him that it was out of the question."

"Who informed him?"

"The Central Committee. The Secretary in charge of State Security."

"Do you know why?"

"Safety."

"Safety?"

"Yes."

"But why?"

"It was too much of a risk."

"But why?"

"Ask them."

"Who?"

"The Security Department."

"Right." Jeff rested his back on the seat as he considered what he had heard. "But they allowed him to continue his investigations?"

"Yes."

"He could interview prisoners but only in Wrexham."

"Yes."

"You are sure you cannot recall any of the names of the prisoners he interviewed?"

"Yes."

"Were there any records of the interviews?

"His Lordship made notes."

Cleveland guessed as much and could imagine what had happened to the paperwork. "Do you know if there was any other supporting information? Was the interview filmed or recorded?"

"No."

"That's a pity. It would help to know who he spoke with and what about."

"The Prison records would provide that information."

Jeff had already thought of this. He considered his options for gaining access to the names. He scribbled, *'Prisoner's names? Ask Purcell'* in his notebook. "How were the interviews arranged?"

"By letter."

"Not by telephone."

"No."

"That seems a very old-fashioned way of working."

"He was an old-fashioned man."

"And the Judge made his own arrangements?"

"Yes."

"How did he go about booking appointments?"

"He had contacts at the Security Department and sent them a list of prisoners he wanted to see. They would round them up and let him know when they could be in Wrexham."

"Round them up?" Cleveland leaned on the table again. "Why would they have to round them up? Wouldn't they be in their cells?" Cleveland detected a sarcastic tone in the reply.

"There are no cells on the islands. Each island jail is well secured. Nobody can escape. The prisoners live wherever they choose."

"What? They live where they want to?"

"Yes."

"Nobody tells them where to go?"

"The Admins don't. Some prisoners get invited to live in the better areas."

"Invited? By whom?"

"The gang leaders. They have their areas and select new prisoners to join them?"

In Jeff's mind, a prison was a building with cells. Learning that once delivered to jail, prisoners lived where other prisoners let them was a shock. However, it did explain why the Judge was not allowed onto the island.

"How do you know this?"

"I have ex-comrades who work in the PHC and on the islands."

Jeff leaned back in his chair. "When did you learn you would be going to Wrexham?"

"The day before, sometimes two days before."

"How often did you make the trip? Weekly…monthly…" He waved a hand, inviting MC to reply.

"Three times a week in the month before he died."

"That's a lot of driving?"

"It is."

"There and back in a day?"

"Yes."

"That must have been exhausting?"

MC stared ahead.

"You were okay with driving all that way?"

"It was my job."

Jeff had a thought. "Did he interview any prisoners from the other island jails?"

"No."

"He never held interviews in Portsmouth?"

"No"

"Only in Wrexham?"

"That's what I said."

Jeff wondered why the prisoners of Anglesey were of such interest to his Lordship and pressed for this information. He sensed that MC either did not know or would not say. He raised more general topics, but yet again, made no progress.

Jeff's half-hearted attempts to lighten the conversation with a few admissions about his life brought him nowhere. MC was not the least interested.

Eventually, Cleveland signalled that the interview had ended but suggested he might want to speak to MC again. MC stood to attention, made a sharp heel turn to the left and marched out of the door, stopping only to say, "You never had that cup of tea, did you? I knew that dipshit prick wouldn't get you one."

"Dipshit. That's an unusual phrase."

"I picked it up from an old friend who was in the Navy. It means…"

"I think I can guess what it means."

"That's why you are the great detective." MC grabbed the door handle.

An idea formed, giving Jeff one more question. "Where do you work at the moment?"

"I am between appointments. They might take a while to find me a new role."

"I thought there was plenty of work?"

"There is, but other Admins don't like to work with me. I must wait for an individual assignment."

"I wonder why that is?" Jeff had not intended to vocalise that question.

"They call me an awkward bastard. I have no idea why." MC left the room.

Harding poked his head around the now-open door and saw Cleveland slumped over the desk, his hands locked behind his head.

"I heard you were here. How did that go?"

"The phrase I'm looking for has something to do with pulling teeth."

"Or getting blood from a stone?"

"Exactly." Jeff stood up, kicking back his chair and grabbing his jacket. "That was hard work." He slid his arms through the jacket sleeves, flattened the collar, and then pushed his notebook and pencil into his pocket. "I'm glad to see a friendly face. Did Purcell contact you?"

"Not directly. He went through my LeRA, who apologised for making me work with you."

"What did you say?"

"I'll tell you again." He pointed at the open door. "Who knows who might be listening?"

Harding stepped closer. They spoke in hushed tones.

"Where do you want me to start?"

"With the neighbours. Find out if anybody saw or heard anything. Ask them if they knew the Judge, whether he had visitors or friends, that type of thing. You know the score."

"I do." Harding removed a notepad from his trouser pocket, extracted a pen from one of three in his breast pocket, and scribbled.

"And check his phone logs. I assume he had a mobile."

"We didn't see one, but I'll check."

"Speak with the Wrexham PHC to see which prisoners the Judge met. Contact the Admins in the other zones to see if the judge and MC visited them. If so, where did they go, whom did they meet, etcetera."

"Will do." He quickly added this to his list. "I'll start on that tomorrow. I've got to finish my other duties today."

"What are they?"

"I'm visiting holiday lets to make sure the records are up to date, and then I need to check on some suspicious products that have appeared in New Milton. Afterwards, I head to Dorchester to speak to a community group and then home."

"Where is home these days?"

"Cerne Abbas, a little village on the Sherborne Road."

The mention of Sherborne prompted a question. "Do you know Billy Jensen?"

"Of course, all the Administrators do. He makes himself known, if you see what I mean."

"I can guess." Jeff stepped behind Harding and swung the door shut. "What do you think of him?"

"Billy seems nice enough, but I don't trust him any further

than I could throw him. He's untouchable as far as the Admins are concerned. He contributes to Admin charities and offers holidays at discount rates. He always provides gifts at Christmas. He goes out of his way to show how much he appreciates our work."

"He sounds like a perfect citizen."

Harding frowned. "Nobody is that clean. I've heard stories linking him to bootlegging, counterfeiting, and trading in stolen goods. If I mention anything or ask questions, I get told to mind my business and not believe the rumours. As far as Norman and his cronies are concerned, Billy is as close to a saint as there is."

"If you spot him on your travels, would you keep an eye on him?"

"Do you suspect him of something?"

"Not yet, but I'd like to learn more about Mr Jensen - whom he sees, where he goes, etcetera, etcetera."

"This is off the record, I suppose."

"For the moment."

"Why are you interested? I can't imagine Billy would have been involved in the death of the Judge."

"Let's keep an open mind on that. I am probably just being nosey.

"It just so happens I planned to call into Sherborne this week. I will visit tomorrow."

"Thank you. I'll give you a ring."

Jeff called Purcell and arranged to see him at five. They agreed to meet in Bath rather than Cardiff, as Purcell was attending a function in Bristol.

Norman expressed his delight at hearing Purcell was coming to them. He would be home at a reasonable time.

The meeting took place in a small waiting room in the Roman Bath building. Norman was excited to be involved and suggested that was because he was making a valuable contribution to the case.

Purcell sipped from a water bottle, "Now then, Mister Cleveland. What is so important that you had to see me today?"

"I want a new Administrator. I cannot work with Norman."

Norman gasped. This news shocked him. "Why? What have I done?"

"Where do I start? You are a bully. You are insulting. You question everything I ask you to do. You talk over me and cannot keep this shut." Jeff ran a finger over his mouth. "You openly laugh at me. You tipped off a suspect…"

"Billy is not a suspect."

"So, you don't deny that you told him about our visit?" Norman inhaled. Jeff spoke on, "You have a blinkered vision. Just because someone is generous to the Administrators should not mean they are above suspicion." Jeff pushed his trilby onto the back of his head and stepped nearer to Norman. They stood toe-to-toe. "But the main reason I cannot work with you is I do not trust you. I have no idea who you are talking to about my investigations, who you might tip off about my intentions, and whether you will follow orders."

"I do not work for you."

"Good. Then we understand each other." Jeff stepped away.

Purcell held up his hands. "Gentlemen, gentlemen, calm down. Let's discuss this like adults."

"There's nothing to discuss," Jeff insisted. "I need someone I can rely on, and Norman is not that person."

Purcell studied Jeff's face. "Is this a deal-breaker? If I say no, will you throw your toys out of the pram?"

Norman giggled.

"I am afraid I will. This task you, sorry, Lord Wilson, set me is difficult enough as it is. I can do without a fifth columnist undermining me at every step."

"Norman is one of our best men. I am sure that we can work through these issues."

"I am certain we cannot. I would be happier pottering in my garden, and that's where you will find me if you change your mind." Jeff reached for the door. "Don't worry about how you will break the news to the Committee Secretary. I know him well enough, and I still have his number somewhere. I'm happy to explain my feelings and tell him where to stick the job."

Purcell went a lighter shade of grey. "Mister Cleveland, wait. Let's talk some more."

Norman's eyes blazed with fury as he told the ChiZA. "Let him go. We can do without him."

"Norman, let me handle this."

"You can't agree to this request? He's not even an Admin. There'll be hell to pay. You won't get anyone else to take my place. All co-operation with this..." Norman's thumb swung toward Jeff. "...corrupt bastard will be withdrawn. Cormack will support me. This investigation will go down the pan."

Purcell nodded. "Good point. Thank you. I have no wish to fight you and LeRA Cormack. Jeff, you can go home." Norman could not look more self-satisfied and was still beaming when Purcell added, "I will have to offer my resignation to Lord Wilson, of course." He studied the Admin's face. "You recall that following my predecessor's departure, the Committee Secretary for Security was on the verge of placing this zone under special measures. I only accepted the post to avoid that happening. My final recommendation will be that special measures are necessary to remove the suggestion of corruption. I shall, of course, highlight the lack of support from you and LeRA Cormack. I am sure Jeff will be happy to support my accusations?"

"Of course," Jeff said. "I will help all I can."

"Thank you," Purcell replied. "Lord Wilson will listen to you. He will also greatly delight in appointing someone new to this zone - possibly ambitious, eager to prove themselves, and keen to make changes." He looked at Norman. "You might have to pick up the dead or something equally unrewarding. Not to worry. I am sure Cormack will be thrilled to work with you. Your LeRA is not a man to bear grudges, is he?"

Norman fell quiet, standing very still as he pondered the

threat. When he eventually spoke, his voice was tinged with disbelief. "You wouldn't dare."

"What have I got to lose? I never wanted this job." The ChiZA said. "I tell you what." Purcell took out his mobile. "I'll get the ball rolling immediately by ringing Lord Wilson." He pressed a few buttons. "I hope you've brought your bus pass. All privileges will be withdrawn immediately. You'll have to find your way home."

"Hold on a second. Don't do anything rash or hasty."

Purcell lowered the phone. "What would you suggest I do?"

"Anything that means we don't have to involve Lord Wilson."

"Are you saying that you will step down?"

"I suppose I am, but you won't get a replacement."

"We'll see about that." He prodded Norman in the chest. "Don't ever threaten me again. If you cross me, I will come down on you and Cormack like a ton of bricks. I know what goes on in your region, and I tolerate certain activities because, generally, things work well, but don't ever take me for granted. You put a foot wrong, and you and Cormack will be deep in shit. Do you understand?"

"Yes."

"Yes, what?"

"Yes, ChiZA."

"Good. Now get out of my sight while you still have a job."

Jeff watched the Admin leave the room.

"Norman is well respected among the Admins," Purcell said.

"I can't think why."

"He has connections. Once word gets out that he's been dismissed, I fear I will struggle to get anyone else to work with you."

"I have Harding to help me with the investigation."

"Harding doesn't have use of a staff car."

"Can't you get him one?"

"Not with Norman on the warpath. I have no say over regional vehicles. Norman and Cormack will cause as many problems as possible."

"Well, let me drive myself. I can borrow a car. My brother has one."

"Impossible. I can't have you running around the zones, causing mayhem. I need someone to keep an eye on you."

"Then you'll have to find me a driver."

"I will see what I can do, but I doubt I will find anyone by the morning." Purcell drank from his bottle.

Jeff thought the answer was simple and uttered it with relish. "What about MC?"

Purcell sprayed water across the room as he tried to avoid choking. "MC? Why would you want MC?"

"Why not? MC is out of a job and keeps this shut." Jeff touched his lips. "It would allow me to ask more questions about the Judge. MC knows more than has been said. I am sure about it. This will give me the chance to see if I am right."

Purcell checked that Jeff was serious. When the ex-policeman nodded, Purcell said, "Okay, MC, it is. May God help you."

When the conversation with Purcell ended, Norman had disappeared, leaving Jeff to get home alone. Purcell offered to see if anyone was available, but Jeff insisted he would be fine. There was a good, frequent bus service between the City and Marshfield.

Whenever they visited Bath, Jeff and Felicity called in at the Raven on Queen Street for a drink or two. It was their favourite pub. The pair were regular theatregoers, and the Theatre Royal was close enough to walk to the Raven. Jeff often looked forward to the after-show pint more than the show itself.

As he approached the entrance, memories of the last time they visited the pub as a couple came rushing back. They had been to see a play about the pandemic that had garnered rave reviews during its London run. Flissy was not impressed. The improvisation and audience interaction had not been to her liking. If she bought a ticket for a show, she expected to be entertained by it, not to perform in it. Jeff thought he could remember every comment she made on the walk between the two venues.

He entered the pub with a wide grin on his face.

Jeff enjoyed a pint and a chat with three visitors, who were part of a touring performance group from the Party Zone appearing at the Theatre Royal. They could not believe the beer prices were way more expensive than in their Zone. Jeff bought them all a drink and apologised for not being available to take up their generous offer of complimentary tickets to see their show. Sadly, he had other plans that could not be changed. He left to catch his bus before they enquired what his imaginary plans might be.

Marshfield, his home village, boasted two pubs. 'The Catherine Wheel' and 'The Lord Nelson Inn'. The same man owned both. A chef who had relocated from Guildford. He cooked at each venue on alternate days. If the Wheel served food on Monday, Wednesday, and Friday for one week, food would be available on Tuesday, Thursday, and Saturday the next, with Lord Nelson providing sustenance on the other days. Sunday lunch would be provided at whichever bar was open on Saturday, but only until 4 p.m. The bar serving food would be open all day Sunday, but the other pub would remain closed.

The food at the Wheel was Italian, Spanish, and French cuisine, depending on available supplies. The Lord Nelson offered the best British gastronomy. Most of the ingredients were sourced locally. Both offerings were very popular, and customers travelled many miles to eat in the village.

On the days when food was not served, the pubs became a focal point for the villagers. They would put the world right over a pint, a chat, games of cards or dominoes, and the occasional sing-along and bingo.

Jeff fancied a nightcap and sat by Pat and another pal, Harry, in the Lord Nelson. The three widowers had forged a friendship over their love of cricket.

Pat was concerned about Marshfield CC's chances in the new season as their popular and successful coach had moved to a new region.

Harry worried about the shortage of incomers. Rival teams had quickly grabbed new entrants to the zone. Most of the newcomers were younger, having only recently turned sixty. Marshfield's older squad would not compete. Harry was seventy-three and still performed wicket-keeping duties, although he wasn't taking as many catches as he did.

Jeff tried to raise their spirits by suggesting their existing team would give anyone a game. His mates were not convinced. Harry thought Marshfield CC would be lucky to win anything in the forthcoming season. Pat was relieved there was no relegation. Jeff teased them about their negativity. Statistics and skill sets were tossed into the discussion, and the debate continued until stop tap.

Eddie Brogan paced the room, barely able to avoid exploding. "What do you mean Norman has been given the boot? How could that happen? Why the fuck did Purcell take the word of that ex-copper over Cormack and Norman?"

His companion shrugged. "No idea but Purcell was well pissed off with Norman's attitude and threatened to call in Wilson. Norman didn't want that to happen and agreed to step away, but he intends to put the frighteners on Cleveland to make sure he's not getting away with it."

Brogan calmed a little. "For once, Norman has made the right decision. It won't do us any good to be seen shaking things up too much this close to the Committee changes. Make sure whatever action he takes cannot be traced to us."

"Will do."

"Is there a replacement?"

"No. Norman has put the word out that he doesn't expect there to be any volunteers. Cleveland is stuck. He has Harding to help him, but Norman is confident he has him in his pocket. Harding doesn't have an official car and is unlikely to get one anytime soon."

"I like it. The operation gets shut down because nobody wants to work with a bent copper. He's got nowhere to go." Brogan smiled. "Grab your coat, we're off to a club." He checked his watch. "The female students will probably just be arriving after an evening in the pub. It's time to continue their education."

8. A WEEKEND OFF

Jeff relaxed on the sofa, enjoying a cuppa while listening to a repeat of a radio play and thinking about Flissy. A telephone call from Purcell stirred him.

MC had agreed to work with Jeff but could not start until Monday. The ChiZA admitted to being stunned at the speed and enthusiasm with which the offer was accepted. Jeff could not understand why there would be any doubt. Did he not have a warm, winning personality? Purcell suggested MC had spotted a way to antagonise colleagues.

The ChiZA urged Jeff to adopt a diplomatic approach when working with the local Admins. Word had spread about Norman's removal, and LeRA Cormack had rung to vent his spleen. Purcell thought Cormack was playing hardball by refusing to release MC immediately. He didn't believe the LeRA's claim that he had nobody available to act as Jeff's temporary driver. Jeff promised to be friendlier with Admins, but he crossed his fingers as he spoke.

Jeff was happy not to work. It had been a while since he had consumed so much beer, and it had not settled well. He felt out of sorts and would spend the day reading his notes and sorting out a work plan for the following week.

There weren't many notes to read, and it was not long before Jeff sat in his garden, a glass of water to hand, watching the birds squabbling over seeds. The ringing of his telephone once again disturbed his peace.

"Cleveland."

"Good morning, sir. I hoped I would catch you."

It took him a few seconds to recognise the female voice. "Carol Lomax! My God. It's good to hear from you. How are you?"

Carol had been Jeff's Detective Sergeant before everything changed. She had helped him investigate the case against Brogan Junior, which ultimately sealed the police's fate.

"Very well, thank you, sir, but it's not Lomax any longer. I'm a Farnham now."

Jeff remembered she was dating a chemist named Lenny Farnham. "Congratulations. When did this happen?"

Carol and Lenny had been married for six years. They had two children, both in the Youth Zone. The couple worked in the family pharmaceutical business on the outskirts of Nottingham.

She peppered Jeff with questions, and he updated her on his activities and the lives of his children. They discussed how much things had changed since they last met, and Carol repeated how sorry she was about Felicity. Jeff used that as an opportunity to change the topic and asked why she was calling.

"Well, I see you haven't changed." She giggled down the line and then adopted a deep voice. "It's great to hear from you, Lomax, but why are you wasting my time?"

"I didn't mean it like that."

"It's okay. I know you don't like to be reminded of your loss. I am ringing because I understand you are investigating His Lordship's death."

"How the hell…"

"Rowey told me. He's a good mate of Lenny's."

The old boys' network again. Some things never change. "Yes, I have been asked to investigate the murder, but I'm not getting far. There's not a lot to go on. Why are you interested?"

"I have some information that may help you."

"Which is?"

"Not over the phone. This is better shared face-to-face. Are you at home on Monday?"

Jeff wanted to be around to welcome MC. "Does it have to be Monday?"

"It's just that Lenny and I are on our annual narrowboat holiday and heading to see his sisters in Birmingham. We'll get there tomorrow evening. I could spend Sunday with them and take a train to Bath on Monday. I was hoping you could meet me there?"

"Depends on what time you arrive."

"I can work around you. Providing I can get a train back."

"Will you have time to get a pass into the Almost Dead Zone?"

Carol chuckled. "I already have one. That's a benefit of working for a drug company. We access all areas, especially the ones where all the old farts live. They are our best customers."

Jeff found that funny. "I'm glad we have some purpose, even if it is only helping you stay in business." He had an idea. "What time do you arrive in Birmingham?"

"Why?"

"I am going to Aston in the morning to see the kids. I'll be with them until about five, and then I'm free. Can you get there in time to meet at sixish in the city centre?"

"I'll be there even if Lenny has to make the boat go at ten miles per hour."

The pair agreed to a rendezvous and bid farewell. Jeff then returned to the challenging task of watching the birds.

Harding telephoned late in the morning to say that his wife, a nurse, had to work the next day, so he would be free to watch Jensen if necessary. Jeff took him up on the offer and told him to claim overtime. If asked, Harding should say he was undertaking enquiries into the Judge's death. Harding chuckled, telling Jeff that overtime was a thing of the past for him, but he was grateful for the thought. He did not mind undertaking surveillance as he had nothing better to do.

Jeff wasn't sure whether this was the best time, but wanted to be straight with Harding. "I've got some news."

"If you refer to Norman being reassigned, you are too late. HQ is alive with the story. Norman visited me this morning to tell me he's got my back. He said that he knows I am only working with you under duress. Not sure how I feel about that."

"It's linked to that, but…" Jeff deeply breathed, "…I have asked MC to be my driver."

"You've done what? MC? Why did you ask that miserable old

bastard? What were you thinking?" Harding's exhale filled Jeff's ears. "Our job is going to be hard enough because you pissed off Norman. Once word gets out that you've employed MC, we'll get no support whatsoever."

"I thought it would be a good opportunity to find out how much MC knows about the Judge's activities."

"Good luck with that. You will only get what MC wants to tell you," Harding grunted. "I wish you had mentioned this before acting."

"Purcell warned me that I would be persona non grata as far as the Admins are concerned so that I wouldn't get another driver. I thought MC would be better than nothing, and as I said, it would give me a chance to ask questions."

"We should have discussed this. I could be your driver..."

"Purcell said you had not been allocated a car."

"I could use my own. Anyway, I know a couple of Senior Admins who would help me get one just to get up Norman's nose. Norm isn't as universally popular as Purcell believes."

"I didn't know that." Jeff wasn't sure if he ought to apologise. He still believed there was merit in befriending MC if that was possible. "Ah, well, it's done now. We'll have to see how we get on."

"It's on your head. I can always ask Norman to get me a move. Nobody else wants MC."

Marshfield Cricket Club was on the outskirts of the village. Jeff liked the walk to the ground, but it took him much longer than it once did.

He helped his teammates clean up the pavilion and ensure everything was ready for the following week's first friendly of the season.

After sorting the interior, Jeff, Pat, and Harry volunteered to cut the outfield grass. The trio were returning to the clubhouse when Harry asked a question.

"Whose murder are you investigating?"

"Who told you I was investigating a murder?"

"Pat mentioned it last night, but it is all over the village."

Jeff glared at Pat, who mouthed 'sorry'.

"Typical, but it's no secret, I suppose. I've been asked to investigate the murder of Judge McGregor."

"Judge? I thought they got rid of them years ago. Don't the Admins sort everything nowadays?"

Jeff stretched his back, realising he had not exercised so much in ages. "They do, but they've kept a few Judges in place to advise on state business."

"Oh, right." Harry was none the wiser. "Have they made you a special Admin, then? Do you have the powers of an Admin?"

"No. I am just an investigator. I hand all my findings over to the Admins, who will decide the next steps."

"That's a shame." Harry moved his bag from one shoulder to the other.

"Why?"

"Because we could have used you to investigate the thefts at the allotments."

"What thefts?"

Pat spoke next. "Somebody has stolen our bean sticks, and several spades are missing. I thought you'd have heard."

"Not a word. Bean sticks? Who the hell would steal old bean sticks?"

Harry was offended. "They are not just any old bean sticks. These were brought down from Yorkshire. They are made from the finest willow. They are thicker and much stronger than the standard type. We use them for beans and the like, and to hang the covering that provides shelter for our vegetables. Once you put those sticks in place, they never blow down." Harry nodded to emphasise how good these sticks were. "Curtis Carrots got them for us."

Jeff had an allotment but surrendered it after the Shift. He vaguely remembered Curtis, one of the allotment holders, having a contact in the forestry who supplied bean sticks directly from the source. "When were they taken?"

"The other night, we think. Someone spotted an off-road

four-by-four parked in the allotment compound but did not recognise the make or model."

"That someone being?" Jeff had a name in mind.

"Neil."

Little happened at the allotments that Neil missed.

Pat was dubious about Neil's reliability. "He's as blind as a bat at the best of times. Had he been to Malky's, sipping his homebrew?"

"Aye," Harry said.

Jeff chuckled. "Not the most reliable witness."

"He's the only one we have." Harry looked dejected.

Jeff patted Harry's shoulder. "I am sorry. I didn't mean to be facetious. Do you still store the sticks in the big greenhouse?"

"Yes. That's the only place long enough to put them."

Pat spoke, "And lots of people would know that."

"Any signs of forced entry?"

"We don't lock it. We never saw the need."

Until now, Jeff thought. "Have you reported them as stolen?"

Harry grunted dismissively. "No point. The Admins don't give a toss about things like that. They are more concerned with taking backhanders and doing their mates favours."

Jeff offered no argument. "But you should still report the theft."

Pat's response was immediate. "We did."

"And what happened? Did the Admins visit you?"

"Nah, we rang them, and the woman told us to apply to their charity fund for replacements. I told her it's not about the money. It's the principle. We want our property back. As you know, our allotments are sacred grounds to us. We are not happy that someone wandered in and stole our stuff." Pat looked distraught. "There was no need for that. We would share what we have. There was no need to steal anything."

Jeff put a hand on Pat's shoulder. The man was almost in tears. "What else did she say?"

"Nothing. She offered to speak with the Charity Trustees if we wanted, or she could give me the name of some generous benefactors in the area who might like to make a direct donation, whoever they might be."

Billy Jensen's name appeared in Jeff's mind. "Any idea who might have taken them?"

Pat stopped, thought for a second and said, "No. We are on pretty good terms with neighbouring allotment groups, so I can't imagine they would have stolen them. Who else would want beanpoles?"

Harry had no clue.

Jeff asked another question. "How many were taken?"

"We ordered a gross and doubt we used more than a couple of dozen, so about a hundred. Plus, a couple of spades."

"A hundred beanpoles would have taken some shifting." Jeff calculated the space needed. "Would they have fitted into a four-by-four?"

"You know what Neil's eyesight is like. It could have been an articulated lorry. He wouldn't have known any different," Harry suggested.

"Except there aren't many arctics around here these days," Pat said. "And you wouldn't easily get one down that road to the big greenhouse."

"I know that. It was only meant as a joke," Harry snapped. "Chill out."

Pat did not appreciate the response and stopped, turned and faced Harry.

Jeff stepped in quickly to avert an argument. "Was anything else taken?"

"I'm not sure," Harry replied.

"Well, get me a list of everything taken, and I'll see what I can find out."

"Thanks, Jeff, but won't you be too busy with this murder?"

"It won't be too much of a distraction. I'll ask a few people to keep their eyes open."

Jeff arrived home in time for the radio news and stood by the sink, listening while studying the garden. The clouds had covered the sun, making the scene much darker. The wind had risen.

He remembered he needed to buy grow bags for his greenhouse. As he looked at the glass frame, Jeff caught sight of a small bird fluttering about inside. He strained his eyes, keen to get a better view.

How could this be possible? He had not been inside for weeks. The doors and windows had been closed over the winter, and the seals were tight. Nothing could get in. This warranted closer inspection. He raced to the top of his garden.

Two roof panes had been smashed, scattering glass everywhere. A couple of house bricks lay on the floor inside.

Guessing that the missiles must have been launched from the back lane, Jeff went outside to check. Large footprints were visible on the rough path. Two indentations near his boundary suggested someone had stood on their toes to ensure the bricks hit their target. His immediate thought was that Norman was the culprit. If so, Jeff would be annoyed and disappointed that the Admin had resorted to childish revenge. He would not mention the incident and wait to see if anyone spoke of it. He busied himself by removing the glass fragments in the frame, measuring the gaps, and filling the holes with cardboard. The broken glass was collected and left in a bin.

As he returned indoors, Jeff speculated about the reason for the breakage. If it was Norman and a friend's work, then what was their aim? Was it intended to scare or remind him that they know where he lives? He would need to stay alert.

Jeff was about to switch off his radio to go to the cricket club when an advert caught his interest. Three of the best-known television soap operas from the pre-Shift days were being relaunched.

For a well-educated woman from an aristocratic family, Flissy had surprisingly simple tastes. She often teased that it was the reason she stuck with Jeff.

Felicity had been to the best restaurants around the globe, but her favourite meal was sausage, mash, peas and onion gravy.

Her father, who had surrendered his title to stand as a Member of Parliament, took her to all the best London theatres and introduced her to fine plays and playwrights, but Flissy was happier watching the amateur performers at the local community centre.

Her mother loved opera and dragged her daughters to see all the classics. Flissy had no time for the genre. She preferred watching a club singer performing a medley of hits. At least she knew the tunes.

After they married, Flissy accompanied Jeff to shows at the Theatre Royal in Bath, but did not always want to see what he did. No matter how much he longed to see a particular show, if Flissy had said no, Jeff would not have gone without her. He rarely made an issue of it. He knew his wife was happiest when sitting in their lounge watching the soap operas. She watched as many as possible, often using the catch-up facility to watch them again.

Jeff pretended to hate the shows and wished they would end. Flissy knew the truth. Her husband enjoyed the ridiculous plots almost as much as she did.

All soaps were cancelled after the Shift but were now returning on a cross-zone basis. The trailers suggested this would be 'groundbreaking television'. Jeff thought the shows would require new titles as the lives and loves of the residents of a northern street, a Yorkshire village, and a London borough were not exactly cross-zone matters.

He guessed the reinventions would be terrible but looked forward to watching them.

Saturday flew by. The trains were on time, and Jeff was grateful to find a seat. Jill was at the station to meet him. She passed on George's apologies. He had to work but hoped they could catch up when his work pressures eased.

Jeff believed Jill and George had made great life choices. They had good jobs, loving partners and wonderful children. Felicity would have been so proud. He often wished she could have seen them become fine, upstanding adults and parents.

Jill, the elder of his children, was an architect who partnered at one of the largest firms in her zone. The business secured lucrative contracts designing and project managing the building of low-cost housing units to replace the older stock. Her work frequently took her back to the Party Zone. Jeff worried for her safety. He reminded Jill that a lot had happened since she last lived in the Party Zone, and she needed to avoid unnecessary risks. Jill dismissed his concern, reminding her father that the Admins went everywhere with her.

Jill and Stuart had a lovely daughter, Carly, whom they visited as often as possible. She showed her father Carly's latest photographs and beamed with pride as he studied the images. Cleveland was not convinced his daughter and son-in-law accepted the need for their child to be reared elsewhere. He never raised the matter for fear of causing upset. He knew Flissy would never have accepted separation from her children, but times had changed.

Father and daughter went for lunch at a pub in town and got to the rugby ground in good time for the 2 p.m. kick-off. Stuart's team romped home in an absorbing match, although his son-in-law limped off at halftime.

The final would occur two weeks later, and Stuart hoped to have recovered by then. He wanted Jeff to watch the next match as he had become a talisman. Jeff had yet to see the team lose.

Post-match celebrations were held in the rugby club, where Jeff was offered a turkey dinner and a free beer. He declined, telling his daughter and son-in-law to enjoy the celebrations and that he would see them in a fortnight. He had arranged to meet a friend.

He found Carol Farnham, nee Lomax, at the Gas Street Basin in Birmingham City Centre. She sat on a bench facing the canal, reading a book.

They found a table outside a waterfront café. Jeff was surprised at the amount of traffic on the canal. Narrowboats were everywhere. Most were cruising the water while others were moored along the towpath.

"This is much different from the last time I was here." Jeff pointed at the barges. "I had no idea this canal was so well used."

Carol removed her coat and draped it over an empty chair. "Canals have become the main freight link. Seventy per cent of the freight is shipped around the country by narrowboat. They collect from the North and bring down to the South and vice versa, and there's a series of interchanges where goods get taken across country."

Cleveland feigned surprise. "I'm impressed. You are a font of knowledge."

His companion gave him a stern look. "No need for sarcasm. I've been on the water for the last week, so most conversations have involved canals and the need to protect the freight links."

"I never knew you were such a keen…what do they call you? A bargee?"

"Makes me sound like a side dish in a curry house. I'm not, but Lenny is a fanatic. He loves everything about narrow boats and canals."

"I hear it is very relaxing. Is it a safe way to travel?"

The waitress brought their tea. Their sandwiches would follow.

"It's fine in this zone and where you live, but the further North you go, the more protection is needed. Narrowboats running through the Party Zone get hijacked by the gangs. Most freight boats have more guards than crew. Many carry automatic weapons."

Cleveland stopped stirring the teapot's contents. "There are armed battles on the canal's banks?"

She nodded. "Yes. The area around the King Charles III Canal is a well-known trouble spot. The Admins are always out in force."

"Where is that? Manchester?"

"Well done. We call it the Old A because it used to be the Ashton Canal until they changed the name."

Cleveland pointed to the nearby boats. "It can't be easy defending the barges. They only go four miles an hour. They'd be sitting ducks."

"That's why more and more of the canal network is being cordoned off in the Party Zone. Much of it is out of bounds to walkers. The gangs still manage to organise raids and break through the barriers. They seem to know where and when the most valuable cargo is being carried. The guards can't stop them from attacking, but they make sure no cargo is lost without a fight."

Cleveland removed his hat to smooth his hair. "I never thought there'd be a gunfight on the Old A Canal."

"That's terrible."

Sandwiches were eaten, teapots emptied, and the table was cleared. Carol reached for her handbag and took out two bits of paper. She leaned towards Jeff. "It's about time I explained why I wanted to speak with you." She handed him a small photograph.

Cleveland studied the image of a young white man with a pale, thin face and wild hair. "Who is this?"

"That is Arthur Dixon. He was a resident of the Youth Zone until recently, when he had to relocate to the Family Zone."

"And you know him because?"

"In anticipation of his relocation, Arthur established a fledgling, small business selling recycled computer equipment. He visited Lenny to discuss his ideas for new systems to improve stock control and distribution records."

"Couldn't you do that? You were always good with technology."

"I knew my way around various programmes, but that was when we had all singing and dancing PCs. We only have access to more basic models now, and Arthur knew how to get the best out of them. He also knew where to get better equipment. Lenny employed him as a consultant, and his first job was to improve our databases, etc. The guy was a genius. Lenny helped Arthur find somewhere to live that was close to our offices."

"That's good of him. You refer to Arthur in the past tense. What happened?"

"He returned to the Youth Zone to collect the last of his stuff. He had all the necessary paperwork and borrowed the company van for the weekend. He reckoned it would only take a few hours. He planned to move into his new place on the Sunday and would be back at work the next day with a delivery date for our new stuff. On the Monday, our internal IT guy was concerned he had not seen or heard anything from Arthur. There was no sign of him or our van at his new place. The neighbours hadn't seen him since Friday morning. Lenny contacted an Administrator friend in the East Central region of the Party Zone. He paid a visit and found the van parked in the street and poor Arthur dead in his flat."

"That's terrible. How did he die?"

"This is the interesting part. He had a block of wood between his knees, and his legs had been smashed with a sledgehammer."

Jeff's jaw and shoulders dropped so quickly that Carol checked that he was okay.

Cleveland left the canal basin, thinking about the late Arthur Dixon. He had Arthur's address in Hyde, Manchester, details of his ex-employer, and a brief employment history.

Arthur was thirty-one and had spent most of his time in the Party Zone working on the coast. He worked in fisheries and had glowing references from his previous employer.

The endorsements referred to Arthur as highly intelligent but shy. He tended to be a loner. He never discussed friends or mentioned relatives and preferred to be left to his own devices. He would speak when spoken to, but rarely started a conversation. He came alive when discussing computers.

Carol said she had met him several times and described him as a lovely lad. She mentioned a persistent cough, which Arthur assured everyone was nothing to worry about and would soon pass.

Before catching the train, Jeff visited a stationery shop and purchased multi-coloured Post-it notes. From there, he nipped to a quiet supermarket, bought a fresh bottle of whisky, and grabbed a couple of ready meals. He could not get them in his zone, and having spotted them, he fancied one for supper.

Arriving home, he kicked off his shoes and rang Purcell. He asked for permission to visit the Party Zone. The ChiZA was not overjoyed at the prospect. He accepted the similarities in the manner of the murders but could not think of any other connection between Arthur and the Judge. There would be nothing for Jeff to see. The body would be long gone. Purcell believed the potential risk outweighed any benefits.

Jeff argued that the deaths, so similar and close together, could not be attributed to coincidence. He wanted the opportunity to search Arthur's home in case there was evidence that could link the two victims.

Purcell proposed to seek broader counsel before deciding. He would ring him back.

Jeff ate his ready meal. It was terrible, and he left most of it in the food waste caddy. He downed a small whisky before clearing his dining table.

He scribbled notes onto the Post-its and placed them around the table. By the time he had scrawled, amended, discarded and rewritten, he was left with seven Post-its. Two contained the names of the victims. One listed the similarities in the way they died. Another listed the Judge's projects. The last two concerned Arthur's employment record. It was a start. It was not a great start, but it was a start, nevertheless. It was something to build on.

It was Lord Nelson's turn to serve Sunday lunch, and Jeff had arranged to join Pat and the two widowed sisters, Mabel and Margaret, who ran the local craft shop, for a Sunday roast.

Rumours were circulating that lamb would be on the menu, but Jeff was doubtful. He believed it would be chicken or beef as usual.

Purcell's call delayed his departure for the pub. The ChiZA agreed to arrange for Jeff to visit Z18-30 on Tuesday, provided MC and Harding accompanied him. Jeff did not mention his concern about the pair working together.

The lunch was chicken, but the serving staff were confident they would have lamb on the menu within a fortnight. The chef had friends, and lamb was in season.

At just after three, Jeff thanked his friends for a lovely lunch. It was time he made tracks. He had a busy day ahead and needed to prepare. Pat would not hear of it. He returned from the bar with a fresh pint for his mate and a large gin and tonic for Mabel. He and Margaret were popping around to his place to collect books. They would return as soon as possible.

"Subtle as a brick, that one," Mabel said as her sister and Pat left the pub. "Gone to get some books. As if."

It was common knowledge in the close-knit community that Margaret and Pat had become friends with benefits. Jeff was impressed that his friends had an appetite for exercise so soon after finishing a three-course meal.

The men at the cricket club teased Jeff about him and Mabel becoming close. They asked whether their wives needed to shop for hats. Jeff played along, saying it was too soon to say, but who knew what the future held?

It would never happen. Mabel had already announced he was not her type. This was a huge relief. It saved Jeff from explaining that he was only interested in her as a friend.

"She'll not be able to sneak away for a quick one when Celia gets here. She'll put a dampener on our Maggie's passions."

"Celia? Who's that?" Jeff had not wanted another pint, but as it was there.

"Our eldest sister. She runs a holiday caravan park in Port Isaac but rang the other night saying she had lost her permit. The

Admins allocated her site to someone else. She'll have to leave at the end of the year. We are the only family she's got, so she'll come and live with us even though we don't get on."

For some reason, Billy Jensen came to his mind yet again. "Was she outbid?"

"She never had the chance to bid. Celia wondered why she hadn't heard about the license renewal and contacted the Admins. She was told the tender round had closed and a new permit holder appointed."

"That's awful. Can she appeal?"

"They told her it was too late."

"Does she know who the new owner is?"

"She didn't know the name, but this person already has a long list of permits stretching all along the Coast. She is ever so upset. She put her heart and soul into that place." Mabel sipped her drink and then put the glass on the table. "Maggie and I are not very happy about it either. We dread having our big sister on the scene. She's always been bossy and acts like a surrogate mother to us."

"You never know. Things might change between now and then."

"I'm not that lucky." Mabel reached for her glass again. "It's been a miserable week for us. We didn't get the amount of wool we wanted, Celia is being evicted, and some bugger stole our canvases."

"Canvases? As in paintings?"

"As in camping and stalls. We bought them years ago and hire them out when there are fetes, the boules tournament and the like. We keep the canvases in the room above the garage. Maggie went to check on them Friday, and they had gone."

Jeff pictured the sisters' place. The garage adjoined the main house and ran the length of the property. The room upstairs was very long. "Are there any signs of a break-in?"

"I couldn't spot a break-in if I saw one, but I doubt it. As you know, this is a safe neighbourhood. We rarely lock our doors. Not even at night."

"Can you replace them?"

"We can, but they are in short supply and very expensive. It's a good job that we kept the frames in the old workshop. They are still there. We always keep that locked to keep out wild animals. We had an escaped skunk in there once." She shivered. "We'll make sure that never happens again." Her eyes wandered across the room, and she exchanged nods with a friend. "We'll have to get some before the Spring festival. The salesman visits next week. I'll try to butter him up."

"If anyone can, you can."

"Are you flirting with me?"

"Not at all. I am merely expressing my admiration for your powers of persuasion."

"Hmm."

"I never knew you supplied the stands for the village fetes."

"That's because you never attend any of them."

Jeff could not defend his lack of interest in such things. He liked the boules matches, cricket, visiting the pub and the odd trip with friends, but carnivals and fetes left him cold. "Can you claim off your insurance?"

"Unlikely, as the house wasn't locked. What worries me is that the thieves knew where to look."

"Did you always store the items in the same place?"

"Usually. It is a light, airy space with plenty of room to spread them out. It helps to keep them dry."

"What size are we talking about?" Jeff looked at his beer and doubted he could finish it.

"They are various sizes. The smaller ones are like a small kiosk, the bigger ones would form a small marquee. We use them as beer tents."

"Pretty big, then. Who would know they were there?"

"Loads of people know we have them, but the only people who know where they are kept are the villagers who help us dismantle and store the stalls. Some of the Admins know. They borrowed them last year for their charity athletics day. The canvases took some cleaning after that event. They stank of beer and urine."

Jeff's attention had wandered again. Bean poles and canvas. He could only think of one use for that combination, but had no idea where to look.

He escorted Mabel to her house, ensured she was safely inside, gave her the obligatory peck on the cheek, and walked home. He planned a night in front of the radio, possibly with a book but certainly with a nightcap.

His walk was interrupted by an animated Mr Chopra running down his garden path to meet him.

"I'm glad I caught you, Jeff. I wasn't sure how long you'd be with Mabel."

"What's the matter?"

"I heard you are working with the Admins."

"News travels fast."

"I wonder if you could do me a favour?" Chopra did not give Jeff time to consider. "We are having a party at the golf club next weekend to celebrate our Ruby wedding."

Jeff offered his congratulations and hoped he was not about to get an invite.

"Thanks, but they just rang to say that someone has stolen their oven, and they can't get another one. They can't cook food. They can provide cold food, but we wanted chicken portions, pies and the like."

"Nice." Jeff lied.

"We wondered if you could speak with your Admin friends…"

"They are hardly my friends."

"…but you are closer to them than we are. We hoped you might have a word to gee them up. Someone must know something. I mean, how many people can offload a commercial oven?"

"I am sure they will investigate."

"You know as well as I do that they won't get off their arses unless there is something in it for them. They'll forget about it unless someone pushes them into action."

"Can't the golf club just replace the oven? Their insurance

would cover it."

"I suggested the same thing, but there is a two-year waiting list for new ovens."

Jeff lifted his hat and scratched his head above his ear. "I see. I will have a word and see what I can find out. I'm not making any promises."

"Of course, of course. I understand, but I'm sure they'll listen to you." Chopra winked at Jeff. "You'll find out something, and I hope you will keep us informed?"

Jeff was not sure that he would find out very much, but nodded. "Of course."

"Thanks, Jeff. We are very pleased that you and Mabel are so close." Chopra held up a thumb. "You're well in there."

"We are just friends," Jeff said, sensing that Mr Chopra was no longer interested.

Jeff checked his answering machine and heard Purcell's short, terse message. He had confirmed the visit to Z1830 for Tuesday, but there were stipulations. Jeff's party would meet their Z1830 escorts at the Warrington crossing point and be accompanied from there. The regional Admins would always be with them, and the visit would be limited to Arthur's apartment.

Relaxing in his armchair with a glass of whisky, Jeff switched on his radio. His local station repeated classic radio plays on a Sunday evening, and Jeff had tuned in to five of the six episodes of a Sherlock Holmes story. He was looking forward to hearing the finale.

The DJ dedicated his last song to a friend recovering in the hospital and played '(*Sitting on*) *The Dock of the Bay*' by *Otis Redding*.

Jeff leapt from his seat, ran to the table, scribbled a name on a Post-it, and put it in a prominent position away from the others. He threw the pen onto the table with force. Swear words and screams filled the room. Jeff was furious that he had not made the connection sooner.

9. A NEW WEEK

MC rang Jeff first thing to agree on a pickup time. The driver arrived punctually but did not look best pleased.

Jeff tried to present a confident, happy persona. "Good morning, MC. All good."

"Hmm."

"Thank you for agreeing to work with me."

"I had nothing better to do."

"I spoke to Harding. He is pleased you are joining our little team."

"That prick? He won't stick around very long. He's probably already licking Norman's arse to get a new post."

Jeff's smile disappeared, as did his optimism. He shrank in his seat. He had created this mess and had to act quickly to fix things. If he didn't, then this would be a long day.

The pair walked into HQ. MC revealed that Jeff's office had been relocated to the basement because Norman urgently needed the other room. Jeff suspected that a point was being made.

MC walked so quickly that Jeff had trouble keeping up.

When they arrived at the dingy box room, MC did not hold open the door, and it closed in Jeff's face.

The only furniture in their new office was a bookcase, a rectangular table, four metal chairs and three telephones spread around the room.

Harding joined them almost immediately. He greeted Jeff and nodded at MC, who called him a name. "Welcome to our new abode. Norman has made us very welcome."

MC grunted.

"Never mind, we'll get used to it. With luck, we won't be here long." Jeff decided to take the bull by the horns. "Hmm, I wondered if you two fancied a drink after work to celebrate our new team?"

MC scowled and pointed at Harding. "I have no desire to drink with that prick."

Harding thought the same, "No thanks, Jeff. I would rather have my arm severed."

"Come on," Jeff said. "Let's at least try to get along. It might only be for a few days. Can't you let bygones be bygones while we try to crack this case?"

"I'd rather crack open his head." MC turned away.

Harding giggled as he patted Jeff on the back. "We had you going there, didn't we?"

Jeff looked from one to the other, "What?"

MC was smiling.

Jeff realised he had been pranked. "This animosity has been an act?"

His new team members nodded.

Harding said, "We get along just fine. MC rang to tell me about the job offer, and we thought we'd have some fun at your expense."

Jeff was relieved. "I believed you genuinely hated each other."

"Nah, I like MC. We'll all get along just fine." He picked up the three mugs he had placed on the table earlier. "Three teas?"

MC nodded and, as Harding went to the door, said, "He's still an arse-licking prick."

Harding flashed two fingers.

When the three of them were reunited, Jeff explained why he and Norman had parted company and said he was satisfied there was no way back. He did not want things to be difficult for the pair and offered them the chance to walk away.

Harding insisted he wanted to continue. If Norman or anyone else pressed him, his line would be that he was working with Jeff under duress.

MC did not see what the fuss was about. Norman and his mates were a bunch of pricks. The priority was to find His Lordship's killer, not pamper the ego of an upstart, corrupt Admin.

Jeff was grateful for their support and appreciated that he

should have discussed the matter before offering jobs. He would not make that mistake again and promised to involve them as much as possible.

Maintaining the spirit of openness, he said he needed their help with another matter. The Admins sat quietly as he outlined his needs.

An open-mouthed Harding squinted at MC and then gaped questioningly at Jeff. "What do we know about Otis Redding? Otis? Redding? Let me see…he was a soul singer who sang that song about the dock of the bay. I believe he was cited as a major influence by other singers. I think he's dead."

"Not Otis Redding. I'm interested in Otice Reading." Jeff spelt out the name.

Harding was none the wiser. "Who the hell is Otice Reading?"

"He is someone I need to find."

"Why?" Harding asked.

MC joined the conversation. "Are you arranging a celebration or something? Nobody told me there was going to be a party."

"Very funny." Jeff provided a potted history. "Otice started as an entertainer. He was the singer in a band but then went solo, performing classic soul songs in clubs and bars."

"Was he any good?" Harding folded his arms.

"Not really, at least not as an Otis Redding tribute. He was terrible."

"What was wrong with him?"

"He was white, had peroxide hair and carried too much weight. His voice never suited the songs. His pitch was too high. He would have been better suited as a Frankie Valli or Bee Gees tribute. Otice rarely got to finish his set."

Harding leaned forward. "Why did he choose that career?"

"The real Otis' music enjoyed a renaissance at the time, and Otice thought he would cash in. His career hit the rocks when he had business cards prepared with the wrong name. We found out later that Otice is barely literate. His spelling is atrocious."

MC gave a half-hearted shrug. Harding spoke to Jeff. "You want us to look into an illiterate, wannabe soul singer who is white, fat with white hair."

MC cackled.

"He's not so fat now, but I would like your help finding him."

"I thought our job was to help you solve a murder. So far, I've spent most of my time on…" Harding was unsure if Jeff had told MC about his interest in Billy Jensen, "…other matters not linked to the Judge case."

MC stood. "If you two need to talk, I'll see what's in Records about Otice."

"Stay where you are," Jeff said. "Let me explain why I am so interested in him."

MC sat.

"Otice's real name is Gordon Baxter."

Harding looked more perplexed. "I am none the wiser. Who the hell is Gordon Baxter?"

"I'll come to that. After the end of his short-lived singing career, Otice changed his name back to Gordon and established a new business. He made a fortune sourcing and supplying stolen goods to order."

MC let Harding do the talking.

"What sort of goods?"

"Anything and everything. His biggest money-spinner was supplying the goods needed to pull big jobs, but Otice also got hold of hard-to-buy items and was very popular at Christmas. People gave him a list and a deadline. They would agree on a price and off he'd go. His list might include cars, oxy-acetylene, expensive drill bits, guns, dynamite, Lego or model figures. You name it, Otice could get hold of it. He was known as *The Retailer* back in the day."

"And was he more successful at that?" Harding asked.

"Very much so. He became the go-to supplier for all the major crims."

"Was he ever arrested?"

"No. Several police forces pulled him in, but he was never formally charged with anything. Gordy was meticulous when it came to covering his tracks. Not only that, but as I said, he supplied the biggest villains in the country. No sooner did he arrive at a station than some hotshot lawyer would arrive to defend him. He wasn't around long enough to get a cup of tea."

"Did he work in our area?" Harding hoped MC hadn't spotted his slip. He looked, but MC was awaiting Jeff's reply.

"Not as far as I know."

MC spoke. "How did you know him?"

"I interviewed him several times. He is a memorable individual. Very cheeky and quite witty. I first met him when we were investigating a robbery at a bank in Bath. We had a tip-off that he had supplied the plastic explosive and metal cutting equipment, so we went to see him but couldn't make anything stick. The second time, a dead body turned up with Otice's details in a pocket. He claimed the deceased had spoken to him about performing at a relative's birthday party and had been gutted to hear Otice had retired."

"Why are you so interested in him now? Is he involved in the Judge's murder?"

Jeff considered the question briefly, then said, "I very much doubt it. Gordon was a supplier. He never went near the actual crime scene."

"Then why do you want us to check him out?"

"Several thefts have occurred in my area over the last couple of weeks..."

"We need more than that if we are going to ask questions. Your name is already mud in this place, and Purcell would blow his nut if he thought we were diverting our attention to investigate petty local crimes."

MC nodded in agreement.

"Let me finish. These may be petty to you, but they are major incidents to my neighbours. The local Admins aren't interested..."

"Nothing new there," MC said.

Harding offered no comment.

Jeff continued, "I promised to see what I could find out."

"How do you know he's involved?"

"He was in the area last weekend just before the robberies took place. I was waiting in the queue for the cashpoint, and he wandered by. He looks a lot different now." Jeff held a cupped hand to his chin. "He has a bushy grey beard and wore sunglasses and a cap…"

"How do you know it was him? Was he singing?" MC sniggered.

"He looked straight at me and started to greet me with his usual introduction, '*Salutations, I trust the day treats you well*', but he realised who I was and changed it to a straightforward good morning. Over the next few days, there were three thefts in our area, all involving items that are unlikely to have been taken by some opportunist. These things were stolen to order."

"What sort of things?"

"Bean poles, canvas and a commercial catering oven."

"What?" Harding did not believe what he was hearing. "You want us to investigate the theft of random items?" Jeff nodded. "Why would anyone want to steal sticks, canvas and an oven?"

"That's what I want to find out. The items have limited availability at present. I'm told there is a two-year waiting list for replacement ovens, and the other stuff is equally difficult to get hold of. That's why I think the thefts are bespoke."

"This oven, is it a catering type? A big thing?"

"Yes, one of those they use to cook food for events. This one was stolen from the golf club."

"But how the hell would you steal an oven?"

"I have no idea, but it was just the sort of job that Otice thrived upon."

MC had a question. "If you knew who he was, why didn't you say something when you saw him?"

"I didn't recognise him, but, in any case, nothing had been reported as stolen then. I felt there was something about him, but…I don't know…I was distracted. The old memory cells are not what they were. I only remembered when the real Otis came on the radio last night." He leaned forward. "I have no wish to get you into trouble. I am not asking you to do anything other than find me an address for Otice…Gordon. I will take it from there."

Harding turned to MC. "What do you think?"

MC's shoulders rose and fell. "No harm in providing an address."

Harding nodded, "If asked, we say that his name has been mentioned a few times, and we thought we'd check him out."

MC nodded. "Works for me. I'll go and check the records."

"Thank you," Jeff said.

With MC out of earshot, Harding updated Jeff on his enquiries. The Judge's neighbours had seen nothing. One recalled His Lordship returning home on Sunday afternoon, but that was it. Nobody saw anything unusual and had not spotted any strangers in the vicinity.

Jeff suggested that Harding ask around the HQ to see if the Admins had seen or heard anything, but Harding doubted they would learn much. Norman had spread the word that his fellow Admins were not to help Jeff in any way, shape or form.

They studied the list of visitors to the zone. Harding recognised some of the names and said he would be surprised if they had not visited.

The Judge had a mobile phone and had rung several unregistered numbers. Harding had requested that these numbers be investigated, but did not expect a quick response.

There had been no response from the prisons or the other zones regarding the details of His Lordship's movements and interviews.

Harding watched Jensen for several hours on Saturday but had little to report. The man spent most of his time coaxing the builders to get moving. He said it was surprising the workmen managed to do anything. Jensen was constantly on their backs. Mrs Jensen was the first to leave the house. A female friend collected her. Harding guessed they were going shopping. The target and a much younger lady, whom Harding assumed was Jensen's 'maid', went for lunch at the golf club. The pair returned late afternoon, before Mrs Jensen got back.

The next day, Jensen revisited the golf club and enjoyed a round of golf. Afterwards, he went to a large storage unit on the edge of town where he met three men. The four greeted each other like old friends.

Harding learned the site was allocated to 'Jensen Enterprises' on a five-year permit. It was supposed to be used for furniture storage, but Harding spotted four vans sporting the *Sherborne Food Products'* branding, parked in the yard. Jeff scribbled furiously into his notebook and thanked Harding for his efforts.

When MC rejoined them, Jeff announced he had good news. They would visit the Party Zone the next day. Harding wished them well but stopped smirking when Jeff told him he was coming along.

Jeff assured his assistants that he had Purcell's clearances, so they were covered for insurance purposes. Neither MC nor Harding offered an opinion.

The trio spent the rest of the day discussing what they knew and wanted to know. They explored various scenarios before accepting that they would never solve the murder without a decent lead. Jeff hoped their visit to Z1830 would help.

Jeff told MC to drop him in Shepton Mallet. He could get home from there.

The bus to Bath was busy. Jeff found a window seat and rested his head against the glass, planning a nap. He had no worries about missing his stop as the journey ended at the city's bus station. The driver would wake him.

He barely settled when the conversation between two women opposite caught his ear.

The first lady told her companion she was using the bus because someone in the street had scratched her car. She prayed she would get it back before her husband returned after visiting his son in Stirling. It was not the first time the neighbour bumped their car, and hubby would not be happy. He hated the neighbour with a vengeance and wouldn't care that the man had offered to pay for the repair.

Jeff sat up when the other lady expressed amazement that her friend knew where to find the ownership documents. She wouldn't know where to start her search. Jeff wasn't bothered about how they stored their documents. His interest lay elsewhere. He wanted to know how easy it would be to get a vehicle re-sprayed without the necessary paperwork.

He knew that auto repair garages had to satisfy themselves of ownership before commencing any work and took copies of the vehicle's registration document in case of inspection. Garages caught failing to follow the rules risked losing their permits and having equipment and premises seized.

It occurred to him that whoever had stolen Gibbons' car - Jeff's money would be on Jensen – would probably get the car resprayed. There had to be a market for sprayers prepared to operate outside the law. He needed to know who this might be and where they worked. He was confident that one of his Admin colleagues could find out.

Alighting the bus in the village, Jeff rushed to catch up with the owner of his local hardware store. She was walking home.

"I'm glad I caught you. Can you get me two panes of glass?" Jeff took out his notebook and searched for the page where he had listed the dimensions.

"You'll be lucky. I can't get any. What do you want them for?"

"My greenhouse."

"Accident or vandals?"

"It was no accident. Does that make a difference?"

"You might be able to claim off the insurance if it's vandals, but you rarely see them around here these days." She chuckled. "Remember when we could blame the kids for everything?"

Jeff nodded. "It's strange to think that if it was vandalism, then the culprit is probably someone our age."

"There are still a few weird people about." The shopkeeper thought about Jeff's request. "I've got a few offcuts of heavy-duty clear Perspex somewhere. There's not much of it, but you are welcome to have what I got. I assume you wouldn't want a full sheet?"

Jeff confirmed that the off-cuts would be enough. "Why can't I have glass?"

"Shortages."

"There's a shortage of glass? How is that possible? It's made of sand. There's not exactly a shortage of raw materials. The stuff is all around us."

"I have no idea. I've tried ordering some but I keep getting told it is unavailable. You could try the bigger stores, but it'll cost you."

The nearest bigger store was also a bus journey away. "It will have to be Perspex. I'll call in later this week."

"I'll pop them down to you. I'll have to find them first."

Jeff wondered how his mates fared in the weekly quiz without him. He entered the bar and saw Chris, the quizmaster, and his partner John checking the answer sheets. This process took ages. The organisers knew the likely consequences of making mistakes.

'The Stumpers' team had been reduced to five, but the chalkboard at the end of the bar showed them in second place with only the results of the picture round to be revealed.

The demise of celebrity culture required quiz setters to show greater creativity in selecting images for identification. A spare question sheet lay on the edge of the bar. It contained grainy, photocopied images of flowers. Jeff knew none of them and was relieved he had missed the proceedings.

He bought a pint and sat close to Pat and Harry at the end of a row of seats. The pair were avid gardeners and confident of getting ten out of ten in the picture round. They believed they were going to win. This confidence extended to the other stumpers, and the team members debated how they should divide their winnings.

The prizes offered were a three-course meal for two or twelve beer tokens. They decided against the meal as it could not be divided.

The five teased Jeff about missing out and told him not to expect a free pint. He ignored the sarcastic comments about them doing better without him.

Jeff shifted along the seat when he saw Mabel and Margaret heading his way.

The sisters and four others who produced items for sale in their shop competed as 'The Crafty Beggars'. The blackboard showed them as leading the competition.

"Where's the rest of your team?" Jeff asked.

Margaret answered, "They've gone to the lounge. They've just served chips."

Pat walked off.

"Any news?" Mabel sat beside Jeff.

"Not yet, sorry, but enquiries are continuing."

Mabel chuckled. "Once a copper…"

"Afraid so," Jeff replied.

Bobby, a sixty-eight-year-old builder and useful spin bowler, was deep in conversation with his mate Cliff, the opening batsman. They paid little heed to those around them.

"I tell you. It's disgusting that these incomers are getting all the best houses. My missus and me need a bigger place, but they don't have a suitable house. Then Dr Lukic moves in and gets handed a four-bedroom detached on the edge of the village." Bobby clicked his fingers. "Just like that."

Cliff agreed. "These Admins ought to be looking after their own. We are older than these incomers and have been here longer. Why do they always get first dibs?"

Jeff saw the look on Harry's face and cringed. He sensed what was coming.

Harry prodded Bobby's arm. "But they offered you that house, and you turned it down."

Bobby swore, then said, "They didn't give us long enough to

decide. They didn't want us to have it."

Harry extended his index finger at the larger man. "You are always moaning that you can't afford to heat your two-bed bungalow. How would you manage in a four-bed with a double garage?"

"You are missing the point," Bobby stabbed a finger into Harry's arm. "We should be given first choice, not these incomers."

"You were given first choice," Harry pushed the man's hand away. "You turned it down."

"Only because they never wanted us to have it."

Mabel interrupted the argument. "Why do you need a bigger place?"

"The wife's sister is coming into the zone. She was sixty last month and needs to move up."

"Oh, I get it. It's okay for your family, but nobody else's?" Harry waited for a response, got nothing and realised the question was being ignored. "I can't reason with an idiot."

Cliff chirped up, "Where did this Lukic come from then? That's not an English name, is it?"

Harry remained keen to have his say. "Neither is McEwan, but nobody holds that against you."

"That's different. I was born here. Lukic only got in because she was attending a conference in the UK when the Shift hit."

"We are lucky to have her," Harry insisted.

"Says you." Bobby snarled. "You always take the other side. You never stick up for the likes of us." His hand waved between him and Cliff. "You were the same when Frank the Yank moved in. You argued he should be allowed to live here because he knew people in this area. He should have gone to the family zone."

Jeff spotted Frank Wallace's colossal frame and the man's face staring his way and quickly mouthed, "It's okay." He waved a cupped hand by his mouth to suggest Bobby had too much to drink. When Frank nodded, Jeff held up a thumb.

Harry witnessed the exchange between Jeff and Frank and did not want the American coming over. "Keep your voice down,

Bobby. Frank is just over there."

"'king yanks." Bobby looked over his shoulder, grunted and turned back to Harry, mumbling. "But why is he here?"

"He was visiting family when the Shift hit. Where else did he have to go?"

"He could have gone home."

"No, he couldn't." Jeff knew Frank had been on the last flight to leave Heathrow heading to New York when news of the devastation to the Eastern Seaboard filtered through. Frank's plane returned to London.

"He's lucky to be here." Bobby sipped his pint.

Jeff did not believe that being stuck in a foreign land while your wife, children, and other family were lost to the elements constituted luck. He sensed he had missed his chance to reply when Harry snapped at Bobby, "You speak some crap."

Jeff held up his glass, asking Harry if he wanted another. Harry nodded in response but took Jeff's glass. He would get them. Harry had heard enough.

Cliff chipped in. "Why do they have to come here anyway? Why can't they stay where they were? We get landed with all the waifs and strays."

"Good point," Bobby nodded. "It's probably because we get the pension in this zone, and the houses are well-maintained. It's also safer because there are no kids."

Cliff agreed. "There's plenty of room in the family zone. Why do they have to move people in here? We've got a nice community. Why do we have to have these incomers spoiling it?"

In Harry's temporary absence, Jeff felt obliged to offer a defence. "It's the rules. Once you reach a certain age, you move up a zone. Dr Lukic, just like this…" he pointed his thumb at Bobby and resisted saying 'dickhead', "…idiot's sister-in-law has just turned sixty, so had to relocate. Personally, I'm glad to see Dr Lukic. It means another GP in this area. I am delighted she is bringing her skills to this zone."

Cliff had not expected Jeff's interference, but was not backing down. "They should stay where they are. There's plenty of room where they were."

Bobby's mind was on other things. "It's not moving up, is it? It's moving down. The older you get, the further south you go, so it's moving down. You keep moving down until you die and end up in the sea."

"Hmm, fair point," Jeff said. "You either end up as landfill or fish food."

Cliff stepped in again. "But there is no need for the zones any longer, is there? Things have settled down, so why can't we go back as we were?"

Bobby leaned back. "'At's right."

"This would never have happened in France," insisted Cliff.

"No. We'd all be underwater," Jeff suggested.

"Before the shift, I mean, smart arse. There would have been a bloody revolution over something like this. The French never let things lie. Us Brits are too polite. We obey the rules. We protest a bit and then say, 'Oh, okay then,' even though we are still pissed off. The French would riot and block the ports."

"'At's right," Bobby said. "'king French."

Cliff turned melancholic. "I miss having younger people around."

"I don't," Mabel said. "I'm happier as it is. I like being amongst people my age. It's like a huge retirement community. I never liked the screaming shit machines and never understood why anyone would want them."

Jeff enjoyed these debates. When you put five or six people with differing views in a room and stir in some alcohol, you rarely had to wait long for a match to be lit and the fireworks to start. During his working years, Jeff had always been wary of the dangers of a police officer taking sides in debates and usually sat firmly on the fence. He felt differently since he'd retired, especially when Bobby and Cliff's views irked him.

"I don't understand why women want kids these days when they are taken off them at two years of age." Pat returned to his seat with a plate of lukewarm chips.

"It's the best time to have them." Margaret smirked. "Have the fun, look after them for a bit, and then hand them to someone else to bring up. That's ideal if you ask me." She helped herself to Pat's chips. "There's no vinegar on them."

"I'll get some." Pat spotted a vinegar bottle on the table by the bar.

"That's why the population is shrinking," Bobby slurred.

"I think you'll find it increased recently," Harry put two pints on the table. "It was on the news the other night."

"Increased? Wha? Are more people having kids? Who would want a baby these days?"

"They are not given much choice," Harry said. "They've stopped prescribing contraceptive pills, and you won't find a condom anywhere."

"It doesn't bother me." Margaret giggled, winking at Pat, who sat down after handing her the vinegar. "It's all the fun and none of the risk."

"Oh my god," Mabel mumbled. "You are putting me off my drink."

"It's removing a woman's human right," Harry said. "The State is forcing women to have children. It's not fair."

Bobby disagreed. "If they want to have sex, then they have to be aware of the consequences. It might stop this promishh… promiscush…bad behaviour."

"Unlikely," Mabel pinched more of Pat's chips. "The Committee is prepared to take unwanted children at birth. Women who hadn't planned to get pregnant can give up the child at birth. No questions asked. After four kids, women can get sterilised."

"Bloody stupid idea that Youth Zone," Cliff said. "Lock the kids away, teach them manners and how to behave properly and then when they reach eighteen, you put them in a zone with all the partygoers and drug takers. They are like lambs to the slaughter."

"That's why they're opening the Intermediate Zone," Harry said.

"The wha?" Bobby was all ears.

"The Intermediate Zone, where all the eighteen-year-olds will go to get them acclimatised to their new zones."

"It would be better to empty the Party Zone before letting new young ones in. That way, they can continue to behave properly and create a better society." Pat grinned as Margaret nodded and patted the back of his hand. She liked that idea.

Mabel did not. "And where will you put all these people you extract from the Party Zone? In with all the families? That's a recipe for disaster. There'd be nobody left to work in the factories."

Harry spotted the chalkboard being updated and rushed to collect his team's answer sheet. He returned crestfallen. "There must be some mistake," he dropped the paper onto the table. "Three out of ten. Chris has cocked that up."

"He would have to make seven mistakes," Jeff said. "That's unlikely. He checks and double-checks and then gets John to recheck them."

Pat examined the paper. "The images were hard to work out."

Mabel was straining to see the board, and as her eyes focused, her smile widened. "Well, it looks like we got ten out of ten, so the images couldn't be that bad." She turned to Margaret. "Shall we pay for the Craftees' drinks and keep the meal deal?"

Her sister nodded and held up a thumb.

Pat nudged Jeff. "Margaret mentioned their other sister is moving here soon, and she's the brightest of the three. We'll never win another quiz."

"'king incomers." Bobby mumbled as he rose to visit the loo.

MC stuck to the motorways, suggesting it was the quickest route.

There were very few cars on the road. Jeff remembered the days when the M5 and M6 were log-jammed most days.

Harding remained anxious about entering the Party Zone. The media regularly reported atrocities in the area, and he repeatedly warned Jeff and MC that if anything happened to him, his wife would come looking for them. Jeff was confident the local Admins would be well-versed in handling visitors and would ensure their safety.

MC laughed away Harding's concerns. "Grow a pair, you dipshit."

Jeff hoped it would help Harding to think about something else. "Where would I go if I wanted to get a car resprayed?"

Harding pulled a face. "I never knew you had a car."

"I don't, but imagine I did and damaged it. Where would I take it?"

"Are you asking for a friend?"

"No."

Harding still looked confused but answered the question. "Henderson's in Shaftesbury. They are the best in our zone."

"Would they require sight of ownership documents?"

"Of course. They wouldn't touch it without papers."

"That's very conscientious of them. What if I didn't have the paperwork?"

"So, now you want to know where to take an imaginary car you don't have the papers for. How about Toytown garage close to Noddy's place?" Harding thought his comment was funny, but shook his head when his colleagues did not offer so much as a smile.

"He is referring to Gibbons' car." MC's eyes did not leave the road. "He wants to know where we'd take the Rover to disguise it after stealing it."

Jeff was impressed by MC's intervention. "Spot on."

Harding turned to face Jeff. "Is that the car that you think Billy Jensen took? The one that Norm got so wound up about."

MC chuckled. "That prick gets stressed out about everything and anything. It's so easy to wind him up."

Harding grinned and nodded. "You are right there. He probably shat himself, fearing that Jensen would not support this year's charity drive. Norm thinks he is the kingpin as it is his turn to be the coordinator. He is determined to make it a success."

"I'm not buying his raffle tickets," MC said.

"You never do, you tight-arsed bastard."

The driver guffawed.

Jeff had not had an answer. "Where would you take the car?"

"Clean Otto's." The Admins said, in harmony.

"Clean autos?" The name was new to Jeff. "Where are they based?"

"It's not they. It's him. Otto Wagner. He's of German descent."

Jeff had guessed that might be the case. "Where can I find him?"

"Just outside Warminster. He has a couple of lockups there, supposedly to repair bicycles and the like, but I can't see why he needs such expensive spraying equipment to tart up a bike frame."

"Nor me," MC said. "The last time I visited him, he wouldn't let me inside."

"Couldn't you force your way in?" Jeff asked. He leaned on the rear of MC's seat.

Harding's expression indicated that he thought Jeff's idea was ridiculous. "What? And get slaughtered by the LeRA? No chance."

"If you know this Otto is breaking the law, why don't you do something?"

Harding replied. "Because Otto is only doing what he is doing because our beloved Lead Regional Administrator Cormack asked him to perform a task that backfired, and Otto had his arse well and truly slapped. This is Otto's compensation."

Jeff encouraged him to continue.

Between them, MC and Harding relayed the story. The latter did most of the talking.

The tale began with a potted history of Hendersons, who had established themselves as the best place for bodywork repairs and resprays. Mr H, as Harding referred to him, was a stickler for the rules and issued instructions that his businesses only work on vehicles supported by the appropriate documentation. The company flourished, and he established repair centres in other zones. It also helped that Mr H knew several members of the Central Committee.

The LeRA for Z6080, west-central region, had been unhappy that Henderson was making a fortune, but his money was untouchable as far as the local Admins were concerned. Mr H refused to pay backhanders or contribute to the causes supported by the regional Admins. He argued that his business was legit and only supported national charities. Hendersons operated nationally, and he was not prepared to favour one region over another.

LeRA Cormack hatched a plan to discredit Henderson by planting an unlicensed vehicle on his premises. He paid Otto, a longstanding Henderson employee, to admit he was working on it out of hours. Cormack believed that Mr H would reimburse him for keeping the matter out of the media. Once hooked, Henderson would need to make regular donations.

In the event, Mr H was tipped off. When the Admins raided the garage, they found nothing. Otto's claims about working on an illegal vehicle were dismissed. Hendersons fired Otto, and he became persona non grata in the world of car bodywork repairs. The vehicle selected to facilitate the scam mysteriously appeared in the driveway at Cormack's home with 'nice try' painted on the sides.

With no job, Otto blackmailed Cormack into granting him a lock-up and equipment to work under the radar. The Admins knew where and what he was doing, but dared not bother him.

"I meant to ask you, MC." Harding tapped the driver's shoulder. "How come Cormack never ripped into you? Everyone knows that you tipped off Henderson."

MC snorted. "He had a word, but I denied it. I told him I would slit the throat of anyone who repeated such scurrilous allegations." Harding's eyes widened at MC. He only relaxed when the driver winked at him.

"Thanks for that." Jeff could not believe Cormack had not been sacked. "How would I go about visiting Otto?"

"There's no point," Harding said. "Even if you find something to tie Otto to the missing car, we wouldn't be able to do anything."

Jeff was not giving up that easily. "I only want you to tell me where to find him. I will pay a little visit and ask if he's seen or heard anything about Mr Gibbons' car."

"And that's it?" MC was not convinced. "Just a few questions?"

"That's right."

"What if you find something? What happens then?"

"I'll play it by ear. I doubt I will find anything. I can't believe Otto will be so stupid as to have stolen goods on his premises."

"You don't know Otto." MC cackled.

Harding spoke while studying the scenery. "Otto thinks it is safe for him to do what he wants. No Admin would touch him."

He looked at Jeff. "Why do you think Jensen would use Otto? It would be easy for a man in his position and with his influence to get forged ownership documents."

MC knew the answer. "Because under the legislation, garages are supposed to check that the vehicle ID number corresponds with the paperwork.

"Oh, right." Harding did not understand why this would be a problem. "Couldn't Jensen just get a new ID?"

"Getting one is easy," MC said. "Attaching it to the vehicle in exactly the same place as the old one requires skill. That's where people like Otto come in." MC's eyes narrowed. "By using Otto, Billy Jensen wouldn't need to pay for a fake ID plate. Otto could transfer the one from Jensen's old car."

"You know a lot about this. I always thought you were legit."

"I am," MC replied. "A few of the regulars at my local make good money from redistributing unregistered vehicles. I just listen to them."

"And you don't say anything to Cormack?"

MC found that suggestion funny and squealed with laughter. "No, of course not. Why would I? Cormack and Norm wouldn't do anything about it except cream off the top. I am all in favour of people using their initiative to help make a living."

Jeff had been impressed with MC's knowledge, but one thing bothered him. "Do you take action against unregistered cars?"

"No. We encourage people to register and can threaten to seize the vehicle if we think it has been stolen, but we can't compel anyone to register their vehicle."

"Why not?" Jeff asked.

Harding took out a small plastic case containing mints. "Because when they deleted the vehicle licensing records to use the computer capacity for other things, they believed there would not be enough fuel for personal ownership. There was plenty of fuel when they tapped into the Norwegian fields, albeit at a premium price." Harding offered around the mints before dropping one into his mouth.

MC continued the explanation. "The right-wing pricks on the Central Committee support libertarianism and see no need for people to register their belongings. They see it as a slippery slope. The compromise solution was to make registration voluntary, but garages can only work on registered vehicles."

"And Gibbons' vehicle has been registered."

Both Admins nodded.

MC said, "It just happens that I need a word with Otto. I intend to visit him when we get a minute. Would you care to accompany me?"

"Are you serious?" Harding could not believe his ears. "Cormack would slaughter you."

"That, I would like to see."

"You'd be kicked out."

"They can stick the job up their arse. It isn't what I thought it would be. We are supposed to uphold the law, but most Admins are more corrupt than the criminals." He nodded at Jeff via the mirror. "I'll take you to see Otto. Harding can stay in the car. I'll change his nappy before we get out and leave him some bog roll."

Harding mumbled an obscenity at MC, who called him a prick.

They arrived at Warrington to be met by two Range Rovers, each containing four heavily armed personnel. A passenger exited the second vehicle and handed Jeff and his companions a protective vest.

"Is this necessary?" Jeff asked.

"It is," the female Admin replied.

"I knew I should have stayed at home," Harding said.

"Wimp." MC put on the vest.

The lady Admin added, "We'll probably be fine. Most residents are at work, so we are not expecting a welcome party, but we cannot be too sure."

MC drove between the two Range Rovers to Hyde. Jeff kept a close eye on his surroundings. He had expected post-apocalyptic scenery with burnt-out vehicles, barricades blocking their path, and the streets covered with litter and debris. There was no litter, and the roads were empty of cars and people.

"It's spotless," Jeff pointed over MC's shoulder. "There's no rubbish anywhere."

"There's money in recycling up here." There was tension in Harding's voice.

"How come we don't get paid for ours then?" Jeff thought about all the journeys he had made to the skip. "I could have made a small fortune."

"It's not a huge amount, but it incentivises the younger element. Recycling for cash. One of the Committee's better decisions, I think."

MC grunted. "Such a good decision that I wouldn't know where to go if I weren't following a car. There are no signs or street names."

Only then did Jeff spot the patches on the walls of houses where street names once rested. There were no directional signs either.

The convoy passed a supermarket with few cars in the car park but multiple armed guards circling the perimeter.

"That's another sight we don't see down our way," Jeff said.

"Bloody crooks rob the shops and then make a fortune selling the produce on the streets." Harding looked at Jeff. "Little wonder there are so many shortages. The gangs steal everything."

"Have the guards made any difference?"

"At the stores, but the crooks hijack the lorries now."

And the barges, Jeff thought, recalling his discussion with Carol.

The convoy completed the journey unhindered.

They pulled up at what used to be a shopping area. The ground-floor premises were shops that had been converted to living accommodation, some to a much higher standard than others, with two floors above.

Jeff and his team followed the female Admin to the front door. She pressed the intercom and asked to speak to Maisie Khan. While they waited, the Admin explained that Arthur's neighbour was the halfway house manager for those awaiting relocation. Arthur would have been given a living space, but most facilities were shared.

The door was unlocked via a remote control. The local Admin told their visitors to keep their ears peeled. If a siren sounded, the three should evacuate the building without delay. She would wait in the car.

On their arrival on the second floor, Maisie greeted them. Jeff had imagined a middle-aged lady, but then remembered which zone they had entered. Maisie was in her late twenties and wore a lime green tracksuit and blue Crocs. She handed a key to Jeff, telling him she would be in her room on the floor below if they needed to speak to her. Jeff thanked her and promised to return the key on his way out.

Arthur's accommodation consisted of three rooms. Each was small, dark and depressing, with an unwelcoming aroma. The curtains had been closed, keeping out the sunlight.

"That'll be the dried blood," Harding suggested, sniffing the stale air.

Jeff nodded in agreement.

"What are we looking for exactly?" Harding took a supply of plastic bags from his pocket.

"Anything and everything." Jeff's eyes had slowly acclimatised to the darkness. He walked to the nearest window and threw back the curtains. It made the room lighter but no more attractive. "Not much of a home, is it?"

MC studied the furniture. "Did you say the man who lived here was killed in this room?"

"Yes," Jeff replied.

"Poor bugger." Harding looked around the room with its shabby furnishings and mismatched wallpaper. "It's depressing."

Jeff nodded again as he examined the adjoining rooms. "Harding, can you take this room? MC, you look in the bedroom, and I'll do the room there." He pointed to a closed door.

Jeff's search was over almost as soon as it started. It was Arthur's office. A tiny space that housed a desk and chair. An old computer rested on the desk. "That looks like it came out of the ark."

Harding looked in. "Bloody hell, if I'm not mistaken, that's an old Dell machine." He read the faded label on the back of the desktop. "We used to have these back in the day. Shall I?"

"Please."

Harding pressed the power button, and the box started vibrating and buzzing. He pressed a button on the top of the monitor, and the screen quivered. A series of words and numbers appeared, disappearing as the machine went through its boot-up sequence.

"Let me know what you find," Cleveland said, looking around the small space. Apart from the PC desk, the area was empty. "I'll check the other rooms."

Jeff found MC looking under the bed. On the wall opposite the head of the bed, there was a hand basin, and next to it, a square metal cube rested on a shelf. Jeff recognised it as a portable electric oven with two warming plates.

The corner cupboard contained nothing interesting besides several boxes of cheap over-the-counter medication. Jeff examined the labels but found nothing untoward. The other cupboard was bare. He checked the drawers under the oven. They contained a few heavily scarred saucepans.

The bed was unmade, with the quilt tossed back as if someone had made a quick exit. The pillow still showed the indent of a head. He assumed it was Arthur's.

MC confirmed there was nothing under the bed. The bedside cabinet contained several well-worn paperback books and a few graphic novels. Arthur enjoyed vampire stories.

Three pairs of worn shoes were on the wardrobe's roof. Jeff moved them and found a shoebox full of Arthur's papers. He briefly scanned old bank statements, bills, and other official letters, none of a personal nature. Cleveland replaced the lid and carried the box to the living room. "That was a waste of time."

"It was," MC confirmed.

They heard Harding thumping the keyboard.

"Any luck?"

"Not really. This machine is so slow, and this keyboard is … well, you have to thump the keys to get it to register, and the mouse keeps sticking."

"Keep trying. We'll have a look around here."

He placed the box on the coffee table and surveyed the room again. It appeared that anything of value had already been removed.

MC pointed at a thick red stain on the carpet and suggested that was where Arthur had been murdered. It looked like the chair on which Arthur was killed had been moved back beneath the small table in the opposite corner. Jeff pictured a solitary Arthur eating his dinner on that table. Small condiment pots, a ketchup bottle, and a cup and saucer spread across its surface. A knife and fork stuck out of a chipped teacup.

An electric fire stood on a hearthstone next to a radio. Jeff realised that Arthur had no television. As bad as the programmes had become, he could not imagine living without a telly, if only to watch the news and scream at the screen.

His sympathy for the dead man increased further when he examined the two armchairs in the room. One was covered in old newspapers, and the other had a small round cushion on its arm. This chair was closest to the fire and the radio. Jeff sensed it was Arthur's favourite. He saw that MC had given up the search and looked over Harding's shoulder.

Jeff picked up the small cushion and gently squeezed it. It contained only filling, so he discarded it. He lifted the larger seat cushion. As he did so, something fell onto the linoleum floor with a sharp crack. Jeff recognised the old mobile phone. The back cover came away on impact. He put the pieces together and pressed the power button, but the battery was empty.

He saw what he needed on the wall by the radio. He slipped the connector into the phone's side. The scratched screen slowly warmed up as the phone began to charge. He left the mobile on the hearthstone and called the Admins.

"If we get a number for this mobile, can you trace the recent calls?"

Harding stopped typing and turned to face him. "Yeah. We can call it in and ask Technical to do a trace. It might take a few hours, but that won't be a problem." His face turned to the screen. "I think he used this for gaming mostly. All I can find are loads of old classic games. Pretty basic stuff, really, but I suppose if that's all you've got."

Jeff pushed his hat on the back of his head, removed his glasses with his left hand and rubbed his open right palm over his face. "He didn't have much to show for his life, did he?" He replaced his glasses. "Just gone thirty years, living alone in this...hovel. A couple of days ago, we were in a luxury mansion occupied by an old man who didn't want for anything, surrounded by other wealthy people with connections who can get what they want when they want it." He looked around the room again. "What chance do ordinary working-class people have in this country? What future do they have?" Jeff straightened. "Ignore me. I'm probably taking this too personally."

Harding said nothing but stopped hitting the keyboard.

MC stepped back and asked, "Why is his stuff still here?"

"Because it's a crime scene?" Jeff suggested.

"No, MC is right," Harding confirmed. "When they remove the body, everything else gets taken and either sold or recycled immediately. Why did nobody ransack the place?"

"Perhaps Maisie can tell us. You keep looking. I'll go and have a word with her," Jeff said.

Maisie's rooms were more comfortable than Arthur's, and she welcomed her visitor with hot tea and a slice of cake.

Refreshments aside, Maisie was of little use to the investigation. She had been at work on the evening in question and did not return until midnight. Arthur's lights were out, so she imagined he was sleeping. She knew he had a busy week ahead.

The next thing she knew, the Admins were demanding access. They later confirmed there were no apparent signs of a break-in. The Admins returned her key and told her not to let anyone in until told otherwise. They rang to check that nobody had entered the room and advised her that Cleveland would be calling. She had no idea why the room had to be secured.

In response to Jeff's questions, Maisie said that since moving to the region, Arthur had kept himself to himself, rarely having visitors, and spent his time playing on the computer, reading, and listening to the radio.

Maisie thought he had a father somewhere and mentioned a grandmother in Essex. She didn't know where. He rarely went out other than for work, to get food or to top up his mobile. He seemed to be making good use of his mobile. The last few times they met, he had either been to buy or was going to buy phone credit.

Jeff noted her number and thanked her for her time before collecting Harding, MC, Arthur's mobile, and the shoebox. Harding locked up and deposited the key through Maisie's letterbox.

The car was quiet until they left their escorts at Warrington. Harding broke the silence. "Do you have any idea about what connects the two men?"

Jeff had been thinking about little else since getting in the car. "No, except they both lived alone and appear to have died in similar circumstances." He lifted Arthur's mobile. "I'm hoping this will tell us something. Maisie said he had been making lots of calls in the weeks leading up to his death. Perhaps whoever he's been ringing will be able to tell us something." He dropped the mobile and the charger onto the floor. "I'll leave this here. Can you try to get the call log for me?"

"Will do," Harding said. "I'll charge it overnight and place the request before we pick you up tomorrow."

Jeff looked at Harding. "It's only just dawned on me. Why are you sitting in the back? I thought you'd want to be in the front with MC."

"Me? You've got to be kidding. I've been in a car with MC before. Drives like an idiot."

"Prick," MC retorted. "Where do you want to go now?"

"Home, I suppose," Jeff said. "There's not a lot more we can do today. We need to get the details of the Judge's visits and see what is on that mobile."

"This might be a good time to visit Otto. He won't be expecting us. It's sort of on our way home." MC saw the ex-policeman smile.

"What a great idea."

"Hang on a minute," Harding said. "Don't we need to discuss this?"

"You might," MC's tone was dismissive. "I think we've just decided what we are doing."

"I want no part in this. It's okay for you..." He looked at Jeff. "Once this is over, you go back to being a civilian. And you..." he pointed at MC, "You don't give a shit what people think. You ignore everyone. It doesn't bother you if they stick you on litter duty."

"It's only a job," MC said. "You get paid the same for whatever you do."

"But I hope to progress, and I can't afford to scar my record with this."

MC made clucking noises.

"No need for that, MC. If Harding does not want to help us. That is his prerogative. Are you sure you want to help me?"

"Somebody has to." MC stared at Harding. "I'll drop you around the corner."

Otto's lockups were the first two in a row of four on a small industrial estate about five miles from Warminster town centre.

MC banged on the metal roll-up door until a twitchy, slight man stepped outside. He wore overalls with *'Henderson Autocentres'* blazoned across the front,

"What do you want?"

"A word," MC said, pushing past him and through the door. Jeff followed quickly.

Otto soon joined them inside. "You can't just burst in here. I'm ringing your boss."

MC grabbed his shoulder and turned him. "You will do no such thing. Mister Cleveland is working with us and needs some information. You are going to help him. Do you understand?"

"Fuck off."

MC slapped the man's cheek and pushed him onto a chair. "Sit down there and answer Mr Cleveland's questions."

"Or what?"

MC studied the tools available on the workbench and selected a hacksaw. "Or I will take great delight in chopping your fingers off."

"You wouldn't dare." Otto was frightened but bullish. "You'll be done for this."

"So what? I'll be out of a job, but that won't get your fingers back." MC nodded at Jeff. "You ask the questions. I'll have a look around."

Otto sounded like he was about to burst into tears. "But you can't…"

MC turned sharply and leaned, pushing a hand into Otto's chest. "Speak when you are spoken to? Understand? You play nicely, and you'll be fine, but annoy me again, and I'll use this." The saw flashed before Otto's eyes. "It looks a little rusty, so, with any luck, you'll get a serious infection too."

MC wandered off toward the wall. Jeff wondered where the Admin was going, but then spotted the door installed to facilitate access to the unit next door. Otto's eyes followed MC, and Jeff tapped him to get his attention. "I want to ask you about a stolen vintage car."

Otto fidgeted in his seat. "I know nothing about any Rover."

"Who mentioned it was a Rover?"

"I heard about it, but I know nothing about that." Otto's eyes looked for MC. "Why are you so interested anyway? It should be the Admins who investigate theft, not citizens."

"I am employed to work on another matter, and I am keen to ensure there is no connection between that and the missing car."

"Your boss won't be happy. He owes me. I could land him in deep shit."

"I do not care about LeRA Cormack. I report directly to the ChiZA and the Committee Secretary for Security. Believe me, this matter goes much higher than your contacts."

Otto was perspiring and straining his neck to see what the Admin was doing.

"In here," MC shouted.

Cleveland dragged Otto from his seat and pushed him toward the door. They found MC holding up the edge of a tarp covering a blue Rover 70 in immaculate condition.

"Well, well, Otto, you disappoint me. You are more stupid than I anticipated," Jeff examined the workbench and mentally noted the contents.

Harding remained in the car, leaving his fellow Admin, Jeff, and Otto to walk up the drive.

MC stepped back after ringing the bell, keeping a firm grip on Otto.

Billy Jensen looked them over and checked his watch. "Good evening. What can I do for you? I hope this is going to be quick. It's my birthday, and we are going to dinner. My wife has invited several guests."

"We won't keep you long," Jeff said. "Can we come in?"

"No, you can't." Jensen stepped outside, closing the door behind him. "What is this about?" He spotted Otto and held out his hand. "Hello, I don't think I have had the pleasure. I'm Billy Jensen."

MC kept a firm grip on Otto, making it impossible for the man to move nearer to Jensen.

Jeff scratched his chin. "You have never met Otto?"

Jensen pointed at the man. "Nice to meet you, Otto." He frowned at the Admins. "I've never met this man before."

"That is a surprise considering we found Mr Gibbons' car at his lock-up with a set of number plates and a vehicle registration tag for your car on the workbench." Jeff saw that his words had registered and added, "We also found a supply of paint which exactly matches the colour of your Rover."

Jensen pulled his best theatrical look of surprise. "What? Really? This man was going to clone my car?" He looked aghast at Otto. "Why would you want to do that?"

Jeff had heard enough. "Please don't waste our time, Mr Jensen. We all know what's happened here."

"You might," Jensen replied. "I don't have a clue. Please enlighten me."

Jeff played along and suggested that Jensen had arranged for Mr Gibbons' car to be stolen to swap it for his own, which Jeff recalled was in a much worse condition. When Jensen said he knew nothing about the alleged crime, Jeff proposed they could resolve the matter at the Admin HQ. However, as he worked for the ChiZA, this would necessitate a visit to Cardiff. Mrs Jensen would need to cancel the birthday dinner. Jeff asked MC to put Otto back in the car ready to accompany Mr Jensen to Cardiff.

"Hang on a minute," Jensen shouted. "You can't just turn up here, accuse me of a crime and then drag me off to God knows where. I'm entitled to phone my lawyer."

"Please stay where you are, Mr Jensen. As you can see, MC is armed and gets twitchy when suspects try to abscond."

"I am not absconding. I am merely going to phone my lawyer as is my right."

"Ah, yes, civil liberties, I remember them. But as you reminded me at our previous meeting, they are a thing of the past. Do you recall telling me that we are much better off with the Admins taking direct action locally without needing all that palaver involving the Courts? What was it you said? Something about justice these days gets done quickly. This is a classic example of direct action. We can resolve this matter without any need for lawyers. However, you will have to come with us. Step this way before MC becomes impatient."

A smirk appeared on Jensen's face. "You wait until my friends in the Administration hear about this."

Jeff caught the man's arm. "I don't see how they will find out. We'll take you to Cardiff to answer questions before my boss. If we like your answers, you will be brought home. If we don't, then MC will take great delight in taking you to the island jail."

"Is that supposed to frighten me? I will be out of there in no time. I know most of the Admins on the Isle of Wight. I'll be back on the mainland before you."

Jeff's bluff had been called, and he struggled to think what to say next.

MC had no such problem. "Who mentioned the Isle of Wight? I didn't. Did you?" MC looked at Jeff, who shook his head. "I didn't think so. As we will be in Wales anyway, why don't we take you to Anglesey or Ynys Mon, as the Welsh call it? They'll make you welcome there, although I understand it gets cold in winter."

Jensen knew how bad things could get on that island. It was not just the weather that scared him. "You can't take me there."

"Can't I? You will be surprised by what I can do. I have friends on Ynys Mon who would happily put you in a house miles away from a telephone." MC moved Otto forward and then spoke to Jeff over Otto's shoulder. "Come on, we'd better get going. You can phone ChiZA Purcell from the car."

A feeble, forced grin spread on Jensen's lips. "Don't be hasty. I am sure we can sort this out here and now. You win a few, you lose a few, and I realise I have lost this one. I know when I'm beaten and would hate to miss my celebratory dinner. My darling wife has spent ages arranging it. What will it take for all this to go away? How much do you want?"

Jeff bit on his bottom lip as he pondered his response. "I suppose the easiest way to resolve this matter would be for you to buy Mr Gibbons' car. What do you think, MC?"

"That sounds like a sensible compromise."

Jeff held Jensen's eye. "You can do what you like with it afterwards. It will be your property, after all."

This was not the reply Jensen expected, but he liked it nonetheless. "Okay, I assume you would prefer cash."

"Yes, but I haven't finished yet. Mr Gibbons deserves compensation for the inconvenience."

The car collector sneered. "How much? An additional ten per cent?" Jeff did not look impressed.

Jensen nodded. "Twenty, then?"

"That would be acceptable."

"And will a finder's fee be payable to you and MC here?"

"Absolutely not. Knowing that Mr Gibbons gets what he is due will be reward enough for us."

Jeff took responsibility for Otto and asked MC to accompany Mr Jensen into the house to ensure he did not have a change of heart or try to use a telephone.

MC returned holding a bundle of notes.

"Let's get Otto back to his lockup so he can continue his work on Mr Jensen's new car before we deliver payment to Mr Gibbons. MC, do you mind if we help Mr Gibbons with the vehicle transfer documents?"

"Fine by me. It shouldn't take long, and I don't have to drive to Cardiff now."

"Thank you," said Jeff, smiling at Jensen on his doorstep. The man was not happy with how events had unfolded. "You'll get the paperwork in the mail shortly. Thank you very much for all your help. Have a lovely evening, and I hope you've had a very happy birthday."

MC dropped Jeff and Harding at the end of Gibbon's street, promising to return after taking Otto home.

As they walked to the house, Harding asked, "Are you annoyed at me for refusing to get involved in what happened back there?"

Jeff kept walking. "I was a little surprised. The Sergeant Harding I knew would have wanted to see justice done."

"That was a long time ago."

"I suppose it was."

"Come on then, out with it."

"What?" Jeff stopped and faced him. "What do you want me to say?"

"How a time will come when I have to decide between doing what helps me and doing the right thing."

Jeff thought he had probably used those words, but could not remember when. He walked on. "We all must live with the consequences of our actions. It is your choice if you feel comfortable lying down and letting people like Jensen walk all over you. But we both know that once you are on the floor, it is not easy to stand up again without paying a heavy price. I've always tried to stay on my feet, but that's just me."

Mr Gibbons was thrilled that the car and a buyer had been found. He brought out the ownership documents, carefully completed the transfer forms, and triple-checked that he had signed in all the appropriate spaces. Having done so, he reviewed the forms several times and insisted on getting an envelope for them.

As his visitors left his property, Mr Gibbons added, "All I need to do now is find out who is stealing my electricity."

Harding waited patiently as Jeff sought further details. They followed Mr Gibbons around his home and looked at his bills. Jeff agreed that they were much higher than he might have expected. He left, promising to investigate the matter and said he would be in touch.

It looked like every light was on in the house next door, and loud music blared from the upstairs windows. He asked Harding to inquire about the neighbours and ask the regional electricity company for details of their bills.

MC was surprised at the lack of conversation on the journey to Jeff's house and even more astonished that Harding was travelling in the front passenger seat.

Jeff arrived home to hear two messages. The first was from Purcell, and the second was from Doctor Rowe. He returned the calls in the order they arrived.

Purcell had been contacted by one of his colleagues, and Jeff knew who that would be, claiming that Cleveland had overstepped his authority in detaining Otto to demand money from Billy Jensen. Jeff denied both charges. He reminded the ChiZA that he had been made aware of the investigation into the disappearance of Gibbons' car. They visited Otto, hoping he might know someone who might have been involved. Jeff emphasised his surprise at finding the car on the premises, and Otto had volunteered to accompany him to Mr Jensen's house to clear up any confusion.

Jeff repeatedly denied threatening Jensen and insisted that the man had offered to buy the car to close the enquiry.

Eventually, Purcell accepted the explanation and proposed to speak to his colleague to explain what had happened.

When Jeff asked how his colleague had found out, Purcell told him it had been mentioned at a celebratory birthday dinner party he attended.

Dr Rowe had left a home number and answered the call on the fourth ring.

He confirmed that the bone fragments were human and most probably came from the Judge's legs when they were smashed. The rope was a generic brand which was used all over the country. The jelly-like substance was the most exciting find. Jeff found this difficult to believe.

"What could be interesting about jelly? What flavour was it?"

"That's just it. It's not jelly. It's Pulp."

"Wood or paper…"

"This has nothing to do with wood or paper. It is one of the generic names for various drugs created for use in Z1830."

"Created by whom?"

"State chemists. There are three key types. You'll probably never remember their chemical names, so I'll use their street tags. Oasis is equivalent to cannabis. Blur has the same effect as cocaine. The third one is Pulp, which is akin to Heroin."

Jeff realised that when Amelia referred to the bands' names, she had not listened to 90s music. "And the Committee know these exist?"

"They do. They asked for them to be created in order to control supply. The drugs are a combination of chemicals which provide variable highs. The good thing about them is that they are non-addictive, so there is no dependency, nor do they have any downer effect. They provide a reasonably safe hit."

"Only reasonably?"

"There are negative aspects. Some of the chemicals involved are extremely toxic, and prolonged use can lead to cancer and other disorders, including liver failure, kidney problems, blood poisoning, infertility, need I go on?"

"No. Thanks. People put this into jelly?"

"The jelly is created when the Pulp has mixed with saliva and then meets the air. You'll bring it back up if you take too much at once. The Pulp in the vomit congeals when it hits the air."

"Was the jelly the result of someone, possibly The Judge, throwing up?"

"I would say that is a strong probability. I would know for sure if I had something to compare it to."

"Sadly, we don't, and even if we did, I don't know where that would take us. If someone knew the Judge took drugs, then they might choose to rob him when he was high. That doesn't explain why they killed him by smashing his legs?"

"I haven't yet mentioned that high doses of Pulp can leave you immune to pain. There have been cases in the Party Zone of youngsters chopping off their fingers or incurring other horrific injuries, but not noticing until the effects wore off."

"Might someone have given him this drug to alleviate the pain of his legs getting smashed?"

"It's possible."

"But who would do that? Why turn up to kneecap the old man and then give him a drug to ease the pain? That makes no sense." Jeff scratched his free ear. "It suggests that the punishment was intended to kill him and not to obtain information, but, for some reason, the killer decided to reduce the pain level."

"Perhaps our killer arrived after the Judge had taken the drug and did not know that he had?"

"It's feasible, I suppose," Jeff recalled visiting Arthur's flat. "There was another killing which followed a similar MO."

"Lenny mentioned that it was one of his employees."

"There were traces of jelly there, too, but they had been removed by the time I arrived." He was quiet momentarily, getting his thoughts in order. "We might have a killer who inflicts horrific injuries on people, knowing they will not feel anything."

Rowe's breath filled the earpiece. "A killer with a conscience."

11. GETTING NOWHERE, FAST

Jeff shuffled the papers, desperately trying to identify something of value. "These are all the numbers Arthur called in the last few weeks?"

"They are," Harding sat opposite him and reached for the sheets. "This page looks the most interesting." He took out his pen and circled the relevant detail. "Arthur rang a mobile three times before ringing this landline." He placed the paper before Jeff. "Just below that, you can see that the mobile returned his call."

"What do we think? Arthur was desperate to speak to whoever owned this number, but could not make contact, so he rang the landline number."

"Makes sense."

"But whoever it was didn't want to talk on the landline."

"Because Admins might be listening?"

"Probably. It looks like this person rang Arthur back within five minutes and stayed on the line for half an hour."

"We need to find out whose landline this is?"

"Can you make enquiries?"

Harding nodded. "Of course, but I wouldn't hold your breath for an early reply. Everyone will know this came from you. They are unlikely to pull their fingers out unless you ask Purcell to make them do it."

"I'd rather keep that tool in the box for now."

MC spoke up. "You can always ring the number."

"That's an option, but if our hypothesis is correct, and this individual won't speak to someone they knew over a landline, are they likely to speak with us?" He tapped the sheet. "Do we know what area this is?"

"The area code is Blackpool, but it could be anywhere around there."

Cleveland sipped his tea and looked at the lists again. "Did Arthur have either of these numbers on his phone?"

Harding had made notes. "He did. The landline is listed as '*BVS*', and the mobile is '*Pmob*'."

"BVS? That could mean anything."

"Might it be a name? Someone's initials, perhaps?"

"Possibly."

Harding sat back on his chair and folded his arms. "I went to Amsterdam once before the Shift. I'm sure several companies there had letters like that in their names. Could the letters refer to a foreign company? One with an office here."

"No idea. It could mean anything. Let's give it a try. We'll ring them. We'll call the mobile number first."

Harding handed him his official mobile.

MC had a better idea. "You should use Arthur's. The person at the other end might be more inclined to take the call if they think it is from someone they know."

Harding was not convinced. "Unless they know Arthur is dead."

"There is only one way to find out." Jeff selected the number from Arthur's contact list and stopped short of pressing it. "How much credit is on this thing?"

"Enough to make a call or two."

Jeff hit the button, placed the mobile phone on the table, and engaged the speakerphone.

After several rings, a lady's voice answered. "Artie, my darling, where the hell have you been? We've got the order ready to go. I have been waiting for you to call to arrange delivery."

"Hello, this is not Artie. My name is Jeff Cleveland, and I have you on speakerphone. I am accompanied by..." He was cut short.

"How have you got Artie's mobile? Where is he?"

"To whom am I speaking?"

"Never mind who I am. Who are you? Why do you have Artie's mobile?"

Jeff cleared his throat. Giving news like this didn't get any easier. "I am afraid that Arthur, Artie, is dead."

The absence of sound told Cleveland that the news came as a shock.

"Dead? But the doctors said he had months left. What happened?" The line fell quiet for a time before the lady spoke again. "He didn't kill himself, did he?"

There were so many questions forming in Jeff's mind, but it was probably better to answer hers first. "No, I am very sorry to report that Artie has been murdered.

A sharp intake of breath followed by "No…no…no, not my Artie, tell me it's not my Artie."

"I am afraid that everything points to it being Arthur."

"Points to? That doesn't sound like you're sure. It might not be Artie?"

Jeff explained that Arthur had failed to turn up for work and that his body was subsequently discovered at his flat. A neighbour identified him.

"Would that be Maisie?"

"Yes, Maisie Khan."

"She'd know him. She was a good friend of Artie's" The deep breathing continued at pace before the voice added, "You said he was murdered. How did he die?"

Jeff did not delay his response. "He was kneecapped and left to bleed out."

The lady took a moment to settle herself. "Sorry, this is awful news."

"I understand. Can I ask how you know…knew Artie?"

"Of course, of course, but this has come as a terrible shock, and I need to compose myself. Keep this mobile on, and I will ring you back shortly."

"I didn't catch your name."

"I am Persephone."

The line went dead.

"Persephone?" Harding asked.

"Yes. Greek mythology," Jeff said.

MC took over. "Persephone was the Queen of the Underworld.

Hades, brother of Zeus, was King of the Underworld. He took Persephone, the daughter of Zeus, to his kingdom to be his own. Zeus's wife negotiated her release, but Hades was allowed to have her for part of the year."

"His niece?"

"They are Gods. They can do what they like," MC said.

"Well, I never," Harding said sarcastically. "How did I ever get by without knowing that?"

MC continued. "The story of Persephone is a classic. It has all the elements - love, lust, and great emotional power. An innocent maiden is abducted. Her mother is initially ravaged with grief over her abduction, then experiences immense joy as her daughter is returned. But then discovers her daughter must go back to see her abductor every year."

"It all seems a bit farfetched to me."

MC could not resist. "It is a myth, you prick."

Jeff narrowed his eyes. "I wonder how she got that name. Why choose Persephone?"

"It might be her real name," MC suggested.

Harding agreed. "She could have Greek parents. Perhaps her father was a lecturer in Greek mythology?"

"Hmm. I'll ask her when she rings back."

MC was doubtful that would happen. "If she rings back. She has probably changed the SIM, and we will never hear from her again."

The same thought had occurred to Jeff, but he saw no point in worrying about things he could not control. "Did you have any luck getting details of the Judge's visits?"

"Not yet. I imagine they have other priorities and don't fancy wading through stacks of paper. I will ring them again later."

Cleveland linked his hands behind his head and stared at the ceiling. "It was so much simpler in the old days. One tap of a mouse and you were away. All the information you could ever need."

MC pointed at the clock. It was nearly time for the canteen ladies to deliver tea and biscuits. Jeff was advised to check his cup to see if anyone had spat into it.

"Do you think that's why the Admins at the jail are taking so long?" Jeff asked. "They are p'd off with me."

MC doubted that could be a possibility. "What? You think they would care about upsetting Norm? They are miles away in a different zone and region."

Harding agreed. "It's like I said. It's all to do with the volume of work."

"To whom did you speak?" MC picked up a paper and pen.

Harding rubbed his face as he tried to recall a name. "I don't know. I asked for the person in charge of records, told him what I wanted, and he said he would get back to me as soon as."

MC scribbled on the paper and handed it to his colleague. "Next time you ring, speak to Scott Johnstone. He's in charge of the reception at PHC. Mention my name, and he'll get you what you need."

Harding was agog. "You never said."

"You never asked."

"How do you know him?" Harding asked.

"He was in my unit for a while. Quite a few of my old comrades work on the island prisons. Scott was a born administrator."

Jeff told Harding to close his mouth and asked MC, "Is that how the Judge booked his appointments? Through your mate?"

"No, as I told you, His Lordship wrote letters. Everything about his visits was handled very formally. I was kept out of it, but I met a few old friends while waiting for His Lordship to complete his business."

Persephone returned the call moments after the cups and plates were cleared away, and Harding had left to speak to Scott. MC was about to leave Jeff alone until asked to stay and listen to the conversation.

Jeff took out his notebook and scribbled a few comments

as matters progressed.

Persephone apologised for her earlier behaviour. She was stunned by the news of Artie's death. She had expected her good friend to die of the terrible disease eating away at his lungs, not in the horrific manner that he had.

Persephone said she and Artie had been good friends since junior school and had always watched each other's backs. They moved to the Party Zone together but were forced apart by the Admins. They eventually reunited.

Jeff asked questions about Arthur's history and family, but learned little. Persephone refused to provide any detailed information over the telephone. If Jeff wanted to know more, he needed to visit Fleetwood. She would ensure safe passage into and out of the zone. Jeff had always referred to that area as Zed1830. He found it strange hearing it called *Partyzee* or *Zee1830*.

He declined the invitation, saying he would not get the necessary clearance to visit. He asked more questions, but the response left him with no doubt that she would only discuss it in person.

Persephone told him to speak to whomever he needed to and to ring the same number when he had an answer. She would only talk to him. If anyone else rang that number, she would hang up and destroy the SIM card. She closed by saying how much she looked forward to meeting Jeff and stipulating that only one Admin could accompany him. That person could not be from the Partyzee. Jeff promised to be in touch.

"Well, that got us nowhere." Jeff put Artie's mobile on the table. "It will need a charge."

"Harding can do that," MC said. "You had an invite to the west central region of Zed1830, sorry, Zee1830. That's something not many people get."

"Why is that?"

"Nobody gets in. Admins don't even try any longer. Everyone fears that area. The region polices itself. "

Jeff was intrigued. "Seriously?"

"Yes. I've never been there, but I know people who moved here from the Party Zone are full of stories about what happens in that region, even though they have set foot over the border."

Jeff wasn't sure if MC was joking. "If that's true, I can imagine the response I will get from Purcell when I ask for permission to visit."

Harding returned with a big smile on his face. Scott had agreed to fax through the list of prisoners interviewed by the Judge. They would have it the following day. He also asked Harding to pass on his regards to MC. "He said you were a hero. What's all this then?"

"Scott is a piss taker. Take no notice of the dipshit."

ChiZA Purcell was adamant there would be no visit to Z1830 with only one Admin in support. However, after Jeff exercised his powers of persuasion, Purcell agreed to consider the matter further. Jeff closed the call, reminding the ChiZA that finding a connection between the Judge and Arthur could prove crucial in cracking this case.

Once again, Jeff found himself in a state of limbo. He was certain the death of the Judge was linked to one of His Lordship's research projects. Unfortunately, the only living people who would know what had been discussed were the prisoners interviewed, and he did not know their names. The Judge's papers might tell him something, but he was uncomfortable with contacting Wilson directly. He needed to get Purcell to sort something. He saw no arm in reminding the ChiZA. He would press for clearance to meet Persephone at the same time.

In the meantime, Jeff needed something to occupy his time.

When Harding reappeared, Jeff asked him for an update on the news of Gibbon's neighbours' electricity bills.

"I wasn't sure if you were being serious or if that was just something you said to shut him up."

"Is that your way of saying you haven't asked for the records?"

"No, I have them, but I didn't know whether to volunteer that information or wait until you asked. Hang on a second."

The bills for the house next door to Gibbons were astronomical. Jeff could not understand how people could use that much electricity. Their bills would have been much lower had they illegally tapped into Gibbons' supply.

"Does the regional electricity company have anyone we can speak to? Someone who might help investigate Mr Gibbons' usage?"

"I am ahead of you there. I've got the number for the customer liaison manager for that area. I rang him, and he agreed to accompany us on a visit. I've got his mobile number here. He said he would drop other visits to help us. Should I give him a call and tell him we are on our way?"

"Why not? There's not much else we can do."

MC waited in the car outside Gibbons' house while Jeff and Harding met with Mr C Stewart. His lapel badge identified him as "Stuey".

The man was keen to help and knew his managers would expect him to support the Administration in any way possible. However, he hoped this exercise was not a waste of time as the company had already checked and rechecked Mr Gibbons' usage and supply.

Seeing the Admins had company, Mr Gibbons said how much he welcomed Stuey's help. The lad was very popular with all the other locals as he was always so helpful and efficient. Stuey blushed.

When Gibbons repeated his belief that his electricity bills could not be that high based on his existing consumption, Stuey remained calm and attentive. He listened to Mr Gibbon's complaint as if he were hearing it for the first time. He suggested they check the meter and the incoming supply point again.

Stuey took them to a metal box near the garage. "If anyone is tapping into the supply, this would be the easiest access point." Stuey opened the box using a key from his kit. It needed a firm twist to unlock it.

Inside was a meter resting on a wooden board and an array of wires. Stuey shone his torch around and muttered. "As I thought, there's nothing amiss here." He pointed to one pair of cables. "That goes to and from Mr Gibbons' house." He looked under the meters. "Nothing under here to suggest any tapping. If someone steals electricity, we expect to see something untoward." He faced Jeff. "I cannot see how anyone is using his electricity. Perhaps there is faulty equipment? Mr Gibbons might use more electricity than expected." He locked the metal door. "I'll undertake a thorough inspection of the property and install usage meters so that he can tell at a glance what he is using."

Gibbons excused himself to answer his telephone.

"Might there be a problem with the meter?" Jeff asked.

"It's possible," said Stuey. "Although the consumption levels are consistent. If there were a fault, I would expect sudden peaks. Let's see what the meters show. They will accurately record his usage. Often, the customer is unaware of what individual appliances cost them."

"I see," Jeff said. "I appreciate your help. Can you ring Admin Harding if you find anything?"

"Of course I will, but give it a couple of weeks. Mr Gibbons knows we are monitoring his consumption and may keep his usage artificially low..." He saw Jeff's eyebrows raise.

"Believe me, it wouldn't be the first time a customer has tried it on."

"I accept that, but it is not unheard of for a meter to be faulty either."

"Fair point. We'll soon find out. I'll be in touch."

MC was leaning against the car and handed Jeff a sheet of paper.

"What's this?"

"The address of that ex-soul singer Otice Reading. Our Resident Records teams got it for me."

"That's great, thank you." Jeff studied the address. "He lives in Basingstoke."

"He must be either loaded or well-connected," Harding suggested. "Those properties are much sought after."

Jeff mumbled in agreement, already working on the best bus route to Basingstoke.

"Shall we go there tomorrow morning?" MC asked, then saw the surprise in Harding's eyes. "You don't have to come. We don't want to force you to do anything that might blot your copybook."

"I hadn't said anything," Harding replied.

"You didn't need to," MC said.

"Now, children, let's play nicely." Jeff climbed into the back seat.

Harding took the other rear seat and was fastening his seatbelt when Jeff said, "Seriously, though. This is my enquiry, so don't feel pressured to come along. Otice has never been violent, and I'm sure I'll be safe."

"I have nothing better to do," said MC.

"Thank you." Jeff turned to Harding. "If you have to be elsewhere, MC and I can manage."

Harding pointed at MC. "You can't rely on that old fart to find the way around." MC flashed two fingers.

Harding added, "I'll be there. I want to see the legend, that is."

"I wondered whether you'd pay a visit, Mr Cleveland." He checked out the car with two Admins standing beside it. "Ah, I see you have friends in the Administration." Otice stepped aside, allowing Jeff to cross his threshold, then pointed at the car. "Are they coming in?"

"Not unless you want them to?"

"No," Otice replied, "I'm happier speaking to you. Go straight through. I like to spend my mornings in the conservatory. I've just made coffee. Can I get you one? I have the real stuff. It's very nice."

"I don't doubt it, but I won't. Thank you. I'll spend a long time in the car today, and my bladder isn't as efficient as it used to be."

"Comes to us all. Please take a seat. "

Jeff wasted no time explaining that he found it too much of a coincidence that he spotted Otice, and then several unusual items went missing from his village.

Otice did not deny his involvement and said he had known it had been a mistake greeting Jeff. He hoped he had not been recognised, having lost weight and grown a beard. Jeff said it was the greeting that had given Otice away. Recalling his name had taken a while. Otice did not know whether to be insulted or delighted.

Jeff asked where the items were, but Otice would not say. He was sure Jeff understood that speaking about the theft would damage his reputation. He was also new to the zone and did not want to upset the residents. As Jeff was only a citizen, not an Admin, Otice was not obliged to answer his questions.

"I know I am not an Admin, but I thought you would prefer to speak to me rather than the Admins."

"I have nothing more to say."

"Not even if I ask my minders to deliver you directly to an island jail."

"Won't bother me, Mr C. Lots of people owe me favours. I

wouldn't be kept there for very long."

Jeff jumped at the chance to use MC's bluff. "I bet you know loads of people on Anglesey, having only recently left that zone."

The comment took Otice by surprise. "Anglesey? Why would I go there? The island jail for this region is the Isle of Wight."

"It is, but the Admins can take you to any island. You have a choice to make. Help me, or Otice might find himself sitting on the dock at Holyhead."

"My name is Gordon. Nobody has called me Otice for years."

Jeff held up a hand to apologise. "You either help me, or I hand you over to them."

"You wouldn't do that. You were always one of the good guys. You were always fair. You were always very kind to me."

"Times change. I'm under pressure to get results, and I don't cope with pressure as well as I used to."

Otice angled his head and looked at Jeff. "You wouldn't really let them take me to Anglesey, would you?"

"It's not up to me. They can do what they want. Much depends on what you decide to do. It's in your hands."

"I can't tell you nothing, Mr C. I simply can't."

"That's a double negative, which suggests you can tell me something."

Otice's face was etched with the pain he felt trying to decipher Jeff's comment. He gave up. "What if I were to suggest places that might be worth a visit so the Admins can see what they can find?" He liked this idea and quickly added, "Admins have the power to search where they want, and they could say someone spotted the items being delivered and tipped them off. What do you reckon?"

"That works for me, but would there be a trail back to you? Would your customers get suspicious?"

"Nah, I get my orders delivered through a middleman. I can say I didn't know where the items were going." He sipped his coffee. "Anyway, I already know where to get another oven so Bl…they won't be stuck for long."

Otice scribbled a couple of addresses onto a pad and ripped out the page to hand to Jeff, who could not read it.

"Your writing hasn't improved. Tell me the addresses. I'll write them in my book. That way, if anything unfortunate happens to me, there won't be evidence incriminating you."

"Good thinking." Otice took the paper, ripped it into small pieces, and relayed the addresses. "You won't tell anyone that I told you? Not even those Admins outside?"

"They know not to say anything. Anyway, if they do, I'll insist my visit was a waste of time."

"Thanks very much for this, Mr C. I appreciate you keeping the Admins off my back. If I can do you a favour at any time, ask."

"It's funny you should mention that." Jeff found and then removed a page from his notebook and gave it to Otice. "No rush."

MC and Harding confirmed they would not tell anyone else about the visit to Otice and listened carefully to Jeff's plan.

Harding exited the car at the Admin HQ. He would collect a few colleagues to visit the new Italian restaurant on the Southsea seafront, where they would insist on seeing the paperwork linked to their newly installed oven. After that, they would confiscate it and arrange its return to the Golf Club.

Jeff and MC drove to a recently extended camping site in West Lulworth. An extension covered land that had previously been categorised as agricultural. MC knew the site and the owner and could guess how the reclassification was agreed in record time.

They had no trouble finding the park. Massive signs directing visitors had been erected along the access road, and the gates were wide open.

MC parked outside the most prominent building, labelled '*Shop, Reception & Offices*'. Jeff counted four other vehicles in the car park.

The site manager joined them and asked why they were visiting. The site was not yet open to paying guests.

Jeff did the talking. He said this was a routine call. Various items of camping equipment had gone missing in the area. As a courtesy, MC and he were visiting sites in the region to check if anything else had been taken.

The site manager assured them that nothing was missing, and the Admins did not need to worry about his site. He mentioned that the park had only recently been developed by William Jensen, who was well known to the Administrators as a generous benefactor.

Jeff ignored the inference and said his primary interest was the theft of tents and glamping equipment. The site manager repeated that they were in the wrong place. Nothing was missing, and they had no glamping tents. Mr Jensen had plans to develop neighbouring fields, which might involve superior tents, but he had not yet gained full approval.

MC's request to view the other fields was refused. The manager was adamant that the pair could see everything they needed from where they stood, so they did not need to go further.

The Admin was not persuaded and asked to see the visitors' book, which all sites were obliged to maintain. The manager advised that, as the current guests were friends of Mr Jensen, staying on a trial run to ensure everything worked as it should, the visitors' book was empty. The guinea pigs were from the Party Zone, friends of Mr Jensen's son, selected because they deserved respite for one reason or another. The manager stretched their patience with his tales of Jensen's generosity and how his employer prided himself on his desire to help those worse off than himself.

Jeff struggled to hide his delight at MC's grimacing as the manager gushed about Jensen.

MC said it was time for them to visit the camping area. Again, the site manager blocked their path. He reassured them that all was well and saw no reason for them to venture further into the campsite. This was private land, and the signs clearly stated it was open to residents only. MC put an arm around the man's shoulders and whispered that letting them look without anyone being arrested for obstruction would be the better option.

The manager was confident there was no need for such action. He told them to stay where they were while he contacted his employer for approval. Jeff and MC waited for him to enter the office and then wandered off.

The smart tents varied in size and shape and were spaced around the fringes of a well-trimmed field. Shower blocks stood in two corners, with outside taps for water collection. Brick barbecues had been erected at various points. Several guests sat around a vast, unlit fire pit, which occupied a central space.

"Where would you hide anything here?" Jeff thought aloud.

MC grunted, pointed and then shuffled to a gate. A sign hanging on the metal bars made clear that this was private land and was not part of the campsite.

The Admin pointed at tyre marks, suggesting a vehicle had passed through recently. The tracks continued into the area behind the trees. The trail led them to a large barn.

MC held up a hand, telling Jeff to wait, pulled open the barn door, and then pointed at a Land Rover parked in the corner next to several bundles of bean sticks.

"Well, fancy that," Jeff said, smirking. He looked in the open back of the vehicle and pulled up the edge of a large, rolled canvas. "I wonder how this got here?"

"You have no business breaking in here." The site manager hurried into the barn. "This is private property."

"The door was open," Jeff said, then fell quiet when MC spoke.

"I think you'll find that as a Committee appointed Administrator, I can access wherever and whenever I like." MC was in no mood to be messed about. "Do you have a problem with me undertaking my duty?"

The site manager stepped back. "No, no, of course not. I meant you should have waited until I could accompany you."

Jeff did not need to contribute. MC was on a roll. "Why? So that you could dispose of this evidence?"

"I see no evidence. All I see is an off-road vehicle containing what looks like canvas and a load of old bean sticks. I have no idea what they are doing here. They have nothing to do with the campsite."

"Then you won't mind if we take the Land Rover and these other items back to HQ for processing."

"Has a vehicle of this description been reported stolen recently?" Jeff asked MC.

"I'm not sure, but I know that no vehicle of this description has been registered to these premises." MC thought for a second. "They have several minibuses and quad bikes, but no Land Rover."

The manager looked flummoxed. "That's because we only acquired it last week. We haven't used it yet as we haven't registered it properly. I will get on to it today."

"So, you do own this vehicle?" MC let out an impatient sigh.

"Yes."

"Can you explain why it was used to ferry stolen goods?"

The manager shuffled his feet, scratched his head and began several sentences unsuccessfully. "Well, we err...The thing is... Um, we err..." Jeff and MC let the man select his best lie and stood, smiling patiently. Eventually, words flowed more coherently. "What I am trying to say is. We had the vehicle delivered last week and stored in this barn until we completed the necessary paperwork. As far as I know, nobody has used it, and I have no idea how these other items got here. We rarely use this barn. It will probably be demolished when we expand. Nobody would have been in here for days...weeks, probably."

"Well, somebody has," Jeff said. "That canvas and those sticks were stolen last week."

"I meant nobody from the park." The manager took a deep breath, calming himself down by waving a hand in front of his face. "I apologise for my rambling, but I have only worked here a few weeks and am mortified that someone could have stored these items here without me knowing. You said they were stolen?" Jeff nodded. "I am horrified that these items have appeared here during my watch. I am sure Mr Jensen will be equally upset."

"I very much doubt that." Jeff heard MC titter. The site manager started to speak, but Jeff interjected. "What I mean is that I am sure Mr Jensen has much more important things on his plate than stolen poles and a bit of canvas."

"Yes, yes, of course." The site manager interlocked his fingers and stood with his hands in front of his stomach.

"What to do, what to do." MC was expressionless, eyes fixed on the site manager.

Jeff stretched his mouth and then scratched his hair under his hat. "We don't want to have to report this, do we?"

His driver looked at him sternly, but the expression soon softened. "No. It would mean a mountain of paperwork."

"And we haven't got the time to spend on that, have we?"

"We could do without it."

The site manager's shoulders relaxed. "Thank you."

"That's okay," MC said. "But we haven't finished yet."

The site manager stiffened again. MC nodded for Jeff to speak.

"We'd like you to return these items to their rightful owners and, perhaps, pay an amount as compensation for their anxiety and inconvenience."

"Of course, of course. I am sure that can be arranged.

Jeff wrote in his notebook and handed a page to the site manager. "The first address is the owner of the canvas. The second is the contact details for the allotment society and the name of the person to speak to. We will leave it to you to decide how you explain it. Get them back today, and we'll say no more about it. Agreed?"

"Yes, of course. I will get on that straight away.

"Good," Jeff said, pointing at the paper. "If you ask these people, they can probably tell you where you might purchase these items legally."

The man nodded mutely, tucking the paper into his pocket.

Jeff and MC returned to the car.

"Leaving those things there was unbelievably stupid," Jeff said, securing his seatbelt.

"They didn't expect anyone to investigate," MC replied. "Billy Jensen won't be happy."

Jeff smirked.

They both said, "Good," simultaneously.

MC's contact, Scott, fulfilled his promise, and the list of people visited by the Judge was waiting for them by the time they returned to the office. Jeff and MC spent the afternoon checking names. One appeared several times. Bruce Dixon.

"There might be a connection to Artie," MC said.

"I was thinking the same thing."

"If the pair are related, might someone kill Artie to stop Bruce from talking to His Lordship?"

"Possibly, but we need to establish a connection between the Dixons. It may be a coincidence." MC did not believe that, but Jeff added, "In any case, if there is a link, why kill Artie and the Judge? It would make more sense to kill His Lordship and tell Bruce to keep his mouth shut."

"I'll ring Scott and ask what he knows about Bruce."

"Thanks." Jeff continued studying the names. He identified several repeat visits, but none had met the judge as often as Bruce Dixon.

There could be no doubt that Purcell was irate. "What the hell do you think you are doing?"

Jeff had answered the telephone in their room, believing it would be a wrong number. Hearing Purcell shouting at him caught him off guard. "Good afternoon to you, too. What have I done to upset you?"

"You know full well. You're picking on Billy Jensen. I have had another complaint from Cormack and calls from members of the Central Committee. What the hell is going on?"

Jeff chose his words carefully. "I have not spoken to Mr Jensen since he agreed to purchase the missing car. What has been alleged?"

"You visited one of his holiday parks and commandeered equipment necessary to extend his campsite."

"Was that Mr Jensen's site? Well, I never. What are the chances?"

"Don't treat me like an idiot."

Then stop acting like one, thought Jeff. "I did visit the site, where I found what can only be described as top-quality bean sticks and a quantity of canvas."

"Are these items relevant to your investigation?"

"Indirectly, yes."

"How?"

"They were stolen from friends and neighbours of mine, and if they had not been found, then those friends and neighbours would have bothered me for updates on the search for them. This would seriously impact my ability to fulfil the task I was set."

Purcell sounded like he was struggling to stifle a cough. "Neighbours, you say?"

"And friends."

"Had these items been reported as stolen?"

"Yes, but as always, the Admins did not take the matter seriously."

Purcell did not comment on the attitude of the Admins. "How did you discover their location?"

"I met an old source who told me where to look."

"A snitch, you mean?"

"That is a very Dickensian term. We called them informants in my day."

"Who is this mysterious person?"

"I can't say."

"And you visited alone?"

Jeff mumbled, "Yes."

"I am told that a person matching MC's description was present."

Jeff said nothing.

"Well?"

"Well, what? You haven't asked me anything."

"Was MC with you?"

"Yes. If you recall, MC is my driver and is very noticeable and memorable. You insisted I always be accompanied by an Admin. However, MC played no part in repatriating the stolen items."

"That is not what I heard. Two sources told me that MC accompanied you to the site and threatened the site manager."

"Then you heard wrong. MC remained by the car while I entered the premises where the items were kept. The manager found me and was very embarrassed at getting caught with stolen goods. He offered to return them to their rightful owners without delay. MC drove me back here. I can only surmise that the site manager did not want to admit that he had willingly surrendered the goods, so he concocted a story to make it sound like he had no choice. He added MC into the mix for good measure."

"If you put MC on the line now, all this would be corroborated?

"Yes, but MC is not here, having been asked by me to check the background of a prisoner that the Judge visited several times."

"What's the prisoner's name?"

"Bruce Dixon." Jeff hoped his answer would hold Purcell's interest. It did.

"Dixon? Where have I heard that name before?"

"You agreed I could visit the Party Zone following Arthur Dixon's death. MC is trying to establish whether there is a connection between the two."

"You think Bruce Dixon is a relative of Arthur?"

"That is a strong possibility."

"Are you suggesting the deaths of His Lordship and Arthur Dixon might be linked to the interview with Bruce?"

"Again, that is a possibility."

"I see. Do you have any idea what the link is?"

"Not yet. We would probably have a better idea if we had the Judge's interview notes. Without them…"

"If those notes exist, they are in the possession of Lord Wilson."

Purcell's silence gave Jeff his opportunity. "I doubt there is much chance of getting him to release them. Perhaps I should meet Bruce and ask him what he and the judge discussed?"

"You'll do no such thing." Purcell made a soft whistling noise as he pondered. "Let me make a few enquiries, and I'll get back to you."

"How long is this going to take? You said you would consider my request to visit Fleetwood, but I've heard nothing…"

"You only asked yesterday."

Jeff was not about to concede. "Speed is of the essence in cases like this. Evidence gets hidden, stories are created, people become unavailable."

"Leave it with me, and I will get back to you by the close of play today."

"Promise?"

The line went dead.

MC handed Jeff two A4 pieces of paper, attached by a paperclip. "What's this?" Jeff asked, studying the manuscript notes on the top sheet. "Your writing is almost as bad as Otice's."

"It was the best I could do in the circumstances. Scott prattles along at ninety to the dozen. His accent doesn't help, and there are only so many times you can ask him to repeat."

MC summarised the discussion. The records at Wrexham showed that Bruce had a wife, Colleen, living in Camberley and two children. The elder, Stacy, was a nurse in Swindon. The son, Arthur, was last registered at an address in Manchester.

"Bingo!" Jeff exclaimed.

"That's not all," MC said. "Arthur served time with his father in Anglesey. He was locked up after an incident involving drugs, but was released at the personal request of His Lordship. Arthur moved to Manchester."

"Why? Why didn't he go back to Persephone's region?"

"No idea."

MC motioned for Jeff to look at the bottom sheet. "That's from his Admin file."

Jeff struggled to decipher the script but eventually read it all with help from MC. He let what he had learned sink in.

"The Judge arranges for Artie to leave jail. He moves to Manchester. His employment record shows a job working on old buildings before he moved to a fish market at Fleetwood. Then, there is a gap before he sets up his own IT business. After that, he moves across the border into the Family Zone. Why did he work in the market if he was a whizz at IT?"

"Perhaps there is not much call for IT in that area?"

"Possibly." He stared at MC. "We need to visit Persephone."

"Purcell isn't keen on that idea."

"Then I have to persuade him," Jeff said, reaching for the telephone. If he wants to speak to you and asks about our visit to the campsite, tell him that you waited by the car and had no role in me taking back the stolen goods."

"I never had you down as a glory hunter."

"Nothing like that. Purcell is not happy with our little detour and is looking for someone to blame. I was trying to keep you out of it."

"No need. If the prick doesn't like what I do, I will be happy to suggest he sticks the job where the sun doesn't shine."

Jeff said nothing. He had hoped for a little more appreciation of his efforts.

When he returned, Harding was in a great mood. The oven had been safely retrieved, and the golf club steward was thrilled. Harding and his Admin companions received a complimentary cold lunch and drinks and were told there would be a free round of golf waiting for them whenever they wanted one. Harding accepted the offer despite not playing the game. He thought his brother-in-law might enjoy it.

The good humour disappeared when Jeff told him that Purcell had sanctioned a return to Z1830 to interview Persephone. Harding initially calmed down after Jeff told him he would not visit, but became angry again, suggesting he was being sidelined because of the incident with Otto. Jeff calmly reminded him that Persephone only sanctioned one Admin companion, and MC was his designated driver.

12. IN THE PRESENCE OF A GODDESS

It was as if someone had flicked a switch in MC's brain since they last met. The Admin barely uttered a word when Jeff got in the car until they arrived at Bamber Bridge.

The village, some three miles south-east of Preston, home to the Briggers, was the rendezvous chosen by the host Admins.

The silence suited Jeff. He lost himself in memories of an enjoyable weekend. Marshfield CC was hammered in the cricket by a team from Bromley. Harry dropped two catches, not that it made any difference to the score. The opposing batters crucified the Marshfield bowlers. Boundaries came thick and fast. Pat blamed the fact that the opposition had five players who had only recently turned sixty. He proposed writing to the ChiZA to complain. Jeff wished him luck with that.

When Pat discussed his proposal with Harry, the pair realised they had a more direct route to the people in charge. Jeff was 'well in' with the Admins and could have a word. Jeff dismissed any suggestion that he held authority or influence. He was only employed on a consultancy basis. Nobody in power would listen to him. His friends found that funny. Harry spoke of how Jeff had no sooner been told about the canvas and stick robberies than the items were returned. Mr Chopra joined the discussion. He revealed how he had asked Jeff for help finding a stolen oven, which had been quickly recovered.

Such success at solving thefts had not been heard of since the good old days before the Shift. The villagers could tell the Admins were anxious to stay on Jeff's good side.

No matter how much Jeff denied holding any influence, nobody believed him. His fate was sealed when another neighbour reported that the work on the new bowling green had almost been completed and looked good. People had complained about the mess for weeks. It was no coincidence that these things had happened since Jeff took on the case.

On the positive side, Jeff did not have to put a hand in his pocket on Saturday night. Neighbours insisted on paying for his drinks. Matters worsened on Sunday when regulars at the pub praised Jeff for lamb being on the menu for Sunday lunch. None had been available for a year, and then, out of nowhere, there it was. Once again, free beer appeared before him.

A loud grunt from the front reminded Jeff he had business to undertake. MC pulled up alongside a Range Rover. Two Admins came to the car.

"Mr Cleveland. We have orders to escort you into the western region. We'll all travel in our vehicle."

"There must be some mistake." Jeff put on his jacket as he stepped into the air. "MC and I are making the journey alone."

The local Admins were not persuaded. "You are joking? That is out of the question. The western central region is a notoriously dangerous area for non-residents. It would not be safe for strangers to enter unprotected. Our ChiZA insists you do not travel without Admin support."

Jeff was ready to protest when the Admin said, "You either enter with us, or you go back home."

Jeff looked at MC, who shrugged, and the pair transferred to the back of the Range Rover.

The vehicle stopped. The local Admins told their guests to sit tight and insisted Persephone's followers were not to be trusted. She had total control and had been known to change her mind in the blink of an eye. The driver wound down his window by a few inches.

Until that moment, Jeff hadn't realised they had not stopped at an official checkpoint. The barrier guards wore casual clothes and caps, their faces covered by masks, with short baseball bats tucked into their belts. Most carried heavy-duty automatic guns. He guessed this was the border entry to Persephone's region.

Additional armed guards circulated behind the enormous

fences erected on either side of a gate and barrier. Massive boulders stood metres from the fences to stop vehicles ramming through the wire.

One of the border guards approached while three others aimed their weapons at the visitors. The Admin driver spoke through a partially opened window. "Mister Cleveland, to see Persephone."

The guard peered into the visiting car. "I can only let two people through. Mister Cleveland and one other." He studied the four and pointed at MC. "That one can go in, but you two are local. You can wait here."

The Admin in the front passenger seat leaned across the driver. "Our orders are to accompany Mister Cleveland. We'll take him back if we cannot come through."

The guard shouted at a colleague who walked to their hut and returned a few moments later, holding up a thumb and tilting it ninety degrees to the left.

"Go through, but take the first left, follow the road to the very end and park up. Someone will be along to get you shortly."

"What's keeping them?" The Admin driver asked.

"Patience." His colleague rubbed his hands with glee. "Just think, we will be the first Admins to see Persephone. We'll be heroes."

"And rich." The driver's mouth could not have beamed wider. "ChiZA has promised us a fortune if we see enough to identify her."

"That is assuming she exists."

"And she lets you live," MC said.

Jeff covered his mouth as the two locals turned to gawk at MC.

"Are you always so fucking cheerful?" The driver turned away.

"I need a piss." The passenger Admin pointed at a wall running behind an abandoned building. "I'll nip around there. I won't pee long."

The driver was not amused. "Haha. Take your gun."

"Of course."

Moments later, the Admin passenger emerged from his makeshift lavatory with his hands on his head. He was followed by four teenagers carrying weapons. One held the Admin's gun.

The driver swung open the door, knelt and aimed at the gang. "Stop right there. Put down your weapons."

"Or what?" One of the youngsters stepped forward. He had a rifle strapped around his shoulder, which he put behind his back. He held out his arms.

"I'll shoot." The Admin driver readied his pistol.

Jeff's eyes roamed from the approaching gang to the Admin driver crouched behind the car door, and then to MC. "We are sitting ducks." He started to open the door, but was restrained by MC.

"Stay where you are. This car is bulletproof. We are safer inside. Don't forget that Persephone is expecting you, and if she is as powerful as those two idiots suggest, nobody will annoy her. Sit tight."

Jeff was unsure whether to believe MC. He found it hard to be reassured by someone sweating profusely and breathing heavily. Water droplets covered MC's bald dome.

The Admin driver fired, hitting one of the gang members in the shoulder, and the body hit the deck. The rest of the gang readied their weapons to unleash a tirade of bullets.

"This is it," Jeff said.

MC tapped the back of Jeff's hand. "Keep calm."

Someone behind the car fired a gun.

"Enough." A male voice instructed.

The gang lowered their rifles and bowed their heads. The Admin driver stood with a smug look on his face, which disappeared when he was disarmed from behind and had a pistol barrel held to his head. He hoisted his arms into the air. "Okay, okay."

A masked face looked through the window at Jeff. "Mister Cleveland?"

Jeff nodded.

"Come with me."

"My driver needs to accompany me."

The masked face studied MC. "Looks like an Admin. We don't let in Admins."

"I don't blame you," Jeff said. "But Persephone agreed I could bring a plus one."

MC slowly emerged from the car and studied the surroundings before standing by Jeff at the rear of the Range Rover.

Three more figures emerged from a van parked behind the Range Rover. The three had their heads and faces covered. Two carried weapons. The third was unarmed.

The weaponless individual walked casually toward Jeff. One hand appeared from the deep pocket of a long coat and pointed at the local Admins.

The Admin driver was pushed forward while his colleague, who had been caught short, was unceremoniously picked up and dropped at the feet of the person in the long coat. The visible hand grabbed the driver's chin, pulling him up on his feet.

"Why are you here? You have no business being here. What are you doing here?"

Jeff realised the long coat wearer was female.

The prisoners winced as two rifles were pointed at them.

The Admin passenger spoke. "We were ordered to accompany Mr Cleveland."

"Why? I promised Mr Cleveland that he and his companion would be safe. They are here at my request. I have no intention of hurting them." The female adjusted her hood. "I repeat, why are you here?"

The Admin passenger turned away and was about to run when a rifle butt smashed into the back of his knee. He collapsed onto the floor, holding his leg.

The Admin driver's voice quivered as he answered. "Our ChiZA insisted we stay with them."

The hood nodded. "That figures. I imagine he has promised you a bounty if you identify me."

The Admin driver said nothing before he, too, slumped on the floor after a boot landed on his shoulder.

"He did indeed." Jeff had seen enough. "They mentioned it on the way here."

"Bast..." The driver was cut short by another sharp kick to his back.

Long coat turned her attention to the young gang. Three were tending to the one who had been shot. "What do you think you were doing, attacking my guests?"

The gang members looked up, fearing what was about to happen.

"Why aren't you wearing masks?"

The boy holding his friend who had been shot said, "We didn't know they were there."

Jeff intervened. "They weren't attacking us. They were probably spooked when the Admin went for a pee behind that building."

"Is that what happened?" The hood put her hands on her hips. "I'm waiting."

A different boy nodded. "It is. We saw him taking a piss and asked him why he was there. He pulled his gun on us. He was going to shoot until he saw there were four of us. We weren't going to do anything until..." he pointed at the admin driver, "...that dickhead shot at..."

"Enough," said long coat. "You know that we don't mention names in the presence of the Admins. Take your friend to the sick bay and get that wound tended. After that, you can clean the staff cars."

"But..."

"No buts. I would have done far worse if it weren't for Mr Cleveland's intervention. The least you could have expected would be clearing the shit from the gutting plant for the next twelve months." She pointed at each of them. "Think yourself lucky that I am in a good mood. Otherwise, I might not have let you keep all your limbs."

Long coat whispered to her men and pointed at the Admin

visitors. She then said, "As these two appear to have problems with their bladders, lock them inside the toilets. Secure their hands behind their backs and pull down their trousers. If they need to go, they can. You two…" Jeff and MC looked at her. "Get in the van. You are coming with me."

Long coat sat in the front. Jeff and MC, escorted by two armed guards, sat on a bench in the van's rear. The windows had been covered so they could see nothing of the world outside.

The journey was completed in silence. MC relaxed more as the trip continued.

The van parked up in one of the bays in front of an office block. Jeff and MC followed into a meeting room on the ground floor.

"I had planned to meet you here and take you on a tour of the area, but that…" she waved her hand, "…episode has slowed us down." She removed the hood and padded jacket, discarding both on the conference table. She had bright pink hair with a chain tattoo around her wrist. "Don't worry, I wouldn't have chopped off any limbs. That was for the visiting Admins' benefit. I must maintain my reputation." Jeff and MC were unsure how to react. "Where are my manners? We haven't been properly introduced. I'm Persephone." She pointed at Jeff.

"You must be Mr Cleveland. Who are you?"

"I'm his driver."

"That's nice for you, but what is your name?"

"You don't need to know."

"That's not very polite. I've told you mine, and I expect to know yours."

"That's MC," said Jeff. "Colonel M C Sands."

MC muttered, "Prick."

Persephone's eyes narrowed. "Not the Colonel M C Sands? The hero of the Berlin massacre? Is that you?"

"Berlin massacre?" Jeff was interested. "What Berlin massacre?"

"Haven't you heard about the bravery of my new friend?"

"I'm not your friend."

"Give it time. You'll learn to love me." Persephone stood face-to-face with MC. "Shall I tell Mr Cleveland, or will you?"

"You seem to like the sound of your voice, so feel free to continue."

"A few years before the Shift, the British Army was on manoeuvres in Germany with NATO allies. A group of soldiers, including MC here, enjoyed a cool beer on a warm Saturday afternoon. The bar they were in was attacked by terrorists who killed five of the group and left four badly injured." She studied MC's face, hoping for a reaction. There was none. "This is the brave part. Twelve soldiers escaped unharmed because MC killed all the attackers. The first were killed using these." She held up her hands. "And MC then used the terrorists' weapons to kill the rest. Over thirty terrorists died."

"I didn't kill them all," MC was agitated.

"No, but without your intervention, there would have been no survivors. I heard that you shared the guns you captured, allowing others to fight their way to safety. You even stood over the injured rather than running for cover."

"They couldn't defend themselves," MC said. "I was doing my job."

"And very well you did." Persephone held out a hand, which MC eventually took. "It's a pleasure to meet you. Lots of my friends would like to meet you if you have time afterwards."

"I'd rather not. Thank you."

Jeff had not heard about the incident and asked why that might be. Persephone suggested the authorities did not want to create panic and played down the seriousness of the attack. The official reports showed that three terrorists and two soldiers died in an isolated attack by a group of deranged, disgruntled students.

"How did you learn about it?" Jeff asked.

"We have many ex-military personnel in our ranks. After a few beers, they start to reminisce. It's not long before your name gets mentioned." She beamed at MC, who did nothing. "Colonel M.C. Sands is an absolute legend." Persephone let go of MC's hand and swept her arm across the table. "Come, sit. We have much to discuss."

Jeff and MC sat on one side of the table, and Persephone sat opposite in the middle of four of her people. Three of the four kept their masks in place. The fourth removed the scarf wrapped around her face but kept her cap on.

Persephone asked Jeff to explain his role, progress to date and why he wanted to speak with her. She said she knew most of it, but others around the table did not.

Jeff admitted he had been surprised to be asked to investigate the Judge's murder by an old boss who now worked in the Security department. He summarised his actions to date. There was little helpful information at the house, and interviews with those in regular contact with His Lordship did not help. His investigation was going nowhere until he learned of Artie's death. He refused to reveal how he found out but was sure the similarities between the two murders merited further investigation. The discovery of Artie's mobile phone resulted in a call to Persephone. The rest was self-evident.

The opposing delegation asked several questions about Jeff's support team, likely suspects and next steps. Jeff answered them as candidly as he could. He told them he had two assistants, MC, who raised a hand, and Harding, who wanted to attend, but Persephone had stipulated that only one administrative assistant was allowed. They had no suspects but thought the Judge's death might have been a result of one of two enquiries he was dealing with. He gave the broadest outlines, summarising what he knew about the Judge's work, but could not disclose any of the Judge's findings as the papers had been removed before he got involved. His next step depended on what they found out during this visit.

Persephone eventually hushed her colleagues' murmurings about how the Admins were not bothered about the murder of their friend. One male voice at the end of the group suggested the Golden Balls had killed Artie, and there was no link to the

Judge's demise.

Persephone said she knew a little of the ex-policeman's reputation and trusted him to investigate thoroughly. She promised to provide whatever assistance she could to identify the murderers. If Jeff needed any help, he only had to ask. Her only proviso was that nothing they said could be shared with the Admins. All requests for assistance had to come from Cleveland or MC, whom she introduced again. MC shied away from any suggestion of being a hero.

Jeff appreciated the offer and asked Persephone to provide background on her links with Artie and his role in her organisation.

She said she had known Artie all her life. At the time of the forced relocations, Persephone was studying at Durham University, hoping to pursue a career in the theatre. When Durham University was closed, she was moved to the East Region Z1830, the University Zone. Persephone was allocated to York University but told to follow a course in teaching. There were too many actors.

Artie was already there and gaining attention for his IT skills, particularly his ability to develop and adapt software. It was rumoured that he would attend one of the Oxbridge Universities for postgraduate studies and a master's degree. This was never a serious proposition as far as Artie was concerned. He was continually skint, his father was always in trouble, and his mother could not afford to fund him.

Persephone was reunited with Artie at a pub in York. While they were firm, close friends, there was never any romance.

Artie had a steady girlfriend, whom Persephone referred to as Cathy Bach, and was devoted to her. When Cathy left the University, Artie went with her. The pair moved into the West Central Region and secured a flat in Sheffield. He worked on numerous clearance and regeneration schemes, and Cathy worked in a doctor's surgery. She had studied medicine, initially planning to become a GP, until her plans changed. Cathy never spoke about why she left university. Artie did not press the issue.

Persephone kept in touch with her friends, who made a beautiful couple. Both were lovely on the outside and the inside. She thought they were settled, and it shocked her when Artie announced they were moving on. This would have been after a year or so in Sheffield. Persephone decided to go with them. She had relationship issues that affected her studies. She quit her course, and the three travelled across the Youth Zone. They shared many adventures before reaching Liverpool, where they found jobs working on the fishing boats. This resulted in a move to Fleetwood and the beginnings of their own fishing business.

In their early days in their new area, franchises frequently became available. It was thought there was nothing worth fishing for, and the older crews left the industry to move to the next zone. The younger generation shied away from a career on the seas, regarding it as pointless. The three of them and other friends had no such qualms. After securing their first franchise, it was easier to get the next one. Persephone had lived in Fleetwood for over eight years and ran the UK's most extensive and successful fleet. Their priority in the first few years was recovering anything that might be salvageable. The seas and coastlines were full of valuable items, and it was not difficult to make a living. They still dealt in salvage, but most of their revenue came from supplying fish nationwide.

She regarded herself as lucky. She made good business deals, employed trustworthy staff, paid them well and took no messing from the gangs in the other regions seeking a share of the action.

She said that her people had erected the fences that secured their region. They now controlled the West Central Region Z1830 and kept it safe. Jeff asked who they were keeping it safe from and learned that each of the other regions in Z1830 had its lead gang.

The lead collective in the West Region, which neighboured Persephone's domain, was *'The Taffia'*. She agreed it was a rubbish name. They were no threat as they constantly squabbled amongst themselves.

The East Region, aka the University Zone, was the domain of 'The Dons' - an intellectual bunch led by friends of the ChiZA for that zone. The East Central Region was controlled by 'The Stretford End Elite'. She was impressed that Jeff recognised the link to Old Trafford, the home of the once-famous Manchester United Football Club. Persephone did not believe there was anything elite about the idiots in charge and referred to them as 'The Golden Balls Brigade' after one of United's old idols.

Persephone's crew was 'The BVs', which, she said, was to wind up their neighbours. The initials stood for 'Brass Vaginas', and the name was apt because strong females held most leadership roles.

The region was a collective, socialist regime, with everyone getting a share of the wealth. Some earned more than others, but nobody would take on additional responsibility without that differential.

Persephone spoke with great pride as she repeated the BVs had secured most of the fishing rights for UK waters and had become too strong for anyone to oppose them. They had warships that they moored offshore and several tankers, which the Central Committee hired to deliver goods around the UK coast.

They ensured their fleet, whether lorries, narrowboats, or ships, prominently displayed the BV logo. This kept them immune from attack and hijacking.

Jeff asked why the BVs were so feared and how they got their arms. The questions brought a long pause to Persephone's otherwise open and friendly responses. She spoke softly to the lady on her left and then nodded as a reply was whispered into her ear.

"We are going to tell you the truth, but if one word of what you hear today gets back to the Admins or the Central Committee, and we have friends who will tell us if it does, you and your family, your son your daughter and your grandchildren will be in grave danger." She pointed a finger at Jeff and then spoke to MC. "That goes for you, too. Understood?"

MC said nothing.

"We won't say a word," said Jeff. "Unless this is in any way related to either of the killings, in which case, if we have to present it as evidence, we will refer to it as speculation."

Persephone told them of visits to other lands and discovering human life elsewhere. The Central Committee preferred not to mention these discoveries but wanted to know what had been found and where. Persephone only partially cooperated as the Committee continued to class her people as terrorists, a term she abhorred.

Reminding Jeff of the dangers of repeating any of this conversation to Admins, she confessed her modern-day explorers encountered sizeable numbers of struggling, hungry survivors who were often well-armed and equipment-heavy but short of food. Tentative trade arrangements had been established, and regular exchanges took place.

She refused to elaborate on which areas of the World or what goods were traded. The trade missions boosted the BVs' coffers, including gold and currency reserves, making them the country's most affluent and best-armed gang. She joked that the BVs had access to more weapons than the Army and Admins combined. However, her gang was committed to peace, and their arms cache was maintained as a deterrent. Nobody, and she emphasised the word "nobody," messed with the BV's territory, business, or transport.

Jeff was impressed but wanted to learn more about Artie. That was, after all, the purpose of his visit.

Persephone said Cathy and Artie split when Artie was arrested while trading drugs in the Golden Balls' region. Persephone could never believe Artie would do such a thing. He had a well-paid role, which he loved. He never took drugs, not even if he felt unwell, and had only visited the neighbouring zone area to collect a supply of PCs supposedly uncovered in a warehouse in Warrington. He travelled alone, without permission. The

Admins grabbed him and sent him to Anglesey without trial. She was convinced that Artie had been set up, possibly to remind her that her people were not untouchable. Cathy never forgave Artie for leaving her and refused to have anything further to do with him. The only saving grace from this incident was that Artie's father was serving time on the island for GBH.

Fate played a strange hand when a Judge interviewed Artie's dad in his review of the island prisons. Around this time, Artie became ill. The doctors on the island sent him to a mainland hospital, where he was diagnosed as having Mesothelioma, probably a result of working with asbestos without proper equipment and safeguards. The cancer spread to the major organs, and Artie was told he had no more than a two-year life expectancy. Artie's father begged the Judge to convince the authorities to release his son, who had already served a long sentence for such a petty crime. The Judge gained him a pardon in return for Bruce's full co-operation in his investigation.

A condition of his release meant Artie could not return to the BVs. He had to move to the FamilyZ. He was housed in Hyde pending relocation.

Jeff thought it strange that Artie had been killed in such a horrific way when he was dying anyway. He asked if Persephone knew why.

"Possibly because they discovered he was linked to the BVs. They have hounded me for years, but still have no idea who I am. They got close once, by accident. They attacked me when I agreed to attend a peace conference. They ambushed us once we were over the border. I wouldn't have survived if it weren't for my partner."

"What did your partner do?"

"He is an excellent driver and quickly got the car out of there. Sadly, not before they shot out the glass. He suffered facial injuries but is fine now."

"I assume you have not attended any other negotiations?"

"You assume correctly. It would be too risky. I have a much larger target on my back these days. The other gangs and their Admins are desperate to find out who controls the BVs to trace our families. They can't reach us but hope to threaten those we love. The bounty for information keeps rising."

"Aren't you worried that someone might let something slip?"

"It's always a risk, but my people can be trusted. In any case, we do not reveal personal information. That's one of the reasons we adopted fake names." Her eyes misted over. "Artie would never use a pseudonym. He did not see himself as a threat to anyone. I think an Admin found out who he was, told the gangs, and they tortured Artie for information about us."

"Would he have said anything?"

"I doubt he had much to tell. Artie never really got involved in the BV business. He set up our IT systems, helped us create false identities, and prepared fake papers. He enjoyed thinking up funny pseudonyms for people. He never asked who got what name. He knew who Cathy and I were, but would never sell us out. Other than that, he probably only knew people by their false names."

"Does everyone in this region have a pseudonym?"

"Everybody who needs one. That tends to be the senior officials and those who look after us. For example, this lady here is Anna Conder. She is my closest companion and confidante. Her sister is our treasurer and is called Cath Edral."

"What about Cathy Bach? Is that her real name?"

"No. Incidentally, Cathy works in this building. This is one of our infirmaries. She is not interested in anything other than helping the sick. She is a dear friend. Cathy adopted her new name on my advice. I fear her family would be in grave danger if outsiders learned how close we are."

"You use these fake names at all times?"

"Pretty much. It helps people get familiar with them. We never use real names or show our features if we go near the border."

"Do the Admins keep a close eye on the border?"

"Yes. They try to hide, but you can see the glass from their binoculars gleaming in the sun. The Admins also send spies in to try and identify us."

"What do you do with them? Feed them to the fishes?"

The laugh was deep but short. "We are not barbarians, Mr Cleveland. Once they see what we offer, these spies usually stay and join us. We watch them, and if we like what we see, we let the word get out that they have been identified as spies and punished." She used her fingers to illustrate inverted commas around 'punished'. "We do that to keep their families safe. They stay with us until it is time to relocate them to the next zone."

"What if you don't like them?"

"They get dropped off on Anglesey. On the island, not in the sea."

"Thank goodness for that. I am surprised you follow the relocation rules. I imagined you would have shut up shop here."

"There comes a time when our people want to be closer to families and loved ones and possibly start their own family. They cannot do that here, so we help them resettle."

"By finding them a place to live, a job and a new identity?"

"We do whatever needs to be done. If they have a problem in FamilyZ, they know where we are. We are always on hand to help whenever and however we can."

Jeff had envisaged the PartyZ as a world where dogs eat dogs. He had not expected such loyalty. "What about you? When will you relocate?"

"I should have done it three years ago."

"Why haven't you? Are you fearful you won't be safe?"

"I am afraid of nothing and no one, Mr Cleveland. Plus, I doubt anyone will recognise me when I adopt a new persona, grow my hair, wear it in a different style and colour and wear glasses."

"I suppose not. Is there a family waiting for you?"

Persephone trapped the side of her nose, suggesting it was for her to know and for him not to find out. "My family is all around me," she said. "Seriously, though, I am hopeful of moving on soon. My partner and I have already identified a place to live, surrounded by trustworthy people. I need to complete one more project, and then we are off. A successor has already been identified and can be relied upon to continue the work."

"Do you mind if I ask you what that project is?"

"Do you mind if I tell you to mind your own fucking business?" Jeff sat back, more shocked at MC laughing loudly beside him than by the response.

At the end of the table, the masked BV got up to open the door when it was knocked. Two unmasked men entered carrying trays of food. A third pushed in a trolley bearing drinks.

"I thought you might join us for lunch, Mr Cleveland. We planned to take you to one of our better restaurants, but Shaun and his team have done an excellent job after our plans were changed at short notice." She thanked the three men individually as they removed the foil from the food trays and placed them on the table with drinks.

"Thank you. This is very kind," Jeff said, rising to study the metal trays, which contained multiple small portions. "May I ask what's what?"

Shaun explained that apart from the sauté potatoes, all food was fish-based. There were prawns in garlic, scallops on black pudding, cod goujons, mini hake bites and calamari. Slices of baguette were piled onto the ends of each tray.

Jeff swallowed hard and looked at MC, who appeared uncertain.

"Is there something wrong?" Persephone asked.

Jeff sat again. "I'm not very hungry."

"You are a very poor liar, Mr Cleveland. Tell me what's wrong."

"We never see fish these days. We are told that the seas are toxic, making fish inedible. I imagined that was why you diversified into other lines of business."

Persephone reached over, collected a supply of the scallop dish, and ate it almost in one chew. "There is nothing wrong with the fish. The seas were more toxic before the Shift than they are now. Granted, supplies became limited for a while, but Mother Nature recovered surprisingly quickly. With a little help from our contacts at the various aquariums we encounter on our trips, we have reintroduced missing species. There is now an abundance of a wide variety of fish. We make sure we limit what we remove, and we further restrict what we make available to the zones, but that is a business decision. I don't need to tell you about supply and demand."

Jeff gingerly collected a portion of prawns and popped them into his mouth. It tasted delicious. He took a second or two to determine if the taste came from the meal being well prepared or simply because it had been so long since he had tasted fish. The prawns melted in his mouth.

"My God, that is stunning."

"Well, dig in. There is more where that came from."

MC and the others tucked in, but the masked members of the BV delegation took the food to a corner and ate with their backs to their guests. Jeff watched them for a time, interested in the chain tattoos on their ankles.

"And you say that you distribute this across the country?" Jeff was enjoying a battered hake bite.

"We do," Persephone said, polishing off a third goujon.

"It never reaches our zone, does it MC?"

"Not as far as I know," MC was enjoying the scallops. "It probably stays with the Committee members in London."

"If I were you, I'd ask your friend in charge of Security why that is," Persephone said.

"Committee members are only there to look after themselves," MC replied before taking another portion of the fish.

With lunch cleared away and the conversation, which covered a wide range of subjects, reaching a natural conclusion, Persephone suggested returning the visitors to their rendezvous point. She was sure the toilet-bound Admins would appreciate stretching their legs.

Jeff promised to keep Persephone informed of developments

and said he would contact her if he needed help. As they left the building, he spotted a large food store on the opposite side of the road. People wandered about without a care in the world, with not a trace of any guards. He laughed.

"Something funny, Mr Cleveland?"

"No, nothing funny. I am impressed that your supermarket does not need protecting."

"Why would we need protection at our shops? Our people are civilised. We look after one another."

"And if anyone were caught stealing, you'd chop their hands off." MC walked on.

Persephone roared. "Yes, that as well, but we've never had to resort to such drastic measures." She pushed MC's shoulder. "You are a cheeky bastard."

Jeff noticed a lady with sorrowful eyes and a white jacket studying them from a ground-floor window. Persephone followed his gaze and waved at the observer. Jeff made the connection.

"Thanks again," Jeff said as he stood back to allow MC to enter the van. He leaned toward his host, pointed at the spectator, and whispered, "Tell Cathy I've seen her mother, and she's keeping well."

"How…"

Jeff's fingers moved to his face. "It's the eyes. I have only seen one other pair that looks so sad. Don't worry. I won't mention it to anyone else. We'll be in touch."

The BV guards loaded the two regional Admins into the van. They threw the keys to the Range Rover to MC, who was told to leave them over the front wheel of the local Admin vehicle when they collected their car. MC was advised to get Jeff out of the PartyZ without delay.

Jeff was instructed to ring Persephone when he and MC were in the FamilyZ, at which point they would transfer the regional admins to their vehicle. Jeff questioned whether this was necessary and was assured it was. The ChiZA would demand to interrogate Jeff and MC, which would mean an extended stay. Persephone did not want the local Admins to cause any delay in Jeff's departure.

The border guard waved them through, and MC drove toward home. Jeff made the call, then sat quietly in the back, thinking about what he had heard.

One thing had staggered him, and he wasn't sure whether to mention it or wait for another opportunity. He wanted to ask, but felt nervous about the reaction he would get. He considered how best to approach the matter subtly.

MC moved the rearview. "It wasn't as bad as I feared. The locals are quite civilised."

"I found it quite scary when they started firing. I imagine you are quite used to that sort of thing, but I have never been so close to a gunfight."

"You never encountered armed criminals in your time in the police?"

"No. There were plenty around, but fortunately, they never came near me. "Jeff waited too long to ask a question and was hit by another.

"How long were you in the police force?"

"A little under thirty years. I joined after leaving university. I was going out with a girl who had two years to go on her Masters, so I joined the local force to stay in the area and be near her."

"They tell me a woman is usually involved in the big decisions."

"Yeah, but I misread the signals. She dumped me as soon as I finished training."

"You made a good career out of it, though."

"It was not intentional. After she ended the relationship, I was all set to join the Navy."

"Why would you do that?"

"Because there was no foreign legion in the UK."

MC laughed. "What changed your mind?"

"I was on security at an event at the University at which the Secretary of State for Education spoke. He was not very popular at the time because of the tuition fees. I met this girl called Felicity and arranged to meet her the next night."

"Was she a student?"

"No, she was the daughter of the Secretary of State. I didn't know it at the time."

"Was it love at first sight?"

Jeff did not have to think about his response. "For me, I think so, but not so much Flissy. I sensed she liked me, but did not want a steady boyfriend. She was fiercely independent. She also travelled a lot, which kept us apart."

"Travelled as in holidays?"

"No, with work. Her father's family bought a chain of off-licences that they turned into upmarket wine shops. Flis was training to be a buyer and had to visit the suppliers."

"So, how long did it take for you two to get together?"

"We went out for a few months, but I started to think I was wasting my time. Flis didn't share my commitment. I had the chance to relocate. I'm from the East Midlands, and the force there was recruiting. I applied for a transfer. I told Flis my plans, expecting her to wish me luck, but she got really upset. She told me that people in a relationship didn't make plans without discussing them with their partner."

"And you stayed where you were?"

"No, I relocated, and Flis came with me. She pioneered working from home and made the trip to her HQ when needed. Her overseas trips continued as she had a choice of airports."

"The rest is history." MC smiled in the mirror. "Was Flis ambitious for you? Is that why you got to where you did?"

"Not really. I was very happy being a bobby on the beat. I liked the interaction with people and helping them resolve issues. I was never ambitious, but we married and took on a mortgage that was too expensive for us, really. Then we found Flis was pregnant with my daughter, so I needed to up my game. I passed the Sergeant's exam and moved to a suburban station.

It was a quiet post but suited me because we had our son soon after. When we'd adjusted to being a family, I became itchy for a return to the action. I got a post in the City, joined CID and found my forte."

"Did your wife go back to work?"

"She never stopped. When her father died, she inherited the business."

"Was that on merit or age?"

"Both. She had a sister, a few years younger, who was more interested in spending money than earning it. She didn't care about the business, provided she got her share of the profits."

"Does she run the business now?"

"No. Flissy was canny. She foresaw that the deregulation of alcohol sales would decimate high-street wine sellers. She sold the business and spent the next few years doing charity work, volunteering and the like. Then, a few years later, she was offered a position with a supermarket as a wine buyer. After that, she had a better offer and then another. She was away on a meet-the-seller trip when the Shift caught her."

"I am sorry to hear that."

"Thank you. It hit me very badly. I was a mess." Jeff ran a hand over his face. "Can I ask you a question?" He saw the driver's eyes looking at him through the mirror.

"If you must."

"Why did you join the army?"

"It was in my blood. My father was an officer in the Bermudan army and was seconded into the British army. My mother and I relocated to the UK when I was about seven."

"And you wanted to emulate your father?"

"I never really thought about it like that. I don't think I did. As a child, I only ever wanted to be a teacher."

"What changed?"

"Fate intervened. My mother died when I was ten, and Dad could not afford to stop working. He secured various scholarships for me, and I was shunted from school to school, mostly as a boarder. When I got into a military training college, I knew where my future lay."

"Were you a naturally gifted soldier?"

"I have no idea what you mean by that, but I suppose I realised I had found my vocation. The hardest part was the elocution lessons, which helped me hide my natural accent."

"You still had an accent after living here for so long?"

"I did. My father's friends tended to be West Indian, and I fell in with their children."

"Why didn't you keep your accent?"

"I was told it would be best to speak like a local."

"The Queen's English and all that nonsense. Typical. Anyway, it didn't do you any harm. You did very well." MC's shoulders rose and fell. "Was your father proud of your achievements?"

"Very. He kept telling me how proud he was." MC chuckled. "Although he wanted me to speak like a West Indian. He pretended to struggle to understand my posh British voice."

"Was he still serving when you joined?"

"Yes, but his career had stalled. He became determined to do everything possible to help me progress." These were clearly happy memories for MC, whose face had lit up. "The look on his face when I was made Colonel, he could not have been happier. He was beaming like a Cheshire Cat when he had to salute me that first time. It was a beautiful moment." MC was briefly lost in memory. "He retired shortly afterwards."

"What did he do after ...what do they call it, he was decommissioned?"

"Very good. Dad had a new family by then. My stepmum was a nurse at the camp, and they had two boys. He lived off his pension in a dilapidated house in Eastbourne that he often threatened to renovate, but my father was useless at DIY."

"I know that feeling. Did your half-brothers join the military?"

"No, neither of them showed an aptitude. One is a doctor and works in London. The other is an artist. He lives in Cornwall. The four of us meet up regularly. My stepmother lives in Brighton."

"And your father?"

"He died when the Shift hit."

"I am sorry to hear that. Where was he at the time?"

"In Bermuda. He was visiting my uncle, who had suffered a stroke."

"That's terrible."

"It was a bad time, but could have been much worse. My stepmother and brothers were supposed to go with him, but Dad had a message that my uncle was fading, so he went ahead. Then...the shit hit the fan."

It did indeed, Jeff thought. "Do you miss the army?"

MC fell quiet, pondering the reply. "Not really. I had...I felt that we were not doing the right things."

"Like what?"

"If you don't mind, I have no wish to talk about it." The steely gaze returned. MC's eyes became fixed on the road ahead. Jeff nodded, and the car fell silent. Jeff never got to ask about Berlin.

MC's mobile rang as the car left the FamilyZ, entering Z6080. The driver put it on speakerphone, and they heard ChiZA Purcell asking where they were and whether it was too late for them to turn around. He said the Administrators in Z1830 had questions for them.

MC left the ChiZA without a doubt that there was no chance of the car turning around. Jeff agreed but promised to tell Purcell what they had discovered so that he could report it to his counterpart.

Purcell attempted to stamp his authority. He shouted that if he gave an order, he expected MC to obey it. MC laughed, called him a prick and ended the call. Jeff was not surprised Purcell did not ring back.

As they approached their region, the mobile rang again. This time, Harding warned them that Purcell was on his way over. "He's well pissed off with you two. What have you done?"

MC chuckled loudly.

Jeff urged MC to quieten down. "We left the Party Zone quicker than the local Admin expected. They want us to return."
"Are you going to?"
"No chance," MC said, "we are on the way to HQ."
"How did it go?"
"We'll tell you when we get there," Jeff said.
MC added, "It wasn't as bad as I feared. You would have enjoyed it."
"I doubt that very much."
Jeff leaned forward until he rested his elbows on both front seats. "How do you know Purcell is visiting? Did he speak to you directly?"
"He rang Cormack and told him to reserve a parking space and ensure you did not leave until he had spoken to you."
"Shall I take you straight home?" MC asked with a wry smile.
"No need for that." Jeff rubbed his ear. "I bet Cormack enjoyed that exchange."
Harding chuckled. "I imagine he loved it, but I didn't witness it. Norman told me. He said he did me a favour by telling Cormack I had no part in it. He promised to put in a good word to get me moved from working with you."
"Will you go?"
"Not if you don't want me to."
"I don't," Jeff said.
"I do," MC shouted, closing the call.

Harding met them in the car park and took them to the rear fire exit. They reached their office as Norman was leaving their room. The Admin looked embarrassed. "Ah, there you are. ChiZA Purcell is waiting for you." He did not hang about and headed back upstairs, whistling a tune Jeff recognised but could not name.
Jeff studied the surroundings. It did not look as if anything had been taken. "What was he doing in here?"
"Giving you a message?" Harding speculated.
"But why was he in here? You can see the whole room from the

corridor. He could tell we were out."

MC opened the only cupboard in the room. "Our papers are still here. But they are not in the same order that I left them. Look..." MC held out a few sheets of names provided by Scott. "...I stored them alphabetically, but these have been messed with."

"Do you think Norman was looking for something?" Harding asked. He saw Jeff nod. "What? We don't know anything. Not really."

"He doesn't know that, and keeping him guessing does us no harm. I suggest that we carry all relevant papers with us. If anyone wants a report, we can write one, but I don't want anything left in this room."

"Gotcha," said Harding.

MC said, "Roger that."

Purcell waited for them in a room on the entrance level. His tone was businesslike and nowhere near as friendly as it had been. He had lots of questions and told his Admin driver to take notes.

Jeff apologised for the nature of their departure from Z1830 but explained that they were given specific instructions from Persephone to leave the area without looking back. They could not be sure they were not being followed.

The ChiZA condemned the failure to follow protocol. Visitors were expected to be received and sent on their way by the host Administration. Jeff said nobody had told him. He was sure MC did not know that either. They both looked at Jeff's driver.

"Negative," MC said,

Purcell apologised, saying he should have arranged for Jeff to be adequately briefed.

"Talking of briefs," said Jeff. "Were the Party...Z1830 Admins okay?"

MC chortled.

Jeff thought the ChiZA wanted to laugh, but he did not.

Purcell wet his lips and said, "Yes, they are fine. The only injury is to their pride. They suffered a significant loss of dignity by being stripped of their trousers and underpants. Their ChiZA is livid that they were captured, but he was even more angry at you for leaving before you could be debriefed."

When Jeff commented that the Z1830 Admins had been debriefed enough for all of them, he and MC burst out laughing.

Purcell slammed a fist onto the table and reminded them this was a grave matter. Persephone and her supporters were rebels and terrorists, acting against the State by effectively declaring independence. The Army and the Admins stood ready to take back control of the area, but were fearful of the loss of civilian life. They needed to know more about Persephone's capability to formulate a plan to oust her. To this end, Purcell proposed that Jeff and MC return to Z1830 to answer questions.

Jeff dismissed that suggestion with a wave of his hand. "You've got to be joking. They risked our lives by insisting we were accompanied when I had agreed it would be MC and me. They didn't give a damn about our safety or the reason for our visit, which, as you will recall…" He pointed at Purcell, "…was to gather information that might help us discover who killed two people. Had I known that you…" he pointed at the ChiZA again, "…only agreed to let us go there to get information that might lead to bloodshed. I would not have gone."

"Me neither," MC added.

Purcell looked flummoxed but unrepentant. "I agreed no such thing."

"Well, they obviously thought you did and saw us as an opportunity to get intel on Persephone."

"I would have thought a man with your experience and intelligence would have realised the opportunities…"

"That role was never mentioned. Had it been, I would not have agreed to do it. I accepted the task of trying to identify the Judge's killer, and you permitted me to investigate how and where I chose. I did not sign up to be an Admin spy. If that's what you expect, you can stick the job…"

"Not this again." He saw Jeff was not about to back down. "Okay, okay, can we calm down and start again?"

"You started it," Jeff snapped.

"He's right, you did," MC confirmed.

Purcell did a double-take as his attention moved from Jeff to MC. "I fear you are reading too much into the request to meet the Z1830 Admins. They only want to ask you a few questions about Persephone. What she looks like? Whether her gang is well-armed? How many of them there are? Where is their base? That sort of thing. You would only be with them for a day or so."

"I won't be there for five minutes because I am not going," Jeff insisted.

"Nor me," MC said.

Jeff spoke again. "Tell them to either ring me or send someone down here to ask their questions. We have nothing to hide, but I have no intention of visiting them. For your information, please feel free to pass this on. We could not see Persephone's features as she always wore her hat, glasses, and mask. Isn't that right, MC?"

"It is."

"We were bundled into the back of a van and taken to God knows where, so we have no idea where their base is. Do we MC?"

"No."

"We only encountered about a dozen armed personnel, so we cannot gauge how many foot soldiers there might be."

Purcell nodded slowly, absorbing what he had heard.

Jeff calmed, "I did not mean to lose my temper with you, but the actions of the Admins put our lives at risk, so please forgive me if I do not trust them. We were granted free passage to Lytham, but then we got involved in a gunfight outside Preston."

"A gunfight?" Purcell looked horrified. "Nobody mentioned a gunfight."

"The other Admins would probably prefer to forget that fact, as they got captured and locked up while masked gunmen took us away. The Party Zone Admins put us in danger by drawing first. You can understand why I am reluctant to return."

"Me too," MC said, coughing, struggling not to laugh.

"I understand," Purcell clasped his hands. "In that case, I will tell my counterpart to send someone here if they wish to question you. I will sit in on that discussion."

"Thank you," Jeff said, "is that it?"

"I would like to hear what Persephone told you about Dixon. Did you learn much?"

Jeff prepared to sit but turned to MC before doing so. "If you want to go and grab a cup of tea, I can update ChiZA Purcell. You must be shattered after all that driving."

MC left the room.

Jeff revealed what he knew and how he believed the Judge's death was linked to one of the projects. He needed to know more about what the Judge was investigating and wanted more information on the discussions with prisoners.

Purcell said he was awaiting a response from Lord Wilson and would chase his office. He asked if Jeff still wanted to visit the Wrexham PHC, which would mean a return to Z1830. Jeff thought he might try to speak to the prisoners by telephone.

The ChiZA offered an alternative. When he eventually spoke to Lord Wilson, and he was confident he would, he would request that the Judge's papers be made available to Jeff, possibly in a locked room. Jeff would not be able to copy or remove any of the documents. Jeff welcomed this proposal and did not mind the prospect of a visit to London.

As Purcell prepared to leave, Jeff said he had one last issue he wanted to discuss privately. Purcell's Admin was instructed to leave.

"I think the only reason we are still alive and unharmed is that Persephone recognised MC's name."

Purcell had not expected to hear that. "Really? Do you think Persephone is ex-military?"

"I doubt it, but she suggested that some members of her gang are. MC appears to be a legend among them. Something about heroic deeds. Do you know what that's about?"

"Have you asked MC?"

"No. I tried to discuss MC's service record, but didn't learn much. The look on MC's face left me in no doubt about the response I'd get. There was a distinct reluctance to discuss it with Persephone. All I know is that there was a massacre in Berlin."

Purcell thought that might be the case. His version of the story was almost the same as Persephone's. MC was the lead British officer during manoeuvres with NATO allies in Germany. The exercise had gone very well, and to celebrate, the senior officers arranged to have a farewell get-together at a bar on the outskirts of town. They were attacked by militants running at them from all sides. The gang was shooting and screaming. The bullets splayed everywhere, hitting a few of the soldiers who sat with their backs to the road. The surviving soldiers were unarmed and scattered and ran. MC stayed, grabbed one of the attackers, took his gun and then used that to kill him and others, collecting their weapons as they fell. The other soldiers saw what was happening and returned, taking the guns offered by MC and using them against the enemy. MC's bravery saved the lives of many senior officers that day. Thirty terrorists were killed, primarily youths aged between fifteen and twenty, including two who worked at the restaurant.

"Incredible. Did MC get a medal, the VC or anything? Does MC stand for Military Cross?"

"I have no idea what MC stands for. We are too scared to ask. Medals were offered but declined. There were also medal offers from other countries, but they were refused too."

"Why did MC do that? If there was justification for recognition, then that was it. They gave me one for solving crimes, but I never had to put my life at risk. I never saved the lives of any of my colleagues."

"MC refuses praise for doing the job expected. It never gets mentioned."

"Do you think there might be some PTSD?"

Purcell nodded. "I'm sure of it, but I'm no expert. MC was offered counselling, but…"

"I can imagine. What happened afterwards?"

"As far as the incident is concerned, the powers that be did not want to create panic, so they reduced the number of terrorists and attributed the attack to ill-prepared anti-NATO campaigners. It quickly got hushed over."

"What about MC?"

"Became a legend, moved to a desk job for a while, but was then asked to retire."

"Why?"

"MC had become convinced that the military was in a no-win situation and their actions were pointless. How can you win against an enemy that does not fear death? MC emerged as a very vocal advocate of talking being better than shooting. That did not go down well. It was damaging morale."

"I cannot believe MC being vocal about anything. It can be difficult to get a conversation going."

"Seems to have taken a shine to you, though."

Jeff stood. "Why would you think that?"

"From what I hear, MC hasn't referred to you as a prick or a dipshit…yet."

"You haven't heard the latest." Jeff winked at Purcell before leaving the room.

As ex-DCI Cleveland returned to the office, he spotted Norman loitering in the corridor. Jeff guessed he was eavesdropping on conversations between Harding and MC.

"Can I help you?"

Norman had not seen or heard Jeff's arrival and did not know what to say or do. "No, I'm heading to the loo, and I thought I would check if you had finished with Purcell."

"You mean ChiZA Purcell?"

"Yes, of course, um, I wondered if he fancies a cuppa."

"You know where he is. Why don't you ask him?" Jeff was about two meters away. "Don't forget to have that wee and ensure you wash your hands."

Norman pulled a face and hurried away. Regaining his composure, he whistled the same tune as earlier.

"What the hell is the name of that song?" Jeff asked, walking through the door.

Harding had not heard anything. "What song?"

"That bloody song that Norman is whistling."

MC held up the cups to see if anyone else wanted a drink. The others nodded and muttered, "Thanks."

"He only whistles it when you are around. It's an old song by Nick Lowe called 'I love the sound of breaking glass'." MC sang the tune all the way to the kitchen.

13. BROTHERLY LOVE

Jeff was delighted when Purcell rang to tell him Lord Wilson would bring the Judge's papers to Cardiff the following Monday. The Security Secretary was due to visit anyway and proposed killing two birds with one stone.

The agreement was that Jeff could read the papers without making notes, removing documents, or copying their contents.

MC's elderly stepmother had been taken poorly, and the driver needed time off. Jeff told MC to take as long as required and then called his other assistant to say he would not be in the office.

Harding suggested spending his time making informal enquiries about Jensen. Jeff warned him to be careful, but Harding dismissed his concerns. It was an excellent opportunity to rekindle his surveillance skills. He lost the knack of working undercover when he became desk sergeant.

The office of the ChiZA for the Youth Zone rang and asked a mountain of questions. Jeff gave only brief replies. He was in no mood to be helpful and, in any case, had other matters on his mind.

The rumble of a van engine broke the silence in the village. Jeff saw the neighbour's curtains twitching as he walked down his garden path to greet his visitor.

"Groover," shouted the man stepping out of the van.

"Great to see you, Rosie." Jeff hugged his brother.

"Now, what is so important that I had to drive eighty miles to see you rather than you popping on one of your beloved trains to visit us? Lowri would love to see you. She sends her love."

"Bless her. Give her my love. How the hell she puts up with you, I never know." Jeff placed an arm across his brother's shoulder and took him into the house.

"So, what is it? You sounded very circumspect on the phone. Can you sound very circumspect? Is that a thing?" His brother sat at the table.

"I know what you meant," Jeff said, making tea. "I need your help…"

"Typical. What is it this time? Have you tripped a switch or something?"

Jeff chuckled. "I'm not that bad. I still remember a little of what Dad taught me."

"Yes, I know. Mainly, if in doubt, ring Linc."

Jeff handed a mug of tea to his brother. "There's milk there." He pointed at the table.

"Why didn't you simply pour it into the cup? My God, Flissy did a good job educating you, didn't she? You'll be offering me biscuits on a plate next." Lincoln howled as Jeff did just that.

"Two things."

"This sounds serious. Go on, big brother."

"Firstly, I want you to have Dad's chair and the family tree."

Linc was speechless. His mouth dropped open as he stared at Jeff. "Seriously? Why? Don't your kids want it?"

"Nah, not since they discovered it is worthless. "Jeff chuckled again. "No, I haven't mentioned it to them yet. It should have come to you. You were always more interested in the family heritage than me."

"But you were the firstborn."

"I know, but I think you'd get more pleasure out of it." Jeff pointed toward his living room. "It's in there, but you can't have it until we've completed the second thing."

Lincoln Roosevelt Cleveland sat quietly, sipping tea and devouring dipped digestive biscuits as his brother told him why he needed help.

"Well, I can't find anything so far." Linc put the widget back in his toolbox. "Nothing suggests unusually high consumption on this side of the meter." He faced Mr Gibbons. "You are sure you haven't been using the welding equipment we saw in the garage?"

"Positive. I have not used it since my wife died. We used to create and sell metal art at the markets, but there doesn't seem to be any point these days."

"Why?" Jeff asked. "Because there is no demand?"

"No. I've lost interest and can't be bothered."

Linc said he understood. "And there are no other power points apart from those you've shown us?"

"No. You saw the one on the outside wall and the one in the garage. There are no others apart from the car charging point, but I haven't used that in years."

Jeff and Linc looked at each other. "What car charging point?" they asked at the same time.

"The one we had installed when my wife got her promotion. The dealership gave her an electric car, but we had to pay to install the charging point."

He led the brothers into the garage and moved a pile of old furniture.

"I put this stuff out here when my wife fell ill, and we had to move a bed downstairs. I am not sure whether to bin it, try to sell it or put it back."

Linc studied the coffee table. "Too good to throw out. If you don't want it, I suggest selling it."

"Take it if you like it. I owe you something for coming all this way to help me."

"You owe us nothing," Linc replied, wanting to help Gibbons move the items quicker but not wishing to appear impatient.

"There it is."

The charging unit was deep in the back corner of the garage. The light from the ceiling barely reached it, so Linc adorned his head torch.

He examined the connection. "This is not a standard issue. The supply board stuff usually has their logo and a part number on the front."

"That's because Stuey did us a favour. He did it for a fraction of the cost, and fair play to him, he checks it every year even though I never use it."

"Did he tell you why it needs checking?" Linc asked.

"To make sure nothing has gone wrong with it. He worries that the company will kick off if that connection causes a fault, so he keeps a close eye on it. I told him to take it out, but he thought I might need it at some point. In the meantime, it was doing no harm."

Linc lay on the floor and gently felt around the base of the point. "What's behind here?"

"Behind the wall, you mean?" When Linc nodded, Gibbons added. "There used to be immaculately maintained church gardens, but it's an overgrown wasteland now."

"How do you access it?"

"Why? Have you found something?"

"Err, no, I am just curious. I have always been nosey, haven't I, Jeff?"

Jeff had no idea why his brother had asked the question, but he went along with him. "Oh yes. Our father always reckoned Linc wanted to know the ins and outs of a cat's bottom."

Gibbons giggled.

Linc added, "I also like old churches. I like the architecture etcetera. I wouldn't mind taking a look while I'm in the area. If the church is still standing, that is. Down our way, they've all been flattened. They haven't been replaced with anything apart from empty land."

"The church is still there. I hear a band practising in it some nights. It's quite a modern church, not much architectural interest. The original burnt down, and they replaced it with one that had a community centre underneath. Nobody goes near it now apart from the band. They sound pretty good. The main entrance is down the road, first left and then left again. The road to the vicarage where Stuey lives is okay, but the grounds are overgrown."

"Stuey lives there, you say?" Jeff held out a hand to help his brother stand.

"Yes, him and four other electric company workers. They are

all permanent Transzers, and they get houses nobody else wants. Stuey mentioned that the vicarage costs a fortune to heat, but there are five of them, so they split the costs."
Jeff looked at his brother, whose face expressed an interest in further exploration.

The grounds were severely overgrown. Linc led the way, using a thick stick to sweep aside the bramble and long grass. Eventually, they reached the boundary of Gibbons' property. A line of rubble and chippings, mostly hidden by weeds, led away from the rear of the garage and across the wasteland.
"Someone has created an improvised channel."
"Is that for a new supply line?" Jeff asked.
Linc nodded. "It looks like one. Let's see where it goes." Linc carved a new path and followed the stones to the church. "I thought this would lead us to the vicarage."
"Why did you think that?" Jeff removed a bramble branch from his trouser leg.
"Gibbons mentioned Stuey telling him how expensive the place is to heat. I thought he might have tapped into Gibbons' supply." He pointed at the building. "But it stops here." A cable emerged from the stones and ran up the church wall for a couple of feet. Linc surveyed the grounds. "It doesn't look like anyone else is about. Shall we investigate?"
The church door was unlocked. Inside, they found only a variety of musical instruments, many linked to amplifiers. Linc scuttled about, nipping outside and then in and around the back of old pews that lined the walls. "The electricity to power the instruments comes from the main line. You can trace the cables. I am not sure where the other supply goes." He stood at the altar. "I am guessing this area is about three feet higher than the ground outside, so the supply probably goes into whatever is underneath."
"Would there be a crypt in a church like this? It is not that old."
"I doubt it. Gibbons told us there used to be a community centre underneath.

They walked the perimeter and, on two sides, found windows at ground level that had been blacked out.

At the rear of the building, there was an entrance to the basement door. Jeff recognised an odour.

Linc persuaded the door to open, and the brothers walked down a few steps to a narrow corridor crammed full of movable coat stands and chairs gathering dust. They eventually found a second door.

The smell was much more pungent here. Jeff turned the metal handle, saw the glow of heat lamps perched above cannabis plants, and heard the buzz of extractor fans.

"That's where Mr Gibbons' power is going," Linc suggested.

Jeff could barely believe the scene. "They haven't left much space to get between the trays."

"Perhaps they don't need to because they are small people. Maybe they are Oompa Loompas?" Linc suggested.

"Willy Wonka's cannabis emporium. I don't remember reading that sequel to the kids when they were little."

Linc jumped as the door swung open. An out-of-breath Stuey stood staring at the pair. He looked more frightened and anxious than the interlopers. His voice shook. "Can I help you? You do realise that this is private land."

Linc spoke to Stuey. "You have an alarm on the door."

"We do."

"I should have looked for that."

Jeff ran a palm over his mouth. "That would never have happened back in the day."

Stuey recognised the visitor. "Mr Cleveland. What do you want?"

"This is my brother, Linc. He is an electrical engineer, and I asked for his help investigating why Mr Gibbons uses so much energy. It looks like we now know."

Stuey looked from one Cleveland to the other. The resemblance was unmistakable. "It's nice to see you again, and it is a pleasure to meet you." He waved at Linc.

"This is quite an operation," Linc swept an arm. "All this

product and no overheads. Nobody is ever going to search an old church. It's far enough away so no one notices the smell. Nice spot."

"We think so," Stuey replied.

"Can we talk outside? I fear this aroma will get me high." Jeff covered his nose and mouth.

Stuey led them into the open air, closing all the doors behind him. "My little secret is out."

"Not so little. You've cost Mr Gibbons a fortune."

"I regret that. It was only intended to be temporary while we arranged for the church to be reconnected to the mains. Now that we have, I'll disconnect him. I'll do it next week."

"I think he needs to be reimbursed for his role in establishing this cottage industry," Jeff suggested.

"Okay, I'll slip him a few quid."

Linc pursed his lips. "It will take a bit more than a few quid. Those lights use a lot of power. Take it out of your profits."

"We don't make that much. We have other overheads." Stuey pointed to the front door. "That'll need a new lock."

"Don't give me that. You must be raking in a fortune with that amount of stuff."

Jeff nodded. "I didn't think there would be much demand for this. I heard there were stacks of Committee-approved stuff on the market. Who buys it?"

Stuey stuffed his hands deeper into his jeans pockets as he explained that their cannabis was not used for recreational purposes. It helped supply a local, small pharmaceutical company that sold Cannabidiol (CBD)-based products at affordable prices. Most raw materials for CBD goods were provided by Admin-sponsored producers who kept supply low and cost high, making CBD products too expensive for the average citizen.

Stuey became involved because his Aunt needed CBD oil to help her cope with her anxiety. The finished products were more affordable because they supplied the raw materials at cheaper prices than the Admins.

"A right little Robin Hood," Linc suggested.

Stuey bit into his top lip.

"But I bet you make something out of it?"

"There are five of us who manage the production. We share any profits, plus my aunt doesn't have to pay for her medicine."

Jeff had another question. "How do you get this to the pharmacists without the Admins knowing? I presume they know nothing about this?"

"No. If anyone learned about this, the Admins would take over the operation and sell it to the bigger companies. We try to keep it very hush-hush. We harvest, pack it and take turns delivering it. Nobody suspects an electricity supply van entering a factory."

Linc knew this to be true. "And I imagine you get paid cash to keep it off the books."

Stuey nodded. "Yes, we get paid per kilo."

"It must be quite lucrative," Linc suggested. "That watch, jeans, and trainers are not cheap."

"I see where you are going with this. How much do you want?"

"Us?" Jeff looked at his brother and back at Stuey. "We don't want anything, but Mr Gibbons deserves a share, especially as he has contributed so much to production."

Linc added. "You can give him a cash refund every month. Tell him you've managed to trace the problem but can't work out how much he has been overcharged, so the company would like to offer him…we'll agree on an amount, and you pay him in cash to avoid VAT and the like."

Jeff was impressed. "You've done this before."

"I used to have contracts with the supply company. You'd be surprised how many things get swept under the carpet."

"And that's it? You only want me to reimburse Mr Gibbons? You won't tell the Admins?"

"I have no interest in lining their pockets. Make sure you give Mr Gibbons what he is due."

The three agreed on a monthly payment, and Linc promised to check with Mr Gibbons to ensure the arrangement was maintained. He warned Stuey that if they had any problems, Jeff would tell his Admin pals, who would probably book him in for an extended holiday on the Isle of Wight.

"What's happened to you?"

Jeff was confused by the question. "What do you mean?"

"My big brother would never have accepted an arrangement like that. He would have wanted to close the site and report it to the authorities.

Jeff looked out the van window. They were nearly at his home. "Things change, and I suppose I have changed with them. My first thought was to shut it all down, but who would that help? Certainly not people like Stuey's aunt."

Are you telling me you believed all that bullshit?"

"I did. Stuey strikes me as a fine, upstanding young man."

"Who rips off older people?"

"He tried to rip off one older person. There are plenty of others who love him. He knows he's been nabbed, and he will learn from it. Mr Gibbons will get a refund, and anything that stops the Admins getting a cut is worth doing in my book."

"Working with them hasn't enhanced your view of the Admins, then?"

"Not one iota. A few are okay, but the majority are corrupt. They make my blood boil. I wish I'd never taken this case."

"How is it going?"

"Not brilliantly. I have no body, fingerprints, forensics, suspects, or motives...I have nothing at all apart from speculation. I cannot even travel to the murder scene without permission. Even then, I have to be accompanied and the local Admins get pissed off that I'm there." He didn't mention the shooting.

"You'll sort it."

"I'm not so sure. I am walking on eggshells, trying not to upset anyone. I annoyed an Admin the other week, and he put a brick through my greenhouse."

"Bastard. Glass is expensive."

"So I discovered."

"Did you report it?"

"No point. I have no real proof. I can't imagine the Admins would take any action even if I did. I'm better off saying nothing and learning my lesson."

"What you really mean is you are going to bide your time until an opportunity for revenge, or justice, as you'd call it, presents itself."

"Exactly."

"You never could let anything go."

"Anyway, enough about me. You haven't mentioned how Lowri is responding to treatment?"

"She's doing well. She'll never be as mobile as she was, but she's accepted that."

"Glad to hear it. Are Jimmy and Nancy moving down to help you with caring duties?"

"I'm still waiting for a reply from the Admins. I've tried convincing them that having my son and daughter-in-law around would be mutually beneficial. We'd get the help we need, and as Jimmy is a qualified electrician, he could take on jobs. There is a shortage of sparkies in my area. I could take on twice the work if I had support. They don't seem interested."

"Have you offered money?"

"Knowing my luck, I'd try to tempt the only honest Admin in the zone and get whisked off to the Isle of Wight."

A delivery van with a 'BV Fresh Fish' logo had parked in front of his house. Jeff's heart sank.

"Who is this? What do they want?" He knew Linc would have no idea, but he felt a need to say something. He feared he was about to get a message from Persephone. Jeff left Linc in his van while he went to see the van driver.

The man stood at Jeff's front door. He had a huge polystyrene container at his feet.

Jeff spoke from a few yards away. "Can I help you?"

"Depends on who you are."

Jeff told him his name and showed his identity card.

"This is for you. It's off a mutual friend." The driver tapped the side of his nose and winked.

"But I haven't ordered anything."

"I know, but our mutual friend wants you to have this as a token of appreciation. I am to tell you that your efforts in discovering who murdered our other friend are greatly appreciated. You mentioned that you don't get fresh fish. You do now, and there's plenty more where this came from."

Jeff had a hand on his chin. "But how much is in there? Is that box full?" The driver nodded. "I can't eat all that."

"Our mutual friend thought as much, but still wants you to have it. It's no problem if you give some to your neighbours."

Linc's curiosity had gotten the better of him, and he joined his brother.

The man pointed at the new arrival. "Give some to him. He looks malnourished."

"Cheeky bugger," Linc said.

"Only trying to get you free fish." The driver returned his attention to Jeff. "You can give it to the pub if you like, but there is a condition. If you dispose of any to a business, there must be some community benefit. If you sell it, then you must contribute to a local charity. Our friend has friends everywhere, remember." Another tap on his nose. "Right, I'd better be off. Nice to meet you, Mr Cleveland. Enjoy your fish, and I'll see you again soon."

Jeff and Linc emptied the contents onto his kitchen table.

"It'll take me years to eat all that," Jeff said.

"I'll take some off your hands." Linc picked up a bag. "Lowri is quite partial to a bit of smoked haddock."

"Take what you want."

"I'll have to visit more often. I get a chair, a family tree and free fish. It was worth coming."

Linc was on his way home after helping to store the fish.

Jeff made one last sweep of his garden and spotted a strange package inside the greenhouse. Initially fearful that Norman and his friends had left him another message, he examined the item without picking it up, taking great care to avoid any booby traps.

The package had been covered in a blanket with a typed note taped to one corner. It read -

> "Salutations. Here is the replacement glass you requested. It is bullet - and brick-proof, so you shouldn't have any further problems. If you do, then you know where I am. I have included a couple of spare panes to be on the safe side."

14. REUNIONS

The white shirt was as pristine as ever, although larger, with more body fat to cover. The cufflinks were gold and rectangular, each with a small red diamond in the centre. The right arm extended across the table before the hand pointed to a chair.

Jeff sat down.

"You didn't take long."

"Once I found what I needed, the trail was easy to follow."

"Did you find anything interesting?" Lord Wilson rested his chin on interlocked hands.

"The same as you did, I imagine. You could have saved me time by telling me what was in the journals."

"I wanted to reassure you that I am being open."

An Admin delivered tea and Welsh cakes.

"Thank you. ChiZA Purcell raves about these. I am looking forward to trying one. You can leave it there. We will help ourselves."

The Admin placed the tray on the table and left the room.

Jeff's journey to Cardiff followed the same route and encountered the same issues as his previous trip. However, his final destination was slightly different this time.

On arrival, he again entered the red brick building but was taken down a corridor and up flights of stairs until he entered a glass tunnel leading to a smaller lift than before.

Exiting the elevator, Jeff saw several armed security guards waiting outside glass-fronted meeting rooms. He was directed into the smallest room, and the Admin switched on the light before closing the vertical blinds, assuring Jeff he would be outside should he need anything and that nobody would enter without Jeff's permission.

Jeff was left to explore the contents of cardboard boxes and told he could take as much time as needed. Ninety minutes later, Jeff had seen enough and was taken to meet his old boss, who waited in a large chamber. Once again, armed guards patrolled the perimeter.

"What is this place?" Jeff chose a cake.

"It was the debating chamber for the Welsh Parliament. It is a lovely building. We often hold Committee meetings here when we fancy leaving London."

Jeff nodded as he ate. Having swallowed, he started to say something, but Wilson held a finger over his lips.

"Carling."

An Admin appeared and stood in front of the Committee Secretary. "Yes, sir."

Jeff read the letters 'CCAS' on the woman's shoulders as he ate more cake. He assumed that was Central Committee Admin Support, but his mouth was too full to ask.

"Ensure we are not disturbed, and tell your team to sweep the corridors regularly. I don't want any snoopers," Wilson instructed.

"Yes, sir."

Carling shouted at the armed guards, waved an arm in a circular motion and pointed at the main entrance. They all headed in the same direction.

"Sorry about that, but walls have ears."

Jeff sipped his tea. It was a cut above any other variety he had drunk in recent years. He savoured the taste. "Who else has read those papers?"

"Only you and I. Let's keep it that way. They are stored securely; other than me, only Carling knows where."

"Do your Committee colleagues know the journals exist?"

"They know we recovered papers from Kendal's office, but not what they contain. I told them they were not much use. I released a couple of earlier editions containing no specific times, dates, and places to reassure them after ensuring the text was brief, lacked detail, and did not mention names. As far as my fellow committee members are concerned, the journals are rubbish, and I plan to destroy them."

"What will you do with them, more importantly, the information in them?"

Wilson placed his cup on the saucer and leaned forward. "That's what I wanted to speak to you about. Do you have any suggestions?"

Jeff's lips tightened. "It's a tricky one. How do you tell the Secretary-General, the most powerful man in this country, that the Judge was convinced his son, who happens to be the Chief Zonal Administrator for Z1830, is a rapist, people trafficker, drug smuggler, bootlegger, murderer…"

"Let's just say he is not a good man." Wilson rested his elbows on the arms of his chair, brought his hands together, and extended his index fingers over his lips.

"If word of Brogan's excesses got out, there would be riots," Jeff said.

"Why do you think that?"

"Because if I were a parent with a child in that zone, I would be up in arms after hearing what Brogan has done."

Wilson waved away Jeff's concern. "The vast majority of children…sorry youths entering Zone 1830 are perfectly safe."

"Define safe."

"What do you mean?"

"Youngsters today are brought up in Shangri-La. They are fed, watered, clothed, and taught to behave like perfect citizens."

"What is wrong with that?"

"Nothing, but when they reach eighteen, they are moved to an area that is far from perfect. They get dumped in regions controlled by gangs. They are lambs being fed to the lions. To make matters worse, the very people appointed to protect them are the worst abusers of all."

Wilson smoothed his hair. "People like Brogan Junior are in the minority."

"But he and his friends are untouchable. I now understand why Persephone is keen to keep the admins out of her zone."

"How was your visit to Persephonia?" Wilson leaned forward again. "Don't believe all the stories about it being Utopia. Residents of that zone are repressed, and their every movement is controlled."

"Have you been there?"

"I don't need to visit to know how bad things are."

"You would be shocked. From what I saw, the residents of that region moved there voluntarily and are happy to stay. They appear well fed, safe, and well-treated."

"She is hardly likely to let you see the real picture, is she? You were a PR exercise."

"I can only say it as I saw it."

Wilson shifted his bottom until he sat upright. "We are not here to discuss Persephone, although I am disappointed you were taken in. I find it hard to believe you could be so gullible."

Jeff offered no comment.

Wilson smoothed the leg of his trousers. "Coming back to Brogan, you can see my dilemma."

"I can, but I have a question. If you knew about these journals, why did you ask me to investigate the death, knowing I would hit a brick wall?"

"At the time, I didn't know what the journals contained. I sent my team to collect papers relating to Kendal's investigations and was amazed to discover how much he had written. I had already decided we needed to start an investigation into his murder while the trail was hot. I told Purcell to contact you. You were the first name on a long list."

A thought had occurred to Jeff while Wilson spoke, but he lost it. He asked a different question. "Why me?"

"I know your methods. You are thorough and committed and cannot be bought. You have all the necessary attributes to undertake a task of this magnitude."

"It is nice to know that I was the first choice, but if you knew my methods so well, you would know I like to see all the evidence."

"You've seen all there is to see."

"Not really. You let the body be burned and go to a landfill."

"I am not sure what good keeping it would have done. I doubt you would have found anything. We have no forensics teams or labs any longer. There was no point in delaying matters."

"We might have found something on his clothes, in his hair…"

"And you might not have. Look, Jeff, there is no point in crying over spilt milk."

Jeff resisted saying what was on his mind and replied, "The Judge believed Brogan was involved in the death of his great-grandchild. That might give Eddie a reason to shut him up. That makes him a suspect, but we cannot take this any further without annoying his dear old dad."

"We may have a name, but we cannot call him a suspect. There is no evidence to support the theory that Brogan killed Kendal. He was attending a charity event on the night of the murder and was seen by over a hundred guests."

"He might not have committed the murder, but could have sanctioned it."

"How could he have known what Kendal was investigating?"

"Word probably reached him from the other prisoners. Gossip spreads quickly. He might not have known about the journals, but he could have heard something about the Judge's interest in his extracurricular activities."

Wilson rested his intertwined fingers on his stomach. "It's possible, but he doesn't know what is in the books."

"No, although he will now know I was brought here to read them. Your Admins might be loyal and trustworthy, but from my experience, most of the others are corrupt…"

"That's a bit harsh."

"Doesn't stop it being true. Word will get back to Brogan."

"Not from my team. In any case, he won't be able to do anything about it. He can't exactly tell his father what a naughty boy he's been and how Kendal found out."

"Accepted, but my involvement puts me and my family at risk."

Wilson hadn't followed Jeff's train of thought. "How?"

"Brogan has been relaxed and confident, believing there is

nothing to link him to the murder of the Judge. The only person who potentially knew what the investigation had uncovered had been killed. Now, he discovers that there are records and that I have seen them. That puts me and mine at risk."

"That's a little melodramatic, don't you think?"

"Not really. If Brogan becomes fearful, he might decide to act. He might have already silenced one possible witness."

"We have no evidence linking him to Kendal's murder."

"I am not talking about the Judge."

"Then who are you talking about?"

"His Lordship helped secure the release of a lad named Arthur Dixon, whose father had been interviewed by the Judge and provided extensive detail on Brogan's activities."

"Dixon? I think Kendal mentioned him. Why is he important?"

"He was murdered in the same way as the Judge."

Wilson shot forward. "When? How?"

"Around the same time as His Lordship. He was kneecapped and left to die at his bedsit in Hyde."

"I was not told." Wilson's hand covered his mouth. "You believe these events are related?"

"Two murders, same MO, murders occurred around the same time. The only link appears to be the Judge. What would you think?"

"Did Arthur know anything of the Judge's findings?"

"I have no idea, but the suggestion that Arthur's father had collaborated with the Judge could have been enough for Brogan to send a message."

"A pretty strong message."

"Yes, and I may be getting a message soon. Brogan will not welcome me snooping in the Judge's footsteps."

"Shit." Wilson stood and walked around. "We need to prepare a good cover story, get the word out that you were here to look at papers from the Judge's office after nagging me to see them, but they were worthless. You wasted your time." He lost himself in thought. "We can say that the papers are confidential, so they are not for general release yet, but concern Kendal's authorised duties." He rubbed his neck. "That'll work. You didn't spend that long in the room, which can be used as evidence that you thought it was a waste of time. What do you think?"

"It might work."

"Yes, I think it will. I'll get on to it right away. I'll have Carling let something slip to the local Admins. She can complain about a wasted journey and a day out of her life she'll never get back." Jeff was quietly impressed by his ex-boss's improvisation. "That still leaves us with the problem of what to do with the evidence."

"It buys us time. I am sure you will think of something."

"Cheers for that." Jeff stood to stretch his legs. "You say Brogan Junior was at a charity event with a hundred people."

"He was. It was a fundraiser for the Party Zones' Games occurring across his zone next year."

"Is there any way he could have sneaked off early?"

Wilson's mouth distorted as he considered this. "It's possible, but the event took place in Nottingham. He would have needed a helicopter or a 'plane to get from there to Bournemouth and back in one night. They are not easy to obtain."

"Do we know where he was the following morning?"

"I don't."

"Well, he could have taken his time getting back." Jeff gently tapped an index finger against his chin as he processed the information. "We don't know the exact time of death, only that Amelia found the body shortly after eight."

"So, I understand."

"What if Brogan…"

"If it is Brogan."

"What if the killer arrived early in the morning and was completing the deed when Amelia arrived?"

"And left without being seen?"

"It's possible. We need to know when the function ended and where Brogan went afterwards."

"That will not be an easy conversation."

"It's impossible to have without raising alarms," Jeff admitted.

"Let's park that thought for a moment. Are we in agreement that Brogan's attendance at the event did not necessarily stop him from making the journey to Bournemouth?"

"We are."

"In that case, I'll double-check the names of all those passing through the borders on Sunday night and Monday morning."

"I thought Purcell had provided that information?"

"He has given me a list of names, but, as far as I know, nobody has checked with the people concerned to see if they actually crossed zones at that time.

Wilson momentarily looked bewildered but then understood. "You think somebody might have used their names or passes to gain access?"

Jeff resisted making a sarcastic comment. He remembered the question he wanted to ask earlier: "How did you know there were papers and journals, and where to find them?"

"Kendal told me. He gave me the location of his safe and the combination."

"Was he fearful of being attacked?"

Wilson rubbed his chin, considered his response, and said, "I don't see any harm in telling you now. If you must know, Kendal didn't have long to live. He had an inoperable stomach tumour, and he knew his time was coming to an end."

This tied in with what Jeff heard about the Judge's eating habits from Amelia and Millie. "The bastards tortured a dying man."

Wilson nodded.

"Arthur was also dying. He had mesothelioma. That's why the Judge helped to get him released."

"Poor bugger, but is the connection relevant?"

"It might explain the timing." Jeff realised Wilson had not made the connection. "If the killers discovered that neither the Judge nor Arthur had long left, then that might have forced their hand. They had to discover what the pair knew and who they had spoken to before it was too late." Another thought went through Jeff's mind. "Did your team tidy up the Judge's office?"

"No, I don't think so. They were only there to collect the journals and didn't stay very long. Why is that relevant?"

"Because there was no mess."

"The local Admins might have cleaned up."

"They didn't. I asked them." Jeff's fingers massaged his eyes. "This is all very weird. The Judge was tortured but had been bagged…"

"Bagged? He had a bag on his head? How did you learn that? Nobody told me."

"One of the Admins who found the body mentioned it. The question is, why would they do that? If they tortured him, they would have to keep taking off the bag to ask him questions. Why torture a frail old man? Why not just look for the information they needed?" Jeff pulled at his lower lip. "Perhaps they searched and happened to be the tidiest killers ever."

Wilson rubbed his temples. "Maybe they thought Kendal had kept it all up here. Perhaps he told them something, but then he died, and they panicked and ran off."

"It's possible," Jeff had considered the same situation. "We will never know for sure. They might have got what they needed from the Judge and Arthur and then put them out of their misery. They killed them to keep them quiet and to leave a message for others. They might have had second thoughts, which explains the use of Pulp."

"What Pulp?"

"We found traces of the drug Pulp on the floor in the Judge's bedroom and Arthur's living room."

"You think the killers administered drugs to ease their victims' pain? That's bizarre. Who would do that?"

"The most caring assailants I ever encountered."

The pair discussed further possibilities until Carling returned, advising that it was time to depart for Wilson's next appointment.

"It's been a pleasure seeing you again." Wilson shook Jeff's hand.

"Likewise. I hope I can get the result you want."

"If anyone can…"

Jeff walked to the door.

"Oh, Jeff," Wilson saw his ex-colleague turn. "I meant to say, if you hear anything about a robbery at Maynard's Glass Works, can you let me know?"

Jeff swallowed hard. "Maynard's? Isn't that on the Gosport Road?"

"It is. They had a break-in, and the thieves got away with some costly, reinforced glass. It was a prototype for use in armoured vehicles. Sam Maynard is worried that it might get into the hands of a competitor. He is very well connected, and questions were raised at Committee."

"Would you like me to investigate?"

"Only if you hear something or if you have the time. It has been reported to the Admins, but I don't hold much hope. Your priority has to be catching Kendal's killer."

"Of course. If I hear anything, I will let you know."

"Thanks, Jeff. I appreciate it."

Jeff left the room wondering whether his ex-superior knew more than he let on, but was pleased he and Pat had installed Otice's gift the previous evening.

Jeff rang Purcell and then updated Harding and MC on his activities that day. He repeated that his visit to Cardiff had been a complete waste of time. The papers revealed nothing. Purcell was grateful to be kept in the loop.

Harding had no idea where this left their investigations. Jeff asked him to double-check the list of people entering Z80+ and confirm they had made the trip. MC, who was not in a chatty mood, grunted. They agreed on a meeting time for the following day.

Jeff relaxed in his usual chair. There had to be a way to get at Brogan, but how? Brogan senior would undoubtedly shut down any official enquiries into his son. He had enough power and influence to ensure the case was closed. If Brogan Junior was as bad as the evidence suggested, and Jeff had not been impressed when they met many years previously, then retaliation would not be far away.

Jeff was considering options for dealing with Brogan when his thoughts were disturbed by the doorbell.

An Administrator stood on the step. Jeff recognised the badge of a Senior Administrator from the East Region of his zone. The visitor had long hair tied in a ponytail, a beard, and glasses. The strap of a leather satchel hung across his chest.

"Can I help you?"

"It's me, McCallum. Can I come in? We need to talk, but…" he surveyed the world beyond Jeff's front garden. "…not out here if you don't mind."

Jeff opened the door a little wider and studied the man. He recognised the voice but not the face. If it was McCallum, he looked different, with multiple scars around his eyes, cheeks and nose. "McCallum? What is your Christian name? Tell me your number."

The visitor chuckled before giving his name and number. He also recounted the last time they had spoken.

Jeff did not want to be reminded of their last meeting. McCallum was being investigated for allegations that he had planted evidence that had resulted in the arrest of one Edward Charles Brogan. At the time, McCallum was a young PC employed to maintain security outside Brogan's house while it was searched. Brogan had been accused of sexual assault and grievous bodily harm. He denied all charges despite overwhelming evidence. His defence maintained that the items that incriminated their client had been placed there by police officers. McCallum did not get a chance to clear his name. The Shift hit, the planet fell apart, and everything changed. That was the same day Jeff last spoke to Flissy. The day he thought his world would end.

"Yes, come on in."

Jeff ushered his ex-colleague into the living room and offered him a drink. McCallum asked for water but agreed to join Jeff in having something stronger.

"How long have you been an Admin?" Jeff asked as he handed him a whisky.

"I'm not." Connor McCallum pulled the front of his shirt. "I find it easier to get around wearing this. Nobody tends to bother me."

Jeff pointed at the epaulettes. "Did you choose that region because it is far from here, making it unlikely anyone would recognise you?"

"You are still as sharp as a pin." McCallum gave a wry smile. "I have several options to choose from."

Jeff did not doubt it. "What do you do these days?"

"Why do you want to know?"

The abrupt reply was out of character. "Sorry. I'm making conversation. Isn't this what people do when they meet people they haven't seen for ages? Ask questions."

"Why are you so interested suddenly? You didn't give a shit about me when I could have used your help."

Jeff felt hurt but knew the comment was valid. "Yes…I am very sorry about that, but I was in a bad place…"

"Not as bad as where I found myself. You hung me out to dry."

Jeff nodded slowly. "I never meant to. After Flis…my wife died, my life fell apart in more ways than one. I was assured your case had gone away. It was only much later that I found out what had happened. I am so sorry."

Connor sipped the liquid. "It did go away for a while, but then they hit me with a multitude of charges, all of which were complete bullshit. I could have done with you or someone like you in my corner."

"Didn't anyone help? Wilson?"

"He turned up at one of the so-called hearings, spoke for a while about my exemplary record, but wouldn't reply to questions from my solicitor. He was as much use as a chocolate teapot."

"Wilson or your solicitor?"

"Both."

"I am not sure what I can say. Apart from sorry."

"We can't change things now, but I was staggered when you completely ignored my messages."

Jeff had no response. He remembered the McCallum of old. A naïve, gentle young man. This reincarnation seemed much harder, sounded more cynical, and had an edge to his tone. Jeff could imagine the new McCallum planting evidence. He eventually said, "I rarely spoke to anyone other than my children for a long time. I was a mess."

"I survived. To answer your question, one of my jobs is to undertake private investigations. I help people trace missing family members and friends."

The atmosphere improved slightly, and Jeff seized the opportunity to change tack. "Is there much demand?"

"You'd be surprised. Most of my clients are wealthy and are prepared to pay for what they want. Several high-profile people have used my services in recent months. Obviously, I can't disclose any details due to client confidentiality." He sipped the whisky and put the glass on the side table.

"I understand."

"Besides being a PI, I am a freelance writer for several newspapers." Jeff looked impressed. "Do you read 'The Weasel' column in your weekly rag?"

Jeff rarely read the feature. It primarily provided titbits of scandal involving the rich and almost famous. That was of no interest to him. "I've seen it."

McCallum held out his hands.

"That's you?" He nodded in appreciation. "Does it pay well?"

"It's okay. I do similar columns for newspapers in other zones. It helps to fill the coffers. I also undertake building and gardening work during the summer months."

"You are making me feel very lazy. I tend to do sod all, and even that knackers me out." Jeff recalled details about the ex-constable's old life. "You used to do carpentry. Is that still an interest?"

Connor nodded. "It is, and I also have the qualifications for plumbing. Next month, I should qualify in basic electrics."

"I am impressed."

"It's not impressive, but you know what they say - we must adapt to survive."

That phrase again. "Where are you living these days?"

"Here and there." McCallum did not believe that would be a good enough answer and added, "I'd rather not say because I don't want to make things awkward for you."

"How could you make things awkward for me?"

"I have information you need to know, but you cannot say how you got it. I do not want anyone to visit me to ask how I came by it."

Jeff removed his glasses and scratched his nose. "What information?"

Connor ran his tongue over his top lip, "Eddie Brogan knows you have seen the Judge's personal papers. He is desperate to know what you've discovered."

"How the hell…"

McCallum explained he had taken a job which resulted in a visit to the University region of the Party Zone. He was employed to trace the daughter of an industrialist who hadn't visited her father as arranged. McCallum feared the girl's absence was due to ChiZA Brogan. After making discreet enquiries, McCallum found the girl safe and well. She had received a better offer and attended a week of parties in Harrogate. His client was impressed at the speed of McCallum's investigation, but far from happy with his daughter's actions.

Before discovering the truth, McCallum had met a contact at the University and asked if Brogan might be responsible for the girl's disappearance. The man had dismissed the notion. He doubted that the new Brogan would get involved in such matters. He was a changed man. Eddie was working hard to clean up his act and had started schemes to improve the lives of citizens in his zone. There were rumours that he would soon join his father on the Central Committee. The Secretary for Employment was retiring.

"Good for him. What does this have to do with my investigation?"

"Because my contact rang me yesterday to tell me Brogan is obsessed with your probe into the Judge's murder and what you might learn from reading His Lordship's papers. He said Brogan knows you were visiting Cardiff today to meet with Lord Wilson. Brogan is desperate to learn what you discussed."

"He is very well-informed." Jeff was still not sure of McCallum's motives and proceeded with caution. "As it happens, I did meet with Wilson today and was given access to confidential papers. Sadly, they told me nothing that would help identify the Judge's killers."

"Thanks for telling me that. I don't care what you discovered. I just wanted you to know that you are on Brogan's radar, and that can be a dangerous place to be. The man is a sociopath who thinks he has a divine right to do what he wants. Heaven help anyone who crosses him."

"Noted. Why did you think Brogan might be involved in the disappearance of your client's daughter?"

"Because I believe he is the same as he ever was. He and his sidekicks have a history of sexual abuse, people trafficking, slavery, drugs and...well, you name it, they do it. People like that will never change. He is protected because of his father, his position as ChiZA and the knowledge that those around him do not dare cross him. He gets away with murder... literally."

"That is quite an accusation. Do you have evidence of this, or is this a continuation of your vendetta against Brogan?"

"Yes, and yes." McCallum took a sip. "I try to stay invisible to that bastard, so I dare not ask too many questions. He would have me killed if my head appeared too high above the parapet. Fortunately, I rarely need to ask for information. If I hang around the Universities long enough, I overhear loads of stories about young boys and girls whose lives have been ruined by Eddie fucking Brogan and his sidekick Billy Jensen the Second."

That was too much of a coincidence. "Would Jensen the First be the so-called entrepreneur with a passion for classic cars?"

"You've heard of him then. Sneaky little twat. He's nothing more than a glorified spiv. He bribes or threatens people to get what he wants. He hijacks lorries to get goods he sells back to the state. He and his son, with help from Brogan, hold the monopoly on shipping people around the country to work for next to nothing - modern-day slavery. With Brogan as ChiZA and Jensen Junior as the LeRA for the University region, they control the Dons and all the criminal activity in the Party and Family zones. Jensen Senior is not without his enemies. In his last region he was exposed as an Admin informant who got his rivals banged up. When the families of his victims discovered his little secret, he scarpered into this zone, pretending to be an honest businessman. I don't believe it. As we speak, Jensen Senior is probably extending their networks in this area."

Jeff thought the same and wanted to hear more. McCallum duly obliged. "Rumour has it that when Brogan joins his father on the high table, Jensen Junior will become ChiZA. Brogan has plans to put his friends into key jobs in all regions and zones. Jobs for the bad boys. They are all evil bastards." Connor wiped his lips and downed most of his remaining whisky. "Sorry about that. It eats me up knowing what they have gotten away with and how they continually get rewarded for being such horrible human beings." He shivered. "You know Brogan was implicated in the death of the Judge's great-granddaughter?"

Jeff chose not to mention that he had read this in the journals. "Why would you think that?"

"Mary was a bright student with a promising future who was selected to work in Zone HQ. Her role involved accompanying Brogan on his visits across the country and working in the Youth Zone, delivering awareness seminars to the next generation. I heard nothing to suggest Brogan interfered with Mary. Her friends knew she was becoming increasingly anxious about Brogan's activities. She suspected he selected Youth Zoners, whom he brought to the Party Zone to experience life there. Many did not return. Some simply disappeared, while others committed suicide. Mary tried to get the authorities to stop these visits and asked questions about the missing. Nobody did anything."

The Judge had not included this level of detail. McCallum had more to say.

"Mary planned to leave her job in HQ to help His Lordship on a series of research projects for the Committee. A week before she was due to depart, she was found dead at the bottom of a cliff in Scarborough. Brogan, Jensen and other colleagues had taken her there for a farewell party." McCallum's tone turned angrier. "Not surprisingly, because of who she was, they held an inquiry which decided it was 'Accidental Death'. Brogan gave evidence that Mary had too much to drink and wandered off before they could stop her. Friends maintain Mary never touched alcohol."

Jeff wondered about McCallum's motives for telling him all this. Was his ex-colleague setting him up by loading the bullet for Jeff to fire? "Did His Lordship ask any questions at the inquest?"

"Not as far as I know. I think it was all done and dusted before he heard about it. The Central Committee discussed the matter and decided it was a tragic accident. The Judge had other ideas and started questioning Brogan's activities under the guise of reviewing the powers of the Admin. I guess Brogan had him silenced before he could say too much."

"And now you believe Brogan fears I am about to reopen the issue?"

McCallum drowned the dregs from his glass. "I have no idea what his concerns are. I very much doubt he fears you. Why would he? Brogan is untouchable. The only person with enough influence to take the matter further is dead. Brogan probably wants to know where you are going with the investigation so that he can prepare his defence."

Jeff pondered these developments as he filled their glasses. He handed one to his guest.

"Cheers."

"You're welcome." A question formed. "How did you get into this zone? Do you have a pass?" Jeff asked.

"I have many." Connor reached into his bag and extracted a bundle of credit card-sized pieces of plastic attached to a metal ring. He handed it over.

"What are they?" Cleveland studied the plastic identity cards. Each contained a different name but no photograph. "Where do you get these?"

"Easy enough if you know where to look."

Jeff turned over a few before handing them back. "There are no photographs. How did you get through the border?" Jeff's experience crossing boundaries made him believe it would be impossible to get through border control without the correct documentation.

"It's easy enough if you use the crew doors".

"What are the crew doors?

"Doors that Admins use to avoid the queues at border checkpoints." He found Jeff's confused expression funny. "There are at least two in and out of every zone."

"How come I've never heard of them?

McCallum laughed. "You need to get out more."

"Very funny. How do these crew doors work?"

"It's simple. They operate on the same principle as the ones at the theme parks in the old days. They put doors in out-of-the-way places, so the public never sees the characters emerging. The Admins appear as if by magic."

"Where are these crew doors?"

"To access this zone, I used the one outside Gloucester. There is another near Stevenage."

"And these are what? Checkpoints hidden in trees?"

"Nah. They are usually empty buildings straddling the border. The one outside Gloucester is the old airfield at South Cerney. The one in Stevenage is an abandoned petrol station.

Generally, you walk into the old buildings to a massive turnstile-type thing that goes from floor to ceiling, run a pass through a reader, and step through."

"Doesn't anyone keep guard?"

"During office hours. I've never seen anyone there overnight. I came in just after midnight this morning and had no problems."

Jeff slumped backwards, pointing at the identity cards. "All it takes is one of those?" Connor nodded. "And Admins use these doors without anyone else knowing about it?"

"The card reader identifies who has gone through and when. I don't know how often anybody looks at the records. The IT is very simplistic. There is a PC attached to the turnstile. When you use the card, it confirms the name, and the turnstile moves." He waved the cards. "These are in the names of ex-Admins. They are always adding new staff to the database but rarely remove those who die or leave."

Jeff's mind had moved onto practicalities. "If visiting Admins used the gate, how would they get from the airfield? Can you bring a car through?"

"You could, although you would need access to the main office. The Admins that I've seen crossing at night drive into the yard in one zone and walk through. They appear to have a vehicle waiting for them on the other side."

"What they leave a car there? Isn't that risky? What if it gets stolen?

"Perhaps they get their colleagues on the other side to leave a pool car for them with the keys over the wheel. All I know is that Admins rarely bring in cars from other zones, as it makes the natives restless. Nobody notices outside Admins wandering around, but for some reason, locals take exception to strange cars."

Jeff recalled his visit to Boscombe. "Is it possible to access the records of people who cross via these gates?"

"Someone with a little IT knowledge and time could get that information from the PC. I haven't tried. I don't tend to hang around."

"If you passed through after midnight. Where have you been until now?"

"That's none of your business. I have friends who help me get to and from the gate."

Jeff brought his glass to his mouth and held it there, pondering whether to ask his next question. He might be about to disclose valuable information, and was unsure whose side McCallum was on. He released it anyway. "There is no record of Brogan or anyone else from his area entering the Old Fogies Zone by the main checkpoint. Could he have passed through the crew doors?"

"Of course. Admins often use the doors. However, as there is only one gate into Z80+, outside Poole, most Admins in that area use the main checkpoints as they are more convenient."

"You know a lot about these gates."

"I have to if I want to get around without being noticed."

"I need to see the records and find out who crossed through the crew doors on the night the Judge was killed."

"Brogan and Jensen were at a charity function."

"I know, but we have no time of death for the Judge, and it might be possible that they left the event and travelled to the Judge's house and back overnight."

"They could have done that easily. I have it on excellent authority that they left the event with two young women before eleven and were not seen again until the following evening."

"How do you know this?"

McCallum tapped the side of his nose. "I cannot reveal my sources, but the girls were back in their dorms by midnight."

"They didn't spend the night at the hotel."

"Not according to my sources."

"That gives Brogan plenty of time to get to Bournemouth and back."

McCallum considered the logistics. "The roads would be empty, and Jensen is known for driving at speed. It's probably worth further investigation."

"I'll get on it."

Connor saw Jeff stifling a yawn. "Not keeping you awake, am I?"

"No, not at all, sorry. I usually catch a nap about this time, but it might be good to miss it. I might sleep better tonight."

"Are you having trouble sleeping?"

"On occasions."

McCallum reached into his bag and withdrew a packet of pills, which he offered to Jeff. "Try these."

"What are they?" Jeff turned the foil container but saw no name or brand.

"Nighttime Flyers."

Jeff looked concerned. "Which do what?"

"Give you the best sleep you'll ever have. Don't worry, these are legit. Fully approved by the Central Committee." Jeff turned the packet over in his hands. McCallum sensed he was not convinced. "After the Shift, many people suffered stress and anxiety, and productivity fell. There was a threat of food shortages. The Committee wanted something to help people relax. A Welsh scientist came up with these. The pills give you a deep sleep and include an extra something that provides you with fantastic dreams. You wake up calm, refreshed and ready for anything."

"Is this extra something a bit like LSD?"

"No, it is a combination of natural ingredients. Your doctor will prescribe them, but be prepared for a barrage of questions about why you need them. They don't want to be dishing out date rape drugs. Not that I imagine there is much need for such things in the GOGzone."

"GOGzone? Why do you call this the GOGzone?"

"Because it's full of grumpy old gits," Connor said without a hint of humour. He pointed at the pills. "Take one in a cup of water."

"Can I drink it with tea?"

"I suppose you could. I am not a fan of the stuff these days.

Each tablet gives a good four hours of sleep. You can decide whether to take another when you wake up or two before bed. I'd try one to start with. See how you get on."

"Why do you need them? Do you have trouble sleeping?"

"Not usually, but when I am working, I need to sleep when I can, whether I feel like it or not. I pop a Flyer and am fast asleep ten minutes later."

"Is that why they are called Nighttime Flyers? Because you fly off to sleep."

"No, although the name is apt. They were originally registered as a relaxant. The sleep element was an unexpected bonus. They got the name because the inventor's great-grandfather used to be in a heavy rock band called Nighttime Flyer back in the day."

Jeff studied the foil, unsure whether trying one would do him any harm.

Connor checked his watch. "I've got to be going. I have somewhere to be."

"I hoped we might have a longer chat. Stay a bit longer."

"I've said what I came to say, and I must go. It's not as if we were ever friends, you were my gaffer, that's all. I am pleased you're keeping well, and good luck with your investigation. Sleep well. If I learn anything else, I will be in touch."

Jeff pointed at Connor's face. "What happened there?"

McCallum touched his cheek. "I had a slight disagreement with a car windscreen. I should have used the door."

Jeff watched McCallum walk down the road, open his bag, and extract an apple. This reminded Jeff that he had not eaten. Sod it, he thought, not attracted by the options in his fridge, freezer or larder, I'm going over the pub.

The Wheel was busy, but when the restaurant manager spotted Jeff, he collected him and found a table near the bar.

"A pint?"

"Yes, please," Jeff was surprised to receive such a warm welcome. "What have I done to deserve this?"

"The chef is delighted with the fish. It is flying out the door. He's left an envelope behind the bar. I'll bring it when I return with your beer."

"Envelope? What's inside?"

"Payment for the fish."

"I don't want it. I told him to give it to the Community Fund."

"I know, but Chef thought you might like to make the donation. It is thanks to you that we have fish on the menu."

"I prefer to stay out of it." Jeff did not want a repeat of the attention he received after finding the missing items. He dreaded thinking about what it would be like if word got out that he could supply fish.

The man leaned into Jeff's ear. "Chef is hoping you might be able to get more."

"That's possible. Let's keep it between us. There is no need for anyone else to learn of this arrangement."

"Of course. The special tonight is salmon…"

"Not for me, thanks. I am happy for others to enjoy the fish. I'll have a medium-rare steak, chips, mushrooms and whatever sauce you have available."

15. GATES AND OTHER OPENINGS

Three men huddled around a small table in the shabby room. The door was only closed once they had double-checked that the corridor was clear and nobody was loitering outside. Harding carefully surveyed the room to check for listening devices.

Jeff was confident he could trust Harding and MC, but knew he could not yet share the findings of his trip to Cardiff. He maintained the lie that the journals had not told him anything new.

Both MC and Harding commented that Jeff seemed in a good mood. He appeared relaxed and had more energy. Jeff confessed to sleeping well but did not mention the pills.

Bringing the conversation back to business, he asked Harding for an update.

The Admin had completed his double-check on the visitors to the Old Fogeys Zone, and most had checked out.

"Most?" Jeff was intrigued. "Which ones haven't?"

"Two sisters, Gloria and Melanie Richardson."

The names meant nothing to Jeff. "What's the problem?"

"I rang them, and they refused to talk to me over the 'phone."

"I wouldn't speak to you either," MC confirmed. "They are clearly women of taste."

"Thank you, smart arse. But they are happy for me, well us, to visit. I have their address. They live outside Salisbury."

Jeff saw an obvious solution. "You live near there. Couldn't you drop in on your way home?"

Harding shook his head firmly. "I'm not going on my own!"

His colleagues looked bemused until Harding told them about the female with an alluring voice answering the call saying, "Bonjour, Moulin Rouge. How may I be of service to you?"

MC roared.

Jeff looked at MC, not getting the joke. "She was having a bit of fun with him. What's wrong with that?"

Harding answered. "You haven't heard it all yet. I asked to speak to Gloria or Melanie and was advised that Madame Charmaine and Mademoiselle Bridget, whom she pronounced as Bridge-eat, were busy with clients and unavailable."

"Then ring them back." Jeff stared at MC, whose shoulders were shaking. "What's wrong with you? What do you find so funny?"

"They are prostitutes," MC chuckled, "they must have been entering Z80+ on business."

"That's right," Harding nodded repeatedly. "She told me to make an appointment to see the ladies and promised me a good discount if I was a first-time visitor. I was gobsmacked, and then she suggested I see Mademoiselle Bridget first because Charmaine got the better reviews. I should save the best for last. I hung up."

MC roared again. "You old dog. I never knew you had it in you."

Jeff could not resist tittering. "Good to hear there is life in a couple of the old boys in that zone."

"They are the only ones who can afford it." Harding looked dejected.

"If you want to visit, I'll organise a whip round. I am sure you could get something for a fiver," MC said. Harding flashed a V-sign.

"The whip would probably cost extra," Jeff quickly added, "Not that I know, of course."

All three giggled loudly until the door swung open. LeRA Cormack stood in the doorway. "I am happy to see you are having fun."

Jeff had never met the man but knew immediately who had entered the room. He sensed he did not like him, but tried putting his bias aside. "Yes. Working with a smile is always better than being miserable." Jeff spotted Norman lurking in the corridor, smirking. "Isn't that right, Norman? You like a good laugh, don't you? Or do you prefer to whistle while you work?"

"Just so long as you are working and not taking the piss," Cormack smirked. "I would hate to learn that taxpayers' money is wasted on this investigation."

MC was about to speak, but Jeff extended an index finger, advising restraint.

"I doubt we are wasting much money compared to the rest of this office." Jeff fixed his eyes on Cormack. "But I suppose at the end of the day, providing the income exceeds expenditure, everyone is happy. I was only thinking about that the other day. I wondered how much of the income from this region makes it into the Treasury coffers."

"What are you suggesting?" Cormack had raised his voice and stepped closer. "Are you saying we are corrupt?"

"Absolutely..." Jeff said, leaving a deliberate break between words and forcing a cough. "...not. I am interested in how much money the Admins make...sorry, I meant take in their everyday business. I've always been fascinated by money." Jeff held up a hand. "I don't expect you to know the answer. I'll ask Secretary Wilson when I see him next."

Cormack retreated. "I hear you met with Wilson yesterday. Did you learn anything?"

"If I did, it is none of your concern. You remember that I work directly to ChiZA Purcell, who then reports to Secretary Wilson."

A weak smile appeared on Cormack's face. "I am due to speak to Purcell later and could save you the trouble of contacting him."

"Thanks for that, but I've already spoken with him ."

Cormack feigned surprise and turned to Norman. "That's funny, Norman. I could have sworn there was no record of a phone call to Purcell from this room this morning."

Norman sneered at Jeff as he spoke. "Nothing. No outside calls at all. I do hope Mr Cleveland is telling us the truth."

"Why wouldn't I?" Jeff asked. "I spoke to him yesterday."

"Good try," Cormack smirked again. "ChiZA Purcell was out all day yesterday and did not return to the office."

"I know. That's why I called on his mobile, but when he failed to answer, I rang him at home."

"You have his home number?"

"Of course. Don't you?"

Cormack and Norman left the room.

Before they reached the stairwell, they heard the other three laughing loudly as MC repeated, "Absolutely...not", with the obligatory cough.

Jeff made the tea and placed them on the table. MC and Harding joined him at the centre of the office. The three had spread themselves around the small room while making calls.

"It's very cramped in here." Harding turned around. "Do you want me to see if we can get a bigger office?"

"It's fine," Jeff wasn't fazed. "It's not as if we spend much time here, and I don't want to give Cormack or Norman the satisfaction."

"Norman hates you." MC looked at Jeff over the rim of the cup.

"I can't please everyone. I'm relieved I don't have to work with him." Jeff licked his lips after drinking. "I suppose I'll have to watch my back now. Norm and his mates are going to be gunning for me."

MC was about to put the cup down, but had a change of heart. "They wouldn't dare."

"Why is that? Are you going to protect me?"

"No," MC said. "There is no need. Lord Wilson has issued a decree that you are to be helped and promised swift retribution for anyone who works against you. The ChiZAs know the consequences of anything happening to you. Cormack is already on a warning and only kept his job because Purcell didn't want to rock the boat too much when he took over. Norman clings to Cormack's shirttails. They protect each other. Neither of them is brave enough to do anything."

"You know that Norman is still telling everyone he quit?" Harding sipped his tea. "He reckons he couldn't stomach working with a corrupt ex-copper."

Jeff's head leaned and then straightened. "I prefer to have

people around me that I can trust."

"What's Harding doing here then? Nobody trusts him."

Harding mouthed an obscene response. MC blew him a kiss.

Jeff was happy to see his assistants getting along. There was a good atmosphere in the room, or as Flissy might have said, *a good vibe*. He seized the opportunity to broach a subject that might upset the harmony of his new, small team. "I can trust you two, can't I?"

"Yes," Harding said.

MC nodded. "Affirmative."

"I was hoping you could do something for me, but before I say anything, I need to know you won't tell anyone else, certainly not your colleagues.

Harding confirmed his lips were sealed. MC pledged not to say a word to anyone.

Harding quickly added. "It wouldn't make any difference because nobody listens to you."

"Prick."

Jeff waited for Harding to cease cackling before speaking. "I need you to get me the records of people passing through the crew doors on the night of the Judge's death."

Harding almost dropped his mug. He took a deep breath. "Do you think an Admin is responsible for the murder?"

"No, not necessarily."

"That's hardly an endorsement. Why do you need that information?"

MC listened intently, elbows on the table.

"To make sure that no Admins from other regions entered this zone and then crossed into the Old Fogeys using the crew doors."

Harding's expression showed his concern. "How did you hear about the crew doors? Only Admins know about them."

MC's eyes lit up as words emerged. "You can be a naïve prick sometimes. They tell us to keep the gates secret, but loads of non-Admins use them."

"Like whom?"

"I can't name them all," MC considered what to say next. "It could be friends of Admins. People who have paid to be allowed to move contraband between zones."

Harding dismissed that suggestion with a firm headshake. "Nah. That could never happen."

"It happens all the time. I bet citizens use them more than Admins."

Harding was not persuaded. "How would anyone get through? You need a pass."

"Not if you bring a lorry through while the gate is manned. Slip the guard a few quid, and you're in."

"No Admins would do that." Harding saw MC's expression and guessed his colleague did not agree. "Anyway, if that happens, then there will not be any records to find." Harding folded his arms and sat back.

Jeff spoke up. "I'm not interested in lorries. I want the names of Admins who used the gates after the guards had left."

Harding's arms unfolded as he leaned toward Jeff. "You do think it's an Admin."

"Not necessarily," Jeff insisted. "I want to see if anyone used both doors to enter and leave this zone, and then we can check that nobody entered using fake passes or borrowed one from an Admin."

"Never happen." Harding's arms had folded again. "No Admin would risk lending a pass, and our passes certainly can't be faked."

"What planet are you on?" MC's arms raised in despair. "Admins are always lending their passes, and there are loads of fake ones around. I am regularly offered cash to let mine be copied."

Harding's jaw dropped. "Do you take it?"

"What do you think?"

"I've never been offered anything."

"Nobody wants to be you."

Harding showed a finger.

Jeff took a breath. "I don't like having to ask, but..." he paused, unsure whether to use the lie. He decided there was little chance of him getting caught out, "...when I spoke to Wilson yesterday, he assumed we had double-checked all the doors. I suggested that we had."

"I have no idea where the records are kept," Harding said.

"The easiest thing to do is to check the PC at the gate," MC pointed at Harding. "You know a thing or two about computers. You could get in and access the records. It can't be that difficult. You've said yourself our IT comes from the ark."

Harding nodded slowly. "It would have to be out of hours, and I would need help."

MC was happy to participate. "It would probably be better if Jeff stayed away. A citizen hanging around at the gate out of hours would look strange."

"I'd like to come along." Jeff looked at the Admins. "If only to keep watch or something?"

Jeff, MC, and Harding pulled up at the South Cerney airfield just after six the following evening.

A tall, metal fence stretched across the front of the airfield perimeter and continued for miles in either direction.

The buildings outside the airfield looked new. They were prefabricated factory units, and the signs showed that multiple businesses occupied them, including upholsterers, tailors, manufacturers of wooden products, and specialist eyeglass manufacturers.

The Admins told Jeff to wait at *'The Flightdeck Café'*. They would not take long. Harding said the task could not end soon enough for him.

The café was on the ground floor of a corner unit. Jeff peered in through the glass and saw a man mopping up. He was relieved to find the door unlocked and poked his head inside. "Are you still open?"

The mopper nodded. "Yeah, we close at eight. My last customer spilt a mug of coffee. I had to clean it up before the floor gets sticky. What can I get you?"

"Tea, please. Milk, no sugar. I don't care which variety."

"You are in luck. We have the good stuff at the moment. Can I get you something to eat?"

Jeff collected a menu on the way to a table. The food options listed on the laminated sheet were extensive.

"I am not used to having so much choice."

The café owner smiled. "We try our best to provide something for everyone."

"Is it mostly factory workers you cater for?"

"And the Admins." The man jerked his head towards the window. "They use the airfield for training and the like. Admins come here to eat because the food in their canteen is terrible."

"Most places would struggle to compete with this menu."

"Thank you. What can I get you?"

Jeff had no idea how long his colleagues would be but believed he had time for *butcher's sausage and chips*. He declined the offer of an egg and beans.

Several customers entered and left the premises while he waited. They collected bags of food, and most promised to see Viv the next day.

When it arrived, Jeff's meal was satisfactory at best. He guessed it was frozen sausage and chips, and, in a way, it was a treat. Frozen products were not readily available in his region.

"You do a good trade with takeaways," Jeff said when Viv returned to collect the empty plate. "I'm not surprised. Those chips were to die for." He was never sure how convincing a liar he was.

"Nice of you to say. I'm afraid I can't take any credit. It's a ready meal. They bring them in frozen. All we do is heat them."

Jeff looked surprised. "I would never have guessed. Do you mind telling me where you got them? I could use a few of them in my freezer for days when I can't be bothered to cook…which is most days."

Viv guffawed and leaned in to whisper even though nobody

else was in the room. "We get them from the Admins. They use part of the airfield for food storage. Lorries arrive all the time to distribute goods around the zone. We buy what is left over. They always bring in more than their local distributor needs."

"Who is the distributor? Perhaps they deliver to my area."

"Jensen Food Products seems to be the main one, but smaller vans are always arriving and leaving."

Jeff decided it was better not to ask any more questions. He was wary of his host becoming defensive. "This is an ideal spot for a cafe. We've got nothing like this where I live." He immediately wished he had not uttered the last sentence. It provided an opening to questions about where Jeff lived. He thought of a story to use if asked why he was there. He needn't have worried.

"We are lucky. Admins need to get the food off those premises, so we get offered quite a bit. We pay cash. We have big freezers out back and can usually take all their leftovers. Everybody's happy. It helps that we are the only café takeaway around here. We soon sell it all."

"You are lucky to be in the right place at the right time. The Admins must be grateful for you helping them with their surplus stock."

"It's a good relationship. It also helps that we keep an eye on the airfield outside of business hours."

"Do you live close by?"

Viv pointed upwards. "We live upstairs. My missus is a light sleeper. If anyone uses that gate out of hours, she knows about it."

"Does that happen often?"

"More than you'd think. They have late-night training events and stocktaking, so people come in and out of the airfield at least three nights a week."

Again, Jeff decided against being overly nosy. "It must be weird living in a factory unit."

"You get used to it. I'm quite useful with the tools and have built a few walls and the like. It looks like an ordinary flat."

"Chef, builder, security guard. You have a lot on your plate."
Viv stood proud. "I like to keep busy."
Jeff looked at the airfield. "It's a big site."
"Yes"
"I'm surprised the Admins don't keep people there twenty-four seven."
"They do for a few nights each week, but it is pretty quiet the rest of the time."
"If you spotted something untoward, would you stop anyone leaving the airfield?"
"What do you mean?"
"Well, say your wife spotted someone coming out of there in the middle of the night looking shifty or out of place."
"Ah, right. I'm with you. No, we note it and then tell the Admins. If there is a vehicle, she writes down the details. We pass the info on and leave it up to them to follow up. I'm too old to be brave."
"Me too." Jeff had another task for MC and Harding. "I am sure the Admins appreciate your support. Not everyone would be so helpful."
Viv had never seemed taller. "We do our best."
"I'm sure." Several customers entered, allowing Jeff to ask. "How much do I owe you?"

The Poole gate was at an abandoned council depot. Once again, the area was sealed off by tall fences. Sadly, there was nothing for Jeff to do but remain in the car, keeping his head down.
He read the scribbled lists provided by MC and Harding, becoming excited when he read Brogan and Jensen's names. The computer log recorded them entering Z6080 via the crew gates shortly after 1 a.m. and leaving at 9 a.m. This allowed them ample time to get to the Judge's house, do the deed, and return.
Jeff was amazed that Brogan and Jensen had used their passes. It would make more sense for them to use fakes. Could someone be setting the pair up? Jeff dismissed the notion,

doubting anyone would be daft enough to mess with two high-ranking Admins, especially one whose father was on the Central Committee.

The more likely scenario was that Brogan and Jensen considered themselves untouchable. They probably thought they could come and go as they pleased, and nobody would question their reasons.

Harding had a broad smile on his return to the car. "Yup, it's them. Two other people accompanied them. I assume they were also Admins. Names of Cornwell and Essex."

MC sat in the driver's seat. "Those names sound made up, but if they were, why would Brogan and Jensen use their actual names?"

"Probably never thought anyone would investigate," Harding suggested. "I checked the log, and nobody has performed a search of the database for years."

"Do you recognise any of these names?" Jeff asked.

"Nope. I've never heard of them," Harding replied.

"Can you check that they exist?"

"We can," Harding noted. "However, this is turning out to be more work than I expected. I thought you were investigating with us acting as chauffeurs."

"Aren't you enjoying being a copper again?" MC asked.

Harding was astonished that MC knew about his previous role but tried to ignore it. "Are you going to take us home or what? I'm starving."

The mention of food prompted Jeff to ask a question that occurred to him in the café. "Would they have opened the main gates when they crossed zones?"

Harding spoke for both. "No. They probably walked through using the turnstiles."

"Then how did they get from one gate to the other?" Jeff asked.

Harding considered the question. "They could have arranged for someone to leave a pool car in the car park."

"Norman," MC suggested.

"Possibly," Harding replied. "We can check if he booked a car and, if so, when he returned it."

MC's mouth tightened. "But that won't prove he left it for Brogan and company. It could have been used for any purpose."

"He might have collected them," Harding suggested.

Jeff raised another issue. "Which Admin office looks after the airfield?"

"East Central," Harding said, "LeRA Irvine's crew."

Jeff had not heard of Irvine. "What are they like?"

MC replied. "Irvine doesn't get on with Cormack, but some of his Admins are friendly with Norman. Several of them will be attending the charity fundraiser next week."

Jeff had seen the posters around the office. "Do you know any of them?"

Harding said not.

"What is it you want to know?" MC fastened the seatbelt.

Jeff told them of his conversation with Viv at the café and the couple's records of overnight visitors.

Harding doubted anyone would pay much attention to snooping citizens.

MC mumbled something and then said, "Not everyone is like you. I have an old comrade whose area covers the airfield. I'll ask him."

"Great," Jeff said, "make sure you do it subtly. I don't want to set any hares running."

"Being as bald as a coot, MC never worries about hairs," Harding teased.

MC grunted, "Prick," and started the car.

The following day, Jeff was about to leave for quiz night when MC entered the office, waving a sheet of paper.

"My comrade tracked down the information supplied by the woman at the café. They have a file in which they store her snippets in date order. A car with this registration number..."

MC waved the paper again. "...was parked at the airfield after eight p.m. She knew that because they were shutting up shop. The vehicle left at about one a.m., containing four men in Admin uniforms, and returned around zero eight forty-five. She was confident about that because the upholstery girls were collecting their breakfast rolls. They arrive at the same time every day."

"That's brilliant. Thanks." Jeff was pleased with that news. "All we have to do now is track the vehicle."

"It's already done," MC winked. "It is an Admin pool car for this region, and it was signed out to your friend Norman, who brought it back the next day."

"Impressive."

"I knew you must be good for something." Harding grinned. "You've done my work for me."

MC cackled loudly. "No change there, then. Dipshit."

Higher Admin Norman Draper sat in his lounge, double-checking his figures. The fundraiser promised to be a huge success. The tickets sold and sponsorship received exceeded all estimates. All that remained was for Norman to decide how much to skim off for his administration charges. He started to work through a few options but was interrupted by his mobile phone. The caller's name appeared on the screen.

"Stokesy, how are you? If you are looking for tickets for the fundraiser, you are in luck. I have a few remaining."

His caller wasn't interested in tickets. She'd overheard a conversation between a colleague, Abel, and one of his old army buddies earlier that day. Her attempts to garner information failed, Abel was an awkward old sod, especially where his old army mates were concerned, but she knew the discussion involved a car.

Once Abel had left for the day, Stokesy searched his desk and bin. She found a scrap of paper with a registration number on it. She checked the database and found it was an Administration car allocated to Norman's region.

Norman knew the vehicle's make, model, and location. What he didn't know was the reason behind the enquiry.

He thanked Stokesy, closed the call, and jumped into his car.

The regional HQ's front doors were secured, and Norman knew that opening them would activate an alarm. He did not want anyone to know he had been there, so he walked around the building.

The rear door could be opened with a key and no fuss.

Cleveland and Co.'s investigation room door did not have a lock. Norman had allocated them this space, knowing the door would always be open.

He examined the office, paying particular attention to the waste bin and solitary cupboard, but found nothing of value. The team must have taken their papers with them. His best bet was to return during the day, preferably when Cleveland and MC were out. Norman hated Cleveland and did not trust MC. He was confident he could get the third member of the team to tell him what he needed to know. After all, Harding needed his help to get reassigned.

16. UNSATISFACTORY OUTCOMES

Jeff absently climbed into the front passenger seat, put on his seatbelt and closed the door.

"Good morning," MC pulled the car away from the pavement.

The words woke Jeff from his stupor. "Oh, yes, good morning, MC. How are you today?"

"A bit more with it than you, I think. Heavy night?"

"Sorry?"

"Did you have a heavy night? Have you been to the pub celebrating what we learned yesterday?"

Jeff leaned on the door and gazed out the window as his hand squeezed his chin. "No, I didn't go out, but I have been thinking about what we've learned. I've been awake most of the night wondering what to do with this information."

"You tell Wilson."

"What good would that do? It's not enough for an arrest."

MC laughed. "Arrest? You didn't seriously think that Brogan would get arrested? You were asked to investigate the crime and report back. There was no mention of an arrest. Arrests are things of the past. The best you can do is write your report and hope Wilson does something with it."

"I expected more."

"Tough. It's a different world these days. We may not like all the changes, but we have no choice."

"I suppose you're right." Jeff took off his hat and placed it on his lap. "Anyway, what makes you so happy? Most mornings, I can barely get a word out of you."

"One minute, you complain that I don't speak; the next, you say I talk too much. There is no pleasing you." MC winked at him. "I am only teasing. I have really enjoyed the last couple of days. It's been good to do something meaningful, something to get the little grey cells working again."

"Crikey, you've turned into Hercule Poirot."

The sound of MC's laughter filled the car.

Harding reviewed what they had learned. "We have a witness who saw a car leave the airfield on the evening the Judge was killed. That witness noted the number plate and saw the vehicle return the following day. That vehicle was signed out to Norman."

Jeff and MC nodded.

"The café owner reported seeing four people in the car, but we cannot confirm who they were."

Jeff and MC shook their heads.

"The gate record shows Brogan, Jensen and two others passed through the crew doors into this zone. We can assume, and Jeff, there is no need to remind me what assume does…"

MC was in before Harding took a breath. "You are already an ass."

"You have a way with words. It's a pity you don't use them more often." MC chuckled. Harding continued. "It is fair to assume that it was those four individuals in the car."

"I think so," Jeff said, "and our calculations suggest that the times that they left and returned allowed plenty of opportunity for them to get to the Judge's house in Z80+." Jeff closed his notebook and tapped it on the table. "Even if they took a comfort break or two, it is still possible for them to get there and out before the body was discovered."

MC spoke next. "If they drove like Harding, they'd only just make it back to the airfield by zero-eight forty-five."

"I am not slow, I'm careful." Harding paused for a second. "But how can we prove the four passengers were Brogan, Jensen and co?"

"We can't," Jeff confirmed.

"We know they crossed through the crew doors," MC said.

Jeff did not want to burst MC's balloon. He had never seen the ex-soldier so enthused. "But we obtained that information illegally. We didn't have permission."

"Permission? Harding and I are Admins. We don't need

permission."

Harding was still not convinced. "We know someone passed through the crew doors using those names, but we cannot prove it was those four. From what you said, it could have been anyone using duplicate passes."

MC refused to be deterred. "What are the chances of people using Brogan and Jensen's names?"

"Very high if they are trying to set them up," Harding suggested.

Jeff had thought the same thing. "We need the data from the crew doors between the Youth and Family Zones."

Harding did not see the point. "That still won't prove it was those four."

MC's index finger hit the table. "It would show that four people left the Youth Zone intending to travel to Bournemouth."

Harding once again disagreed. "We can speculate that's where they were heading. They might have visited a friend or an old aunt or uncle. Anyway, we have no chance of getting proof that they left the Youth Zone. Brogan's lot won't give us anything that might implicate him."

Jeff blew hard. "You're right. We can't even ask for it as we would be tipping him off that we are interested in him."

MC relaxed with hands locked behind the shiny dome. "That is not a bad thing."

"I can't see how," Harding said, "Brogan might have a moment of concern, but that is all it would be. He knows we can't prove anything. We daren't challenge him. As far as mere mortals like us are concerned, Brogan is untouchable. He only has to sit tight, say nothing and keep his head down. We need unassailable evidence."

His colleague smiled. "You are overthinking things. We don't need hard evidence to make Brogan break cover. We need him to believe we have that evidence."

Harding looked at Jeff. "Do you understand what that means?"

"Not really. Go on MC."

"Sun Tzu…"

"Who the hell is that?"

MC dismissed Harding's interruption with a shake of the head. "I'm coming to that, you prick. Sun Tzu was a Chinese general and strategist who developed military strategies later compiled into '*The Art of War*'.

Harding looked at Jeff again. "Have you heard of this?"

"No, but I'm hoping MC will enlighten us."

"Sun Tzu's philosophies have been adapted and applied throughout history. Emperor Napoleon used a tactic where he made his enemies believe his forces had a particular weak point. They attacked that weak link expecting little opposition, but Napoleon's forces swept around them and stopped them from escaping."

"I read about that when the film starring what's his name Phoenix came out." Harding's mood lightened, and he was about to comment on the film when MC spoke again.

"That tactic is based on deception. When we are able to attack, we must seem unable."

"But we are unable." Harding's elbow rested on the table, and he rubbed his forehead with his fingers. "There is no deception in that."

"I'll put it another way. Let me finish this time. Appear weak when you are strong and strong when you are weak."

"So, we are going to pretend there are more of us than there are." Harding pointed to the others. "How do we make three become three hundred? Because that is the least we would need to take on Brogan."

MC waved a hand, telling Harding to calm down. "It's not all about numbers. We can appear strong by claiming we have more evidence against Brogan than we do. If we put the word out that he is our number one suspect and we have discovered enough evidence to prove it, Brogan will want to know more."

Harding still wasn't convinced. "All he'll do is get Norman to find out what we know and then discredit it. His father has enough friends to make all this go away. We are wasting our time."

"If you were Brogan, would you put your future in Norman's hands?" MC studied the others' faces. "Nor would I. From what I've heard, Brogan has always been very hands-on. He likes to sort things for himself. Once he learns he is on our radar, he won't be able to resist paying a visit."

"How do you propose to let him know he is our prime suspect? Shall I ring him? Hello Eddie, we're after you. That won't look like a trap, will it?"

MC laughed. "Sometimes, Harding, you should engage what little brainpower you have before you open your mouth. We need to be more subtle than that. We'll prepare a case against him. Jeff can write it up, and then we'll leave it for Norman to discover. "

"Norman is not the brightest, but even he will see through that. He told me he came to check the room and was impressed with how tidy we left it."

Jeff was relieved they had maintained a clear desk policy and had not left paperwork in the office. "Norman would be suspicious if we suddenly leave incriminating evidence around?"

"He would," MC confirmed. "That's why we hide it behind a ceiling panel and get Harding to grass us up."

"Hang on a minute…"

"It has to be you. You are the only one of us that Norman would believe. You don't have to tell him where to look or what the evidence is. You could, I don't know, take him for a pint to ask whether you are any closer to reassignment. He's bound to ask how the case is developing. You tell him Jeff is very close to a conclusion, but won't discuss it with us because he doesn't trust Admins. You could also mention something about Jeff being weird because you came in the room and found him standing on the table, looking for listening devices."

Harding nodded. "I get it. Norman will also look up there."

"With any luck."

"Bloody hell, MC. That's a master plan." Jeff was impressed. "How long did it take you to think of that?"

"As I was saying it. We had to think on our feet in my old job."

"They trained you well. Brilliant work."

"What is it?" MC saw Harding put his tongue into the gap between his bottom lip and teeth. "What's eating you?"

"We spread the word that we have enough evidence to condemn Brogan and also reveal when we plan to use it." Harding's eyes flitted from one face to the other as each nodded. "What if he comes down here, kills us, and wanders off with the evidence? Cormack and Norman won't shed a tear over our deaths." He pointed at Jeff. "They would probably clap at yours. We would be the victims of persons unknown.

"Brogan isn't stupid, he knows Wilson would demand answers and would not stop until he gets them. We just need to lure him from his lair." MC's eyes narrowed. "What about this? The office will be empty next week because of the Charity Fun Day. You let slip that Jeff will be here that day, writing up his report, ready to give it to Lord Wilson the next day. Brogan has already confirmed he is attending the fun day…"

"Who told you that?" Harding had heard no mention of this.

"Norman and Cormack were discussing it the other morning. Jensen Senior is arranging for them to bring in a surprise that they will raffle off. Norman was so excited he almost wet himself."

"They discussed this with you around?"

"They didn't see me. Cormack's office door was open, and I took longer than necessary to pass by."

"Fair play," Harding smiled. "You are craftier than I realised."

Jeff sought clarification. "We somehow let slip that we have a case against Brogan in the hope that he uses the visit to the fun day to make a detour here to…what? Kill us and steal the evidence?"

"I knew this would be a shit plan." Harding scratched his chin.

MC was not deterred. "We lull him into a sense of false security. If he arrives and finds Jeff…say, typing up a report…"

"Can you type?"

Jeff waved away Harding's question. "Go on MC."

"Jeff gets him to talk about what happened, which we record... and before you ask Shithead, I have an old portable recorder we can use. You and I wait until Jeff signals, and we capture Brogan."

Harding clapped sarcastically. "Masterful. We hang out in case Brogan falls for our scam, but we don't know when he will arrive or what he intends to do. He could walk in, shoot Jeff, take our evidence and get out."

"Do you have a better idea?" MC locked eyes with Harding, who admitted he didn't.

"This might work." Jeff whistled as he thought. "We need to shorten the window and find reasons why you pair will be out of the office."

"But we will be in the office, armed and ready." MC grinned.

"Only Brogan won't be able to see us because we are either invisible or so well camouflaged..."

"Prick," MC snapped. "What else is on this floor?"

"Nothing apart from cupboards and storage rooms ..." A light went on in Harding's brain. "We wait in one of those! How will Jeff tell us when to move?"

"We'll think of something. We could use our mobiles?" MC looked at Jeff. "Did you ever get a mobile?"

"No," Jeff said.

"That prick Norman has kept it. I know it arrived because I saw the package from Purcell."

"Don't worry about that now. The first challenge will be getting word to Brogan without raising his suspicions."

"What do you want me to say?" Harding asked.

"I think I know how to make it more convincing," MC's grin widened as the thoughts developed.

Norman could see nothing but good things coming his way. This would be the making of him. Brogan would reward him handsomely for what he was about to do. Who knows, he might usurp Cormack as the new ChiZA. Happy days were here at last.

He had not expected Stokesy to get in touch again so soon. She told him Abel had been drinking with them that afternoon and let slip that MC knew the Admin vehicle was signed out to Draper. Abel claimed that the ex-copper had already gathered enough evidence to identify the Judge's killer. Abel's contact refused to specify who they were chasing but suggested it was a senior Admin. Norman was intrigued to hear that Cleveland had prepared a timeline of events for a final report. That report would go to Lord Wilson and ChiZA Purcell in the next few days.

Then, to cap a day of great fortune, Norman bumped into Harding as he left the office. His colleague looked depressed and ignored Norman's suggestion that he cheer up. Harding was not confident that things would look better tomorrow.

"Better for whom?" Harding snarled. "What does tomorrow hold for me? Another day working for that…that corrupt ex-copper. I didn't want the job in the first place, but I'm stuck with it. It wouldn't be so bad if he told me what was happening. I'm supposed to assist him, but all I do is fetch and carry. He doesn't even trust me to see any of his papers. Any news of my move?"

"I'm working on it." Norman put his arm around Harding. "Look, a problem shared and all that. Are you in a rush to get home?"

"No, my wife is working this evening. I can please myself."

"Let me take you for a pint, and you can tell me what's upsetting you. I will speak to Cormack tomorrow and demand you get your move."

Norman and Harding had parted in the pub car park.

"Leave it with me. I'll speak to Cormack first thing. He's had enough of that bent bastard hanging around his office. He reckons there is a terrible smell when Cleveland is in residence".

"Thank you, Norman. I am sorry to burden you with my problems."

"It's not a problem. We're mates. In any case, I asked you to tell me. It is awful the way you've been treated. We've been friends for a long time. I can't have you being depressed because of work." He patted Harding's back. "Now you get home safely, and I'll see you tomorrow. Leave it with me."

"Cheers, Norman, I appreciate it."

Norman stood on a chair, eased aside a ceiling panel and felt around in the void. Finding nothing, he replaced it and moved another. On his third attempt, he discovered a case.

The bag contained papers detailing zone crossings, estimated travel times, names of people using crew gates and notes on cars entering and leaving the crew gate areas.

Norman read enough to substantiate what he surmised after his chat with Stokesy. Cleveland had identified ChiZA Brogan, LeRA Jensen, and two others as key suspects. The four were recorded entering Z6080 and moving onto Z80+. Cleveland's note indicated that the timings of their crossings provided ample opportunity to get to the Judge, complete the task and return before the body was discovered. Norman and Cormack were highlighted as assistants providing Brogan's gang with vehicles to cross zones without detection.

A separate sheet listed why Brogan wanted the Judge dead. Lord McGregor strongly suspected Brogan was involved in the death of his great-granddaughter. The Judge's investigations unearthed cases of false arrest, people trafficking, and slavery, together with a multitude of other offences.

Another page was dedicated to Jensen Senior's illegal business activities and how Brogan, Jensen Junior, LeRA Cormack, and Norman had benefited from them.

Scribbled notes illustrated what the suspects stood to gain from forthcoming changes to the Central Committee. It was as if Cleveland had been listening to Norman's conversations with his boss.

Norman took a deep breath. It was not good news that their plans had been rumbled, but it was fortunate he discovered

Cleveland's findings before any damage was done. He sat, head in hand, thinking what to do. Would he fix things by destroying the paperwork? No, that would do no good. Cleveland would only write it out again. Thoughts could not be unthought.

He used his mobile to take photographs of everything in the case. From what Norman had learned of the man, now that Cleveland had his suspicions, he would be like a dog with a bone. He would not let the matter go. Norman could not be sure if Cleveland knew more than was in the papers and whether he had spoken to anyone else about his suspicions.

He replaced the briefcase and eased the panel back into position. Norman knew what he needed to do next. It was time to earn his reward.

17. JUNIORS' PLAYTIME

Chief Zonal Administrator Edward Brogan held the telephone receiver away from his mouth, mimed stifling a yawn, and winked at his companion.

Billy Jensen Junior giggled into a pillow as he stretched on the sofa.

"Yes, Dad, of course, I understand, but..." Brogan fell silent, listening. "Okay, Dad. I will think about it. I'll see you soon." He hit the button to close the call and sighed.

"What does he suggest?"

"That I shouldn't do anything. He says it will all blow over, and nobody will care what Cleveland says in his report." Eddie walked the short distance to the fridge, extracted two cans of beer and handed one to Jensen before slumping onto the other sofa. "I'm not so sure. I think it would be better to meet him face to face and persuade him of my innocence."

Jensen opened the can and sipped the liquid. He wiped his lips with the back of his hand. "What makes you think he'll listen to you?"

"Because for everything else he might be, Cleveland is not stupid. He will ask himself, why I would bother to make that trip if I were guilty. He'll appreciate that a guilty man would never travel halfway across the country to express his innocence. If I were guilty, I would stay out of his way, relying on my connections to guarantee that Cleveland could not touch me."

"Why did your old man tell you to stay put?"

"Politics. He's confident he has the support needed for me to join the Committee, and once selected, nobody will care about what I might have done before. In the meantime, Dad will dismiss any accusations, saying they are groundless, and Cleveland and I have a history..."

"Which you do because he tried to nail you for that sexual

assault."

"Thanks for reminding me. Do you think I had forgotten about that? You can be a right dickhead sometimes." Brogan drank again. "If I stay away from Cleveland, he will tell everyone I am frightened of the truth and hiding. That might cause problems."

"Whereas if you travel to see him, he'll think you are threatening him."

"Why would he think that?"

"I would."

"It's lucky for me that Cleveland isn't as stupid as you. He'll realise I am innocent."

"Or stupid."

"That's rich coming from you. Unlike you, I see the bigger picture. I think strategically. You barely think at all."

"Why are you so worried about all this shit? Your dad has it under control. He has the power to make this go away."

"He thinks he does, but old Kendal had many supporters on the Committee. If Cleveland's report points the finger at me..."

"Norman suggests it will."

"Indeed. Then the vote on my joining the top table might be closer than dearest daddy expects."

"Which Committee members need persuading?"

"Wilson, Williams and Rayer were very close to Kendal. I wouldn't be surprised if they have spoken to a few other members."

"How could they? They haven't seen the report yet."

"Don't be so naive. Wilson met Cleveland the other day and probably already knows what the report will say."

Jensen sat forward. "That's your defence. The two people pushing the guilt your way are ex-coppers who could never accept you were innocent of the previous crimes that brought about the end of the fuzz. Once people see that, they'll side with you."

"Billy...Billy...Billy, can you really be that stupid?" Brogan blew air through tight lips. "Some Committee members know I was guilty of that previous offence but kept quiet, knowing my father would look after them."

"They've done very well out of it."

"They have, but Daddy won't be around forever. They might secretly worry that I am being installed as a successor, and they won't require much persuasion to believe Cleveland's report. I need to get on the front foot."

"How?"

"By proving my innocence to Cleveland and showing everyone that I'm a changed man."

"I still think it's risky."

"Why? What do I have to lose? If I fail in my quest, things will be the same as before. I rely on my father to get me through this. If I time my visit correctly, nobody will know I was there…nobody that matters anyway. If I succeed in persuading Cleveland of my innocence, then…" He spread his arms, "…I'm quids in."

"Cleveland might see it as intimidation. I think you'd be better off maintaining your innocence from afar. All the evidence shows you haven't done anything. We were at that Charity dinner. We have girls who spent the night with us…"

"We think they spent the night with us. We both passed out, remember."

"Yeah, but they were still around when I woke at four. We ordered more champagne."

"We only have your word for that. I was zonked. When I got up for a piss, there was nobody else in the room."

"But they have already given statements that they were with us."

"They told some Admins, who work for me, that they were with us, but is that all they said? Have they only told their story to my Admins?"

"Who else would they speak to?"

"My enemies."

"Nah. They wouldn't be dull enough to point fingers. They know how dangerous that would be."

"You're probably right, but I don't like leaving things to fate."
Jensen stood and stretched. "I agree with your dad. It is better to leave Cleveland to do his worst and then discredit him. We have stacks of evidence to show you are innocent. Your father has the power. All Cleveland has is a load of unprovable accusations. Everybody knows this man has a huge vendetta against you."

Brogan crumpled his can, threw it into the recycling bin and collected another. "I'll give it some further thought." He popped the can. "But I can't take too long. That report will hit Wilson's desk next week. If I am going to speak with Cleveland, it makes sense to do it when visiting the area on other business."

"You are still going to Norm's fundraiser?"

"Of course. Norm might be an idiot, but we need him to step up as LeRA when Cormack gets Purcell's job."

"Is he up to it?" Jensen mocked Norman's mannerisms as he grabbed his foot and mimicked Norman's voice. "My feet are aching." His hands went to his back. "And my back feels like it is in two." His palms covered his belly. "And I'm a big fat lazy fuck to boot."

Brogan roared. "But he's easy to manipulate, and the other local Admins like him. We'll need their support to do what we've planned."

18. NOT YOUR TYPICAL FUN DAY

MC followed Jeff into the office and complained, not for the first time, that Norman couldn't have given them a smaller room.

Jeff ignored his driver's moans. "It's dead here today. Are we sure that everyone is at the fundraiser?"

"Yes," MC confirmed. "They can't find the time to do their jobs properly, but when it comes to splashing money at one of Norman's so-called charity events, they have all the time in the world."

Harding caught the end of MC's comments. "Don't be upset. I wasn't asked to buy a ticket either."

"Nor me," Jeff was not disappointed. "At least we can talk freely without fear of someone listening."

"We can," Harding replied. "Cormack has arranged for all calls to be diverted to other regions to ensure we are not disturbed."

"That was very generous of him." Jeff had seen enough posters but hadn't absorbed the details. "Where is this fundraiser taking place?

"At one of Jensen's parks, the one near Weston," Harding collected the mugs left from the previous day. It was his turn to make the tea.

"What time is Brogan supposed to do the presentation?"

Harding looked at his watch. "About one o'clock. Norman arranged it so that it would make the evening news."

"That will make scintillating television," MC joked. "Couldn't they find a three-legged dog?"

Jeff laughed.

"I guess we will be getting a visitor sometime after two." Harding set off to the kitchen.

Jeff turned to face the laptop. "That's providing you know who takes the bait."

The three took their usual places around the small table. Jeff and Harding nursed their teas.

Harding pointed at the laptop. "Isn't it strange how, within thirty minutes of your conversation with Purcell, when you rang to inform him when you would submit your report, Cormack offered you the use of a computer and a printer?"

"Cormack must be keen to get rid of you. He never lends his laptop to anyone." MC studied the machine and checked the printer. "He hasn't left you much paper. He probably expects a short report."

"Have you thought more about what you'll put in it?" Harding asked.

"I have thought of little else," Jeff said before emptying his cup. "At the moment, no matter how I try to dress it up, we have no concrete evidence that Brogan and his cronies killed either the Judge or Artie. All we can do is present the facts and hope that results in action."

Harding put his mug on the table. "Unless Brogan takes action."

"We'll soon find out," MC looked pensive. "This needs to work. Without evidence that Brogan Junior is involved, nobody will challenge his father. We are relying on circumstantial evidence."

"For once, I agree with you," Harding said, "we know who is responsible and why they did it, but we still need to supply proof."

"Well, today will be a special day, whatever happens," Jeff replied, "we have probably reached the end of our time together. I want to say I have enjoyed working with you. We became a good little team at the end."

Harding and MC nodded.

Jeff drafted his report, seeking views from the other two as he went along. Having finished what they hoped would be the final draft, MC suggested they celebrate with chips. Harding said he needed to go to the cashpoint and would accompany MC. Jeff assured them he would be fine on his own. It was not yet twelve-thirty.

The printer churned out Jeff's report, and he fidgeted in his chair to reach it. An outside door opened and closed.

Jeff shouted, "That didn't take long. I haven't got the plates ready."

"Hello, Jeff." The tall, broad Admin with a receding hairline stood in the doorway. He held a semi-automatic service pistol, which moved with his glare as he swept the room. "All alone, I see. Good." He joined Jeff at the table.

Jeff thought about Guy Garvey, the singer with the band *Elbow*, who once sang about the *'Simian Stroll'* and his failure to perfect it. He believed Garvey could have done worse than mirror Brogan's movements. Back straight, head fixed in position, shoulders moving in a circular motion, feet at ten to two, hands swinging back and forth. He reminded Jeff of a great ape walking upright.

Jeff hit the button on his concealed mobile and told himself to stay calm. "Eddie Brogan. It's been a while. If you are looking for the Admins, I am afraid you have missed them. They are all at the fundraiser."

"I know where they are, Jeff. Thank you. I will catch up with them later. It's you I wanted to see, Jeff."

Cleveland looked around the room.

"Are you expecting anyone?" Brogan asked.

"No. It's just that you have used my name a few times already. I assume you are doing that to let me know you are addressing your words at me, but as far as I can see, it is only us here, so why bother?"

"I've always known you were a cantankerous old bastard, Jeff."

"Flattery will get you nowhere. I thought you were presenting the grand raffle prize at the fun day."

"I left that to Billy's old man. Only fair as he is the one donating it."

Jeff's head rose and fell. "What did you want to see me about?

Brogan grabbed a chair, dragged it across the floor to the table and sat opposite Jeff. He placed the pistol on the wooden surface. "I want you to stop trying to pin Kendal's murder on me. I had nothing to do with it."

"I see." Jeff pushed his seat back, rested his joined hands on his belly and stretched his legs. "What makes you think I would do that?"

"Don't play the innocent. I have friends who know exactly what you have planned for me. I did not kill Kendal."

"What about Artie?"

"I only recently learned that Artie died."

"And I am supposed to believe that?"

"Yes, because it's the truth." Brogan leaned nearer. "I have no idea when Artie was killed, but I can prove I had no role in Kendal's death. Billy and me picked up two female students and spent the night with them in a hotel." He smirked leerily. "The staff will verify it. We ordered room service on arrival and again four hours later. We drank champagne, but it was probably only expensive sparkling wine. Billy and me left after breakfast and stopped in Sheffield on the way back. I can tell you the places we went. There were plenty of other people around."

"That's very convenient. You have rehearsed your story well."

"It is not a story, and the events are not convenient. I'm speaking the truth. We never went through the gates or asked Norman to book us a pool car."

Jeff slid his chair forward, rested his elbows on the table and interlinked his fingers. "Then how do your names appear on the lists of people who used the gates?"

"Someone cloned our cards. It happens all the time."

"Yet another convenient coincidence."

"It doesn't make it a lie." Brogan's tongue appeared through tense lips. "Do you honestly believe I am so stupid that I would use my pass to cross zones if I intended to kill Kendal?"

This was the third time Brogan referred to the Judge by name. "I had no idea you were on first-name terms with His Lordship.

"He's a friend of my father. He's been around me all my life." Brogan put his elbows on the table and ran his palms across his hair. "I am telling you the truth, Jeff."

"You said that the last time we met. Why should I believe you this time?"

"Because I was young and stupid then. I've grown up now, and I haven't killed anyone. I know how this looks, but someone is setting me up."

"Again, why should I believe you?"

"Because I am telling the truth."

"The evidence doesn't lie."

"Your so-called evidence against me is flimsy, and the Committee will laugh at you."

"In which case, I'd have thought you would be keen for me to submit my report, although you have no idea what's in it."

"I know enough." Brogan tapped the side of his nose. "You are going to say that we crossed the zone, but we never did." He put an index finger to his chest. "If I had wanted to cross the zones, I would have used a fake ID. Had I used my pass, I would have deleted the computer record. It's quite easy to do, and nobody would have known I was there." Jeff let him continue. "Why would me and my boys use our own passes? Only one of us needed to swipe a card, which could have been a fake."

"How would that work?"

"Having swiped, it is easy to keep the turnstile open. Admins do it all the time if they carry stuff through."

This was news to Jeff, but not relevant. "Who would be brave… or daft enough to set you up and why?"

"I don't know who, but the why might have to do with my being appointed to the Central Committee."

Jeff acted like this was news. "Wow. Congratulations. I had no idea there was a vacancy."

"Don't pretend you didn't know."

"Whose job are you taking?"

"There isn't a vacancy at the moment, but there will be in a couple of weeks."

"I find it hard to believe someone with your abysmal record would get the position. They must be desperate to fill spaces."

Brogan's eyes narrowed, and he rested his hand on his pistol. "I know you won't believe me, Jeff, but I've changed. My father told me it was time to clean up my act. I have a family legacy to continue, and I was unlikely to get the support I needed from other Committee members if I continued doing what I was doing. I have sorted out my life…"

"So, no more slavery, pimping, bootlegging, drug running and so on?"

One hand remained on the pistol while the other stroked the chin. Brogan said, "I had that coming, I suppose. Yes, I have made mistakes…"

"You were and are a terrible person. A dreadful human being."

"I wouldn't go that far."

"I would, and I think His Lordship thought the same. He believed you were responsible for the death of his great-granddaughter."

Brogan's eyes and mouth opened widely. "Did he write that in his journals? I heard they weren't much use."

Jeff had spoken before considering his words, but he saw a way out. "They weren't. I learned that during my investigation. A few people repeated it."

"Probably that bitch Persephone and her crew. You can't believe a word she says." Jeff gave a slight shrug. "I was in Scarborough when Mary died, but I had nothing to do with her death. It was a tragic accident. What happened was not my fault."

"It never is."

Brogan took a deep breath. "We took her to Scarborough to celebrate her new job. She must have had too much to drink. Mary was never much of a drinker, and we left her behind in the pub. It was a tragic accident, but I never touched her."

"Even though she might tell the Judge what you had been up to?"

"Do you think he didn't know? Every time we met, he told me I was a disgrace. He hated the way I abused my power and asked me how much money and control I needed. Kendal used to say, 'The greater the power, the more dangerous the abuse...'"

"Edmund Burke."

"What?"

"They are Edmund Burke's words."

"How did you know that?"

"By reading books. You ought to try it sometime."

Brogan massaged his temples. "I couldn't see it at the time. I was young, and it was very easy to get carried away."

"What did Kendal say about Mary's death? Did he suspect you were involved?"

"I think that in the beginning he accepted that Mary had been alone and tripped or jumped. Then that bastard Weasel published a column about it, suggesting Mary was with me and had been pushed. Kendal became obsessed with pinning Mary's death on me. When that failed, he went looking for anything and everything he could use against me, but I have no idea if he found anything."

"Is that the real reason you cleaned up your act?"

"It had something to do with it. I never hurt Mary. I liked her. She was a nice kid."

"Aren't they all?" Jeff thought his comment would provoke a response.

Brogan's eyes narrowed, but he kept his cool. "Mary's death was an accident."

"You are repeating yourself, but I still don't believe you, nor did Kendal."

Brogan was becoming frustrated. He took a deep breath and shook his shoulders. "Okay, I don't suppose there is any harm in telling you this. We were all in a pub. I met..." Brogan used his fingers to highlight inverted commas, "...a smart young lady from Bridlington. We left before the others and were getting friendly on a bench when I heard a scream and people shouting. We went to look and saw that Mary had slipped down the cliff. Billy said he had moved to kiss her. She wasn't ready, pulled away and fell. It was a tragic accident."

"Why didn't you say this in the first place?"

"I didn't want to drop Billy in the shit. He's always had to put up with grief because of who his father is, and I didn't want to risk coming clean in case they made an example of him. I told him to say we'd moved on to the next pub, but Mary never showed. When we searched for her, we found her body on the rocks."

"I find it difficult to believe that Kendal believed that lie."

"Well, he did until the Weasel column. After that, he was always pissed off with me, slagging me off every chance he had."

"I can imagine how that might make you angry enough to want to kill him."

"No, you've got it wrong," Brogan shouted. "I had nothing to do with his death." He rubbed his palms on his eyes. "I never told him what happened, and, other than speculation, he had no evidence linking me to the tragedy. When my father told me about the forthcoming Committee vacancy, he said he could no longer rely on Kendal's support. I needed to clean up my act to persuade other doubters that I was a changed person. That's what I've done. I avoid taking stupid risks."

"That's quite an epiphany, from devil to saint, as quickly as that." Jeff clicked his fingers.

"I tried." Brogan brought his gun close and put his arms around it on the table. "I should have done it years ago. I get all the rewards without the hassle and fear of being attacked."

Jeff did not understand how Brogan going straight had kept him safe from enemies, but he had other matters he wanted to explore. "Who gets your job when you get promoted?"

"Billy Jensen."

"Of course. Why doesn't that surprise me?"

"Billy will make a great ChiZA. He is a man of the people."

Jeff smiled on the inside. "Whether the people like it or not. All change then. Yet more jobs for the boys."

"You make it sound corrupt, but the Committee will make the changes. It will be their decision."

"I rarely gamble but would bet that you have already discussed the next steps with your father." He watched the smirk develop. "I knew it. I cannot believe he only wants you there to continue the legacy. This sounds to me like a power grab."

"We have spoken about possibilities."

"Such as?"

"Why are you so interested?"

"You say someone is setting you up, but why would anyone do that? Maybe someone is wary about what you will do in your new role."

"Very few people know about the plans."

"Well, someone is seeking to discredit you and your father. Framing you for these murders kills two birds."

Brogan leaned back. "You agree that I am being framed."

"Not at all. I see no reason why anyone would want to frame you. As I said, it would be easier to kill you." Jeff shuffled in his seat, making himself comfortable.

The ChiZA gripped his lower lip between his teeth. "Not everyone is as bright as you."

Jeff angled his head as he studied Brogan. "What if it isn't you, they, whoever they might be, are trying to stop? Who else stands to gain from you joining the Committee?"

"Billy gets my job, and we'll move Purcell on."

"Will he get the job in the Old Fogeys zone? I know he's keen."

"He is. His in-laws live there, and his wife is anxious about them, but he won't get his wish. We have someone else in mind. Purcell will be pensioned off and offered a house in the ROFZ. We'll let him and his missus live there as carers. That should keep him sweet."

"Who replaces him?" Jeff could guess the answer.

"Cormack."

"With Norman taking over from Cormack?"

Brogan smiled.

Jeff interpreted that as a yes.

MC appeared from nowhere and shouted for Brogan to stay still. "I will shoot if you move." The Admin's gun was aimed at the visitor.

Brogan raised his arms and stood.

Jeff held up his hand, palm facing MC. "Easy, MC."

"I got your signal. Sorry that it took me so long to get here."

Jeff waved for MC to come into the room. "No problem. As it happens, ChiZA Brogan and I have been having a chat."

MC nodded at the pistol on the table. "So why does he need a gun?"

Brogan said, "I mean no harm. I simply wanted to tell Jeff he shouldn't believe circumstantial evidence." Brogan pointed at his pistol. "I'll put this away." He reached out to collect his weapon.

"Leave it there," MC ordered.

Jeff noticed a shake in MC's grip as perspiration appeared on the bald dome. He picked up the pistol. "I tell you what. I'll move it over…"

Jeff never completed the sentence. Two loud explosions filled the room. Jeff clenched his eyes, covered his ears and ducked. He could still make out the sound of metal scraping over the floor and a loud thud, which he assumed was a body hitting the deck.

"Fucking hell Billy! What have you done?"

That screech came from the last person Jeff expected to hear. He'd believed MC had shot Brogan and feared the worst. He was in no hurry to learn the truth. He shook his head, sat up and slowly opened his eyes.

Brogan shouted again. "What the fuck have you done?"

A newcomer entered the room. "I was saving your life."

Jeff saw a motionless MC spreadeagled on the floor with blood all around. He felt his heart race and his breathing quicken.

"The bastard had a gun pointed at you. What was I supposed to do?" Jensen Junior kicked MC's foot and shrugged when there was no movement.

Jeff moved toward the fallen ex-soldier.

"Stay where you are. Sit back down," Jensen pointed his gun at the ex-policeman. "It was self-defence. You heard my warning. It's not my fault if MC ignored me."

"I heard nothing." Jeff slumped in his seat and took several deep breaths, which he let out slowly, trying to divert a panic attack. He looked at MC and rubbed his cheeks as moisture formed on his eyelids. He straightened. "That was cold-blooded murder. MC did not deserve that."

"I told MC to put the gun down."

"I didn't hear you shout," Brogan stroked his lips and chin. "What the fuck have you done, Billy? You've killed a fucking war hero." His hand moved onto his hair. "How are we going to explain this?

"I thought it was MC or you."

Brogan spoke again. "I had it under control. I told you to stay in the car."

"I saw you had company."

Brogan's second fingers massaged his eyes as his palms covered his cheeks. "How the fuck are we going to explain this?"

Billy Jensen Jr suddenly exuded confidence. "We'll get our arses out of here, and nobody will know any different. We'll have plenty of witnesses who will vouch for us."

"And what about him?" Brogan's thumb pointed at Jeff. "He's not going to keep quiet, is he?"

"Then we kill him too and make it look like a double murder."

"Somebody would have heard the shots," Jeff thought he noticed a passing shadow in the corridor and wanted to hold their attention. Words were not easy to come by as his eyes kept returning to the dead Admin. "I expect one of the neighbours is already on the phone to report it."

Billy smiled. "Nice try, but I've been here loads of times. The third floor has a shooting range, so the locals are used to the sound of gunshots. I don't think anyone would have noticed. Even if they did, who's going to investigate? They're all at the Fun Day." He tightened his grip on the gun handle and raised his arms, aiming. "Let's get this over with."

"I don't suppose we have any other choice." Brogan stood.

For months after the Shift, Jeff wanted to die. Now that there was a probability his time was up, his mind was filled with reasons to live.

Harding shouted, "Drop your weapon."

Billy turned but was beaten to the draw. Three bullets hit him in quick succession, and he crumbled next to MC. Brogan stepped forward but stopped when Harding told him to back off. Once again, Brogan's hands were aloft.

Keeping his gun aimed at the visitor, Harding kneeled to touch MC's neck with his spare fingers and gave a slow shake of his head.

"I never meant for that to happen," Brogan rubbed his hands over his head. "I only wanted to talk. Billy always acts before he thinks."

Harding stood. "You trained the monkey, so you must take responsibility for its actions."

"I want no part of this," Brogan insisted. "This had nothing to do with me."

If looks could kill, there would have been three bodies. Harding waved for Brogan to sit. "You really are a snivelling little shit, aren't you. I just heard you talking about killing Jeff."

"That was Billy's idea…"

"But you agreed with him. I have a good mind to blow your head off and claim it was self-defence."

"If you were going to shoot me, you would have done it at the same time as you murdered Billy. You'll think about it now, and it will be harder to fire again."

"I wouldn't bank on that if I were you," Harding snarled. "Anyway, it wasn't murder, it was self-defence. My actions were reasonable after what your friend did to MC."

"Can we calm things down a little?" Jeff had two trains of thought running through his mind and needed time to consider the better option. "Where would more killing get us? We'd have another death to explain."

Harding did not see this as a problem. "We can remove the bodies without questions being asked."

"And how would you explain their mysterious disappearance? Do you think for one minute that nobody will investigate?

Others almost certainly know their plans for today. Questions will be asked."

"Yes, yes," Brogan said eagerly. "I told loads of people where we were going. They are expecting me back."

"It's a risk I am prepared to take."

"Well, I'm not," Jeff insisted. "It won't only be us affected should anyone discover the truth. The lives of our family and friends will never be the same."

Again. Brogan was quick to add his thoughts. "Jeff is right. My father will ensure you and everyone attached to you will suffer."

Jeff mumbled, fingers wiping his lips. "We need to think of another way. Killing him is not the answer."

Harding stared at Jeff. "I can't believe you are going to let him off for murdering MC."

"I didn't say anything about letting him off, but technically, he didn't kill MC. Jensen did, and then you killed Jensen. We can explain that, but we are in a much worse situation if we shoot him." Harding looked ready to kill. Jeff added, "Please lower your weapon, sit down, and we can work out how to handle this situation to everybody's advantage."

"I agree with Jeff," Brogan said quickly. "Nobody was supposed to die, especially not MC. MC is…was a fucking hero."

Harding sat but refused to holster his weapon. Jeff removed Brogan's gun from the table, disarmed it and put it on the floor. A smug grin had formed on Brogan's face. "Are you going to take me to the island jail?"

"Possibly, I don't know yet."

Harding spoke to Jeff but pointed at the ChiZA. "If you take him there, he'll have left the holding centre before us. He and his mates will ambush us on the way home."

Brogan cackled. "You know me too well, but if you let me go, we can agree on what to say and do. I give you my word. I will honour our agreement."

"I don't find that much of a reassurance." Harding retorted.

"I need a drink," Jeff said. He looked at Harding. "Is it safe for me to leave him alone with you while I see what Cormack has stored in his office?"

"That's a great idea." Brogan held up a thumb. "I know he keeps a bottle of Scotch in his desk drawer and glasses in his filing cabinet."

Harding looked dumbfounded. "What? He kills MC, and now we'll enjoy a drink together. Do we toast absent friends?"

Jeff held Harding's stare. "We can if you wish, but as I see it, we cannot bring MC back, and we have to decide what to do with our uninvited guest. Our choices appear to be to kill him and face the consequences or find a way out that keeps us and our families safe. There is no point taking him in. We either kill him or set him free." Jeff was not yet ready to outline the plan taking shape in his head.

Harding stood behind Brogan and pulled his head back. "You think we can trust this shitbag to keep his word? He'll say anything to get out of here, and then he'll blame it all on us. We are fucked however we play it, but at least I would get the satisfaction of killing him."

"There is no need to shoot me." Brogan extended his arms. "I am no danger. I told Jeff that I'd cleaned up my act. I will go along with whatever we agree. What if you suggest that Billy went rogue? He came here without me…"

"His best mate's only been dead two minutes, and he's already dropping him in the shit. What chance do we have?"

"Let's discuss this when I get back. Keep a close eye on him, but please don't kill him."

"No promises."

Jeff returned carrying glasses of whisky. He placed one before Brogan and Harding, keeping the third for himself. "I don't normally drink this early in the afternoon, but…"

Brogan lifted his glass and took a mouthful of the liquid. "What whisky is this? It tastes a bit weird."

"Tastes fine to me," insisted Harding.

"You've forgotten how good the real stuff is." Brogan was

smirking again. "You can't beat a nice single malt."

Harding swallowed slowly. "Unfortunately, we can't all rely on Daddy to provide little luxuries."

"Leave it with me," Brogan winked. "I'll send you a bottle. See if you can taste the difference."

"It isn't the best," agreed Jeff. "The bottle said it is blended, but I have no idea what's been blended. For all we know, it might be brake fluid."

Brogan chuckled a little too keenly. Harding kicked the ChiZA's foot and drank in silence.

Jeff and Brogan bounced ideas off each other until Jeff decided it would be best if Brogan denied coming to the office. He would maintain that he left the fun day because he felt unwell and returned home. Billy stayed behind.

Brogan liked this idea.

When Jeff reported the deaths, he would say Billy panicked when MC arrived. Jensen was threatening Jeff when Harding appeared. Harding had no option but to shoot.

Brogan smiled, delighted at how the story did not refer to him. The one matter that Jeff could not resolve was how Brogan would leave the area. He could not take the pool car as it had to remain at HQ, along with Jensen's body, to give the impression that Billy had travelled alone. The other two offered no solution. Harding was in no mood to contribute, and Brogan sat drinking whisky with a fixed smile.

It was left to Jeff to suggest they give Brogan a lift to the crew gates, where he could collect the car they used to cross the Family Zone. Jeff would give him ample opportunity to leave the area before reporting the deaths. Nobody was likely to question his story.

Brogan loved the plan. He was confident it was safe to leave the bodies unattended as the local Admins were unlikely to return to HQ. They were too busy enjoying the free booze and food laid on by Jensen Snr.

Jeff asked how their plans might impact Billy's father. Brogan thought Jeff was asking out of concern. He assured him that Billy Jensen Sr would not be affected. Fathers cannot be held responsible for their sons' crimes. Jeff thought differently and wanted to come down hard on Jensen Sr, but remained silent.

Harding downed his whisky and stood. "I've had enough of this. I suppose I have little choice but to go along with it. I want you to know I am not happy." He pointed at Brogan. "You should be held accountable for MC's death."

"Billy shot MC, and his accountability will be established." Jeff emptied his glass and checked his watch. "It's time we made a move."

"Hmm," snarled Harding. "I'll have to put fuel in the pool car. He handed his gun to Jeff. "In case he tries anything."

Harding had just unlocked the car door when he heard the unmistakable sound of gunfire. He raced to the office to find Jeff standing in the doorway holding Billy and Harding's pistols. Brogan was slumped over the table.

"What have you done?"

"Change of plan," Jeff said cooly, returning the pistol to Harding. "I cannot abide the prospect of that little runt getting away with his role in the death of MC, someone who is worth a thousand times more than those two delinquents put together."

"What did you do?" Harding checked the body. "Did you shoot him? I can't see any blood."

"No, I dropped a sleeping pill or two into his whisky. I believe they've kicked in and should keep him quiet for hours...seven or eight possibly." He removed the mobile from MC's belt.

"What kind of sleeping pill?"

Jeff showed him a foil tray. "Nighttime Flyers."

"Where did you get them? Were they prescribed?"

"Not exactly."

"You know that you should only take them one at a time, especially if you've never taken them before. They contain a muscle relaxant and can cause you to lose control of bodily functions."

Jeff grimaced. "It's too late now. You'd better get us a larger vehicle; I wouldn't want to be stuck in the back with him if he shits himself."

"Where are we going?"

"I will explain in a moment. I need to make a call first."

Harding checked his gun. "Why have you emptied my cartridge?"

"I emptied yours and Billy's."

"Why?"

"Because someone will ask why we surrendered to Brogan if we had a loaded gun of our own?"

"Surrender? We didn't surrender." Harding looked at the bullet holes in the wall. "I don't understand."

"Our story will be that Brogan entered carrying his gun. I sat him down, and he was blabbering about being set up. MC arrived and aimed. Billy shot MC, and then you fired at Billy."

"Isn't that pretty much what happened?"

"Yes, but in my version of events, you missed each other a few times."

"I wouldn't miss. I am a good shot."

"Well, maybe you were upset by MC's death. Anger and grief affected your aim."

"Okay. I emptied the cartridge, and then what?"

"Brogan pulled out his gun and took us into Cormack's room, where he made you pour three whiskies. He dropped a Nighttime Flyer in each of ours and forced us to drink. We crashed out, and when we awoke, Brogan was gone. We reported MC's death immediately and…" Jeff read the contacts list on MC's mobile. "That's the one I want. Let's hope he's available."

"Who? Where are we taking Brogan?"

19. REPERCUSSIONS

Jeff rubbed his face for the umpteenth time, looking like a man struggling to comprehend what had happened.

Purcell was suitably sympathetic. "We can do this some other time if you'd rather. It's been a traumatic day for you."

"No, thank you. I'll be fine." Jeff's hand briefly covered his mouth. "I have never witnessed a murder before. I've investigated many, but I'd never seen one. Now I've seen two deaths in one afternoon, one of them MC's…" He fell silent.

"It must have been terrifying."

Jeff nodded. "Does it sound selfish to admit that I am relieved Brogan decided not to kill us, too?" Jeff's facial muscles relaxed.

"No, I think that is a perfectly normal reaction."

"I wish I knew where he was. I don't like the idea of him being free after what he did. I am terrified that he will come after me and my family. He might appear on my doorstep…"

"We'll never let that happen."

"Thank you," Jeff said, knowing that scenario was impossible.

Earlier that afternoon, Harding left HQ in Brogan's pool car to give the impression that the ChiZA had fled. When he reached the airfield, he left the car keys in the door well.

Jeff followed in an Admin van with Brogan secured in the back. It felt strange to be driving again. He did not find it easy. The gears reminded him that he needed to depress the clutch fully.

Jeff waited while Harding walked through to the neighbouring zone and found the vehicle Brogan and Jensen used to cross the Family Zone. Harding placed the keys to that car over the wheel and returned to the van.

The pair headed to Shrewsbury, where MC's friend and Army colleague Scott met them. Jeff had suggested meeting at the Wrexham Prisoner Holding Centre, but Scott disagreed. Other, non-military Admins at the PHC might insist that Brogan get taken to the Isle of Wight, as is the right of Admins. Scott proposed transferring Brogan directly to Anglesey.

Scott had called several old squaddies who served with MC and now worked on the island. When he rang to seek their help, they were distraught at the loss of a much-loved and respected senior officer. They looked forward to getting acquainted with the man responsible for the Colonel's murder. Brogan would not get off lightly. If the guards did not finish him, the island was home to many who hated Brogan, including Bruce Dixon.

Jeff and Harding returned to HQ, using the time in the car to test each other on their stories.

Purcell listened carefully and said he understood when Jeff needed frequent breaks to breathe and drink. These breaks were not forced. It was a struggle for Jeff to keep it together. He guessed adrenaline had played a large part in his actions immediately after MC's murder, but reality hit on the journey back from Shrewsbury. He was finding it difficult to cope with the speed at which events unfolded. He had never expected anyone to die, certainly not MC.

Jeff sipped the whisky. "Does anyone have any idea where Brogan went?"

"We will ask those closest to him, but personally..." Purcell looked solemn. "...I fear he is already dead."

Jeff feared he had let something slip or Harding had revealed more than they agreed, but tried not to appear concerned. "Why?"

"We found the pool car that Norman and Cormack booked for them on this side of the crew gates. It was intact. Sadly, nobody saw it arrive. On the other side of the border, we found the vehicle used to cross the family zone. Somebody had slashed the tyres and scratched 'XTZ' on the car door."

"XTC?" Jeff guessed Harding was responsible for the punctures and the scratches, but did not understand why he chose those letters.

"No, it's a Zee. The logo of 'Exterminate The Zones'. They are a terrorist group operating in the Z3060."

"Exterminate? That's a clumsy term." It reminded him of the Daleks and early evenings sitting around the telly with his children.

"They probably decided on a logo and retrofitted the words around it." Purcell scratched his chin. "We assume someone spotted Brogan and Jensen crossing the zone this morning and awaited their return. The tyres were slashed so that they couldn't go anywhere. Then, when Brogan arrived, they grabbed him."

"What will they do? Ransom him?"

"Unlikely, I imagine that the next time we see ChiZA Brogan will be in a photograph sent via the mail."

"Dead?"

"Almost certainly."

"That's…terrible."

"Indeed."

"Do these XTZ people take many prisoners? Are the crew doors dangerous for Admins?"

"XTZ are not interested in everyday Admins. They target senior ranks. That's why we never travel alone and are always armed."

"Brogan had a gun."

"I know, but he was on his own. They probably caught him unawares."

"Wasn't there anyone on the gate?"

"No, it is supposed to be manned during working hours, but the staff were given the day off. I fear LeRA Cormack and his counterparts in the other regions will face repercussions."

Couldn't happen to a better man, thought Jeff. He pointed at the laptop. "I was about to finish my report when Brogan arrived. I suppose I had better add a postscript outlining today's events."

"No. There is no need. I spoke to Lord Wilson, who will visit you tomorrow. He does not want anything in writing. He suggests a paper trail could be dangerous."

"Tomorrow? Where? Do I need to come here?"

"No, he knows where you live. He'll visit you at home."

Great, thought Jeff. He could do without that.

The ChiZA stood. "I think that is enough for one day. I appreciate your help, Je… I never expected things to turn out like this. I am very sorry about what happened."

"Thank you." As Jeff emptied his glass, he realised he had no means of getting home. He did not fancy a bus trip.

Purcell must have read his mind. "I'm staying over tonight, but my driver can take you where you want to go."

The rear doors of the van that carried Brogan to Shrewsbury were open, and two bodies lay on the floor inside, covered in blankets. He recognised MC's shoes and placed his hand on one of them.

"Rest easy, MC. I am so sorry. You deserved far better than this." Tears trickled down Jeff's cheek as he put both hands to his face. An arm reached around him.

"Come on, let's get you home. There's plenty of time for grieving." Harding eased him toward MC's car.

"Thank you. I thought Purcell's driver was taking me?"

"I said I'd do it. I've been interviewed, and I can go home."

Jeff sat quietly in the front passenger seat.

"I can't believe MC managed to drive with the seat so close," Harding said, putting on his seatbelt. "There again, there were many things I never understood about MC." The car moved off.

Jeff wiped his eyes again. He did not want to talk about the Colonel. "How did your interview go?"

"Okay, I think. I kept to our story, and the two Admins seemed to accept what I said. Purcell called in after he had finished with you. He thanked me for my efforts and bravery and told me to go home. That's when I asked where you were and volunteered to be your driver."

"Thank you. I appreciate it." Jeff rubbed his eyes again.

"Puncturing the tyres and scratching the second car like that was a great idea. It was good thinking. I'm impressed."

"I will take that from the man who created such a brilliant story to get us out of the proverbial. I would never have expected that from Squeaky Clean Cleveland."

"What did you call me?" Jeff gave him a look. "Squeaky Clean Cleveland?"

"That was your nickname back in the day. SCC."

"Who called me that?"

"We all did. You never put a foot out of line, always obeyed the rules and remained whiter than white."

Jeff smiled. "It was all an illusion. I bent enough rules in my time. I was fortunate that I knew how to cover my tracks."

"It never did anyone any harm."

Jeff hoped that was true.

Lord Wilson arrived at three the next day. The sun was shining, and he insisted on viewing Jeff's garden. He even asked if they could take tea outside.

"It is a lovely spot," said Wilson, relaxing in the garden chair.

Jeff wished he had wiped the seat, fearful of staining Wilson's shiny white shirt. "Thank you. We loved it immediately. It's the main reason we bought the house."

Wilson's eyes surveyed the scene. "I can imagine." He sat upright and cleared his throat. "I hate to do this, Jeff, but please run me through your findings and the sequence of events that resulted in....what happened yesterday."

Jeff summarised the investigation results and recited the story he had given Purcell. It was more straightforward this time. The more a lie gets repeated, the easier it is to believe it.

Wilson nodded, sympathised and spoke in anger at the appropriate times.

When Jeff had finished, Wilson asked, "Do you think Brogan might be telling the truth that he is not responsible for Kendal's death?"

"He insisted he had nothing to do with it, but he would, wouldn't he? The evidence, some of which I accept, is circumstantial, does point to him."

"I cannot comprehend how Eddie could have been so daft to use his pass to cross the zones?"

"I wouldn't say daft, but he is extremely arrogant. It would not surprise me if he had never considered the possibility of anyone checking the crew doors. He relied on his alibi and expected us to accept that he was being framed. He mentioned witnesses who would vouch for his movements after the charity event."

"Ah, yes, the young students he and Jensen picked up." Wilson stretched his mouth. "Purcell told me about them last night, so I had one of my men contact the girls this morning. He only managed to track down one, but she was resolute that she and her friend did not spend the night with the pair. She said they went to the hotel with Brogan and Jensen, but nothing happened. The girls were instructed to order what they wanted from room service and charge it to the room. Their companions had business to attend to and left. They never saw Brogan and Jensen after midnight."

"Which gave them plenty of time to travel to Bournemouth and back."

"Indeed. My men also contacted Admins Cornwall and Essex..."

"They exist?"

"They do. Why do you think they don't?"

"I thought the surnames seemed a little contrived."

"They exist right enough and are good at their jobs. They are orphans named after their counties of birth. The pair admitted to collecting Brogan and Jensen and travelling to Bournemouth, where they served as lookouts. They never questioned what happened inside the house, but Brogan and Jensen carried a large block of wood and a sledgehammer. When they got back to the car, the pair had no baggage and were covered in blood."

"What about Artie?"

"Cornwall claims to know nothing about that, but Essex said Jensen had tried to get him to help. He refused, so Brogan and Jensen travelled alone. Essex has been fearful of what retaliation Brogan will dish out. At least he won't have to worry about that now."

"Wouldn't it be dangerous for Brogan and Jensen to cross to another region without backup? I've heard rumours that the rival gangs are at war, and the Admins are not welcome."

"Don't believe all you hear. Brogan and the gangs have an uneasy peace treaty. They are engaged in a struggle against a common enemy."

"The BVs?"

"Exactly, so Brogan would have been safe to cross." Wilson stood, readying to leave.

"Purcell believes that Brogan is dead. Do you agree?"

"He seems convinced." Wilson's mouth closed, and his face contorted as he thought. "I tend to agree with him, although we will never know for certain unless a body turns up."

Jeff pushed himself out of his chair. "Let's hope he doesn't."

"I agree. It would be much easier if he stayed out of sight."

"Easier? Why?"

"We will shortly have the written testimony from the female student and the Admins who assisted in the death of Kendal. That, together with your evidence, should be enough to convince doubtful Committee members of Eddie Brogan's guilt. The question is how his father responds."

"Whether he accepts the findings or tries to quash them?"

"I don't see him accepting them, but what happens next hinges on how many committee members he can persuade that the evidence is a witch hunt against his family. Apart from rumour and conjecture, we have no actual evidence that Eddie Brogan murdered anyone."

"He came here to silence us."

"I know that. You know that. Unfortunately, from how you and Harding described events, it could be argued that Eddie came here to protest his innocence."

"Sorry about that. Perhaps we should have waited before speaking to Purcell. I find it difficult to believe Eddie Brogan travelled all that way to tell us we were wrong. He could have done that by phone or getting Cormack to state his case." Jeff swore to himself. "I should have thought things through before speaking to Purcell."

"You had a lot on your plate, and watching that happen to MC couldn't have been easy. You won't believe me, but it is not your fault - it is mine. I should have released Kendal's journals and brought all this out into the open. I missed an opportunity."

"Release them now." Jeff immediately realised that was a silly suggestion. "You can't because Brogan Sr will claim the journals have been falsified or that you are trying to use them for political advantage. He'll make it look like you are part of the conspiracy."

"Exactly. I thought I was being clever by withholding them, but now I've boxed myself into a corner. Release and risk ridicule, or keep them hidden and allow Brogan to get away with his crimes. Kendal's journals are compelling reading and would leave even the Secretary General's closest supporters in little doubt his son was a bad egg."

"It might not come to that," Jeff said. "The Committee might decide it is time to exorcise the devil..."

Wilson interjected. "Sadly, for some, that would be like turkeys voting for Christmas. They enjoy their power, and Brogan protects them."

Jeff's eyes narrowed. "There might be another way."

Wilson sat down again. "Go on."

"Have you heard of the Weasel?"

"Of course. We have no idea who writes that rubbish, but we use the column. It's useful for testing new proposals before making a formal announcement."

"I wondered how there are so many mysterious leaks. What if someone released extracts or a whole journal to the Weasel?"

"Nice idea, but I would still get slaughtered for not saying anything before. I like my team and wouldn't want them to be investigated."

"What if it wasn't your team? What if, unbeknownst to

anyone, you didn't collect all the journals? You thought you had them all, but a few were kept from you and given to the press. The Weasel could insinuate that local Admins initially kept them to protect their links with Brogan, but when the shit hit the fan, they didn't want to be caught holding them. The journals could be handed over without the source being revealed. You would then order an urgent investigation into who had them."

Wilson nodded. "There is something in that. A few of the Committee were sceptical about my claims that there was little of relevance in the journals. This could explain why..." Wilson stood again.

"If you can get the Weasel to stick to the script."

"We may not know who the Weasel is, but we know that person is no friend of Brogan's." Wilson had a massive grin on his face. "I'll get on to that straight away. Do you know what? That idea is quite brilliant. I would never have believed Squeaky Clean Cleveland could be so devious."

"Don't you bloody start..." Jeff wanted to avoid questions about who else might have referred to it and why, so he added, "...I had enough of that when I was working. I'd rather that remain forgotten."

20. VISITORS

Jeff spent hours sitting in his garden, staring at everything but noticing nothing. He was lost in grief and self-blame.

He wished he had seen Billy Jensen arrive and told MC to drop the gun. That might have saved the Colonel, but would it have resulted in additional deaths? He had no way of knowing how far the pair might have gone to cover their tracks.

The only thing he knew for sure was he would never unsee the images of MC's body on the floor.

Had he taken the right decision by taking Brogan to certain death? Jeff squeezed his eyes and told himself it no longer mattered. Brogan got what he deserved. The evidence pointed to him and Jensen killing the Judge, and they were both culpable for the murder of MC.

Jeff shivered, realising that darkness had fallen. He had no idea what time it was, but he sensed he should stop thinking and get some rest. He hoped for a sleep with happy dreams, but knew he only had one Flyer left. Once that had worn off, his mind would probably replay the nightmares. Still, something was better than nothing.

He made a mug of tea, switched off the lights and went to bed. With a pillow behind his back, he slowly sipped his Flyer-flavoured drink.

He could not escape reliving what had happened and felt tears rise.

Jeff wondered what Flissy would have said. He guessed it would probably be, '*You've got the bastard. That's all that counts. Well done. Now, can I please get to sleep?*'

The Flyer worked its wonders, and he drifted off with his bedside lamp still on, unaware that his first thought on waking would be that the muscle relaxant had resulted in him wetting himself.

He would soon realise that he had let go of his cup, and it

emptied its contents over the blanket before rolling onto the floor.

Not usually a fan of daytime television and all too aware that the Committee sanitised all news spewed out by the three channels, Jeff found himself unable to take his eyes off the screen. The repeated mentions of his name in the news and the suggestion that he was the intended target of the two renegade Admins made Jeff uneasy. He hated the thought of being in the limelight.

The media had been in overdrive for 48 hours since the unfortunate events came to light. Extensive and surprisingly truthful reports of the tragedy came with a plea for further details of the whereabouts of Eddie Brogan. The newspapers detailed a special report from the Weasel suggesting that Brogan had been named by His Lordship Kendal McGregor as the murderer of his great-granddaughter.

The articles included a long list of monstrous crimes believed to have been committed by Eddie Brogan. Jeff wasn't sure if that list had been released by Wilson or created by McCallum.

Speculation mounted about the position of the Secretary-General, with commentators suggesting his position had become untenable.

For his part, Jeff had no desire to discuss the matter and thought it better to avoid people. He decided to remain indoors with the curtains closed, but soon realised the flaw in that plan. It would only be a matter of time before visitors arrived at his door, probably bearing cake, offering condolences, and full of curiosity. Once inside, it would be hard to get rid of them. There was merit in going outside and meeting people on his terms.

Jeff opened the drapes, slipped on his jacket, checked his pockets and stood by the front door. He planned to visit the High Street and eat at whichever pub served food.

He took a deep breath and reached for the lock, but never opened it. Jeff was not ready for company and questions. He returned to the lounge, where he removed his jacket, kicked off his shoes, reclosed the curtains, lay on his sofa and barely moved for two days.

The noise of someone unlocking the door made Jeff jump. "Who is it? Who is there?"

"It's okay, Dad, it's only us." Jill entered the room accompanied by her brother.

"How...What?"

George spoke. "Lord Wilson rang suggesting you could do with the company. It sounds like you've been through hell. Why didn't you ring?"

Jeff stood in the centre of the lounge with tears running down his cheeks. "It's been..."

"It's okay, Dad." Jill wrapped her arms around her father. "You don't need to say anything if you don't want to."

George hugged the pair. "Take your time. We are not going anywhere."

Jeff spent the next three days chatting, reminiscing, laughing and going for walks. George politely told anyone who approached that his father could not talk about what happened and did not want to be disturbed. People understood and told him Jeff knew where they were if he needed anything. On the fourth morning, the three were chatting in the garden when Jeff asked, "Isn't it about time you two got back to your families and work?"

"Well, that's charming," Jill said, "you can't wait to get rid of us."

"It's nothing like that," Jeff replied, "I've loved having you here, but you have other responsibilities, and I know how busy you are with work."

George shook his head. "It's okay. Lord Wilson told our bosses to give us a week off. I'm sure I can get a few more days if needed."

"That's a lovely idea, but things must return to normal at some point. You've both been fantastic. I don't know what I would have done without you."

"Are you sure, Dad? It took you a long time to recover after Mum." Jill fixed her eyes on her father.

"I know that, but I am feeling much better. In any case, it's costing me a fortune having to feed you."

"You cheeky sod," George exclaimed. "We offered to pay, but you wouldn't have it." The three laughed.

Jill said, "You still owe me for the milk and biscuits I bought yesterday. Shall we call it twenty quid?"

The siblings laughed at their father's curt response.

Pat and Harry called shortly after the children left, asking if Jeff would join them for the pub quiz. After some coaxing, Jeff agreed, admitting it was time to face the neighbours. His friends promised to protect him from too many questions.

They agreed to meet outside Jeff's house at their regular time.

Counting down the minutes until departure, Jeff sat in his chair, listening to the radio while rehearsing how to respond to enquiries. The more he thought about it, the less confident he was that he could fully explain what happened and why.

He reconsidered the evidence again.

The only suspects he could link to the murders of the Judge and Artie were Brogan and Jensen. They had motive, means and opportunity, but something wasn't right.

If Brogan learned that Kendal was investigating his activities, why did he leave the scene without discovering what the Judge knew? If he had searched, would Brogan spend time hiding his tracks by tidying up? He had a strong alibi, why would he care if he left a mess?

The Judge might have told him what he wanted to know, but surely Brogan would have expected the Judge to have notes. Why leave without the paperwork that could implicate him?

The manner of the Judge's demise still bothered Jeff. Why torture an old man after giving him drugs to ease the pain and gagging him? There was no logical explanation for doing this.

Jeff had a theory about why Artie had to die. If Brogan feared the Judge had shared his findings with Bruce, who, in turn, had told his son, then with the Judge and Artie out of the way, nobody would listen to the rantings of a convicted criminal? In any case, who was Bruce going to tell? He was stuck on an island miles away from anyone.

The biggest issue that Jeff could not resolve was why Brogan needed to kill anyone. All he had to do was bide his time. His father was powerful, he was protected, and both victims were dying. There was no need for him to rush into action like he did. Could arrogance have driven Brogan to act so recklessly?

So many questions. Jeff told himself he was overthinking things. He had spent too long on his own, dwelling on the murders and was in desperate need of a break. A quiz and a few beers would do him good. It was time for him to think about something else.

If only it were that easy. The locals were bound to be inquisitive, and even if he said nothing, there would still be whispers and pointed looks.

Jeff pulled his hands down his cheeks and squeezed his chin. He knew that he should be delighted that the case had been resolved to everyone's satisfaction. Purcell rang to say that the testimony of the female students and the two supporting Admins eliminated any arguments that might have cleared Brogan and Jensen. He congratulated Jeff on a job well done.

Jeff was impressed at the speed with which Wilson's team identified and questioned the witnesses. From his recollections of his ex-boss, the man had a penchant for dithering but could not shift the feeling that he was missing something.

There was one aspect of the case that Jeff had no doubts about. Brogan and Jensen were responsible for the death of MC.

Jensen, aided and abetted by Brogan, had committed cold-blooded murder. MC's PTSD meant there was little chance of a bullet leaving the gun. MC's hands had been shaking, and the Colonel was getting more anxious by the second. Billy took the cowardly route by shooting MC in the back. That action alone made it easier for Jeff to satisfy himself that his subsequent actions were justified.

It was time to face the music. Jeff slipped on his jacket and shoes and was about to switch off the radio when the presenter announced they were heading to the offices of the Central Committee, where the Secretary General was making a statement.

Jeff listened as Lord Brogan announced he was stepping down while enquiries continued into the actions of his son and William Jensen Junior. There was no mention of the friendship between the two. The Secretary General's words made it abundantly clear that Billy committed the murders and Eddie had panicked. Lord Brogan asked anyone who knew his son's location to come forward. He was certain things could be cleared up, but Eddie needed to come forward. He was not in trouble. There were plenty of people who wanted to help him.

Jeff smiled as he recalled his father's often-repeated words to his sons. *'There are lies, damned lies and political statements. Don't believe the lying buggers. They will tell you what they want you to know, not what you need to know. With enough spin, they will distract you from what matters so that you focus on what they want you to believe.'*

He switched off the radio and headed toward the door, still grinning at his father's advice. Turning the latch, a thought entered his head that took the air out of his lungs. Jeff stumbled into the telephone chair as his mind raced.

He grabbed his mobile, pressed the buttons, and, ignoring the pleasantries, said, "We need to talk. Let me know where and when."

Early the following day, Jeff was awoken by someone making good use of his doorbell. He peeked through the curtains to see who it was.

A 'BV Fish' delivery van had parked across his drive. The rear doors were open, and two men were removing boxes. Jeff had not placed an order, so what did they want?

He dressed quickly, ran downstairs and opened the front door. "I haven't ordered anything."

A lady wearing a baseball cap pulled down on her head said, "I have an urgent delivery for Mr. Cleveland." Jeff was speechless. He had not expected a personal visit. "Do you mind if I come in?" She did not wait for an invitation.

Jeff and Persephone sat on opposite sides of his kitchen table.

"I was not expecting you to come here."

"It sounded like an emergency."

The men from the van each placed a sizeable cool box on the worktop.

Persephone nodded at them. "Thanks, lads. I will be out in a bit."

Jeff watched the men leave. One wore shorts, and his chain tattoo was visible above the edge of his trainer. "Thank you for the fish."

Persephone laughed. "Isn't that the ending to a hilarious book?" She lost her smile. "What do we need to talk about?"

Jeff stretched his mouth, licked his lips and exhaled. "I wanted to run something by you."

"Sounds interesting. I'm all ears."

Jeff had forgotten his manners. "Sorry, would you like a drink?"

"I'm fine, thanks, but you have one. You're the one who has just got out of bed."

Jeff smoothed his hair. "I can wait. Okay. Well. Where to begin."

Jeff scratched his forehead. "I've always lived by the motto that if something appears too good to be true, it probably is."

"I can understand that." Her eyes narrowed as she studied his expression. "Is this about the fish? Do you think I will be asking you for favours in return?"

"I very much doubt there is any favour I could ever do for you."

"That's where you are wrong. You have already done me the biggest favour of all by discovering who killed Artie. I assure you, I do not expect anything else from you and will remain forever in your debt."

"Who killed Artie, Arthur. Yes, that's a good place to start. What if Brogan wasn't responsible for that murder?"

Persephone narrowed her eyes and placed her palms on the table. "Why would you think that? You got a confession out of him, well, as good as. He fled to avoid the repercussions."

"Brogan denied playing any part in the killings of the Judge and Artie."

"He was never going to confess. He's too much of a coward."

"Maybe. The evidence suggests that Brogan is the killer, but I can't understand why he needed to murder anyone. He did not need to act. The victims were unlikely to live very long. Brogan knew he was safe from prosecution, so why take risks?" Jeff locked eyes with his guest.

"Perhaps he did it because he could. He thought nobody would investigate, and it tied up any loose ends. He hadn't counted on your old boss asking you to get involved."

"Possibly, but why did he travel all that way to persuade me of his innocence? With his father's power and connections, what difference would my view make?"

"Word might have reached him that you had more on him than he realised."

"That was part of our...well, MC's plan, but I never expected him to fall for it."

"Well, it looks like he did and having made his decision, Eddie may have seen his visit as an opportunity to silence you."

"He had ample chance to do that before MC appeared, but he seemed keener to talk."

Persephone shrugged. "I have no idea why Eddie visited you. People say he is a sharp cookie in many ways, but he often lacks common sense. I heard that he feels compelled to act if an idea enters his mind." She saw Jeff's head shake. "Why are you worrying about this? You've found the culprits and are being lauded as a hero. Eddie's done a bunk. If he were innocent, he would have stuck around."

"You might be right, but don't you think it's all been a little too straightforward?"

"You've solved the case. Just leave it at that. You've put the jigsaw pieces together and solved the riddle."

Jeff scratched his chin. "The jigsaw analogy is a good one. When I started the investigation, I had no pieces, no box and absolutely no idea what I was doing."

"I imagine that is a regular occurrence for a policeman. That's why you do what you do. You build a picture as you go along."

"I suppose so, but in this case, with hindsight, others were handing me the pieces and subtly telling me where to put them."

Persephone reclined. "I don't understand what you are getting at. You spoke to people, they told you what they knew, and then you followed the trail until you found the killer. That sounds like typical police work to me."

"It's rarely that easy. I had absolutely nothing to go on, but then, all of a sudden, I had a trail which took me to the killer."

"Again, isn't that what happened in your job?"

"Sometimes, but from my experience, very few cases were as linear as this one. Clue A fell into my lap, which took me to B, onto C and so on."

"I don't follow. As I said, isn't that what the police do?"

"In my day, we rarely had the clues presented on a plate."

Persephone shook her head. "I have no idea what you are on about."

"Let me try again." Jeff sighed. "When I took on this case, I did what I've always done. I visited the crime scene, spoke to potential witnesses, put a team together, etcetera, etcetera. Then I learned of Artie's murder. Again, I visited the site and discovered the mobile."

"You had a bit of luck…"

"Was it luck? What are the chances of me finding his mobile after the Admins had visited?"

"They might not have searched too closely."

"Or they may have been instructed not to search and seal the place until I arrived. Maisie said the Admins told her not to let anyone in until told otherwise."

"Why would Brogan do that?"

"Who said it was Brogan? He denied even knowing Arthur was dead. I think the Admins were working to someone else's instructions."

"This is all very Machiavellian. Everything I've heard on the news supports the theory that Eddie and his cronies killed His Lordship and Artie."

"That's what I was supposed to think. What if it didn't happen that way?"

"What if it did? You look tired, Jeff. You are clearly overthinking this. I should leave and let you get some rest."

"Please let me finish. All the clues point to Eddie, but the big question remains unanswered. Why did he do it?"

"Who knows why people act as they do?"

"I suppose so, but I cannot understand why Eddie became so desperate to kill the Judge and Artie in quick succession? The pair might have had evidence to incriminate him, but what could they do with it?"

"Make things difficult."

"How? His father controlled the Committee. Eddie could have denied all charges and sat tight, knowing that his accusers would die shortly anyway."

"If he knew that."

"His father probably told him about the Judge's condition, but I don't think he knew that Arthur was poorly. Not that it makes any difference." He sighed. "I can't think of any reason why Eddie would cross the zones to kill anyone. There was no need for him to take risks"

"But everyone knows he did."

"Everyone believes that he did. Most reports suggest he silenced the people who stood in his way and had to complete the task before his appointment to the Committee became public knowledge."

"Seems reasonable."

"But I have an alternative scenario."

"Go on."

"What I am about to say assumes that Brogan was not interested in killing anyone, but his enemies were desperate to bring him down." Persephone's mouth was sealed, and she remained still. Jeff continued, "If I approach things from this angle, things become clearer."

"How?"

"From what I hear, Eddie was being lined up to replace Lord Falshaw, the Secretary for the Environment."

"Doesn't he have Alzheimer's?"

"I have no idea. Wilson only told me that Falshaw would not stay in post much longer. His behaviour has become very erratic."

"What difference does that make?"

"The culprits knew Falshaw wouldn't be around long and needed to discredit Eddie before his appointment was formally announced. That's why they arranged the murders"

"So, none of this was Eddie's fault? Do you realise how mad that sounds? I'm sorry, but you need a break. Go and see your kids or spend some time at the beach. Eddie committed the murders to stop His Lordship and Artie from making things awkward for him."

"Then why didn't Eddie search for the evidence against him? I find it impossible to believe he left without looking through the Judge's papers."

"He might not have known there were papers."

"What? Do you think he never considered that the Judge made notes? If I were Eddie, I would have searched the house."

"Perhaps he did."

"Unlikely, the place was immaculate."

"He may have been disturbed?"

"Doubtful. It is more likely that whoever is responsible for the death of the Judge left his journals in place to ensure there would be an investigation." Persephone fell quiet again. Jeff filled the void. "Don't you think it is a strange coincidence that His Lordship told Lord Wilson the combination to his safe a few days before he died?"

"Is that what he did? Perhaps he was tipped off that Eddie was coming for him?"

"If that were true, Wilson would have arranged extra security. I think Kendal knew when he would die because he was involved in the planning."

Persephone pulled a face. "You cannot be serious?"

"It all makes sense: the call to Wilson, the visit to see his children, and MC being given the day off on the day his body was found. Kendal was putting his house in order, ready for death."

"That's an outrageous suggestion."

"Is it, though? Is it really?" Jeff leaned forward, putting his elbows on the table and interlocking his fingers. "What if Kendal, Artie and a person or persons unknown heard that Brogan was being lined up to replace Falshaw? They knew they could only stop that by discrediting Brogan and exposing his activities. The Judge couldn't present his evidence to the Committee because much of what is in the journals is hearsay. Brogan's father would dismiss it as lies spread by his enemies." He paused, looking to see if her expression changed. It didn't. "The Judge had to die, and Brogan had to get the blame."

"Why would the Judge make some kind of suicide pact?"

"Because he was dying anyway and didn't want to go to his grave knowing a bastard like Brogan would join the top table. Not after he learned that Eddie was involved in Mary's death."

"I thought she fell?"

"As you well know, the Weasel suggested she was helped on her way. Eddie told me it was an accident and, unsurprisingly, blamed Jensen."

"Typical. And Artie? Why did he need to die?"

"To highlight the links between his father and The Judge. I had to believe that Artie had information that would incriminate Brogan."

"Are you suggesting the Judge and Artie were prepared to die, and the culprits, whoever they may be, turned up with blocks of wood, kneecapped two dying men and let them bleed out?

That's barbaric."

"Unless the Judge and Arthur were already dead before the so-called torture started. Even if they weren't, it is highly unlikely they felt any pain. They were given copious amounts of Pulp to dull the pain and Nighttime Flyers to send them into a deep, happy sleep. They probably felt nothing." Persephone still showed no emotion. "The deaths were staged. Arthur first. He made a show of having to move his stuff to his new home and borrowed the work van, knowing it would be missed. Someone would ask questions."

"I see."

"The Judge followed shortly afterwards. Both murders mimic a form of torture used by the gangs in the Party Zone, making it appear likely the killers were from there."

"It's possible, but if the killers weren't Admins, how could they have crossed the borders without papers?"

"Do you expect me to respond to that?"

"I'm all ears."

"You know how, by using the crew doors and the fake IDs. It is only with hindsight that it dawned on me that Connor's visit was never meant to be a warning."

"Connor? Who is Connor?"

"Your partner."

"I don't know who you are talking about."

"Connor's visit was to speed things up. I was taking too long and needed to be pointed in the right direction. He casually told me about the crew doors and how there is a record of people using the turnstile. Then he showed me how easy it is to obtain fake IDs."

"Are you suggesting this Connor is involved in this?"

"I am, and you are, too. Not that I could ever prove it."

"What about the witnesses? The two girls and the Admins who confessed to helping Brogan."

Jeff smiled. "You are determined to keep up this pretence, aren't you? The girls probably drugged Brogan and Jensen and left them without an alibi. I think Cornwall and Essex were your men from the start. I forgot to ask if they had tattoos."

Persephone's lips broke into a wide smile. "They don't. It would have been too dangerous for them."

Jeff nodded and bowed his head. "Thank you. What is the significance of the inking? Do you have one on the wrist because you are the leader?"

"No, my tattoo is on my wrist because I went with Brogan of my own free will. There are many like me in the BVs. Only his victims have tattoos around their ankles."

"To signify slavery?"

"Something like that." Persephone nibbled her bottom lip. "I will deny saying anything to substantiate your claims."

"I thought you might. I don't intend to tell anyone else. I just wanted to discuss it with you."

"I can see why it had to be you investigating this case."

The comment caught Jeff off guard. "That was probably because Lord Wilson was my old boss, and he couldn't think of anyone else."

"That's rubbish. Kendal told Wilson that if anything untoward happened to him, he wanted you to be involved in finding out what happened. He was certain that you would get to the bottom of it." Jeff had no idea how to respond, so Persephone continued, "We had a bet with him that he was wrong. We expected you to reach the obvious conclusion and leave it at that. Everyone else I've spoken to is delighted with the outcome, but you? You just couldn't let things lie. As we lost the bet, we'll have to make a sizeable donation to charity."

Jeff replayed her words in his mind. "I can't believe the Judge had that much confidence in me."

"He thought you were one of the best detectives he had dealt with. He said you were always thorough, concise and honest when facing him in Court."

Jeff sat back. "I had no clue."

"He rated you very highly," Persephone remembered something else. "One of the reasons he gave to explain his confidence in you concerned your chair. Kendal wouldn't tell us what that was about. He said we had to ask you. What is important about a chair?"

"It is not any chair." Jeff smiled. He had forgotten he had mentioned his father's fake heirloom to the Judge. He recited the story again for Persephone's benefit, concluding, "That's why I get twitchy if something seems too good to be true."

"A sad but interesting tale." Persephone stood. "Well, I had better be going. You need some tea and toast. I hope the pub chef makes the most of the fish."

"How did you..."

She smiled and tapped the side of her nose. "I make it my business to know".

"I couldn't eat it all..."

She held out a hand. "Relax. I gave instructions that you should use it however you wanted. I am pleased the Community Fund's coffers are growing thanks to the pub owners' donations. Do you have any idea what you'll use it for?"

"I don't tend to get involved in that sort of thing."

"I hope they seek your advice. The proceeds of that lot..." She pointed at the boxes, "...should provide quite a boost."

"Thank you, but I'll probably stay out of it." Jeff did not wish to appear rude, but he needed to know. "Why did you come here? I could have met you halfway. I thought it was dangerous for you to leave your region."

"The world is a safer place for me now. Thanks to you."

"I wouldn't be too sure. They haven't found Brogan's body."

Persephone smiled. "Are you going to maintain the pretence?" She laughed. "Don't worry. I know where to find Eddie if I want to, although the tide might have moved him."

Of course, she would know, Jeff thought. Who did I think I was kidding?

She spoke again. "There is no need for anyone else to know, though. You did me and many others a huge favour by getting rid of him. We owe you."

"You owe me nothing. All I did was hand him over. Harding and MC had done all the heavy lifting. MC..." he struggled for words.

"MC paid the ultimate price." Persephone reached into her thick-padded body warmer and removed a brown envelope, which she put on the table. "I almost forgot. This is for a memorial for MC. If you need more, ring me."

Jeff picked up the envelope, which was full of fifty-pound notes. "Are these real?"

Persephone cackled. "Of course they are real, you cheeky bastard. Do you think we deal in fakes?"

Jeff put down the envelope. "Thank you. I hadn't thought about that, but..."

"You've had a very traumatic time."

Jeff nodded and took a breath. "A memorial is a lovely idea."

"The least that should be done."

"You said the world is safer, but isn't that only short-term? Brogan will get replaced, possibly by someone worse."

"I doubt that. Eddie was a one-off. He had the history and the connections. I should have realised sooner, but there you are. He got away with so much because of his father. Thankfully, the old man won't be around much longer. This is a sea change not just on the Committee but across the country. Your old boss, Lord Wilson, has already put out feelers about a peace treaty. The other gangs are keen. It'll be interesting to see how that works."

"Does it have a chance?"

"No reason why not. Our rivals are fed up with looking over their shoulder to see if we are after them. We'll agree to leave them alone if they leave us alone. We'll retain our weapons and independence, but we are willing to compromise so long as the others do the same."

"Long live Persephonia."

She roared. "I hadn't heard that, but it won't be Persephonia. I am handing over the reins." She placed her hands on her stomach. "My partner and I are having a baby and moving away."

"Congratulations to you and Connor. You will make great

parents."

Persephone's face turned serious. "How did you know about Connor and me?"

"When we first met, you mentioned your partner helping you from an ambush. When Connor called to see me, he said his scars came from a collision with a windscreen. I put two and two together. I wish the two of you and your baby every happiness. Connor is one of the good guys, but don't tell him I said that."

"He said you are a good man and a great detective."

"You are being kind, but I very much doubt that. I hung him out to dry. I should have supported him."

"Connor knows you had a lot on your plate. As it turns out, losing his job and meeting me are the best things that happened to him. He and I set up the BVs and have never looked back."

"Isn't he an investigator and column writer?"

"Sort of. He has others to do the work and gather the information. He oversees things. It would be too dangerous for him to travel the country. Eddie knows…knew him and…well, you can guess what would happen if he found Connor."

"I can. How did you two meet?"

"He ran from the gangs, and I crossed the country with Artie and Carrie. The four of us met and travelled together. Connor and I became an item."

Persephone said Connor had the idea to enter the fishing industry and accidentally thought of the gang's name. When they discussed how to crew the boat, he suggested that hundreds of Brogan's Victims needed a job. Word spread, business expanded, and the rest is history.

"You never mentioned why you needed to get away. Had Brogan harmed you?"

"He hurt me, but not like you think. It was my fault. I fell for Eddie almost as soon as I saw him. I thought he was stunning. He had an attitude like he didn't care about anyone or anything. It took me a long time to realise that it wasn't an image thing. Eddie genuinely didn't give a shit. He believed life was for living, and good times were there for the taking. Believe me, he took them. I thought we were in love, but then I caught him and Jensen with a couple of younger girls in our apartment. He didn't even try to deny it. He dismissed me for being neurotic. After that, the more I dug into his activities, the less I liked him. Drugs, rape, prostitution, murder, slavery…"

Jeff nodded. "I get the picture."

"I met Carrie, and she was so sweet. She and Artie were a lovely, loving couple. Eddie spotted her, and…you can imagine what happened." She wiped her mouth. "What he did to her was unforgivable." Her voice faded as her eyes welled up. "He did the same to Artie's sister. That's why Bruce went after him. He treated his dogs better than he did people."

"Would you like a glass of water? I have something stronger if you like."

"It's a bit early. Anyway…" Persephone rubbed her stomach. "…I'd better not."

Jeff had forgotten. "Sorry."

She dismissed it with a wave. "Carrie was broken…"

"That's not surprising."

"…Artie and I got her out of there. We weren't sure if Eddie would send his thugs after us, so we crept around, constantly changing direction and identities. We bumped into Connor outside Bury."

"Where his father lived."

"That's right. He was living a quiet life, but then a gang member recognised him, and they torched his house for being a bent copper. He didn't deserve that. He had only been doing his job."

"He had a raw deal."

"He did, but he bears no resentment. He doesn't let it take him down. He is witty, makes me laugh, and is very sweet. People underestimate him. Connor is a sharp cookie, quick on the uptake, and a great strategist."

It was an opportunity too good to miss. "Was it Connor's plan to stage the deaths to make it look like murder?"

"He may have suggested it." She moved closer to Jeff. "I must make a move. The boys have a couple more deliveries. It's good to see you again and in one piece. You need your breakfast." Her eyes skimmed the room. "You have a lovely home."

"Nice to see you too. I wasn't lying. I won't be sharing the revised conclusion with anyone else."

"I know." She pointed at the boxes. "I hope the fish goes down well. We had no idea what was needed, so we've included a mixture."

"Thanks."

"Perhaps next time you could give us an order? Tell us what they'd like."

"Nah, let's keep them guessing. You send what you have the most of, and they can do their best."

She giggled. "Okay."

"You never told me where you are moving to?"

She studied his face. "I'll tell you because I trust you, but if you say a word…"

"I wouldn't dare."

She chuckled again. "Scotland. We've secured a new fishing franchise."

"How the hell did you get that? I thought mentioning BV would set the hares running in the Administration."

Persephone winked at him. "The Admins have no clue we are linked. We applied via an associate based in Grimsby. Nobody asked any questions. It proves that, in the main, Admins are lazy bastards who cannot be bothered to do their jobs properly."

"I know of three exceptions to that rule, but other than them, I agree with you."

"You'd better not say a word about my plans," she said, running a finger across her neck. "You know I can find you and yours."

"I thought you said you were safe."

"We are, but would rather stay that way. We don't want any

renegade gang members or Admins tracking us down. We want to be left alone to lead a quiet life."

Jeff thought, where you'd be able to rear your child, you've got it all planned, so why not? He said, "Once this media frenzy has calmed down, I will be joining you…by living a quiet life, I mean. Don't worry, I'm not planning on moving in with you."

Persephone laughed loudly. "You will always be welcome, but I'm not sure life will ever be so quiet for you again. There is much for you to do."

"Like what?"

"You'll find out soon enough." Persephone shook his hand, hugged him tightly, and whispered into his ear, "Look after yourself, and if you need anything, anything at all, give me a ring." She stepped back and held up a mobile. "This is going to be my Jeffphone." She kissed his cheek and departed.

21. VISITING

A couple of weeks later, Jeff and recently promoted LeRA Harding arrived in the village of Gorran Haven in Cornwall. They found the house, the directions were spot on, and the view exceeded their expectations.

MC's half-brother, Christian, answered the door, welcomed them, and took them to the patio. The paved area overlooked the beach, and they sat on wooden chairs while an older lady slept on a lounger with a blanket over her.

Christian explained that his mother had been granted permission to live with him, and carers had been appointed. They spent most dry afternoons on the patio. She said the sound of the sea reminded her of being back home when she was young and lively. He found that funny, as his mother usually fell asleep as soon as she sat.

Harding let Jeff take the lead. He explained that money had been donated to pay for a monument to honour MC. Jeff knew Christian was an artist and hoped he would accept a commission to design and create an appropriate memorial.

Christian was delighted to accept and grabbed a sketch pad. The three discussed options and agreed that a statue of MC in uniform would be appropriate. Jeff recalled the reference to the first time MC's father had to salute her and suggested that might honour both. Christian knew where to find a photograph of that. He visualised the image, and his pencil flittered over the page until a rough outline appeared.

Jeff and Harding loved the concept but said they would let the family decide. More money was available if necessary. Christian offered to keep the cost down. He knew where to source a supply of bronze figures that could be melted down and reused.

Mrs Sands woke up and called for her son.

Christian said, "I'm over here, Mama. Maxine's friends have

arrived to discuss the memorial."

His mother squinted through her glasses. "Which one is Mr Cleveland?" Her West Indian accent was noticeable.

Jeff stood and approached her. "That's me, Mrs Sands. I am pleased to meet you."

They shared a weak handshake.

"Maxine liked you. She didn't like many people, but she told me she liked you. She thought you were honest and committed to justice, and she admired that."

"I liked her too, not that I knew Maxine for long. She was quite a character."

"She was damaged. Maxine was never the same after Berlin. That day changed her forever. We tried everything, but nothing worked."

"It was a courageous thing that Maxine did. It's bound to leave a scar."

"Scars never fully heal, do they? There is always a mark. Maxine was scarred all the way through." She sat up. "She felt so guilty. We told her it was not her fault. Nobody asked those terrorists to attack. Maxine said they were only teenagers who had been brainwashed. Her reactions were automatic; it was how she was trained. Afterwards, she believed she should have tried to disarm them instead of killing them. No matter how much we told her that she did the right thing, she would not listen. She was like her father in that way. He used to overthink things. They were so alike." She smiled at her son. "Unlike Christian and his brother. They don't think about anything." She let out a loud laugh. Her son shook his head in disbelief, causing his mother to laugh again.

They left the Sands and returned to the car, ready for the journey home. Harding's mobile rang, and he answered the call.

"That was ChiZA Purcell. Lord Wilson wants to see us when we get back." He unlocked the car.

"What does he want?" Jeff wondered if the Brogan/Jensen case might get reviewed.

"He didn't say. He told us to meet them at HQ."

It felt strange to be back at regional HQ. Jeff wondered whether their old office space had been renovated, but he did not dwell on the issue.

Purcell appeared and shook his hand. "How are you?"

"I'm getting there."

"If there is anything I can do."

"Now that you've mentioned it, there is something."

Having heard Jeff's request, Purcell ushered him into a side room, where Wilson waited. Purcell left, promising to make the enquiries into Jeff's problem.

Wilson smiled. "Good afternoon. How was your trip?"

Jeff told him about the initial design for the statue and his confidence that MC's brother would create something unique.

"That's wonderful news. If you need anything from us, let me know. I am sure the Committee would want to contribute to such a worthy cause."

"We should be fine," said Jeff, accepting the offer to sit. "We have had contributions from all over the country. MC was well known and, obviously, well respected."

Wilson looked slightly deflated when he heard his input was not required. "Let me know where you want it positioned, and I'll sort it."

"Thank you. We were thinking about the grounds of the military training centre. It might inspire future generations."

Wilson smiled and nodded. "That's a great idea. Very fitting."

"It was MC's stepmother who suggested it."

"Even better."

"So why did you want to see me? I don't wish to appear rude, but we have a cricket match starting at six."

"Of course, of course. I wanted to tell you that the Committee has appointed a new Secretary General."

Jeff knew Wilson had been using his influence and playing kingmaker. "At last, which idiot did you get to take the job?"

Wilson looked hurt. "Actually, they voted for me."

"Oh well…congratulations, that is good news. You must be very pleased." Jeff hoped he wasn't blushing.

"It is quite an honour."

"I'm sure."

"As you can imagine, my first weeks, hopefully, months, will be a honeymoon period, and I want to use that opportunity to make a few changes that not all my fellow Committee members will like."

"I see." Jeff appreciated the urgency but had no idea why Wilson needed to share this with him. "Good luck with that."

"One of those changes concerns you."

This made Jeff nervous. "Me? What can you have in mind that will concern me?"

"I want to establish a new cross-zone investigation team."

"What? Like a police force?"

"We cannot call it that, at least not yet. What I have in mind is a team that can investigate cases that traverse zones. The zonal administrations do not work very well together…"

"Unless there is money in it for them."

Wilson ignored the comment. "…and cases important to one zone fail to progress because a neighbouring zone has different priorities."

"Why is this of interest to me? Do you want me to help set it up?"

"I want you to run it." Jeff's eyes widened. Wilson added, "Your success in solving Kendal's murder means you have several fans on the Committee. If you are involved, they will agree to this project going ahead."

"I never thought I'd be offered a job today." He ran a hand down the back of his head. "What sort of cases?"

"Anything. Domestic, commercial, environmental, and industrial. If there is a suggestion of wrongdoing that affects more than one zone, then I want you to investigate."

"Me? I cannot do it on my own. I will need a team."

"I know that. How many do you think you would need?"

"Phew, let me think." His face creased as he thought. "The team would investigate crimes across the whole country. In every region?"

"Yes."

Jeff tapped his right thumb against the neighbouring fingers as he totalled the number of regions that covered. "The Youth Zone is only one region, isn't it?"

"It is, but it covers a huge area with numerous industrial and commercial sites."

"In that case, I am guessing about fifty people."

"You can have twenty-four."

"Okay, that's a start." Jeff would have settled for twelve. "Where would this team be based?"

"I thought you would be co-located with the administrations." Another loud exhale told Wilson that Jeff did not like that idea. "I would prefer the team to be housed separately to emphasise its independence. We might need one or two offices and send investigators into the regions as required. That way, you prevent people from becoming too friendly with the Admins and the citizens in a particular area."

"That would be your choice. I am assuming you would not want an office in London."

"You assume correctly. I think Bath would be a good starting point. I was there the other day, and the *Royal London Insurance* building on the corner of Trim Street has space on the upper floors."

"That is very specific. Does the building have special significance to you?"

"Not really. A friend worked there, and I called in from time to time. It is close to the main services, and I can easily get a bus there."

"A bus? We'd give you a car…a driver if you want one."

"No thanks. A bus will be fine. I like buses. You never know what you might learn."

"Up to you."

"Will this team have access to all zones?" Wilson nodded. "To whom would it be accountable?"

"Me, initially. The Committee needs a few more members, including my replacement, so I'll take responsibility for getting it off the ground, and we'll see how that works out. I am making Purcell the ChiZA in Chief, and I assume you and he will work closely."

"I'm happy to do that, but I thought he was keen to go to the ROF… sorry, I meant Z80+."

"He is, and that's where he'll be based."

"Good. He deserves a break. When would I start?"

"Give me a couple of weeks. There's nothing to stop you from identifying potential recruits."

"Do you want a say on appointments?"

"Yes, theoretically, but it's unlikely. I'd be happy to leave that to you, but please don't focus on ex-police personnel. I am playing a delicate political game here."

"Noted. Who determines what gets investigated?"

"I thought cases would be referred by Purcell, his ChiZAs and Committee members, plus any that you hear of by other means. How does that sound?"

Jeff nodded. "Will this team have the power to take prisoners directly to jail?"

"I assumed so. I was thinking of granting you the same powers as the Admins."

"I'm not sure I like that. Kendal disagreed with that practice. The Admins decide how long prisoners remain on the island without independent review. That is hardly fair."

"Had he lived, I believe Kendal would have campaigned for changes. Are you also suggesting we need new arrangements? There is no appetite for trials in the Court. It takes too long, and the only people who gain from it are the legal bods. Can you think of an alternative?"

"It's not fully thought through, but while investigating Brogan, it scared me how much power he and his counterparts hold. Perhaps we should have a review process. If we are sure a suspect is guilty, we could recommend a minimum stay, but suspects would have the right to appeal. Three independent people look at the evidence and make their recommendation, which might be less lenient than ours. Some suspects could be absolved of guilt. However, others might face tougher sentences."

"That might work. We could use the old Magistrates system as a starting point, but would have to agree on the panel's membership."

"All evidence has to be submitted in writing with no personal details. No hearings. The panel members would never know whose case they were considering. Accusations of bias undermined the old Magistrates' system."

"It did. Let's give it further thought. We don't have to decide today. I haven't got clearance yet."

"Of course. Sorry, I'm getting ahead of myself."

"There is no need to apologise. I am pleased you are interested. Does this mean you would take the job?"

"Oh yes, I'll take it. Let's get back to some proper policing."

"We cannot call this policing. We need to refer to it as investigating. I thought the new unit might be called the 'Cross Zone Investigation Team'?"

"CZIT! No thanks. Let's drop the 'T'. Cross Zone Investigations will do as a working title. We can review as we go along."

"Okay."

"It is somewhat ironic that I am being asked to establish a police force in all but name after investigating the death of the man who shut it down in the first place."

"Kendal did not make the decision."

"I know, but he came up with the recommendation."

"Well, actually, he didn't." Wilson scratched his ear. "It was known as Kendal's review, but there were three people involved in the inquiry. Lord Norman…"

"The idiot who believes everyone should be able to do exactly as they please?"

"He's a libertarian and supports freedom of choice."

"Who was the third member?"

"A representative from the Nobles' House. Lord Dover."

"I might have guessed he'd be involved somehow."
"I thought you'd recognise the name. Kendal was the only one of the three to oppose the recommendation, but had to live with the majority verdict."

Lincoln Roosevelt Cleveland stood on the doorstep holding a bottle of fizz and a tray of homemade lasagne.
"A little gift from us to congratulate you."
Jeff ushered him inside. "And you drove all the way here to deliver it. I am honoured."
"I'm also taking you over to the pub so we can have a proper celebration. Am I okay to stay the night?"
"Of course, but what about Lowri?"
"She's fine. Jimmy and Nancy are with her. They are moving over permanently."
"How did you manage that?"
"As if you didn't know. Your mate Purcell rang the other day to discuss Lowri's illness and what we needed. He told me you'd mentioned my circumstances, and he promised to sort things out. He sorted it all very quickly. Thank you."
"No need to thank me, I did nothing."
"He said you bent his ear, so he was compelled to review the matter."
"I had no idea I had so much influence."
"Don't get carried away. Get that lasagne in the oven, and we'll eat before we head to the pub." Linc opened the fridge. "I can't believe you haven't got any beer in."
"If I'd known you were coming…"
"I thought the world's greatest detective, make that the only detective, would be prepared for any eventuality." He checked his pockets. "I suppose I'd better nip to the shop. Bloody big brothers. They always leave the work to the younger ones."

ACKNOWLEDGEMENT

Confession time. The Zones concept was not entirely my idea. My wife thought of it first and has let me use it. We discussed several ideas but it is fair to say that her vision of the Zones was far more dystopian and oppressive. I developed my own story which assumes that, over time, the British people would adapt and life would return to (a new) normal.

BIG THANKS, as ever, to my family for their support - especially Odette for the idea, and to my regular guinea pigs - Annemarie Thorn and Stephen Phipps who kindly reviewed the first draft. This time they were joined by John Kilner (my Marshfield correspondent) and Julian Morgan who provided technical advice. I greatly appreciate the efforts of Calum Rayer who designed the book cover and Zones map. It could not have been easy working with my sketchy ideas but I think he's done a great job. I am delighted with the final designs.

Thanks to all of you who purchased and read Murder in THE ZONES and/or my earlier books. I hope you enjoyed reading them as much as I liked writing them.

Jeff Cleveland will return but in the meantime, please feel free to leave a review on one of the many sites. You can find me on Facebook and I am also working on a website but it is taking much longer than I hoped.

Keep safe, keep well, keep smiling.

WSAx

ABOUT THE AUTHOR

William S Allin Books

All published by JOKApress and available in ebook/paperback
from Amazon and other booksellers:

The growing up series
SIKES: Misconstrued
DICEY: Trailing
GARGAR: Commitment

A Song for the Season (a short-ish story for Christmas)

Factory Fortnight